The Murder
in the Tower

Due to illness, Jean Plaidy was unable to go to school regularly and so taught herself to read. Very early on she developed a passion for the 'past'. After a shorthand and typing course, she spent a couple of years doing various jobs, including sorting gems in Hatton Garden and translating for foreigners in a City café. She began writing in earnest following marriage and now has a large number of historical novels to her name. Inspiration for her books is drawn from odd sources – a picture gallery, a line from a book, Shakespeare's inconsistencies. She lives in London and loves music, second-hand book shops and ancient buildings. Jean Plaidy also writes under the pseudonym of Victoria Holt.

Jean Plaidy

The Murder
in the Tower

The Stuart Saga

Pan Books London and Sydney

First published 1964 by Robert Hale and Co
This edition published 1971 by Pan Books Ltd,
Cavaye Place, London SW10 9PG
4th printing 1977
© Jean Plaidy 1964
ISBN 0 330 02660 7
Printed in Great Britain by
Cox & Wyman Ltd, London, Reading and Fakenham

CONTENTS

BIBLIOGRAPHY

A Detection of the Court and State of England during the Reigns of James I, Charles I, Charles II and James II, Roger Coke

The History of Great Britain, being the Life of King James the First, Arthur Wilson

James I, Charles Williams

Lives of the Queens of England, Agnes Strickland

The National and Domestic History of England, William Hickman Smith Aubrey

British History, John Wade

King's Favourite, Philip Gibbs

Her Majesty's Tower, William Hepworth Dixon

The Dictionary of National Biography, Edited by Sir Leslie Stephen and Sir Sidney Lee

Abbeys, Castles and Ancient Halls of England and Wales, John Timbs and Alexander Gunn

Political History of England 1603-1660, F. C. Montague

History of England, James Anthony Froude

History of England, John Lingard

An Accident in the Tiltyard

FROM HIS chair of state which had been set on the stage in the tiltyard at Whitehall, the King lazily watched the champions as they tilted against each other. James was forty-one and did not himself tilt; he preferred the chase; but his young friends were eager to display their superiority over each other in this harmless way. So let them, mused James. He watched them – such handsome young men, all eager to show their Old Dad and Gossip, James the King, how much better they were than their fellows.

'Fill the goblet, laddie,' he said, glancing at the tall young man who stood behind his chair waiting to perform this service.

The boy obeyed – a pleasant creature; James insisted on having pleasant-looking young men about him; and this one was kept occupied, for the King was constantly thirsty and nothing satisfied him but the rich sweet wine which many of his courtiers found too potent for their taste. James prided himself that he was rarely what he would call 'overtaken'; that was because he knew when he had had enough.

He fidgeted inside his padded clothes, which gave him the appearance of being a fat man; but ever since the Gunpowder scare he had insisted that his doublets be thickly quilted – and it was the same with his breeches, for how could he be sure when someone, resentful against a Stuart or Protestant, might not have the idea to thrust a dagger into him? There were plenty of Englishmen who were not pleased to have a Stuart on the throne; he knew that they whispered about the days of good Queen Bess, and did not care for the Scotsmen he had brought to the Court, nor their Scottish manners either. They thought him ill-behaved at times, and said the Tudors had had a royal dignity which he lacked.

James could laugh at them. He might not have the looks of a King. His ancestor Henry VIII had been a fine-looking man, he knew; well over six feet tall, and men had trembled when he frowned. James was neither tall nor short; his straggly beard was characteristic of the rest of him; his eyes were too prominent; his tongue seemed too large, which resulted in a thickness of speech; and since he made no effort to cast off a broad accent, and sometimes lapsed into Scottish idiom, the English were often bewildered by his utterances.

He was glad to be seated; he never felt easy when his legs were all that supported him, for they were inclined to let him down at any moment. Perhaps they had never recovered from the tight swaddling of his infancy; moreover, he had not been allowed to walk until he was five years old, and there were times when he still tottered like an infant or a drunken man.

His nature was a philosophical one; he accepted his physical disabilities by taking a great pride in his mental superiority over most of his contemporaries. The title of 'The Wisest King in Christendom' had not been lightly bestowed, and he believed that if he put his mind to it he could get the better of Northampton, Suffolk, Nottingham, or any of his ministers.

He scratched with grubby fingers through the padded and jewelled doublet. He disliked washing and never put his hands in water, although occasionally he allowed one of his servants to dab them with a wet cloth. The English complained of the lice which often worried them; but James believed it was better to harbour a few of the wee creatures than undergo the torment of washing.

'In the reign of good Queen Bess,' these English grumbled, 'ladies and gentlemen came to Court to search for honours, now they have to search for fleas.'

''Tis the more harmless occupation,' James told them.

So the Court had deteriorated since Tudor days, had it? But he believed the Tudors had not been such lenient sovereigns. They had demanded flattery – something which James would have scorned, immediately understanding the motive behind it, and not for one moment believing that he was the most

handsome of men. The old Queen had had to be more or less
made love to by her ministers when she was a black-toothed
hag. Was that wisdom? Nay, James knew himself for what he
was and asked for no deception. His subjects had no need to
fear that their heads would be parted from their bodies on the
slightest provocation. They called him Solomon; and he was
proud of it, although he did not much like the jest that the
name had been given to him because he was the son of David.
He was the son of the Earl of Darnley and Queen Mary; and it
was a calumny to suggest that his mother had taken David
Rizzio as her lover and that he was the result.

But there would always be these scandals; and what did
they matter now that the crown which united England and
Scotland was his. The result was peace in this island as there
had never been before, and all because the wisest King in
Christendom, who had been James VI of Scotland, was now
also James I of England.

'Fill up, laddie,' he said gently.

Wine! Good wine! When he was a baby he had had a drunk-
ard for a wet nurse; it had not been discovered for a long
time, and sometimes he wondered whether her milk had been
impregnated with stronger stuff and that as he had been nur-
tured on it he had acquired not only a taste but a need for
it.

A strange childhood his. The youth of royal children was
often hazardous and that was doubtless why, when they came
to power, they frequently abused it. But his childhood was
even more unsettled than most; and that was not to be wondered at when he considered the events which had taken place
in his family at the time. His father murdered — by his
mother's lover — and some said that his mother had a hand in
it. His mother's hasty marriage to the Earl of Bothwell; the
civil war; his mother's flight to England where she had remained a prisoner in the hands of good Queen Elizabeth for
some twenty years. Not a very safe background for a child
whose legs were weak and who had only his wits to help him
hold his place among the ambitious lairds surrounding him.

How he had gloried in that good quick brain of his! He

might not have been able to walk but he soon learned to talk. He could memorize with the utmost ease; his prominent eyes seemed to take in more than those of the grown-up people about him; there was little they missed; and with childish frankness he did not hesitate to comment on what he saw. As soon as he began to talk his wit was apparent; and all those ambitious men who wished him to be no more than a figure-head for their schemes, were often dismayed.

That excellent memory of his had many pictures of the past preserved for him; and one of those which he liked best was himself, not yet five, being carried into the great hall of Stirling Castle by his guardian the Earl of Mar, there to be placed on a throne to repeat a speech which he had had no difficulty in learning by heart. He had astonished them all by the manner in which he could make such a speech; and as he had made it, his observant eyes had noticed that one of the slates of the roof had slipped off, and through it he could see a glint of blue sky.

He could still hear his high, precise voice informing the company: 'There is ane hole in this Parliament.'

From then on men had respected him, for what to him had been a statement of fact had been construed as grim pro-phecy. The Regent Moray had been assassinated, and the Earl of Lennox, James' paternal grandfather who had been elected the next Regent, quickly met a violent death.

The Scottish lairds were certain that their young King was no ordinary child.

James had been gleeful. He could not walk, but while he had attendants to carry him wherever he wished to go, what did that matter? He would walk all in good time; and while he waited for that day he would read, watch and learn.

He had come a long way from that Stirling Parliament to the Palace of Whitehall.

His eyes brightened as he watched the riders. There was Sir James Hay. A pretty boy James Hay had been when his King had brought him to England from Scotland; now he was a very fine gentleman. James had been very fond of young Hay and determined to advance him. A pleasant boy with manners to please the English because they were more polished than most Scotsmen's since Hay had been brought up in France; James had made him a Gentleman of the Bedchamber and young Hay had proved to be a good companion, his nature being an easygoing one and free of tantrums.

He was a little vain, of course, but who would not be, the King asked himself indulgently, possessed of such outstanding physical charm? The young man liked ostentation and, as James liked to bestow gifts of money on his friends, it was no concern of his how they spent it. If their tastes ran to fine garments, lavish displays, well let them enjoy themselves, remembering all the time whose kindly – if somewhat grubby – hand bestowed these favours.

Sir James was followed everywhere by his retinue of pages, all handsomely dressed, though naturally less so than their master, and it was certainly a pleasant sight to see Sir James and his little retinue in action.

James caught the eye of the Queen upon him. Her expression was reproachful. Poor Queen Anne, she was getting somewhat fat and showed the effect of seven pregnancies; yet she still preserved the petulance which he had once thought not unattractive. That was in the days of his romantic youth when he had braved the storms to go to her native land and bring his bride back to Scotland. He could smile now to remember their first meeting and how he had been delighted with his young Danish Princess, how he had in time sailed with her back to Scotland and brought to trial those witches who he believed had sought to drown his Anne on her way to Scotland. Pleasant days but gone, and James was too wise a man to wish to return to youth; he would barter youth any day for experience; knowledge was more to be prized than vigour.

Theirs had not been an unsuccessful marriage, although they sometimes kept separate Courts now. That was wise, for her interests were not his. She was a silly woman, as frivolous as she had been on her arrival, and still believed doubtless that what had been charming at sixteen still was at thirty-two. She kept with her those two Danish women, Katrine Skinkell and Anna Kroas, and it seemed to him their main preoccupation was to plan balls, the Queen's great passion being dancing. But he must be fair: dancing and her children.

Every now and then her gaze would rest with pride on their eldest, Prince Henry; and James could share her pride. He often wondered how two like himself and Anne could have produced such a boy. A perfect King, Henry would make one day; the people thought it. They cheered him heartily whenever he appeared in public. He was an English Prince, they thought, though he had been born in Stirling. Doubtless they would not be displeased when his Old Dad gave up the crown to him.

But there's life in the old gossip yet, thought James.

Then his attention was caught by a figure in the retinue of Sir James Hay. This was a tall, slim young man who was carrying Sir James' shield and device and whose duty it would be, at the appropriate moment, to present these to the King.

That laddie is familiar, mused James. Where can I have seen him before? At Court? 'Tis likely so. Yet once having seen him, would I not remember?

He forgot the Queen and young Henry; he forgot his own brooding on the past.

His attention was focused on the young stranger, and he was impatient for the moment when the boy would ride to the stage, dismount, and come to kneel before him with his favourite's shield and device.

The young man who had attracted the King's attention would have been delighted had he known that James had already singled him out, because that was exactly what he was hoping for.

He had recently returned from France where he had heard rumours of conditions at the English Court. The King, it was said, surrounded himself with handsome young men who, it seemed, had little to do but look handsome – which was an easy enough task if one had been born that way, as he, Robert Carr, certainly had.

This habit of the King's was deplored by his more serious

statesmen, but as long as they were able to keep the favourites under some control they accepted it. There were worse faults in Kings.

Robert Carr, tall, slender with perfectly shaped limbs, a fine skin to which the sun of France had given a light golden tan, features so finely chiselled that strangers turned to take a second look, hair that glistened like gold and was thick and curly, was an extremely handsome young man. Women constantly plagued him, but while he enjoyed their company he did not allow them to take up too much of his time.

He had always been ambitious, and being a younger son in a not very affluent Scottish family had given him a determination, at a very early age, to rise in the world; and he had seen his opportunity when his father, Sir Thomas Carr of Ferniehurst, had found a place for him at the Court of the King.

James had been pleased to receive the boy, for Sir Thomas Carr had been a faithful friend to his mother, Mary Queen of Scots, during her long captivity and James felt the family should be rewarded in some way.

So young Robert had been allowed to come to Court to serve as a page; but he was young and ignorant of Court ways and scarcely ever saw the King in whom in any case he would have been too young to arouse much interest.

He had not been long at Court when that event took place which was to unite the two nations who for centuries had been at war with each other. Queen Elizabeth died and James was declared King of England and Scotland.

It was natural that James should leave the smaller kingdom to govern in the larger, although he had declared in St Giles' Cathedral that never would he forget the rights of his native Scotland and it would be his endeavour to see that Scotland lost nothing but gained everything from the union. James kept his word and many a Scotsman now was lording it below the Border.

Robert had come South in the royal retinue, but James, finding his Court somewhat over-populated by Scottish gentlemen, had found it necessary to placate his new subjects by dismissing some of them in favour of the English. Young Robert had been sent to France, which, he now realized, had been for his good. In that country he learned more gracious manners than those he could have acquired in his native land; and there was no doubt that they added to his extreme attractiveness. In France he learned what an asset good looks were; and the raw Scottish boy had become an ambitious young man.

He considered himself fortunate to have been taken into the retinue of Sir James Hay, himself brought up in France, and handsome enough to have won the King's favour; in fact one on whom young Robert might, with reason and hope, model himself.

The King's presents to those he favoured were varied, and Sir James had been presented with an heiress for a wife. Robert being somewhat impecunious was in need of such a useful acquisition; he had no intention of remaining in a minor position in the household of a favourite when he himself – and it would have been falsely modest to deny this – was far more personable. He lacked experience of course, but that would come with time.

It was a very excited, hopeful young man who rode into the tilting yard on that day.

He could see the King seated on his chair of state, the light catching the jewels on his quilted doublet. James did not wear those costly garments with elegance; but what did that matter when it was well known how he admired that quality in others. Perhaps it was because he was uncomely, bulky and weak in the legs that he so admired physical perfections in others. And there was the Queen – but wise young men did not concern themselves overmuch with the Queen. If a young man could make no headway in the King's Court, then he might try in the Queen's; and there had been cases when the Queen's favour had actually led to the King's. But Anne was not pleased by the King's delight in handsome young men, so at this stage she need not be considered.

There was Prince Henry, himself personable, but very young, of course. He too had his friends and Robert had heard that he used his influence with the King for the benefit of those he favoured. So there they were – the royal trio on the stage, from each of whom blessings could flow.

Determined to have the King's attention, Robert rode close to the stage. But at that moment when he was prepared to dismount gracefully, the horse rose from his haunches, and kicking up his hind legs shot his rider over his head.

Robert rolled over and over. Then he lost consciousness.

Robert Carr who had so meant to impress the King by his equestrian skill had taken an ignoble tumble and lay unconscious before the royal stage.

James rose unsteadily to his feet. He disliked accidents; he was constantly afraid that they would happen to him, and the ease with which they could occur distressed him.

He descended from the stage, and by this time a little crowd had collected about the fallen man. It parted to let the King through.

'Is he much hurt?' he asked.

'His arm's broken for one thing, Sire,' said one of the onlookers.

'Poor wee laddie! Let him be carried gently into the Palace, and send one of my physicians to look to his needs.'

Someone had removed Robert's helmet and his golden hair fell across his pale brow.

James looked at him. Why, he was like a Grecian statue, what beautifully moulded features! The eyelashes were golden brown against his skin, and several shades darker than his hair.

At that moment Robert opened his eyes and the first face he saw among those bending over him was that of the King.

He remembered in a rush of shame that he had failed.

James said gently: 'I've sent for a man to look to you, laddie. Dinna be afraid. He'll look after you.'

He smiled, and it was the tender smile he bestowed on all handsome young men.

He turned away then and Robert groaned.

He had had his great chance but believed he had failed.

*   *   *

That evening James called his favourite, Sir James Hay, to his side and demanded to know how the young man who had fallen in the tiltyard was faring.

'A broken arm, Sire, seems to be the main damage. He'll mend fast enough. He's young.'

'Ay, he's young,' agreed the King. 'Jamie, where is the lad?'

'Your Majesty commanded that he was to be housed in your own palace and given the attention of your own physician. This has been done. He is bedded next to your own apartments.'

'Poor laddie, I fear he suffered. He was so eager to do well in the yard.'

'Perhaps he has not done so badly, sire,' murmured Sir James.

'I'll go and tell him so. He'd like to hear it from me, I'll swear.'

'He might even think it worth a broken bone or two,' replied Sir James.

'What! A visit from his King! You boys all flatter your Old Dad, Jamie.'

'Nay, Sire, I was not thinking to flatter.'

James laughed, nursing a secret joke. His lads were always afraid he was going to single one of them out for special favours. Jealous cubs, they were, fighting together. Yet they never amused him so much as when they jostled for his favour.

So James went along to see Robert Carr, who lay in bed, his beautiful head resting on his pillows. He tried to struggle up when he saw the King.

'Nay, laddie, bide where you are.'

James took a seat beside the bed.

'Are you feeling better now?'

'Y . . . yes, Sire,' stammered the boy.

A very nice natural modesty, thought James; and now there was a faint colour in the young face and, by God, there could not have been a more handsome face in the whole of the Court . . . now or at any time.

'Dinna be afraid, laddie. Forget I'm the King.'

'Sire . . . I lie here and . . .'

'As you should, and I forbid you to do aught else'

'I should be kneeling.'

'So you shall when you're well enough. Tell me now: is it true that you're Robbie Carr of Ferniehurst?'

'Yes, Sire.'

'I've heard tell of your father. He was a good and loyal servant to my mother the Queen of the Scots.'

'He would have died for her as I would . . .'

'As you would for your King? Nay, mon! he'd not ask it. This King likes not to hear of men dying . . . and this is more so when they have youth and beauty. Wouldn't a broken arm be enough, eh? Is it painful?'

'A little, Sire.'

'They tell me it'll be well enough soon. Young bones mend quickly. Now, Robbie Carr, were you a page to me back in bonny Scotland?'

'Yes, Sire.'

'And came South with me and then left me?'

'I was sent to France, Sire.'

'Where they taught you pretty manners, I see. Now you're back at the King's Court, and Robbie, your King's telling you this: he hopes there you'll stay.'

'Oh Sire, my great wish is to serve you.'

'So you shall.'

Robert had heard that the King was always deeply impressed by good looks but he had not believed that they could have such a remarkable effect as his evidently had. The King was as indulgent as a father; he wanted to know about Robert's childhood, what life had been like at Ferniehurst.

Robert told of how he had been taught to tilt and shoot, and how he had become an expert in such manly pastimes.

'But what of books, lad?' James wanted to know. 'Did they not tell you that there was more lasting pleasure to be found in them than in the tiltyard?'

Robert was alarmed, because his teachers had despaired of

him and he was far happier out of doors than in the school-
room; it had seemed more important to his parents that he
should grow up strong in the arm than in the head.

James was disappointed.

'It seems to me, lad, that your education has been most
shamefully neglected. And a pity too, for ye'd have had a
good brain if any had taken the trouble to train it.'

James went sorrowfully away, but the next day he returned
to Robert's bedside. With the King came one of his pages
carrying books, which at James' command he laid on the
bed.

James' eyes were bright with laughter.

'Latin, Robbie,' he cried. 'Now here ye are, confined to bed
for a few days. And already you're longing to be in the saddle
again and out in the sunshine. Ye canna, Robbie. But there's
something you can do. You can make up a little for all ye've
lost, by a study of the Latin tongue, and ye'll discover that
there's more adventure to one page of learning than to be
found in months in the tiltyard. For ye're going to have a
good tutor, Robbie – the best in the Kingdom. Can you guess
who, lad? None but your King.'

In the Court they were discussing the King's latest oddity.
Each morning he was at the bedside of Robert Carr. The
young man was not an apt pupil; but the teacher quickly forgave him this deficiency because he had so much that gave him
pleasure.

It was clear; the King had found a new favourite.

Opposite the entrance to the tiltyard at Whitehall was the
Gatehouse, a magnificent pile, built by Holbein, of square
stones and flint boulders, tessellated and glazed. Several busts
of terracotta and gilt adorned the Gatehouse; one of these
represented Henry VII and another Henry VIII; and it was
known as the Cockpit Gate.

At one of the windows two children – a boy and a girl –
stood looking down towards the tiltyard where a group
slowly sauntered, led by the King who was leaning on the arm
of a tall, golden-haired young man.

The boy was about thirteen although he looked older and the expression on his handsome face was very serious. The girl, who was some two years younger than her brother, slipped her arm through his.

'Oh, Henry,' she said, 'do not let it disturb you. If it were not this one, it would be someone else.'

Prince Henry turned to his sister, frowning. 'But a King should set an example to his people.'

'The people like our father well enough.'

'Well enough is not good enough.'

'It will be different when you are King, Henry.'

'Do not say that!' retorted her brother sharply. 'For how could I be King unless our father died?'

Elizabeth lifted her shoulders. Although but eleven, she already showed signs of great charm; she adored her brother Henry, but she was much happier when he was less serious. There were so many pleasures to be enjoyed at Court, so why concern themselves with the odd behaviour of their parents? At least they themselves were indulged and had little to complain of. Their father might be disappointed because they did not show signs of being as learned as he was, but on the whole he was a tolerant parent.

Henry however had a strong sense of the fitness of things; that was why everyone admired and respected him. He was constantly learning how to be a good king when his time came. He was wonderful in the saddle but did not care for hunting, believing it to be wrong to kill for the sake of killing. Many thought this a strange notion, but it was natural that the son of King James should have odd ideas now and then.

If he had not excelled at all games and disliked study he would have been too perfect to be popular, but his small faults endeared him to everyone.

Elizabeth put her head on one side and regarded him with affection.

'What are you thinking of?' he demanded.

'You,' she told him.

'You might find a more worthy subject.'

She put her arms about his neck and kissed him. 'Never,' she told him. Then she laughed. 'I heard two of your servants grumbling together today. They complained that you had caught them swearing and insisted on their paying a fine into your poor box.'

'And they liked that not?'

'They liked it not. But methinks they liked you for enforcing the rule. Now Henry, tell me this: are you pleased when your servants swear?'

'What a question! It is to prevent their swearing that I fine them.'

'Yes, but the more fines they pay, the more money for the poor. So perhaps the poor would wish your apartment to be filled with profanity.'

'You are becoming as serious-minded as you say I am.'

'Oh no!' Elizabeth laughed. She changed the subject. 'Our father does not like you to visit your friend in the Tower.'

'He has not forbidden me to go.'

'No, he would not. Our father is a strange man, Henry. He hopes that you won't, but he understands that you must; and therefore he does not interfere.'

'Why do you tell me this?'

'It is like the fines in the poor box all over again. So much that is good; so much that is not good. It is hard to weigh good against evil. There is much our father does which you do not like; but he is a good father to us.'

'My dear sister,' said Henry with a smile, 'I sense your reproach.'

'Why do we concern ourselves with matters beyond us? Are you practising vaulting now, and shall I come to watch you?'

'I am going to the Tower.'

At that moment the door opened and a woman entered holding a little boy by the hand; the child was about seven and walked with great difficulty.

'My lord, my lady,' she said, 'I did not know you were here.'

'Come in, Lady Carey,' invited Henry. 'And how is my brother today?'

The woman's face was illumined by a loving smile.

'Tell your brother, sweeting,' she said. 'Tell him how you walked all alone this morning.'

The pale-faced little boy nodded his head and his eyes sought those of his elder brother with adulation.

'I w . . . walked,' he said, 'alone.'

An impediment in his speech made the words sound muffled.

'That is good news, Lady Carey,' Henry told her.

'Good news, of a surety, my lord. And when I think of this little one . . . not so long ago!'

'You have been good to him,' put in Elizabeth.

'He is my precious boy,' declared Lady Carey. 'Are you not, Charles?'

Charles nodded and thickly confirmed this.

Elizabeth came and knelt down by the side of her younger brother. She touched his ankles. 'They don't hurt any more, do they, Charles?' she asked.

He shook his head.

Lady Carey picked him up in her arms and kissed him. 'My boy will be taller and stronger than any of you before long; you see!'

Elizabeth noticed how the little boy gripped Lady Carey's bodice. Poor little Charles, he was the unfortunate one. But at least he was able to walk now, after a fashion; there had been a time, not very long ago, when they had all thought he would neither walk nor speak; and several of the Court ladies had declined the honour of bringing him up because they feared it was an impossible task.

Lady Carey, however, had taken a look at the poor helpless child and decided to devote herself to his care; it was small wonder that she was proud of what she was doing, even though little Charles was an object of pity to most who beheld him.

Elizabeth took her little brother from Lady Carey and set him on a table.

'Have a care, my lady,' implored Lady Carey; and she was immediately at the side of her little charge to hold his hand

and assure him that no harm could come to him.

Henry came to the table. 'Why, Charles,' he said, 'you're as big as I am now.'

Charles nodded. He was intelligent enough; it was merely that his legs were so weak, and it was feared that his ankles were dislocated and he would never be able to do anything but stagger about; moreover some deformity of the mouth prevented him from speaking clearly.

Henry, deeply touched by the plight of his young brother, began to talk to him about riding and jousting and all the sports which he would be able to take part in when he grew stronger. Young Charles listened avidly, nodding from time to time while he smiled with delight. He was happy because he was with the people he loved best in the world – his adored foster mother, his wonderful brother, his sweet sister.

Anne, the Queen, chose this time to visit the royal nursery. She came whenever she could, for she loved her children dearly, particularly her first born who seemed to her all that a Prince should be.

So while Henry and Elizabeth talked to the little boy seated on the table, Anne came in followed by Katrine Skinkell and Anna Kroas.

'My sweet children!' she cried in her guttural voice. 'So little Charles is here with his brother and sister.'

Lady Carey made a deep curtsy; Elizabeth did the same while Henry bowed and Charles looked on with earnest eyes.

'Henry, my Prince, how well you look; and you too, daughter. And my little Charles?'

'Making good progress Your Majesty,' Lady Carey told the Queen.

'And can he bow yet to his mother?' asked the Queen.

Lady Carey lifted the little boy from the table and stood him down where he did his best to make a bow.

Anne signed to Lady Carey to lift him up and bring him to her, when she kissed him.

'My precious baby,' she murmured. 'And what a pleasure to have my family at Court all at the same time.' A petulant expression crossed her otherwise placid face. She loved her children and had longed to be able to bring them up herself. She hated the royal custom which ordained that others should have charge of them. She would have been a good mother – even if she had tended to spoil her children – had she been allowed to.

Now here was Charles more devoted to Lady Carey than to her; and Henry – beloved Henry, a son of whom any parent might be proud – while affectionate, depended on her not at all.

She never saw Henry without remembering her joy at the time of his birth, when she had believed herself the most contented woman alive; but what anger and frustration had followed when she had learnt that she was not to be allowed to bring up her son. That he should be taken from her and given into the care of the old Earl and Countess of Mar had been more than she could endure. James, always the most affectionate and tolerant of husbands, had commiserated with her, but had insisted that the custom of Scotland was that its kings should be brought up in Stirling Castle under the care of an Earl of Mar, and there was nothing he could do about that.

She had stormed and raged, and perhaps her relationship with James had changed from that moment. She had pointed out that a King should be the one to decide how his son should be brought up and, when his Queen passionately desired to nurture her own son, he should have thrust aside custom.

How she had hated the Mars! She had never lost an opportunity of showing that hatred; and as there had been many turbulent lairds who were only too pleased to make mischief, James, who could be very clear-sighted, reprimanded her gently.

'I lived through a troublous childhood,' he told her, 'and ambitious men used me in their schemes against my mother. I beg you, wife, do not seek to bring discord into this kingdom.'

Anne had been young and heedless, and not prepared to

have her wishes set aside. There might easily have been trouble had James been of a different nature; but while he sought to please the Queen by arranging for her to see as much as was possible of her son, he never allowed her to poison his mind against the Mars.

She had never forgiven James; she had continued to fret for her son; but soon she was pregnant again and Elizabeth was born, only to be taken from her to be given into the care of Lord Livingstone and his wife.

There had followed other pregnancies and Anne was in a measure resigned. The children were growing up now and she contrived that they should be at Court as much as possible; they were fond of her; and she tried to forget the grudge she bore against their guardians and gave herself up to the pleasures of ball and banquet.

She had become frivolous; there were some who declared that she had had a hand in the Gowrie Plot, but that was nonsense. Anne would never bestir herself to plot against a husband who had been indulgent to her; there were others who said that she had preferred the Earl of Murray to the King; that was again not true. Anne was no intriguer; she was a thoughtless, somewhat spoiled woman, who, when she became a mother wanted to devote her life to the children she adored.

Now, as she gave herself up to the pleasure of talking to them, Anna Kroas came close to her and whispered: 'The King has entered the Cockpit Gate, Your Majesty. He is on his way to the nursery.'

Queen Anne's expression scarcely changed. 'Is it so, Anna,' she said mildly.

Anna wanted to tell her that she had seen from the window that he had the new young man with him, the one who had broken his arm in the tiltyard and of whom the whole Court was talking. But her mistress would discover that soon enough; Anna hoped the Queen would not show too openly her dislike of the new favourite.

The door was opened and James came into the room, not as a King should come; he was quite without dignity, thought the Queen angrily. Sometimes when his young men were in high spirits she heard his voice weak with laughter. 'You laddies will be the death of Old Dad.'

Old Dad! And sometimes Old Gossip! A fine way for a King to behave. It was small wonder that the English sighed for the days of the Tudors when a King or a Queen was a being, far above them, whose smiles were coveted, whose frowns were feared.

'The family is assembled here then,' cried James with a chuckle.

He was leaning heavily on the arm of Robert Carr who had flushed and was uncertain how to behave when he saw the Queen.

He bowed in an embarrassed way but Anne did not look at him.

'Henry,' said James, 'it does me good to see you so bonny. And Elizabeth.'

The children, Anne noticed with pride, ignored their father's crude behaviour and showed the respect due to a great King.

'Well, well,' laughed James, 'get off your knees, lad. This is no state occasion. Why, Elizabeth, you're taller every time I see you.' He smiled at Anne. ' 'Tis true, eh, Majesty?'

' 'Tis true, Your Majesty,' Anne answered, and her tone was warm as it must be when she talked of her children.

'And I must not forget my youngest. Well, how's my mannie?'

Lady Carey who was at Charles' side, took his hand and pressed it reassuringly while James came close to his youngest son and took his chin in his hand. Charles looked into his eyes, unafraid; no one could be afraid of James unless they had offended him deeply, and even then he would be calmly judicious.

'Prince Charles is walking a little now, Your Majesty,' Lady Carey told the King.

'Good news. Good news. And he is talking?'

Lady Carey whispered to the boy: 'Say Yes, Your Majesty.'

Charles opened his mouth and did his best, but the words were strangled. James nodded and patted the boy's shoulder.

'Well done,' he said. 'Well done.'

Then he laid his hand on Henry's shoulder and pushed him towards the table on which young Charles was sitting. 'Talk to your brother, lad,' he said. 'And you with him, Elizabeth.'

Then he took the Queen by the arm and walked away from the group round the table, towards the window, calling over his shoulder to Lady Carey to follow him.

When they had reached the window he said quietly to Lady Carey: 'The lad does not improve.'

Lady Carey's face puckered. 'But, Your Majesty, he does, indeed he does. He is much better.'

'He is no longer a baby.'

'But he can speak a little. Forgive me, Your Majesty, but he is overawed by your presence.'

'He's the only one in this Court who is then,' said James with a laugh.

Lady Carey was afraid, for the Queen was regarding her with the dislike she had for all those who took her children away from her.

'It cannot go on,' mused James.

'Your Majesty, he *is* improving. I do assure you of that.'

'I've been consulting my physicians about him, Lady Carey, and they believe he should be put in iron boots to strengthen his bones, and the string under his tongue be cut.'

'Oh no, Your Majesty. I implore you. Why, do you not see how he has improved since he has been in my care? The boots would be too heavy for him and he would never walk. He has a horror of them. Your Majesty, I beg of you, do not do this.'

Lady Carey's eyes were full of tears; her lips twitching, her hands trembling. She looked imploringly at the Queen.

'Why should she have the care of my baby?' Anne asked herself. 'She behaves as though she were his mother.'

Lady Carey was so overwrought that she laid a hand on the

King's arm. 'Your Majesty, he is speaking more clearly than he was a month ago. He needs confidence ... and loving care. To cut the string might mean that he would never speak again or at best have an impediment for the rest of his life.' Her eyes were shining with faith. 'I know I can make him well. I am certain of it.' She looked from the King to the Queen and seemed suddenly aware of her temerity. 'Your gracious pardons,' she murmured, lowering her head; and the King and the Queen saw that she was fighting to control her tears.

James looked at his wife, but she would not meet his gaze. She was thinking: This woman loves my Charles as though she were his mother in truth. And I hate her because she has taken him from me. But it is good for Charles to have one who loves him so.

The maternal instinct was stronger in Anne than any other and she could forget her jealousy in her concern for her son. So she said: 'Lady Carey should be given a further opportunity to prove her words. It is true that Charles is better since she took charge of him. It is my wish that there should be no iron boots, nor cutting of the string ... as yet.'

'My dears,' replied James, 'this is the advice of the doctors.'

But the two women stood firm; there was a bond between them; they were so conscious of their feelings for the child, and they shared the belief that the power of maternal love could exceed the experiments of doctors, however wise.

James regarded them with mild good nature. They loved the boy; there was no doubt of that; and there was also no doubt that young Charles loved his nurse.

James often preferred to thrust aside decisions.

'Then for the time let things be as they are.'

Lady Carey seized his hand and kissed it.

'Why,' he said kindly, 'it is the Queen and myself who should be showing gratitude to you, my dear.'

The Queen's mouth tightened. 'I know,' she added, 'that Lady Carey has looked after him as though she were his mother. She could not do more than that.'

James turned to Robert Carr who had been standing at

some little distance while this conversation took place.

'Come ye here, Robbie,' he said. 'Give me your arm.'

'So Your Majesty needs support, even as little Charles?' murmured Anne maliciously.

'Aye,' retorted James. 'I like a strong arm to lean on.'

'There might be stronger and more practised arms,' said the Queen.

And when Robert Carr came to the King she turned her back on him.

James, smiling, went to the children, exchanged a few jocular words with them and then, leaning on the arm of Robert Carr, left the apartment.

James went to his own quarters and when his little party arrived there he dismissed them all, with the exception of Robert, because he sensed that the Queen's antagonism had upset his favourite.

'Sit down, lad,' he said, when they were alone, and Robert took a stool and placed it by the King's chair. He sat leaning his head against James's knee while the grubby royal fingers gently pulled at his golden hair. 'Ye mustna let the Queen upset ye, Robbie,' went on James. 'She never did take kindly to my lads.'

'I thought she hated me,' Robert said.

'No more than many another. The Queen's a kind woman in her limits and it grieves me to plague her. Ours has been a good union, though, and we've children to prove it. Two boys and a girl left out of seven; and the eldest as bonny as children could be. Little Charles . . . well, you heard how the women stood against me, Robbie. But 'tis on account of their fears for the boy. The Queen would have been a good mother if she'd been in another station of life. Queens, poor bodies, are not permitted to care for their own. From the time of Henry's birth she changed towards me, and all because I'd not dismiss the Mars and give her charge of the bairn.'

'I fear that she will poison Your Majesty's mind against me.'

'Nay, laddie. Never. I've been a happy man since my Robbie came to cheer up his Old Dad. Dinna take much notice of the

Queen's little spites. Bless ye, boy, others have felt it before you.'

'Sire, there is something I must explain to you.'

'Your Old Dad is listening, Robbie.'

'Your Majesty has raised me so high in so short a time. But often I feel out of place at Court. Your Ministers look down on me – men like the Howards. I'm not one of them. I'm shabby . . . I'm poor.'

'Give your Old Gossip time, laddie. I'm going to make ye the most grand gentleman among them. Ye shall have fine clothes and in time an estate of your own. Why, I might find you a rich bride. That would be a fine plan, eh?'

'Your Majesty is so good to me.'

'I like to see my boys happy. Now, dinna fret. All will be well. If fine clothes would help you to be happier, fine clothes you shall have. This very day you shall see some silks and satins, brocades and velvets; and make your choice. Why, mannie, there'll be no one to hold a candle to you. Though your Old Dad thinks that's the case without fine clothes.'

'How can I thank Your Majesty?'

'Ye do well enough, Robbie. Now bide quiet a wee while and let me chat with you. Conversation is a pleasant pastime; and when ye've spent a little more time with your books, there'll be conversation in plenty for us.'

'I fear I am a simpleton – and Your Majesty so learned.'

'And you such a winsome fellow and me an old scarecrow. Dinna make protest, lad. I was ne'er a beauty. Which is surprising for my mother was reckoned the foremost beauty of the day; and my father was a handsome fellow. But ye see, I was never cared for as a babe. There were too many who wanted what I had – a crown. And I had it too young, Robbie, for they took it from my poor mother who was a captive of the Queen of England, and they wanted it . . . they wanted it badly. And now I'm no longer a boy; and there are still some who'd like to see me out of the way. Look at these padded breeks. I often wonder, when my subjects press too close, whether one of them is not waiting . . . with a hidden dagger.'

'No one would harm Your Majesty.'

'Oh, laddie, ye've not long come to Court. Did ye never hear of the Gunpowder Plot? Did ye never hear how the Catholics planned to blow up the Houses of Parliament while I and my ministers were sitting?'

'Yes, Your Majesty. Everyone was talking of it at the time and rejoicing in your escape.'

'Aye,' murmured James. 'Yet the scoundrels might so easily have succeeded. Do you know, lad, if one of the conspirators had not been anxious to save the life of Lord Monteagle, if he hadn't warned him to stay away from Parliament, the cellars would never have been searched; we should never have discovered the gunpowder and Guido Fawkes keeping watch. And that would have been the end of the Parliament and your King, Robbie.'

'But Your Majesty had loyal subjects who prevented the treachery.'

'Ay, loyal subjects – and good luck. You can never be sure when they're going to turn, lad. I've had my troubles. You're too young to remember the Gowrie Plot; but I came as near to death then as a man can without dying, and I've no mind to be so close again . . . if I can help it. Oh, Robbie, 'tis a dangerous life, a King's. There was a time when I thought even the Queen was with my enemies.'

James enjoyed reminiscing on the past to his handsome young men; he liked to consider how often he had come near to death and escaped. It was the excuse he offered for the padded garments, for what they might consider timidity on his part. He wanted to assure them that it was sound good sense which made him give such thought to the preservation of a life which had almost been snatched from him on more than one occasion.

'Aye,' he went on, 'I did suspect the Queen, but I'd say now she's never taken part in plots against me. She goes her way and I go mine; but she was a good wife to me, and bore my children. I used to think she had an eye for some of the handsome laddies of the Court. And Alex Ruthven was a fine-looking boy. It was the Ruthvens, you know, who plotted against me. The Earl of Gowrie and his brother, Alexander Ruthven, never forgave me because their father had met the just reward of his villainy. Beatrice Ruthven, their sister, was one of the Queen's ladies and it may be that she brought her brother Alexander to her mistress' notice. I remember a summer's day – it was before young Charles was born – when I was walking with some of my laddies in the grounds of Falkland Palace and came upon young Alex Ruthven fast asleep under a tree. Round the young man's neck was a ribbon – a very beautiful silver ribbon – and I knew it well because I had given it to the Queen. I was a jealous husband then, Robbie. I said to myself: "Now why should this young man be wearing the Queen's ribbon?" And I went with all speed to the Queen's chamber and I said to her: "Show me the silver ribbon I gave to you. I've a mind to see it." And the Queen opened a drawer and took out the ribbon; and there was no denying that it was the ribbon I gave to her.'

'So there were two silver ribbons,' said Robert.

James shook his head. 'Nay,' he continued. 'There was but one ribbon, and methinks I was not at heart the jealous husband I wanted my subjects to think me. I had seen Beatrice Ruthven watching me from behind one of the trees; she was wearing a scarlet dress and she wasn't hidden as well as she thought she was. What did she do? No sooner had I turned and made my way to the Queen's apartments than she tweaked the ribbon from her brother's neck, ran by a short cut to the Queen's chamber, thrust the ribbon into a drawer and gasped out to the Queen what had happened. Why, when I arrived, there was the crafty young woman sitting with needlework on her lap, thinking I didna see how her chest was heaving as she was trying to get back her breath.'

'So the Queen did give the ribbon to Ruthven?'

'Ay, 'twas so. But there was nothing lecherous in the Queen's friendship with the young man. She likes young men to admire her; she did not like my having friends. The rift was there between us; so to pretend she cared not that I spent much time with my friends, she allowed young men to express

their admiration of her. Murray was one; this Alexander Ruthven was another. Ah, that Alexander Ruthven was an enemy of
mine and he met his just reward. Dinna tell me, laddie, that
ye've forgotten what happened to the Ruthvens after what
they tried to do to their King. Oh, but you're but a boy and
this happened before I crossed the Border and took this
crown of England.'

James smiled shrewdly as he looked back, and he could not
resist telling his young friend the stirring story because he felt
he had come out of it well, and he wanted to impress on the
lad that in spite of padded garments he was no coward; he
wanted to teach his dear Robbie the difference between being
afraid and being sensible.

And as he told the story he relived it. He saw himself rising in the early morning of that fateful day in August of the
year 1600. He remembered Anne's watching him sleepily while
his attendants dressed him, for they had shared a bed in those
days. She was big with child, he remembered; Charles was to
be born three months later.

'You are astir early,' she had said. 'Why so?'

He had smiled at her, the excitement in him rising so that
he, usually calm, found it difficult to control. 'That I may kill a
prime buck before noon.'

He did not tell her that he was going in search of a Jesuit
priest who Alexander Ruthven had told him would be at
Gowrie House. This Jesuit, Ruthven had informed him, was in
possession of a bag of Spanish gold and was clearly up to no
good since, of a certainty, he had been sent from Spain to
spread sedition throughout the Protestant land of Scotland.

As he rode out to the hunt James promised himself a
pleasant reward of Spanish gold and, what pleased him almost
as much, a discussion with the Jesuit. There was little he enjoyed so much as spirited conversation, and theological
differences were a delight to him.

Slipping away from the party, and taking with him only a
young gentleman of his bedchamber named Ramsay, he made
his way to Gowrie House where the Earl of Gowrie and his

younger brother Alexander Ruthven were waiting to meet him. Food and wine had been prepared for him and he fell to with enthusiasm, for he was hungry; but he was soon demanding to be taken to the Jesuit. Young Alexander offered to take him and led the way up spiral staircases to a chamber, circular in shape, which James guessed to be the prison-hold of the Gowries; and as the heavy, studded door swung behind him and Alexander, he looked about for the Jesuit. The man was not there; then James noticed a small door in the chamber, but, before he could speak, Alexander had locked the great door and drawn his sword.

James faced the young man and saw murder in his face. His first emotion was anger at his stupidity rather than fear for his life. He had known he was trapped, and that the Gowries had brought him here to murder him.

And they would have murdered him, but for great good fortune. He had been a friend to Ramsay, and Ramsay was ready to risk his life in his service. There had not been many like him; so what good luck that Ramsay had been with him that day! The boy, being anxious because of his disappearance, had prowled about the house searching for him and, hearing his master's cries, found a way of forcing the turnstile and making his way to the circular chamber by means of a private door. He had arrived just in time, for Ruthven had the advantage, and there would certainly have been murder that day at Gowrie House but for Ramsay.

Several of Ruthven's servants, who had been warned to keep all away from the chamber, came hurrying through the private door after Ramsay, and joined in the fight. For some minutes James and his servant held off Ruthven and his; and, seeing how evenly matched they were, one of Ruthven's servants declined to help his master, declaring that he wanted no part in killing the King.

Mar and Lennox, who had been with the hunt that day, missing the King, came on to Gowrie House and, hearing them galloping up, James managed to reach a window and shout down: 'Treason! I am murtherit!'

Lennox found a ladder and climbed it; but it was not until

the Earl of Gowrie and Alexander Ruthven had been killed that the King was rescued.

'And that, Robbie,' James ended, 'was the Gowrie Plot, and it happened in Scotland; and then when I came to England my enemies took a turn with the gunpowder.'

He could see that Robert's attention was forced. Poor laddie, he would have to learn to concentrate.

'Concentration, mannie, is the secret of acquiring know-ledge; did ye know? Train the mind not to wander, however dull the road, however pleasant the meadows by the wayside may seem. 'Twas a lesson I learned early in life. I shall have to give you lessons in the art.'

'Your Majesty has given me so much.'

'And now your mind is on brocade and velvet, eh? And your Old Gossip tires you with his talk of bloody murder. Give me your arm, lad. We'll away and choose the velvet for your jacket and breeks. And we'll see that there's no delay in making them.' He rose to his feet and for a moment swayed uncertainly, till he leaned heavily on Robert. 'But dinna fret yourself for the Queen. She won't love you, boy, but she'll no harm you. The Queen's a good woman, though between our-selves, boy, I've often thought her a frivolous one. Now ... velvet and brocade ... satins and silks. We're going to make Robbie Carr a proper man of the Court.'

Prince Henry rode out of the Palace of Whitehall and turned eastwards. He was soberly dressed and took with him only one attendant, for he was eager not to be recognized. His visits to the Tower were becoming more and more frequent and he did not want them to be commented on lest his father should forbid them. Had James done so, Henry would still have found some means of visiting his friend; he could be stubborn when he believed himself to be in the right, but he was not one to court trouble.

It was pleasant riding through the City, and the journey always delighted him. He was proud of this country which one day, he believed, he would rule. He was determined to bring great good to it; his head was full of a hundred notions; that

was why one of his greatest pleasures was to talk with his dear
friend – the man whom he admired perhaps above all others.
'Men such as he made England great,' he told his sister
Elizabeth, and his eyes would be full of dreams when he spoke.
'When he talks to me, he shows me the world. He ought to
have a fine ship of which he is captain. Would that I could
accompany him on his voyages of discovery. But, alas, I am a
boy and he is a prisoner. None but my father would keep such
a bird in a cage.'

Along the banks of the Thames stood the gabled, tall-chim-
neyed houses of the rich, with their pleasant gardens running
down to the water. He felt daring, riding out almost alone;
but he was determined never to be a coward; he would never
have his garments padded against the assassin's dagger, he
told himself. Better to die than remind everyone who looked
at him how much he feared death.

When he was King he would give encouragement to bold
seamen, and if they disagreed with him on State policy he
would shrug aside such a disagreement. He would never re-
strict his adventures.

He smiled as he looked ahead to where the great fortress,
palace and prison, dominated the landscape.

Many a man had passed into its precincts with the sense of
doom in his heart. There on Tower Hill many an adventurer
had taken his last look on the world; the grass of Tower
Green was stained with the blood of Queens.

Yet he thrilled to look at it – the grey walls with their air of
impregnability, the bastion and ballium, the casemates, the
open leads, the strong stone walls, the battlemented towers.
There was one particular tower he sought – for there his
friend was imprisoned at this time – the Bloody Tower.

Henry felt a shudder of distaste as he entered the gate; the
guards, who knew him well, saluted, well aware whither he
was bound. He had their sympathy; there were many in
London who were not pleased to be ruled by the man from
Scotland; but Henry seemed no foreigner; clearly he defied his
father, in as much as he had made a friend of one of his
father's prisoners.

Henry passed through to the Inner Ward. The wall which bounded this was crowned by twelve mural towers. Now the original fortress lay before him, with its ditch under the ballium wall. Here was the Keep, the Royal Apartments, and the Church of St Peter ad Vincula among other impressive buildings.

Entering the Bloody Tower Henry climbed the staircase to an upper chamber in which, near a small window, a man was seated at a table writing busily. For some seconds he did not notice the Prince. Henry watched him, and his anger was almost like a physical pain; he always felt thus when he called on his friend.

The man looked up. His was one of the handsomest faces Henry had ever seen. Not handsome as men such as Robert Carr were. There was strength in the prisoner's face; arrogance perhaps, something which implied that years of imprisonment could not quell his proud spirit.

'My Prince,' he said; and rose from the table. He walked rather stiffly. The damp cold of the Tower was notorious for seeping into the bones and ruining them.

That such a man should suffer so! fumed Henry inwardly.

'I have come again,' he said.

'And none more welcome.'

'How is the stiffness today?'

'It persists. But I believe I am more fortunate than some. You know I have my three servants to look after me.'

'And your wife?'

'She is at Sherborne Castle with the children.'

Henry was about to speak; but he could not bring himself to do so. He had unpleasant news, but he must break it gently.

He took the arm of the man and led him to the table. How tall he was, how splendid still, though he was past fifty; his face was bronzed with tropical sun, for this was a great traveller; even now as a prisoner he was fastidious in his dress, and there were jewels in his jacket which must be worth a large sum. His hair was well curled; Henry knew that it was the task of one of his servants to attend to this every morning early before his visitors arrived; for Sir Walter Raleigh was visited by the great and famous even though he was a prisoner in the Tower.

'How goes the ship which you are making for me?' asked Henry.

Sir Walter smiled. 'Come and see it. She's a beauty. Would to God I could have her copied full size and set sail in her.'

'And would to God I could go with you. Perhaps some day . . .'

Ah, thought Henry, if I were King, my first duty and pleasure would be to free this man from prison.

'Life is full of chances,' Raleigh told him. 'Who shall say where you and I will be, a year, a week, a day from now?'

'I promise you—' began Henry impetuously.

But Raleigh laid a hand on his arm: 'Make no rash promises, Your Highness. For think how sad you would be if you were unable to honour them.'

Here in the upper chamber of the tower, Raleigh had come to adopt an avuncular attitude towards the Prince. He looked forward to his visits; he admired this boy as much as he despised his father; when he talked to him and reminded himself that this could be the future King of England he ceased to fret for the days of his glory when a woman had sat on the throne, a woman who had become a victim of his charm and had shown him the way to fame and fortune.

He led Henry to the model of the ship, and for half an hour they talked of ships. Raleigh was a man who had been richly endowed; few had ever possessed such gifts and in such variety. He was a poet, an historian, a brilliant statesman as well as an inspired sailor, with a flair for oratory. When he talked of the sea his words were golden; his eyes glowed for a few minutes and Henry could delude himself that the model he held in his hands was sailing the seas and he and Raleigh commanded her.

He almost forgot the unpleasant news he had to give, for Raleigh must be prepared. Not yet, he told himself. Let us enjoy this hour together first.

And later the sailor became the historian and explained to

Henry how he was progressing with the history of the world which he was writing; and when he talked of the Spaniards the fire of hatred shone from his eyes.

Henry knew something of political intrigue and he believed that it was largely due to Spain that his friend was a prisoner. Spain hated Sir Walter Raleigh and was uneasy while such a man was free to roam the seas. How different life in England had been under the Queen. Elizabeth had defied Spain; James, loathing the very thought of conflict, wished to placate that country. He wanted to be at peace, to read the books he loved, to pamper his young men; the only battles he enjoyed were verbal ones.

Men such as Raleigh were no longer Court favourites as they had been in the old Queen's day.

James had known, even before Elizabeth's death, that Raleigh was against his accession and had him marked down for an enemy. Raleigh had plenty of them in England; it was inevitable for one who had so enjoyed the Queen's favour and at one time had been her leading man. He had risen to the peak of power; it was natural that many should long to see him fall to the depths of humiliation.

His great fault was his impetuosity, coupled with his arrogance. He had believed that he might do what others dared not. When he had seduced Bess Throgmorton he had lost the Queen's favour, because she could not endure that he should pay attention to any woman but herself. And a scandal that had been, with Bess pregnant and that other Bess, the all-powerful Gloriana, sending for him and insisting that he right the wrong he had committed and make an honest woman of her namesake.

And his Bessie had been a good wife, always beside him in his misfortune. Their son Walter was a fine boy and little Carew had been born in the Tower, for Bess had her apartments there with him that she might look after him as she swore his servants could not; and there she planned indefatigably to bring about his release.

He told Henry now that he was fortunate ... for a prisoner, as he led the way on to the Walk along the wall, which he was allowed to use in order to enjoy a little fresh air and exercise.

'How many prisoners enjoy such a privilege?' he asked. And Henry knew that he was eager to show him his new experiments in the hut at the end of the Walk which he had been allowed to use for his scientific work.

Inside the hut was a bench on which were several substances in tubes and bottles.

'I'm working on an elixir of life,' he told the Prince. 'If I perfect it, it may well be that people will be living many more years than they do at present.'

'You should have a fine mansion in which to work – not a hut,' said Henry.

'This serves its purpose. My remedies are becoming well known.'

'The Queen said that she had heard your balsam of Guiana was excellent.'

'I am honoured. That balsam is much admired. Only yesterday the Countess of Beaumont, walking in the Tower, saw me on my walk and asked me to send her some.'

'Oh, you should be free. It is so wrong that my father should keep you here.'

'Hush! You speak treason. Why, my Prince, one little word can turn a free man into a prisoner. It is well to remember it. Tell me, what of the new beauty?'

'Carr?'

'I hear he is most handsome and struts about the Court in fine feathers.'

'He is most sumptuously clad now.'

'And the King delights in him. Well, the way seems smooth for him. A rich wife, I'll warrant, who can bring him great estates and a great title . . . Is aught wrong?'

'There is something I have to tell you, Sir Walter.'

'It disturbs you. Do not tell it.'

'But I must. I came to tell it.'

'And is it so bad then that it must be thrust aside?'

Henry nodded. 'It is very bad. Walter, do you care very much for Sherborne Castle?'

Sir Walter had turned slightly pale though this was scarcely noticeable, so bronzed was he.

When he spoke, his voice was harsh. 'Sherborne Castle? Why, that and my land about it is almost all I have left. I have consoled myself that if, by a royal whim, it should be decided that my turn has come to walk out to Tower Hill, Sherborne Castle and my lands will prevent my wife and sons from becoming beggars.'

Henry looked appealingly up at this man whom he so admired; then making a great effort he said: 'My father has decided that Carr must have a great estate. He has offered him Sherborne Castle.'

Sir Walter did not speak; he went to the door of the hut and stood for some seconds on the Walk, staring at the grey walls and battlements.

Henry came out to stand beside him.

'If he had never come to Court, if there had not been an accident in the tiltyard—' Henry began.

Then Raleigh turned to smile at him.

'And if I had not been born, I should not be standing here now. Dear boy, do not say, If this and If that. Because that is life. I am robbed of my possessions. But remember this: I have already suffered a greater loss. My freedom. Yet I continue to live and work.'

Then they went together along the Walk, into the upper chamber of the Bloody Tower.

Never to either of them had it seemed so hopeless a prison.

The Child Bride

THOMAS HOWARD, Earl of Suffolk, had taken time off from Court to visit his country estates, and he had a very special reason for doing so. Thomas Howard, like most of the members of his family, was a very ambitious man; they regarded themselves as the leading family and secretly believed themselves to be as royal as the Tudors and Stuarts. In the past many of them had not hesitated to make this known – to their cost. Suffolk believed he had learned wisdom through the misfortunes of his ancestors; his own father had gone to the scaffold because he had plotted to marry Mary Queen of Scots, and with such an example in the family, Suffolk had no intention of acting so foolishly.

His wife, Catherine, was with him; she did not care for life in the country but she was ready enough to be there on this occasion.

They sat together in the gracious room with the mullioned windows overlooking the parklands; and the expression on their faces showed a certain smugness. This expression was visible on the face of their companion, another member of the Howard family – in fact one might say the head of the House. This was Henry Howard, Earl of Northampton.

Northampton, a man well advanced in years, for he was nearer seventy than sixty, was at this time one of the most powerful men in the country. He had been playing the intricate game of politics so long that he performed with great skill, and in spite of his age he had no intention of relinquishing one small part of his power if he could avoid it.

Being a secret Catholic he greatly desired to bring Catholicism back to England, and his plan for doing this was to arrange a marriage between Prince Henry and the Infanta of Spain. Never for one moment was he insensible of the danger of his position. He had seen his elder brother lose his head; that made him very careful of his own.

Now, at his nephew's home, he was on a very different mission; a pleasant, domestic one; but everything in the life of the Earl of Northampton, as was the case with his nephew Suffolk and his wife, had some political implication.

Northampton was saying: 'This marriage will prove advantageous to us all. James is in favour of it, and while the Scot is a lumbering boor of a fellow, one must not lose sight of the fact that he happens to wear the crown.'

'He is anxious to do honour to any relation of Essex. No doubt he feels remorse because his predecessor, after pampering that young man, allowed his enemies to lop off his head.'

'Oh, the old Queen had to surround herself with handsome men whom she imagined were in love with her, but there were never two she favoured so much as Dudley and Essex. The boy is a pleasant youngster. The union will be good for us all.'

'I have met young Robert. He shows promise. My only regret is that the children are so young.'

'What is it— Fourteen the boy – and the girl?'

'Frances is twelve,' said Lady Suffolk.

'Well she can go back to her lessons while young Robert goes abroad to complete his education. There'll be no question of the consummation yet. I should like to see the child. It is time she was told of her good fortune.'

'I will send for her.'

A few minutes later Frances Howard came into the room. Approaching the group she stopped some little distance from them and dropped a deep curtsy, daintily spreading her blue skirts as she did so. Her gown became her well, but she was so beautiful that nothing could have detracted from her looks. Her long golden hair fell in curls to her waist; her skin was delicate in texture and colour; her blue eyes large and darkly lashed.

Northampton thought: This is not merely a pretty child. This is a beauty.

'Frances,' said her father, 'your great-uncle has come from Court to bring you good news.'

Frances turned hopefully towards Northampton. There was nothing shy in her manner, a fact which half pleased, half annoyed Northampton.

'Come here, child,' he said.

She stood before him waiting while he peered into that oval face seeking some imperfection. He found none.

'How would you like to go to Court?'

'More than anything in the world,' she answered fervently, and her eyes sparkled.

'And what do you think they would want with a child like you at Court?'

'I do not know, Great-Uncle, but I am waiting to hear.'

Was she pert? He was not sure.

'Whether or not Frances Howard was at Court would give little concern, I'll warrant.'

'Yet Frances Howard is to go to Court, Great-Uncle.'

'You are fortunate to have a father, mother and great-uncle, who have your welfare at heart.'

'Yes, Great-Uncle.'

'The fact is – we have a husband for you.'

'A husband . . . for me! Oh, where is he?'

'Do you think I carry husbands around in my pocket, child?'

'I have heard it said that the Earl of Northampton is capable of anything, sir.'

Yes, she was pert; but sharp of wit. What did she need – a place at Court, money lavished on her, or a whipping? He would discover, and whatever she deserved she should have.

Northampton saw that Lady Suffolk was trying not to smile. *She* should be careful. Her reputation was none too good. It was said that she took advantage of her husband's Court posts and accepted bribes for certain services. The woman's morals were not too sound either; and she spent a fortune on her clothes and jewels.

Northampton decided to ignore the girl's comments, telling himself that perhaps he was inviting them.

'You are to have a wedding, child, at Court. The King himself is interested in your bridegroom and wishes to see an alliance between his House and ours.'

'May I know his name, sir?'

'Robert Devereux, Earl of Essex.'

'An Earl. How old is he?'

'Your own age, child . . . or as near as makes no difference. Your mother tells me you are twelve. Robert is fourteen.'

'Fourteen and an Earl already!'

'His father has been dead some years.'

'His father lost his head, I believe,' said Frances. 'I have heard of the Earl of Essex.'

'It is an accident which happens now and then in the best of families,' murmured Northampton.

'The better the family, the more frequently,' put in Lady Suffolk. 'A fact, daughter, which we must all bear in mind.'

'I shall remember,' said Frances.

'I trust you will be grateful to your family for arranging such a good marriage for you,' went on Northampton.

'Is it such a good match?' the girl asked.

'Do you doubt it, Frances?' cried her mother.

'Well, Mother, I have always been taught that there is only one family good enough to mate with the Howards: the royal family.'

Northampton smiled grimly at her parents. 'This girl is but twelve, you say?'

'I remember well enough the day she was born,' said Lady Suffolk. 'Although I must say that bearing children had become rather a habit with me since I married Suffolk. Seven boys and three girls – not a bad tally, Uncle?'

'The Howards could always fill their cradles. They were not like the Tudors – a barren lot. But this child has a ready answer.' He turned to Frances. 'You have a tongue, girl.'

'Why, yes.' She immediately put it out and the expression on her face implied that she enjoyed the gesture.

'Guard it well,' he told her. 'I sense a certain waywardness in it. When you go to Court you must not speak with the freedom you employ here in the country.'

'I understand, Great-Uncle.'

'Now, you must prepare yourself for your wedding.'

'Yes, Frances,' her mother put in, 'we shall have to start at once on your trousseau. You must be worthy of the Earl of Essex.'

'Fine clothes! Jewels!' cried Frances, clasping her hands together. 'How I love them!'

Northampton thought the parents should have had more control over the girl. He now desired her to leave them. He had seen her, assured himself that they had a little beauty who

would be ripe for marriage in a year or so; and that was good
enough.

He waved his hand and her father said: 'You may leave us
now, Frances.'

'Yes, Father,' said the girl; but she hesitated.

'Well?' said Northampton.

'When shall I leave for Court?'

'As soon as your wardrobe is ready,' answered her mother.
'We shall lose no time. The King himself is eager to see you
married.'

'I wonder why—' began Frances.

But Northampton interrupted impatiently. 'It is not for you
to wonder, girl, but to obey your parents. I believe I heard
your father tell you you might leave us now.'

Frances demurely lowered her eyes, swept another curtsy
and blithely left her elders.

In her own chamber, Frances called together three of her
favourite maids. They were well-bred girls who were more like
friends than servants, and their parents were delighted for
them to be brought up in the household of the Earl of Suffolk
who was a man of influence at Court and held among other
offices, that of Lord Chamberlain of the King's Household.
These three were not more than a year or so older than
Frances; but by reason of her rank and personality she completely dominated them.

'Listen,' she demanded. 'It is true – what we suspected. My
parents are here because I am to be married. My great-uncle
himself deemed it necessary to tell me.'

Then she recounted in detail the interview which had just
taken place, colouring it a little to make herself a trifle more
audacious than she had been, taking the part of the Earl of
Northampton and Frances Howard alternately.

'Mistress Frances!' cried one of the girls. 'You'll be the
death of me. And did you, in truth, put your tongue out at my
lord?'

'I did. He asked for it. I fancy he wished he hadn't provoked
me. I wished that someone very important ... someone like

the King or the Prince could have come in and seen me standing there putting my tongue out at the Earl of Northampton.'

'The King would have thought it a great joke, I am sure. He
would have given you a high place at Court and made you one
of his favourites.'

'I should have to dress in breeches and cut off my hair first,'
said Frances, catching at her long curls and holding them lov-
ingly. 'The King has no eyes for girls. You should know
that.'

'Has he not then, Mistress Frances?'

'Do you know *anything*?'

'We dare not listen at doors as you do, mistress,' put in
another girl quietly.

Frances swung round and slapped the girl across the face.

'If I wish to listen at doors, miss, I will. And think again
before you speak thus to me. I can have you whipped; and
don't forget it. I might even do it myself . . . to make sure the
blood is drawn.'

Her eyes were suddenly dark with anger. The girls drew
back. She meant what she said. She could be friendly at one
moment; she could be generous; but if she were offended,
vindictive.

The girl was quiet, her eyes downcast as gradually a red
mark appeared where she had been struck.

Frances turned her back on her and went on: 'I can scarce
wait to go to Court. I'm tired of being a child in the
country.'

'Marriage is but the first step, mistress. And when you go to
Court all the men will—'

'Go on!' commanded Frances. 'Fall in love with me because
I'm so beautiful. That's what you mean, is it not? I wonder
what my bridegroom will think of me. He is only fourteen and
the marriage is not going to be consummated yet. I have
heard them talk of it. They talk of nothing else. I am to go to
Court, be married and then sent back here . . . back to my
lesson books, they say, until I am of an age to share my
husband's bed. I want to tell them that I am of an age now.'

'Perhaps it is better to wait.'

'I hate waiting. I won't wait. I might wait until I'm no longer beautiful.'

'You'll always be beautiful.'

'Of course I shall. I shall make sure that I stay beautiful as long as I live.'

'Everyone tries to do that, mistress.'

Frances was thoughtful. Her own mother was beautiful still, although not as she must have been in her youth. Perhaps it was the fine clothes and jewels she wore that dazzled the eyes.

'I know of a way to stay beautiful,' said a quiet voice, and there was silence, for it belonged to the one who had recently been slapped.

Frances turned to her, her face alight with interest. 'How, Jennet,' she demanded, and all the venom was gone from her; she spoke as though there had been no friction between them.

'By spells and potions,' said Jennet.

'Do they really keep people beautiful?' asked Frances.

'They do everything. There are love philtres to win the love of those who are indifferent. There are potions to destroy those who stand in your way. It's called trafficking with the devil.'

'How I should love to traffic with the devil!' cried Frances, delighted because she was shocking them all so much.

'It's the way to get what you want ... if you're bold enough,' said Jennet.

'I would be bold enough,' declared Frances.

The next weeks passed quickly for Frances. She was constantly being measured for the clothes she would need for her wedding, and when she saw the jewels which she was to wear she declared she had never been so happy in her life.

She knew that when the wedding had taken place she must return to the country, but she was not going to think about that.

In a few weeks' time she would set out for London in the

company of her parents, taking her elaborate wardrobe with
her; she would see that Court of which she had heard so
much; she would actually live at it until the ceremony was
over. She wondered whether she could persuade her parents
to allow her to remain in London. It was a pity that Great-
Uncle was there to make their decisions for them. He would
most certainly not agree.

But Frances was one to live in the present without giving
much thought to the future. She was going to Court; let that
suffice.

Her mother was as excited as she was. Lady Suffolk loved
pageantry, and this wedding was going to be one of the great
Court occasions.

'You see, my daughter, the King is eager for it. And he and
the Queen and Prince Henry will all honour you with their
presence.'

There were dances to be learned. What joy! Frances loved
to dance. There were curtsies to be practised. There was
advice on a hundred points.

'You'll do well,' her mother told her, 'as long as you are
not over-saucy. That might amuse the King, but the Queen and
the Prince wouldn't like it. It is more important that you
please the Queen and the Prince than the King. And I doubt
not that you will.'

'I have heard, Mother, that girls do not please the King.'

'That is something to keep in the mind and not on the
tongue.'

Frances allowed the tip of her tongue to appear between
her perfect teeth.

'Great-Uncle Northampton has already warned me,' she
said.

'Remember it,' admonished her mother.

How she enjoyed those days! The gaiety, the colour, the excitement. What an exhilarating place was London, and what
fun it was to ride through the streets and see the women
curtsy and the men doff their hats as she passed.

Many of them recognized her, and all seemed to be aware

that she was to be married. She sat her palfrey demurely and, with her long hair falling over her shoulders, was a charming sight.

'God bless the little bride!' the people cried.

The bridegroom was somewhat disappointing. She was not sure why. Robert Devereux was a handsome enough boy. But although he was two years older than she was, he seemed younger.

'He has not the incomparable looks of his father,' people said; and others retorted: 'Look where *they* led *him*.'

But all was well now. The Essex wealth and estates had been returned to young Robert, and James the King was eager to honour him.

The youth of the bridal pair enchanted everyone.

'Of course they are too young as yet . . .'

'But what an alliance!'

'It's as well to make it when they're young, for marriage at twelve and fourteen is as binding as at any other time.'

Binding, pondered Frances. She was bound to this shy boy!

They sat side by side at the wedding feast; he scarcely spoke, but she chattered away; and if she was disappointed in him, he was not with her. He thought his bride all that a bride should be.

She explained to him that the man who had written the masque which was now being performed, and who was taking the principal part in it, was Ben Jonson, the leading dramatist and actor who had been engaged for their pleasure.

'Look at the dancers!' she cried. 'And is the scenery not wonderful? Did you know that Inigo Jones made the scenery?'

Robert said that he had heard it was so; and there were not two better artists in the Kingdom than Ben Jonson and Inigo Jones.

Frances clasped her hands together and stared ahead of her at Hymen who was bringing forward his bride; dancers were springing from the great globe which Jonson was turning; and never had Frances seen such an array of jewels, never such dancing that was both wild and graceful.

'Oh what a wonderful wedding this is!' she cried.

'I am so happy because you are,' Robert told her.

'We shall dance together when the masque is over.'

'I do not dance well,' Robert told her.

'I do. I dance beautifully, and people will look at me, not you.'

'Yes,' said Robert humbly, 'I suppose they will.'

'Soon we must speak to the King and Queen,' she told him. 'Are you afraid?'

'A little.'

'I am not. I long to speak to them.'

She stared enrapt at the table at which the royal family were sitting, and as she did so Prince Henry looked in her direction, and for a few seconds they gazed at each other.

Frances felt suddenly angry.

In the privacy of home the Howards always said that the only family good enough to mate with was the royal family.

Frances believed it. That boy seated on the right hand of his father, so handsome in a rather ethereal way, was the one who should have been her husband.

If Frances Howard had been married that day to the heir to the throne she would have been completely happy.

Did she want to be Queen then? Was that her ambition? But she had not thought of that until this moment.

There was something about that boy which appealed to her. She thought: If he were my husband I should insist that I was old enough to be truly married.

Yet he might have been slightly younger than she was. He was aware of her though, she was sure of it.

She turned to look at Robert and a slight distaste curled the corners of her mouth.

He said to her then: 'You know I have to go abroad very soon? I have to learn how to be a soldier and how to speak foreign languages. It is all part of my education. Now that I am married I shall long to come back to my wife.'

Frances did not answer. She scarcely heard Robert. She was

imagining that she was married to Prince Henry and remembering some words she had heard a little while ago.

'It's the way to get what you want ... if you're bold enough.'

Where had she heard that? And was it true?

She remembered then. It was Jennet, the sly girl who always seemed to know so much more than the others.

Robert moved a little closer to her and took her hand in his.

Many watching smiled indulgently, telling themselves that they had rarely seen such a charming bride and groom.

The farewells had been said. Robert had gone abroad; Frances had returned to the country while her parents stayed at Court pursuing their exciting life.

Frances was sullen.

'How long will it take me to grow up?' she had demanded.

Her mother had laughed at her.

'Two years, three years.'

'It is an age.'

'Time passes, child. Go back to your lessons. You'll be surprised how quickly you'll become a woman. Don't try your eyes with too much learning. We don't want their brightness dimmed. And when you come to Court, you'll come as a Countess. Remember that. Farewell, little Countess of Essex.'

And so she had returned. The house seemed like a prison. She hated her servants and her governesses. She did not want to learn lessons ... not the sort that came from books.

She wanted to learn from the delicious experience of life.

Her great comfort was Jennet.

She often made the girl come to her bed and talk half the night of spells and potions, and how, by careful use of them, all that one desired could be obtained.

It was her belief in this which helped Frances to live through the time of waiting.

A Pageant at Whitehall

DURING THE four years which had elapsed since that day when Robert Carr had fallen in the tiltyard at Whitehall he had been the King's constant companion, and it was a source of great irritation to many at Court that the young man remained the first favourite.

Robert, although far from intellectual, had proved himself to possess a shrewd intelligence. He was humble in the King's presence – a welcome change from the manners of some of the petted boys of the past; he admitted that he was no scholar and confessed that he doubted whether he ever would be. But James replied that although he was without knowledge of literature and had had little experience, his dear boy was possessed of a calm, clear mind, which enabled him to reason with logic. He liked well his manners, and his company was the most enjoyable at Court.

Robert made a great effort not to annoy important ministers: he was never arrogant towards them; and when they begged him to lay this or that petition before the King he would always promise to do his best. In time they began to say of him: 'There could be worse. And if the King must have a lapdog this is the best breed.'

Robert was becoming ambitious. He believed that in time he would occupy some of the highest posts in the kingdom. James had as much as promised that he should.

'When ye've acquired a little more *nous*, Robbie.'

In the meantime his doting benefactor had knighted him, had given him a fine estate and promised him a rich wife. The Lady Anne Clifford's name had been mentioned in this connexion.

Robert had not been eager to marry, and he fancied that his reluctance had not displeased his master. Robert was content to wait. He believed that a great fortune could be his and that he must approach it step by cautious step.

When the Earl of Northampton, that wily statesman, had decided to win his friendship, Robert had met him more than halfway. Northampton – the secret Catholic – wanted alliance with Spain and believed Robert might help him to it. Robert was flattered by the attention of the old man but was sorry that, because of it, the Queen disliked him more than ever; and because Prince Henry supported his mother, that meant that the Prince was his enemy.

But Robert shrugged aside this unpleasant fact. He knew that Prince Henry would have been his enemy in any case because he hated all his father's favourites.

The climb was slow but steady; and each week saw the King's affection deepen.

But one day when they walked together in the gardens of Whitehall, James talked seriously to Robert.

'Robbie,' he said, 'I'd make ye my secretary if you were more nimble with your pen. But as you are, laddie, it's difficult. Now if you had a clever scribe who could answer correspondence in your name . . . why then 'twould be an easy matter. Ah, how I wish ye'd stuck at your lessons when you were a wee mannie.'

Robert was thoughtful. There was a suggestion behind the King's words which he might have thought of before.

A great ceremony was taking place at the Palace of Whitehall and the Queen declared again and again that rarely had she been so happy in the whole of her life.

There were to be days of rejoicing, as was only fitting; and there was nothing Anne enjoyed more than balls and masques. Inigo Jones had been summoned and given the task of turning Whitehall into a magic setting for all the pageants and spectacles which would be devised by poets such as Daniels and Jonson.

This was the occasion when her elder son would be invested with the title, Prince of Wales.

James looked on with amusement. Such frivolities were

scarcely in his line; but it was better for his subjects to spend their time in masking than in plotting. The Queen was happy, and he liked to see her so. As for his children, he was proud of them – every one of them; and now that little Charles was walking like a normal boy and had almost overcome the impediment in his speech, he reckoned he could forget the four they had lost, in the three they had. Such a handsome trio too. Where did they get their good looks? From their paternal grandmother, he supposed. That was it. The beauty of Mary Queen of Scots had missed her son and passed on to her grandchildren.

James called on the Queen, knowing that it would be a pleasant call at such a time. He found her in the centre of a bustle, ordering her women to do this and that; almost hysterical, he thought, in her excitement.

'Well, my dear,' said James, 'one would think this was all in honour of you.'

She turned to him, her eyes shining and for a moment he felt old sentiments stirring; she looked like the young girl whom he had crossed the seas to woo. It occurred to him that he had grown old and Anne had stayed young. He did not envy her. Poor creature, he thought, she has the mind of a child.

'It *is* to honour me,' she cried. 'When I see my beautiful one given these honours, they *will* be mine too.'

'You love the boy,' said James with a smile, 'and so do I, for all that he sets himself against me.'

Anne looked petulant. 'Henry would never set himself against Your Majesty if—'

'If I acted in a manner which would win his approval? He is but sixteen, wife. I'm a little more than that. Much as I should like to please you – and him – I must still make my own decisions. But enough of that. Tell me of this masque. Is Jonson giving us some fine poetry, eh? I like that man's work. And Daniel's too. And what of Inigo?'

'You will see all in good time,' Anne told him. 'And I have a surprise for you. He is very excited about it. I do hope he won't be too excited. After all it is but a short time since—'

'Charles?'

She pouted. 'There, you have guessed and 'twill be no surprise.'

'Dinna fret. I'll store the little matter at the back of my mind and be astonished when I see him. It gives me pleasure every time I set eyes on that boy.'

Anne's petulance disappeared and her face was almost beautiful in her maternal love. 'It is a miracle,' she said. 'I cannot thank Lady Carey enough. She has given so much to him.'

'We'll not forget her for it.'

'She has been rewarded, but her greatest reward is to look at him. I could not have done more myself. She gave him the confidence, the tenderness, the love. Oh James, I love that woman, although she usurped my place. I should have been the one.'

James patted her hand. 'But ye're too much of a mother to be jealous of her. What matters it? The task was done. And I'm to see young Charles dance at his brother's ceremony, eh?'

'But it was to be a secret, James!'

'Oh, aye, I mind that. There'll be no one more astounded to see Charlie dance than the King of England.'

Prince Henry, who had his own private establishment at Richmond, came by State barge to Westminster.

It was a glorious May day and the river was as smooth as silk. Lady-smocks and cuckoo flowers decorated the banks and there was pink apple blossom in the orchards of those gardens which ran down to the water. Henry was no longer a boy, being sixteen; old enough to be given the first title under the King: Prince of Wales.

His mind was filled with ideals as he sailed down the river on that day; the spires and steeples of the capital touched him with emotion. One day he would be ruler of this land; and he was determined to make it great. He would devote himself to the task of kingship. He would be zealous, yet modest. He would choose his ministers with care; he would dismiss men such as Northampton, whom he suspected of working for Spain, and Suffolk and his wife who he knew used their

positions to enrich themselves; there would be no room at
Court for men such as Robert Carr. On the other hand his first
task would be to release his dear friend Sir Walter Raleigh from
the Tower. Such men who had proved their worth should be his
premier advisers. England would be a different country under
him. And today, this solemn ceremony would be the first step
towards the change. Life could not stand still. He was young
yet, but this day he would cease to be a boy and become a man
of consequence to his country.

On some of the attendant barges sweet music was being
played; the Lord Mayor and authorities of the City accompanied him; and the river was crowded with smaller craft,
for on such an occasion all those who possessed a boat must
be out to pay homage to the young man who they believed
would one day be their King.

Arriving at Westminster, the Prince's barge drew up at that
jetty known as the Queen's Bridge. It had been erected by
Edward the Confessor and led to Anne's apartments in Westminster Palace. Henry bowed and smiled to the applause of
the people, and when he eventually reached his mother's privy
chamber she was waiting to embrace him with tears of pride
in her eyes.

'My beloved son,' she cried, 'this is in truth the happiest day
of my life.'

It was a few days later when Henry was introduced by his
father to the Houses of Parliament which were assembled to
see the heir to the throne created Prince of Wales.

As soon as this solemn ceremony was over it was the signal
for the pageantry to begin; and in one of the rooms of the
Palace several young women were chattering excitedly as they
awaited their cue to take their places.

These were reckoned to be the loveliest of the Court ladies
and it had been decided that each should represent a river of
England. Among them was one, much younger than the others
and more vivacious; this was the fourteen-year-old Countess
of Essex.

Frances had plagued her parents until they allowed her to

come to Court; though fourteen, she reminded them she was a married woman and, having glimpsed something of the excitement of Court life, she would be driven mad by melancholy if she were forced to spend many more days in the country.

Her father, the Earl of Suffolk, was indulgent. Poor Frances, she was much too gay to be expected to sulk in the country. Let her come. His wife was agreeable. She herself had matured early and believed this would be the case with Frances. The child was safely married, even though her marriage had not been consummated and her husband was far from home. Let her come to Court.

Thus the nymph of the River Lea took her place among the others, and secretly she was delighted because she knew that she could attract attention even among such beauties.

She studied them dispassionately. Were they such beauties? There was the Lady Arabella Stuart – a very important lady, it was true. But she's quite ancient! thought Frances. She must be thirty-five. Thirty-five and unmarried! Poor Arabella Stuart, whom the King watched constantly and did not like much because of her nearness to the throne. There had been plots involving her, and James would never allow her to have a husband.

I wouldn't change places with Arabella Stuart, royal though she may be, thought Frances. Arabella on this occasion was the nymph of the Trent. She was preoccupied, and Frances had heard it whispered that she was in love with William Seymour and determined not to lose him, in spite of the fact that the King would certainly forbid the match.

Frances shrugged aside the affairs of that ancient one. Those of Frances Howard were – or soon would be – far more interesting.

There was no one so beautiful as she was. Certainly not Elizabeth Grey – the nymph of the Medway because she was the daughter of the Earl of Kent – nor the Countess of Arundel – nymph of Arun. There was one though who was attracting most attention, and that was the Princess Elizabeth, who represented the Thames.

But that is only because she is the King's daughter, Frances told herself scornfully.

The Lady Anne Clifford had noticed Frances pirouetting this way and that and came over to her smiling.

'It is your first Court occasion,' she said.

'How did you know.'

'You are so excited.'

Frances clasped her hands. 'Is it not wonderful to be at Court?'

Anne laughed and said: 'Take care. You are too young to come to Court.'

'I am fourteen.'

'So young? I had thought you a little older.'

Frances was delighted. 'It is such a handicap to seem a child!'

'You must be watchful. There are people at Court who would be ready to take advantage of one so young.'

'What people?'

'Men.'

Frances laughed scornfully. 'I shall be the one to take advantage of them.'

Several of the ladies laughed, and agreed that there was something about the nymph of Lea to suggest that she would take care of herself.

In the great hall beautiful scenery had been set up; there were to be several scenes, and the first represented Milford Haven and the arrival of Henry VII. Songs, written by the poets especially for the occasion, were sung, extolling the beauties of the rivers; and all the nymphs were mentioned in turn as they took their places in the dance.

Frances was intoxicated with happiness.

'The beauteous nymph of crystal streaming Lea ...' sang the musicians and for one moment everyone in that great hall was looking towards Frances Howard.

Too soon the charm of Anne Clifford, the nymph of Aire, was being acclaimed, but the words about the nymph of Lea went on and on in Frances' mind.

As she danced with the others after the fashion which they

had practised together, she tried to get as near as possible to that spot where the Prince sat beside his father.

He too had become older since she had last seen him; he was no longer a boy.

He had noticed her, she was sure of it. Every time she took a sly look at him, he was watching.

This is the happiest moment of my life ... so far, Frances told herself.

Anne, the Queen, assured those surrounding her that it was the happiest of hers, for now the nymphs had stood aside and little Zephyr had appeared. His green satin robe was decorated with gold flowers, and wings made of silver lawn were attached to his back. A wreath of flowers had been placed on his flowing hair and Anne's eyes sought the valuable diamond bracelet which she had put on his little arm when she went to see him being dressed.

With him were his naiads, lovely children with their hair hanging loose, garlanded like Zephyr, dressed in pale blue tunics decorated with silver flowers.

The children made a charming sight, particularly as they danced so skilfully to the music which had been written for the occasion.

Applause broke out and there was a whisper of astonishment, for Zephyr, who now danced so elegantly, was none other than the ten-year-old little Prince Charles who, a few years ago, had been unable to walk and in danger of having his legs put into iron supports.

Lady Carey who was standing near the Queen, was weeping, although she did not seem to be aware of it; Anne reached out and taking her hand pressed it.

'Your Majesty . . .' whispered Lady Carey.

But Anne put her fingers to her lips and whispered: 'Well done. I shall never forget.'

The scene of Milford Haven had been withdrawn and another even more striking was presented to view. Waterfalls were visible about a grotto, and in this grotto was a throne on which sat Tethys, daughter of Uranus and wife of Oceanus. This was none other than Queen Anne herself, who was always delighted to play a part in the pageantry. For days she had thought of little but the costume she would wear, and it was truly striking. On her head was a helmet in the shape of a shell; it was decorated with coral and a veil of silver floated from it. Her gown was blue silk, traced with silver seaweed; and her magnificent blue and silver train was draped about her throne.

Seated at her feet were the River Nymphs. Frances had placed herself in the most prominent position, and every now and then threw a glance in Prince Henry's direction, for, she told herself, was it not all in honour of him, and should not every river nymph among them seek to please him?

The poem which was being recited explained what was happening.

Little Zephyr would now take presents from Tethys and present them to those for whom they were intended.

Gracefully he walked to the Queen who handed him the trident she carried and whispered to him. Charles carried it to his father and bowed. James took it awkwardly; and Charles returned to his mother once more and received the sword, which was encrusted with precious gems and was said to be worth four thousand pounds, and a scarf which the Queen herself had embroidered. These were for her beloved son who was now the Prince of Wales.

The assembly applauded enthusiastically and little Charles held up his hand as he had been taught to do, to remind them that this was not all; he then returned to his mother and kneeling implored her in a high, sweet voice, with only the slightest stammer, to come down from her throne and dance, for the Court's enjoyment, with her River Nymphs.

The Queen pretended to consider this while Charles, beckoning to his little naiads, took the floor and once more danced with his charming companions.

Then the Queen rose and the girls who had been ranged about her in the grotto fell into place about her. She led the

way and they danced the stately quadrille which they had practised together for many days.

Anne in her shell-helmet and her blue and silver gown
looked ecstatic. She was completely happy. It seemed to her
on that day that she had all that she desired. She herself the
centre of the dance; James looking on, a little bored but
tolerant, understanding that it was necessary from time to
time to have such pageants; her beloved eldest, now the
Prince of Wales; her daughter a charming, docile girl; her
youngest, over whose state she had shed many tears, now a
normal boy, promising to be as handsome as his brother.

Oh, thought Anne, that this day might last for ever!

Robert Carr who was seated with the King found his attention
wandering from the dancing. He was turning over in his mind
something which James had said to him recently. Why did he
not find himself a clever scribe?

Easier said than done. Where could Robert find such a man?
But how inviting was the suggestion. The King's secretary!
One of the most important of posts – particularly if a man
enjoyed the King's favour. It was only his lack of ability which
was keeping him from reaching the top of his ambition. James
was ready to bestow on him anything he wished; but how
could even James give him a post which all those about him
would know he was inadequate to fulfil?

A scribe? He needed more than a scribe. He needed someone on whom he could absolutely rely, someone who would
be prepared to work for him in secret, someone who knew
how to use words and had a sharp and clever brain. But surely
such a person would want to seek honours for himself. Not if
he had little hope of doing so. Moreover, how could an ambitious man hope to rise more easily than by doing service to
Robert Carr, who could direct the King's attention towards
him?

Like James he was a little bored with the Queen and her
dancing girls.

Then it was almost as though a prayer had been answered,
for while the Queen and the River Nymphs were dancing their

quadrille he caught sight of a man whom he had known a few years earlier and had not seen for some time.

They had been great friends. Thomas Overbury was a clever fellow, a poet, a graduate of Oxford; a very pleasant young man. Older than Robert, he would be about twenty-nine. What had been happening to Tom Overbury since they last met?

His fortunes had certainly not risen as Robert's had. He was at the pageant, not exactly as a member of the Court but from somewhere on the fringe. He had been rather fond of Robert, amused at his lack of scholarship while, like the King, he recognized a shrewd brain and intelligence.

As soon as he could make an opportunity he would seek out Tom Overbury.

An opportunity came during the ball that followed the pageant. The King, unwillingly, must partner the Queen in opening the ball, and Robert had his opportunity to slip away.

As he pushed his way through the crowds, he was met by ingratiating smiles.

'Sir Robert, I have a request to make—'

'Sir Robert, I humbly ask—'

To all he said: 'Come and see me tomorrow. At this moment I am engaged on the King's business.'

Unsure of himself, it was his policy never to make an enemy, however humble. That might have been one of the reasons why he remained first favourite for so long. James liked a man to be easygoing and not stir up trouble.

He took Overbury by the elbow and said: 'My friend, it is good to see you.'

Thomas Overbury's thin clever face lit up with pleasure.

'Why, Robert,' he said, 'it's good to hear such an important man call me friend.'

Robert laughed: it was his habit to feign a modesty he did not feel. 'Important?' he said. 'Poor Robert Carr, whom you used to marvel at because he could just manage to spell his own name.'

'Life is more than a matter of spelling, it seems. Any scholar can spell. There's a surfeit of scholars and only one Robert Carr.'

'I want to speak with you in private ... for the sake of our old friendship.'

'Give the word, and I am at your command.'

'Now.'

'I am ready.'

'Then follow me. We must be quick, for the King will expect me to be at his side.'

Carr led the way to a small ante-room and, when they were there, he shut the door.

'Now Tom,' said Carr, 'tell me when you returned.'

'But a few weeks ago.'

'From the Low Countries, was it?'

Overbury nodded. 'Whither, you will remember, I retired from Court in some disgrace.'

'I do remember.' Robert burst out laughing.

Overbury lifted his finger. 'Do not expect me to join in your laughter, Robert. Remember it was laughter that led me into disgrace.'

They were both thinking of those days which immediately followed the accident in the tiltyard. Good-natured Robert had sought to help his old friend, and it had seemed that Thomas Overbury would bask in the sunshine of Robert's success. The Queen, disliking Robert, disliked his friends; and although she could not harm Robert, he being so warmly protected by his benefactor, the same thing did not apply to his friends.

On one occasion Thomas Overbury – who had recently been given a knighthood at Robert's request – had been walking in the gardens at Greenwich with Robert when Anne had noticed them from a window. She had remarked: 'There goes Carr and his governor.' Neither Robert nor Overbury had heard the comment but, just at that moment Overbury had laughed aloud at something his friend had said. Incensed, certain that he was laughing at her, Anne had declared she would not be insulted and had given orders that Overbury be sent to the Tower.

Even now Overbury shivered, thinking of being conveyed down the river to the Tower, those grey walls closing about him, the damp smell of slimy walls, the clank of keys in a warder's hands, the sound of steps on a stone stair.

Robert understood; he laid a hand on his arm. 'The Queen was angry with you once, Tom,' he said.

'With you too; but she could not harm you.'

'Nor did I allow her to harm you for long.'

Thomas' eyes were narrowed. 'You were my good friend as always. As much when you were at the King's right hand as when you were a mere page in the household of the Earl of Dunbar. Do you remember?'

'I often think of those Edinburgh days.'

'It was a good day for me when my father decided to send me on a visit to Edinburgh with his chief clerk as my guardian. But for that . . . we should not have met.'

'We should have met later at Court.'

'There would not have been the same bond between us, Robert. Then we were two humble youths; now you are humble no longer.'

'Nor are you, Sir Thomas.'

'Humble compared with Sir Robert.'

'I'll tell you a secret. I am soon to be created Viscount Rochester.'

'There is no end to the titles and wealth which will one day be yours.'

'I trust you are going to stay in London now, Tom.'

'Providing the Queen does not see fit to banish me.'

'Why should she?'

'Perhaps because Sir Robert Carr . . . or Viscount Rochester . . . . continued to be my friend. Let me tell you this, I would be ready to risk the one for the sake of the other.'

Robert clasped his friend's hand and said: 'We shall always be friends, I trust. Did I not soon bring about your release from the Tower?'

'And arranged that I should be sent to the Low Countries an exile.'

'It was the only way, Tom. The King does not flout the

Queen too openly. But you see, you did not remain long in the Low Countries.'

'A year seems an age to an exile.'

'Exile no longer. Do you still write excellent poetry?'

'I write poetry, though whether it be excellent or not, as the author it is not for me to say. But I'll tell you this: Ben Jonson has told me that he admires my work, and since I admire his, that is a compliment.'

'The Queen insists that Ben Jonson be called when she wants poetry for a pageant.'

'He's a rare fellow – Ben Jonson.'

'Not too rare, I trust, Tom. I mean I hope there are others who admire your work.'

'I am writing some sketches which I'm calling Characters. I'll show them to you. I think they will amuse you.'

'You will be famous one day, Tom. I am sure of it. You have a great gift. You need a patron . . . someone who will help you make the best of your talents.'

'A patron? Who?'

'Tom, you have seen me rising. I shall go much further. Those who come with me will rise too.'

'What are you suggesting, Robert?'

'I need a secretary – someone who has a gift for words, hard work, and who is shrewd and loyal. I know you well and I know that you possess these gifts. Tom, throw in your lot with mine. I am travelling upwards . . . you can come with me.'

Overbury stared at his friend. He was fond of Robert. He trusted him. Attach himself to the brightest star at Court, the petted boy who only had to whisper his desires in the King's ear for them to be readily granted?

He was an ambitious man but he had never thought such an opportunity possible.

The music could scarcely be heard above the talk in the crowded ballroom.

The dance went on; the Queen was among the dancers, while the King sat looking on with Robert Carr beside him.

The Prince of Wales was dancing with one of the River Nymphs; he had noticed her in the ballet and thought her by far the most beautiful of them all. He was surprised at his interest, for girls had not greatly attracted him until now. This girl was different. She was so vital, so young; her lovely eyes which seemed determined to miss nothing betrayed her innocence; he was sure this was her first visit to Court.

Their hands touched.

'I liked the dance of the nymphs,' he told her.

'I noticed how you watched.'

'Did you? You seemed so intent on the dance.'

'It was all in honour of the Prince of Wales and I was so anxious to please him.'

'Will it give you pleasure if I tell you that you did?'

'The greatest pleasure.'

'Then it's true.'

'Thank you, Your Highness.'

'I fancy I have seen you before at Court, and yet this is your first appearance here. I find that strange. It seems as though . . .

'As though we were meant to meet, Your Highness.'

'Just so.'

'I am surprised that Your Highness noticed me. There are so many girls . . .'

'I suppose so, but I have never noticed them before. I hope you will be often at Court.'

'I intend to be there whenever I can.'

'We must arrange it. I shall hold my own Court at Oatlands or Nonesuch, and perhaps Hampton or Richmond. You must come there.'

'Your Highness, how that would delight me!'

He put her hand to his lips and kissed it. Several people noticed the gesture for there would always be some to watch the Prince of Wales and comment on his actions.

'Tell me your name,' he said.

'It is Frances.'

'Frances,' he repeated tenderly.

'Countess of Essex,' she went on.

He looked startled. 'Now I remember where I saw you before.'

She smiled. 'It was at my wedding.'

But Henry's expression had lost its gaiety. 'You were married to Robert Devereux, Earl of Essex. So ... you are a wife.'

'A wife and not a wife,' she answered. 'After the ceremony my husband went abroad. I have not seen him since. Our parents considered us too young to live as man and wife.'

'But he will return,' said the Prince.

'I know not when. I care not when.'

'I care,' said Henry almost coldly. 'I should conduct you to your guardian.'

'Oh ... please not—'

'It is better so,' he answered.

Frances could have wept with disappointment. He had noticed her; more than that he was attracted by her; and because she was married he wanted to end their friendship before it had begun.

It was true. The Prince of Wales was prim and prudish. He implied that while he was ready to be the friend of a young girl, he was not eager to cause scandal on account of a married woman.

Who would have thought that she would have found such prudery at Court? And in the Prince of Wales!

Frances was not one to accept defeat. In that moment she knew she wanted a lover; and that lover must be the Prince of Wales.

The Prince of Wales Takes a Mistress

THE KING was alarmed and no one but Robert Carr could pacify him. James paced up and down the apartment while Robert sat helplessly watching him. At every sound James started: he could never get out of his mind the treachery of the Gowrie and Gunpowder Plots.

'You see, Robbie,' he said, 'I have enemies. They're all over the Court; and I know not where to look for them. When I think of how the Ruthvens laid their snare for me . . . and how I walked into it, I marvel that I came out alive.'

'There is some Providence watching over Your Majesty.'

'Providence is fickle, Robbie. Guarding you one day and turning its back the next. I'd liefer rely on my head than my luck. And Providence is another name for the last.'

'Your Majesty is unduly alarmed. You acted with your usual shrewd sense; Arabella Stuart can no longer be a threat.'

'Can she not, Robbie? Can she not? There's many a man in this city that would like to see me back across the Border . . . or under the sod. There's many looking for a Queen to put on the throne. They like to be ruled by a woman. Have ye never heard them talk of my predecessor? Ye'd think she was God Almighty to hear some of them. These English like to be ruled by a woman; the Scots would have none of my mother, but the English worshipped their Queen. How should I know that they're not drinking their secret toasts to Queen Arabella?'

'Your Majesty is the true King of Scotland and England, and Prince Henry the true heir.'

'Aye, lad. That's true. And Henry will have many to support him. Have you noticed how they flock to his Court and desert the King's? I wonder they don't shout for King Henry in the streets. That boy will bury me alive if I don't take care.'

'They acclaim him as the Prince of Wales.'

'And they look to the time when he'll be King. Dinna seek to draw the mask over my eyes, Robbie. I know.'

'But that is not to want Arabella.'

'The people like to plot. To the young, life is more worth while when they're risking it. Arabella is as good an excuse for a rebellion as any other. And now she has disobeyed me. In spite of my forbidding her, she has married William Seymour – himself not without some claim.'

'And Your Majesty has acted with promptitude, by committing her to the care of Parry, and her husband to the Tower.'

'Yes, yes, boy, but I like it not. The lady has become a martyr. And a romantic one at that. Before this marriage she was a woman not young enough to arouse the chivalric zeal of other young people. The Lady Arabella Stuart at Court, was welcome. I like not this marriage. What if there should be issue?'

'Your Majesty has sought to make that impossible by separating the pair.'

'You try to comfort your Old Gossip. And you do, Robbie. Now let me look at that letter to the Prince which you've drafted. I fear he is not going to like my suggestions, but we must find a wife for him soon; and I do not see why we should not, in Spain or in France.'

'It would be an excellent step, Your Majesty, for how much easier it is to make peace between countries when they are joined by royal marriages.'

'That's true enough, Robbie. The letter, boy.'

James read the letter and a smile of pleasure crossed his face.

'Neatly put, Robbie, neatly put. Why, bless you, boy, if there's not something of the scribe in you after all. Poet, I'd say. That's succinct and to the point. I can see you've learned your lessons. Ye're going to be useful to me, Robbie.'

James did not ask the obvious question, because he would have already known the answer; and Robert would have given it because he was not a liar.

The boy had found the solution at last. James did not want to know who had drafted the letter. It was enough that it was perfectly done. Robert had found the one to work in the shadows.

The Prince of Wales was holding Court at the Palace of Oatlands. He liked to stay at this palace with his sister Elizabeth, and together they entertained a Court which was different from that of their parents.

Henry had the reputation of being a sober young man; he

could not endure the practical jokes which were a feature of his father's Court. Not that James cared for them; but his favourites played them with such gusto, and because he liked to see them enjoying themselves he joined in the fun. Henry's ideal was to have a Court where serious matters were discussed and there was no practical joking. He wanted very much to bring Sir Walter Raleigh from prison; he was sometimes a little angry with his friend who often gave the impression that he did not regret his captivity; how otherwise, he asked, could he devote the necessary time to his history of the world which he wanted to dedicate to the Prince of Wales?

There was so much that was wrong with the King's Court, Henry told himself and Elizabeth.

'And now they want to make a Catholic marriage for me,' he complained. 'I'll not endure it. Did you know that our father has taken Carr for his secretary and I receive letters from the fellow.'

'I did not think he was literate enough to write a letter.'

'He is. And flowery epistles they are.'

'There are qualities we did not suspect in the fellow then.'

'I dislike him and all his breed.'

Elizabeth smiled. 'I couldn't stop myself laughing when you hit him on the back with your tennis racquet.'

Henry laughed with her. 'I was overcome by a desire to murder him.'

'Yet he seemed to bear no malice.'

'Who can say what goes on behind that handsome face of his?'

'Well, let us forget him, Henry, and think of the ball we are giving tonight. Young Lady Essex pleaded so earnestly for an invitation that I gave her one.'

Henry turned away to look out of the window; he did not want his sister to see that he had flushed. 'She is very young . . . too young,' he mumbled.

'Oh no, Henry. She is sixteen.'

'And married,' went on Henry. 'Where is her husband?'

'It was one of those child marriages. They have not yet set

up house together.' Elizabeth smiled. 'And by the look of the girl I should say that it was time they did.'

'And what experience have you of such matters?'

'Dear Henry, there are some things that are so obvious that it is not necessary to have experience to recognize them.' Elizabeth went on to talk of Arabella. She was sorry for her kinswoman; so was Henry. If he were King, he thought, he would not allow himself to be disturbed by other claims to the throne. His father's claim was so much more sound and he was sure the people had no intention of setting up Arabella. It was his father's terror of plots that made him so nervous.

He said so to Elizabeth; but he was not really thinking of his father and Arabella. He was wondering whether he would dance with Lady Essex that day.

The royal pleasure house of Oatlands was not far from the banks of the Thames. It was built round two quadrangles and three enclosures and its gardens were magnificent. When Frances had passed the machicolated gatehouse and looked at the angle turrets and huge bay windows she had made up her mind that in this mansion the Prince of Wales should become her lover.

Jennet was with her; she had selected this girl for her most intimate maid. She might have found others more servile, but Jennet's insolence – which was always veiled, and only rarely shown even then – appealed to Frances. That girl had a knowledge of matters which Frances felt might be useful to her some time. There was a bond between them. To Jennet she talked more freely than to anyone else. She was certain that Jennet would keep her secrets. Frances often had a feeling that if Jennet had been born in her stratum of society she would have been very like her, and had she been born in Jennet's she would have been another such as she.

The maid knew, for instance, of Frances' hopes concerning the Prince of Wales. She was not in the least shocked that a young girl, married to one man who had never been her husband, should seek to become the mistress of another. Jennet gave the impression that she was there to administer to her mistress' pleasure and that whatever Frances desired was reasonable and natural.

While the maid helped her dress for the ball, Frances glanced critically at her own reflection in the mirror. Jennet, her eyes lowered, assured her mistress that never had she looked so well.

'How old do I look, Jennet?'

'All of eighteen, my lady.'

Jennet would not have said so had it not been true. Frances had matured early.

'And my gown?'

'Most becoming. There'll not be another lady to compare with you.'

'How I wish that they had never married me to Essex.'

'You would not have been a Countess then, my lady.'

'No, but that would not have mattered. I should still be my father's daughter and of a rank to be welcomed at the Prince's Court.'

'You are older than he is, my lady.'

'Oh no.'

'I did not mean in years.'

'I understand you.'

'And, being older, should lead the way.'

'He is not like the others, Jennet. He is a very good young man. He is anxious not to do anything of which he could be ashamed.'

Jennet gave a short laugh. 'When the good fall into temptation they fall more deeply.'

'Sometimes I feel he will never fall into temptation.'

'There are ways, my lady.'

'What ways?'

'I know how to procure a love potion which is certain to work.'

Frances' heart began to beat a little faster.

Then she looked at her own radiant image. She was so certain of her charms that she could not believe they would fail.

If they did, she would begin to think seriously of Jennet's philtres.

There was less ceremony at Oatlands than at St James's or Hampton Court, and almost everyone there soon learned that the Prince, who had never before been interested in women, was attracted by the young Countess of Essex; so when she lured him from the dance into the gardens, no one followed them, believing that it was the Prince's wish that they should be alone.

Frances, who knew instinctively when and how to act in such matters, was certain that if she was to become the Prince's mistress she must induce him to overcome his scruples before he became fully aware of the potency of her allure. Once he realized how eager she was he would set up such a barrier between them that his seduction would be impossible.

Although they were both virgins, Frances was ready to lead the way; moreover, she was determined to do so.

Walking between the flower beds made mysterious by summer moonlight, she pressed closer to him. He hesitated and would have returned to the palace but she put her arm through his and told him how happy she was to be at Court, and particularly to be a member of the Prince's Court.

It was only polite to say that he was happy to have her; and when he did so she raised his hand to her lips and kissed it.

He withdrew it sharply.

'I have offended you?' she asked, her lovely eyes wide with horror.'

'No . . . no. But it is best not to . . .'

'Not to?'

'To . . . to kiss my hand.'

'Would you prefer me to kiss your cheek, your lips?' she cried passionately.

Henry was startled and astonished by the tremendous excitement which was taking possession of him. He tried to analyse his feelings. 'If you were not married . . .'

'But I have never known my husband.'

'You must keep yourself a virgin for him.'

'Is that Your Highness' wish?'

Henry was silent. Then she threw herself against him and cried triumphantly, 'It is not so. It is not so.' Then she took his hand and began to run with him; and as they ran such an excitement gripped him that he seemed like a different person from the sober young Prince who deplored the loose morals of his father's Court.

She withdrew her hand and went on running; now he was pursuing her. She allowed him to catch her in a summer house; and she waited expectantly while he embraced her, listening to the sounds of music which came from the palace.

He was uncertain; but she was not.

Frances Howard had always known what she wanted, and she had wanted the Prince of Wales from the moment she had seen him on the day she had married Robert Devereux.

Jennet knew as soon as she was in the privacy of her own chamber.

Frances stood, her eyes brilliant, while Jennet relieved her of her gown and jewels.

'So, my lady,' said Jennet slyly, 'we shall not have to ask my good friend Mrs Turner to provide us with a love philtre?'

And soon certain knowledgeable members of the Court were telling themselves that the Prince was behaving like a normal young man.

He had a mistress – Frances, Countess of Essex.

Frances knew that she was meant to have a lover. She blossomed and became even more beautiful than before. She enjoyed intrigue and secret meetings. Moreover, it delighted her to be loved by the most important man at Court.

Henry had changed; he was gay and lighthearted, although there were occasional fits of remorse. But, he assured himself, why should he not indulge in a love affair, when this was considered natural conduct by almost everyone at Court? In any case, as soon as he saw Frances, any good resolutions he had made quickly disappeared and he gave himself up to pleasure.

He wished that he could have married Frances. Then he would have been completely happy. He confessed his dilemma to Sir Walter Raleigh who shrugged it aside as unimportant. No one would think the worse of him for having a love affair, he assured the Prince; and Henry at length forgot his qualms.

Those were exciting months. Never had Henry been so immersed in pleasure. To his Court flocked all the most brilliant of the courtiers, and James, watching, feigned a chagrin he did not feel. He was glad to see his son so popular, and if the boy was showing himself to be less of a puritan than before, that was all to the good. In the parks about Nonesuch Palace Henry rode and walked with Frances; they made love in the arbours; and the columns and pyramids, with their stone birds from whose bills streams of water flowed, made a perfect setting for their idyll. In the more stately St James's Palace they were together; and Richmond, where the Prince loved to hold Court, was yet another background for the lovers.

Those who watched them wondered how long this romance would last. Many of the young women planned to take Frances' place in the Prince's affections, for they were certain that soon he must tire of his young mistress, when he had all the Court to choose from.

But Henry remained faithful, and Frances was very sure of him.

She had taken the lead in their love affair and kept it. Often it seemed to her that Henry was a little young. Why, she asked herself, should I have to teach him everything?

He was a Prince – the Prince of Wales at that – yet he was really nothing but a boy.

How different it would be to have a *man* for a lover – someone mature, someone who did not follow everywhere she led but sought to dominate her. Henry never would of course, because Frances was determined to dominate; but it would be exciting if he tried.

Jennet, watching, knew before Frances did herself, that her mistress was tiring of the Prince of Wales.

When Frances received a summons to sup with her great-uncle, the powerful Earl of Northampton, she was not very pleased. This meant that she would be obliged to absent herself from the Prince's Court and, although she was less eager for his company than she had once been, she had no wish to sit down to supper with the friends of her great-uncle whom she suspected would be of his age, or at least that of her parents.

But she knew she dared not refuse such an invitation, for Northampton was accepted as the head of the family, and if she offended him he could prevail upon her parents to send her back to the country.

She was scowling as Jennet dressed her.

'My lady is black as thunder today,' remarked Jennet with a smirk.

'I am wondering whether my great-uncle has been hearing rumours.'

'Nay, my lady. My lord Northampton would not be displeased because the Prince of Wales is your friend.'

'It seems strange that he should want me at table with his dreary old men and women.'

'You'll seem all the more beautiful in such a setting – providing you take that black scowl from your lovely face.'

Frances bared her teeth at the reflection in the mirror. 'Shall I smile like this? Shall I mince and look coy?'

'My lady will suit her manners to the company, I doubt not.'

And Frances, wearing her simplest gown and scarcely any jewels, waited on her great-uncle; and when she was seated at the supper table she greatly wished that she had chosen something more becoming, because she found herself next to a man whom she had previously seen only at a distance, never having been considered of sufficient importance to have been brought to his notice.

She was instantly aware of her great-uncle's deference to

this man; how the company paused when he spoke; how his simplest jokes were loudly applauded; and how everyone at that table was trying to catch his eye.

How handsome he was! Frances could scarcely stop herself staring at him. Never had she seen such a profile; he wore his golden hair somewhat long; and his fair skin was becomingly bronzed; his expression was extremely pleasant but remote, and that remoteness was like a challenge to Frances. He sparkled as he moved, for costly gems decorated his jacket; and diamonds and rubies were set off to perfection on his beautiful white hands.

'My lord Rochester, pray give us your opinion . . .'

'My lord Rochester, you'll be the death of me. I have rarely laughed so much . . .'

His kindly smile was bestowed right and left; on the syco-phantic gentleman opposite; on the fawning lady on his left; on the wondering Frances on his right; and yet, thought Frances, he cares nothing for any of us.

And why should he, when he is, in some respects, the ruler of us all? For the King himself wishes to please him in every way, and if he puts a petition before James, it is granted; a word of advice from Robert Carr, my lord Rochester, and the King is ready to act.

There never was such a man! thought Frances. How irk-some, how maddening that to him she was merely a young woman of the Court, of no more interest than any other.

But it shall not be so, she promised herself.

She plucked at his sleeve. He turned his smile on her, that facile smile which meant so little.

'My lord, I am afraid I am a dull neighbour. You must for-give me. I have not been long at Court.'

'I can see that you are very young.'

'Perhaps I am older than I seem. I have lived long in the country.'

'Is that so?' He was smiling at the man across the table who was doing his best to attract his attention. He did not care how old she was or whether she had lived in town or country. She meant nothing to him. He was unmoved by the beauty which had been irresistible to the Prince of Wales, and as soon as he left this supper table he would have forgotten her.

He *shall* notice me, she vowed.

The violence of her feelings often amazed her. With an impulsive gesture she knocked over a goblet of wine. His puffed, slashed breeches were marked by the wine, and for a moment she had his full attention as she caught the goblet and lifted eyes, wide and frightened, to his. Surely he must now notice how beautiful those eyes were; who else at Court had such long lashes? He must notice. He *must.*

He did for a moment. He flicked his breeches with a careless hand.

'It is of no moment,' he said gently. 'You must not distress yourself.'

'But I fear I have made you angry.'

'Do I seem so?'

'No, but I understand you to be kind. My great-uncle is glaring at me. He will take me to task for this.'

Robert Carr smiled. 'I will be your advocate,' he said.

'Oh, thank you.' She touched his hand and lowered those magnificent eyes so that now he could see their fringed lids. 'But I have ruined your clothes.' A pretty white hand touched his thigh.

He patted the hand and for a second kept his over hers.

In that moment, she told herself afterwards, the importance of this occasion became known to her, for Frances Howard, Countess of Essex, had fallen irrevocably in love with Robert Carr, Viscount Rochester, and first favourite of the King.

Frances was in despair.

She had seen him on several occasions since, and on all these he had smiled at her somewhat vaguely as though he were trying to remember where he had seen her before.

What could she do? It was not easy to meet Viscount Rochester. Every day men and women waited outside his apartments in the hope of seeing him. He was often with the King, and unapproachable.

She felt listless when she was with the Prince of Wales, and constantly she compared him with Robert Carr. The Prince was a boy, a boy who always seemed a little ashamed when they made love. That was not the way to be a good lover. How different Robert Carr would be if he were in love with her.

If he were in love! But he was not very interested in women. Perhaps he dared not be, for fear of offending the King. At times she knew she was foolish to have set her heart on such a man; but because he was unattainable he seemed all the more desirable.

Jennet quickly learned the state of affairs.

'My lady could try a love potion,' she suggested.

'How could I give him a love potion?'

'There are potions a lady can drink which will make her irresistible to any man.'

'Is it indeed true?'

'We could put it to the test, my lady. Give me leave to visit a friend of mine. I will tell her what is wanted and we will see what happens.'

'Do you really know such a woman?'

'Yes, my lady.'

'Where is she?'

'She lives at Hammersmith. Give me leave to visit her and I will put your case before her, without mentioning names of course.'

'There can be no harm in it.'

'Only good, if my friend can make my lady irresistible to a certain gentleman.'

'Go then and try.'

'It will cost money.'

'How much?'

'I must ask. But I think it will cost much money, as you would expect it to, my lady, if it does its work,'

Frances clasped her hands. 'I would be willing to pay . . . a great deal . . . for my Lord Rochester.'

It seemed to Robert Carr that everywhere he went he saw the young Countess of Essex. He was not so indifferent to her as he had appeared to be. She was without doubt the prettiest young girl at Court and he liked her persistence. There was no doubt that she admired him, and was inviting him to be her lover.

He had made inquiries. She was, even at this time, the mistress of the Prince of Wales. How amusing to humiliate that young man. Robert did not forget that blow on the back with a racquet. If it had been anyone but the Prince of Wales he would not have let the incident pass. But he was shrewd enough to know he must not have an open quarrel with the heir to the throne.

Yet quietly to snatch his mistress was another matter.

Why not? James did not object to his young men marrying or taking an occasional mistress. This girl was already married to Robert Devereux, the young Earl of Essex. There could be no harm in a little dalliance. And how furious the Prince would be!

Next time he met her – he would not go out of his way – he would pause and talk to her; he would convey to her that he was not indifferent. It would be amusing to see how far she would go. He had no doubt that she was ripe for immediate seduction.

Frances was jubilant. Everything she wanted would be hers, she was sure of it, because the potion had worked. She had paid highly for it, but it was worth every penny. She had drunk the rather unappetizing brew, and the next time she had seen Robert Carr he had stopped to talk to her. His voice had been caressing; his eyes even more so.

So there could be no doubt that she had become irresistible to this cool young man. She went to her own chamber and embraced Jennet.

'It works!' she cried. 'He has spoken to me. His looks tell me all I want to know. It will not be long now.'

Nor was it.

Robert Carr chose an occasion when the King was resting and the Prince was honouring his father's Court with his presence.

He found himself near Frances in the dance and when their hands touched they clung.

She was ready and eager. He did not need to persuade. It was not difficult to slip away because worldly courtiers had a gift for knowing when two people wanted to be alone, and with such as Carr it was necessary always to forestall his wishes.

They were left uninterrupted for an hour in one of the ante-rooms.

That was an ecstatic hour for Frances; a very pleasant one for Carr.

And from then on Frances knew that this was the man with whom she wished to spend the rest of her life. She was alternately wild with joy, desperate with sorrow.

Why had they married her so young to Essex when she might have married Robert Carr? She knew that he had no mistress; and could have had but few. Yet to him — because of a love potion, she believed — she had become irresistible.

He was the most important man at Court. Why had she thought the Prince was? The Prince was a simple boy, unaware of true passion. She was awakened now, and afire with desire, and no one but Carr could satisfy her.

All the honours that he asked for would be his. He could have any post, any title. As his wife she would be the most powerful woman in the Court.

'Oh, God,' she cried to Jennet, 'how I want to marry Robert Carr.'

There was dancing at St James's. Robert Carr was not there, and therefore Frances was bored and indifferent; she was longing for the evening to be over and wished that she had not come.

Henry had not sought her out, although his manner had not changed towards her. She supposed that he was going through one of his prim periods. Let him. She had no desire for him. From now on there would be one man and one man only in her life.

As she danced she dropped her glove and, seeing this, one of the courtiers picked it up.

Knowing nothing of the new state of affairs and believing that the Prince would be glad to possess his lady's glove, and, after the prevailing custom, count it an honour to wear it, this man carried the glove to the Prince and, bowing low, offered it to him.

The dance had come to an end; the music had stopped suddenly; and all were watching this pretty little scene.

Henry looked at the glove and when he did not reach for it, there was complete silence, so that many heard the words which were spoken.

'Your Highness, my lady Essex dropped her glove.'

The Prince looked at it disdainfully and then said in a clear high voice: 'I would not touch that which has been stretched by another.'

The whole Court knew then that the Prince of Wales had discovered his mistress' infidelity; and that the love affair between them was at an end.

'I don't care!' Frances declared blithely to Jennet. 'I'm glad. I did not want him pestering me. The silly boy with his "I durst not." "I'd liefer not." And "This is sin".'

What a lover! Oh, how different is my Robert.

She frowned a little. 'Yet he is cool, deliberate. He is never impetuous. I always have the feeling when he fails to keep an assignation that he has forgotten we made one.'

'Perhaps,' suggested Jennet, 'there is need of another potion. Perhaps now that you are on visiting terms you could ask him to sup with you. I feel sure, my lady, that a potion drunk by him would be more effective than one drunk by you.'

Frances clasped her hands together. 'I wonder if that would work.'

'My lady saw the first one work.'

'Hush,' said Frances. 'Someone is coming.' She took Jennet's arm and held it so tightly that the maid winced. 'Not a word of this to any . . . understand?'

'Of course, my lady. You know you may trust me.'

'Come in,' called Frances; and one of her women entered.

'My lady, the Earl, your father, asks that you go to him without delay. He has news for you.'

'I will come,' said Frances, dismissing the woman with a wave of her hand. Then she turned to Jennet and her face was a few shades paler as she said: 'Do you think they have discovered that Robert and I—'

'They could not command my lord Rochester, my lady. It is for him to command them.'

'The King . . .'

'My lady, the best way to find out is to go to your father.'

The Earl and Lady Suffolk surveyed their daughter intently. It was clear to her mother that Frances was no longer a child. There had been rumours which had amused her; and although she had never bestirred herself to discover whether they were true or not, she was sure they were.

Frances was her daughter; therefore she would know how to amuse herself, and it was almost certain in what direction.

The Earl said: 'My daughter, good news for you.'

'Yes, father?'

'Your position has been a difficult one. A wife yet not a wife. It has been difficult for Robert too.'

'Robert,' she said blankly, for to her there was only one Robert.

'Robert Devereux, your husband, of course, child. I have news of him which will please you. He is on his way back to London, and expects to be with you within the next few weeks. I have a letter here from him for you. He tells me that he is longing to take you home to Chartley, for now that you are both grown up he wants his wife.'

Frances felt bewildered. Horror, frustration and anger swept over her.

Helplessly she looked from her father to her mother; but

she knew there was nothing they could do for her.

Now that she had discovered the one man who could satisfy her deep sensual needs, now that he was ready to be hers, this stranger was coming back from the past, to claim her as his wife, to take her away from the exciting Court to the dull country mansion, there to bury her alive.

'No!' she whispered.

But even as she spoke she knew that she was trapped.

Dr Forman

RIDING FROM Dover to London the thoughts of Robert Devereux were pleasant. It was good to be home after so long an absence and he was very much looking forward to seeing his wife who was now at Court; but, he promised himself, they would not remain long there. He and Frances would soon be riding northward. He was certain that she would be as delighted with Chartley Castle as he had always been.

He had never craved for the Court life. No doubt this was because he could never really escape from the ghost of his father. The first Earl of Essex – Robert Devereux like himself – had been too famous a man, beloved of the Queen, as great a favourite with her as this man Robert Carr was with her successor; and then, still young, he had lost his head. It was too colourful a life to be forgotten; and to be the son of such a man meant that wherever he went people recalled his father.

No, it would be Chartley for him and his young wife. He would teach her to love the place as he did. She would enjoy being the first lady of the district; and how the people would love her!

He had thought of her steadily during his absence; he remembered how she had smiled at their wedding; how they had danced together; how her eyes had sparkled. Dear little

Frances! It was not his proud prejudice which had assured him
that she was the loveliest girl at Court.

They were very different, he knew. Perhaps that was why
she attracted him so much. He was too serious for his age.
Being some ten years old when his father had gone to the
scaffold had left a mark on him. He still remembered those
years which followed his father's death when poverty loomed
over himself and his family. His two brothers had died when
they were young; but he and his little sisters, Frances and
Dorothy, had often wondered what would become of them.

Then fortune had changed. The King saw fit to restore his
estates; and, more than that, took a special interest in one
whose father he believed had been treated badly by Queen
Elizabeth. Not only had his estates been restored to him, but
he was given a wife – a young lady of rank and outstanding
charm.

He could not wait to see her again, and as he drew nearer
to London he gave himself up to pleasant imaginings of their
reunion.

In an ante-room in the Palace of Whitehall Robert Devereux
waited.

He had seen Frances' father, the Earl of Suffolk, who had
sent for her.

'I'll swear,' said the Earl, 'that you would prefer to be alone
together.'

Robert admitted that this was so, and at any moment now
she would appear.

Then she was there – framed in the doorway – certainly the
most beautiful girl he had ever seen, dressed in becoming blue,
her golden curls loose about her shoulders.

'Frances!' he cried and went to her so quickly that he had
not time to notice the sullen set of her lips.

He took her hands in his; then he dropped them that he
might cup her face in his hands; he kissed her lips. Hers were
very unresponsive.

Dear pure child, he thought, momentarily exultant, but
almost immediately he asked himself whether she was

as glad to see him as he was to see her.

'I am home at last.'

'So it seems, my lord.'

'Oh, Frances, how you have grown! Why, when I went away you were only a child. Are you pleased to see me? I have been longing for this day. Do not think that, although I have been away from you, I have not thought of you constantly. Have you thought of me?'

'I have thought of you,' said Frances; and it was true; she had thought of him with growing regret and repugnance; and his presence did nothing to diminish these emotions.

'I see,' he went on, 'that you are shy of me. Dear little wife, there is nothing to fear.'

She turned away from him and, with sick disappointment in his heart, he sought to cajole her.

'Why, Frances, you are young as yet and—'

She shook herself free of the arm which he had placed about her.

'Please let me alone,' she said quietly but with determination. 'I don't want you to touch me.'

'Have your parents not talked to you? . . .'

'I do not want to listen to my parents. I only want to be left alone.'

He stared at her blankly; then he smiled tenderly.

'Of course, this is a shock to you. You are so young. I forget how young. You did not want to leave your parents, your family . . . but you will grow accustomed to the idea. After all, we are married, Frances.'

The words were like the strokes of doom in her ears.

She was married; and there was no escape.

But hope came with his next words. 'The last thing I want is to make you unhappy, Frances. You need time to get used to me . . . and the idea of marriage. Have no fear. I do not want to hurry. We have all our lives before us.'

'Thank you.' Her voice was quiet and grateful.

Time. If she had time she might think of something she could do to escape this cruel fate.

*   *   *

She was truly frightened; so much so that she gave way to tears.

Jennet tried to calm her; her mistress' tears alarmed her.

'He wants me to go to the country, Jennet. The country! I shall die of melancholy. You know how I hate the country. It is better to be dead than live there. I won't go to the country. What can I do? What can I do?'

Jennet was thoughtful; then she said quietly: 'There are ways.'

'What ways? What?'

'You remember how I procured a powder for you which made you irresistible to my lord Rochester?'

'Yes, Jennet.'

'Well, mayhap I could procure a powder which would make my lord Essex so loathe you that he would wish to be rid of you.'

'Do it, Jennet. Do it without delay.'

'It is not as easy as that.'

'You mean it would cost money. You know I can find money. I have my jewels. I will give anything to escape from Essex.'

'You are married to him and escape will be difficult. It may well be that even if he loathes you he will still make you live as his wife. If he took you to Chartley, loathing you, you would be very little less unhappy than if he loved you.'

Frances paced up and down the apartment. Then she cried suddenly: 'I will see my Robert. I will tell him of my predicament. He is the most powerful man at Court. He will know what to do.'

Robert Carr embraced her with tenderness. His emotions were more engaged than he had believed possible. Frances' vitality was incomparable; she was a passionate mistress; and he would be really sorry to lose her.

On this day she was clearly disturbed.

'Oh, Robert,' she cried, 'you must know what has happened to me. I am desolate. But I know that you will save me. You are all powerful. No one would dare disobey you.'

'Do be calm,' he implored, 'and tell me all about it.'

'My husband is home and he wants to take me away from Court . . . to the country.'

'But it is natural that he should.'

'Natural!' she stormed. 'Why should he not stay at Court? Why should he want to bury me in the country . . . even if he does himself?'

'It is usual for wives to live with their husbands.'

'Robert, you can stand there so calmly! . . .'

'My dear Frances, ours has been a charming friendship.'

'A charming friendship! Is that all it is to you?'

'How I wish it could be more. But you are not free.'

She threw herself against him; she gripped his arms and stared into his face. 'Robert, if I were free, would you marry me?'

'My dearest Frances, you are not free.'

She stamped her foot. 'If I were, I said. If I were.'

'Ah, if they had not married you to Essex, how different everything would be.'

'Then you would marry me?'

Marry a daughter of the Howard family, one of the first in the country – rich, influential? Certainly he would. He had hesitated over Anne Clifford; but he would not over Frances Howard.

'Of course I would marry you,' he said truthfully.

'My dearest. My love!' she cried in ecstasy.

'You have forgotten something, my dear. You are not free to marry, having already a husband.'

'I shall never forget what you have just said, Robert. Never.'

'I shall always remember you.'

'You talk as though we are saying goodbye.'

A look of pained surprise crossed his handsome face. 'Alas, but we are,' he said.

'Robert, I shall never say goodbye to you. I shall never give up hope. You can prevent my going to the country. You can ask the King to command that we stay here.'

He raised his eyebrows. 'That would be most unwise.'

'Unwise! What has wisdom to do with love like ours.'

'Ah,' he sighed. 'You are right. We have been unwise. And I fear the consequences if you remained at Court. What when your husband discovered that we were lovers?'

'Let him discover.'

Robert moved away from her. She was being rather ridiculous. While James had no objection to a love affair he would not be pleased by scandal. James disliked the sort of scandal that could easily arise if Essex discovered he had been forestalled. It could do endless harm. No, the affair was over. He was regretful, but he knew he would grow less so as the days passed. She had been a charming mistress and he had been far from indifferent. In fact, he could sincerely say that he had never cared for a woman as he had cared for her; but that did not imply that he was the victim of a grand passion.

Frances was staring at him in horror. She had sensed the shallowness of his feelings compared with her own, and she was desolate.

He was ready to say goodbye. Perhaps he was eager to do so. He did not want trouble with Essex.

It was early next morning when two soberly dressed women, both wearing hoods pulled well over their faces, rode along the river bank towards the village of Hammersmith.

Jennet had said: 'It will be well for us to avoid the crowded streets which can be noisy.'

'I would not wish to be recognized,' her mistress agreed.

'My lady, are you sure—'

'That I want to come? Of course I want to come, you fool. Did we not decide that it was the only way?'

'Very well, my lady, but if we should be caught . . .'

'Oh, have done! I will take the blame. I will say that I forced you to take me. Indeed, how could it be otherwise? *You* could not force *me* to come, could you?'

Jennet appeared to be satisfied with that.

Her mistress would know how to take care of them both; perhaps she need not have worried about any evil that might have befallen them in the streets of London. Yet she had shivered to think of Lady Frances riding through the streets of the City, which were used by pickpockets and prostitutes, or lewd men out for adventure. She saw that a curl had escaped from her mistress' hood, and in any case a quick glance would give some idea of the beauty which there had been an attempt to hide.

But Frances had determined to come, and who could gainsay Frances when she made up her mind.

Jennet was relieved when they came to the outskirts of Hammersmith and in a short time were pulling up before a house.

They were ushered in by a maid whose sandy hair was plainly worn in a twist at the nape of her neck; there was a shawl about her shoulders; her tight bodice was topped by a linen collar and her skirts were full, though naturally she wore no farthingale.

'Madam is waiting for you,' she said in an awed whisper.

'Then take us to her at once,' commanded Jennet. 'My lady does not like delay.'

A door was opened and Frances and Jennet stepped into a pleasant room. It was small by the standards to which Frances was accustomed, but she realized that it was comfortably furnished. The ceiling was ornamental and there were some good pictures on the walls. A woman who had been sitting by the window rose as they entered and came forward swiftly. She curtsied before Frances; then rising took her hand and said: 'Welcome, my lady.'

Then she nodded to Jennet and bade them sit down while she called for refreshment.

Wine was brought with little cakes which Frances, who had a good appetite, found delicious; but she was too excited to care much for eating or drinking, and was very eager to get to the business which had brought her here.

'Jennet has often talked of you, Mrs. Turner,' said Frances.

'I am honoured,' answered the woman.

She was handsome, richly dressed and had an air of distinction, and although no longer young – she could have been

some fifteen years older than Frances — she was still very attractive. It occurred to Frances that she would not have been
out of place in some Court circles.

'Jennet has told you why we have come?'

'As far as possible, my lady,' Jennet answered.

'You yourself must tell me exactly what you want,' said Mrs
Turner. 'I am sure we shall be able to procure it for you.'

Frances wasted no time. 'I was married as a child, having no
say in the matter. I did not live with my husband who went
abroad. Now I have met a man whom I wish to marry, but my
husband is insisting that I go with him to the country. I
cannot do this. I *will* not do it. I want to be freed from my
husband; and to make sure of keeping the love of the other.'

'Is my lady in danger of losing the love she wishes to
keep?'

Frances said firmly: 'Yes.'

Mrs Turner took up a fan and fanned herself. She was
thoughtful.

Then she said: 'My lady, you were given a potion some
while ago.'

'Yes, that is so.'

'And it was . . . effective.'

'It is for that reason that I am here now.'

Mrs Turner laughed lightly. 'I see we shall get on well.
You speak your mind. I am forthright myself. I must tell you
that I only dabble in these arts. I myself used a love potion
once.'

'It was successful?'

'Most successful. I have been to Court. My husband was Dr
George Turner. The late Queen was very good to him and saw
that he gained advancement. He had a considerable practice
among her courtiers.'

'I thought this must be so,' said Frances, who found a kin-
dred spirit in this woman and was liking her more every
moment. She had expected to meet some witch-like creature,
some drab who would give her what she asked and demand a
high price for it. To find a cultured lady, who knew something

of Court life, was an agreeable surprise and was making this meeting, which she had thought might be an ordeal, very pleasant.

'Oh yes, I have had a comfortable life. Dr Turner was so clever. A kind husband too. Of course I was much younger than he was, and he understood.' She became a little arch. 'It was then I needed the potion. I had fallen in love with a very gallant gentleman. You may have heard of – Sir Arthur Man-waring. The potion I took worked as I wanted it to. I have three children by him now – such darlings. They are all here with me.'

Frances looked a little startled and Mrs Turner went on: 'I tell you this, my dear, to let you know my secrets. You see, I shall have to know yours. And I have always believed that it is fair to share secrets. That is why I tell you ... to let you know that whatever you wish to tell me, it is safe, locked in here.' She touched her silken bodice below the yellow ruff to indicate her heart.

'You are right,' said Frances. 'I did feel a little chary of telling you all that I feel.'

'Then set aside your fears. Some turn their eyes upwards and look pious because a handsome woman seeks a lover outside the marriage bond. I do not. I have done it all before you.'

'Can you help my lady, Mrs Turner?' asked Jennet.

'I am sure I can.'

'Can you give me two potions? One to make my husband loathe me; the other to make my lover continue in such love for me that he cannot rest until I am his wife?'

Mrs Turner was thoughtful. 'It is not so easy to help a married lady to another marriage,' she said.

'But why not?'

'Because it is always a little more dangerous when there is an unwanted husband.'

'I do not understand.'

Jennet said quickly: 'My lady does not wish to harm her husband.'

'Of course not. But the difficulties are there. I think in such a delicate situation I must call in the help of the wisest man in London.'

'Who is that?' demanded Frances.

'My father, Dr Forman.'

'I have never heard of him.'

'You will soon. He gave me the little knowledge I have; but he is well known for his genius. When you have refreshed yourself I propose that we leave for his house. I have told him that he might expect us.'

Jennet glanced anxiously at Frances, but Anne Turner had so won her confidence that Frances was ready to go wherever she suggested.

In his Lambeth residence Dr Simon Forman was waiting for his visitors.

The room in which he would receive them had been made ready; the Countess of Essex would be by no means the first highly born client he had welcomed here. Often ladies of the Court, having heard of his fame, came to beg favours of him; and he sold them dearly.

He rubbed his hands gleefully; it was pleasant to think that a member of the noble family of Howard was coming to consult him.

On the walls hung the skins of animals; there was a stuffed alligator on a bench, and ranged about it bottles of coloured liquid. Painted on the walls were the signs of the Zodiac; and a chart of the heavens was propped up on the bench. Hangings were drawn across the one small window; and candles in sconces had been placed about the room.

Dr Forman was pleased with this room; he considered that it had a desired effect on the applicant before the talk began.

He had a sharp, clever face; he had lived almost sixty years and a great many experiences had been packed into those years. He had always thirsted after knowledge; and it had become clear to him, at a very early age, that he was an extraordinary man. As a child he had been tormented by the strangest dreams; and he had quickly discovered that, by telling these dreams and putting a plausible construction on them, making a guess at what had a very good chance of happening to some of his acquaintances, he very soon earned a reputation for having supernatural knowledge. He decided to exploit this.

Simon Forman was born at Quidhampton in Wiltshire. His grandfather had been Governor of Wilton Abbey but, with the suppression of the Monasteries, was robbed of that post and given inferior employment about the Park.

One of Simon's early occupations was to compile a genealogical tree which, he insisted, revealed that the Formans were a family of some gentility and that several of his forbears had been knights.

His pride had been deeply wounded in his childhood, for poverty was humiliating to one who was certain that he possessed unusual powers. But he never lost sight of the need for education, and when William Riddout, an ex-cobbler turned clergyman who had fled from Salisbury on account of the plague, came to live near the Forman family, Simon was allowed to take lessons with him.

Simon's father had the same respect for learning as his son, and had in fact imbued Simon with this desire to improve himself; and when it seemed that Riddout could teach him no more, Simon was sent to a free school in Salisbury.

He had suffered there under a master named Bowle, who had beaten him severely on more than one occasion, so under him Simon lost a little of his desire for learning; but he was a sharp lad and managed to elude whippings more successfully than his fellow students.

Simon was pleased when his father decided to take him from this school and put him into the care of a Canon of Salisbury Cathedral. This man, whose name was Minterne, lived very austerely, and life in his household was sheer misery. There was never enough to eat and in winter the cold was almost unbearable.

Canon Minterne did not believe in self-indulgence and would not have coal in the house, although he did permit a little wood to be used – but not for burning. 'Exercise,' he told Simon, 'brings more comfort to the body than sitting over fires. If you are cold, boy, do as I do. Take these faggots and carry them up to the top of the house at great speed. When you have reached the top, come down again; repeat this until you are warm. That is the way to enjoy comfort in cold weather.'

The boy had been sorry for himself during his stay in the Canon's house; but he had to suffer greater misery than that of austere living when his father had died and his mother, harassed by poverty, declared that she had not patience with a boy wasting his time on learning, and Simon must earn his keep now.

What humiliation! He, Simon Forman, the possessor of special powers, to be apprenticed to a dealer of Salisbury; moreover one with a wife who thought it her right to lay about her husband's apprentices with a stick when the mood took her. He had no intention of giving up his dream of becoming a scholar though, and found a means of doing this. Lodging in the house of his master was a schoolboy, and Simon cajoled this boy into teaching him by night all that he had learned by day.

When he considered himself sufficiently learned to teach others, he ran away from the merchant's house and became a schoolmaster; he then had a stroke of luck. He made the acquaintance of two lighthearted young men who were studying at Oxford – or pretending to. They needed a servant. This gave Simon his opportunity. While looking after these young men, helping them in their courtship of a certain lady (they were both her suitors, which simplified matters) Simon was able to study at the university – a great asset for future use, even though circumstances prevented his attaining his degree.

He took several small posts at schools after that and, believing that there was more money and prestige to be won by using what he called his miraculous powers than by teaching, he decided to make a career for himself. He studied astrology and medicine and had certain success. It was inevitable though that some should consider him a quack, and he was brought to court to answer a charge of quackery.

When he was bound over on an injunction to cease his practices he went abroad for a while, and on his return set up as a doctor and astrologer in Lambeth. That was in the year 1583. There had been occasions when complaints were made against him, and he was imprisoned for a while; but his reputation was growing; and many wealthy people were coming to him and recommending him to their friends.

Although he was nearly sixty, he was as vital as he had been in his youth; he lived comfortably with several servants to attend to him. The females among them shared his bed whenever he had the fancy to invite them to, which was often – a fact which his wife had found necessary to accept. He was a man who had always been very fond of women – his clientele was largely made up of this sex – and it was a great pleasure to him to hear of their love affairs, their need to attract this lover, or rid themselves of that. He enjoyed a vicarious delight, of which they were not aware, as they sat in this darkened room and allowed him to peer into the secret places of their minds.

It was remembered in some of the poorer districts of London that during times of plague he had come where no other doctor had ventured, and that his remedies had saved many lives. So that he had his followers among the poor as well as the rich.

The authorities might despise him, and from time to time bring him before the justices. They might call him a charlatan and a quack with little knowledge of medicine. Simon would laugh.

'I look to the stars,' he retorted. 'They tell me all I want to know about disease.'

He was vain and longed for the approbation of the world, and like most men of his trade he made long and frequent experiments in search of the philosopher's stone; and because now and then his prophecies came true, like many of his kind and those who followed him, he remembered such occasions and conveniently forgot the many times he failed.

'I came to my present position the hard way,' he often told

one of the maids whose young bodies kept him warm at night, 'and that is the best way, my dear; for when a man has experienced hardship and opposition on his long climb upwards he is ready for any contingency which presents itself.'

Now a rather intriguing contingency was about to present itself.

Frances Howard, Countess of Essex, was on her way to see him.

Frances was overawed by the character of the room into which she was ushered. She was even more impressed by the man in his long black robes – decorated with colourful cabalistic signs – which gave a glimpse of blood-red lining as he moved towards her.

'Do not be afraid, my daughter,' he said.

'I am not afraid,' answered Frances.

'Call him Father,' whispered Anne Turner.

And strangely enough, so impressed was Frances that she did.

Jennet remained standing by the door, her eyes wide with wonderment.

'Be seated,' said Simon Forman.

Frances sat in the chair which was offered her; and Simon placed a crystal ball in her hands. Then with long bony fingers he himself threw back her hood.

Her beauty was startling in this dark room. Even Simon was astonished. His tongue licked his lips. What kind of man is this who needs to be wooed by such a beauty? he asked himself.

His expert eye saw there was more than beauty to this girl. Fire, passion, desire . . . and all directed towards one who was not eager for it.

He could bless his daughter Anne for bringing her to him.

He rubbed his hands together. Now he was going to uncover a spicy strip of Court scandal. He would have the pleasure of brooding on that – and counting the money it would bring him. This one could be considerably milched, he doubted not, for she was young, inexperienced and very eager in her desires.

'My daughter,' he said, 'tell me all as clearly as you can.'

So Frances once more told of the unfairness of her marriage, of her dislike for her husband, of her love of another; and how it was imperative to her happiness that she be rescued from a position which was intolerable to her.

'Can you help me . . . Father?' she asked.

He laughed lightly. 'It does not seem to me to be an impossible task, Daughter. First, there is the young man whose affections are cooling. We can give you a potion to strengthen his ardour. His affections, you say, cooled when your husband returned. Shall we say he is a man who has a horror of being involved in scandal?'

'You could say that.'

'Well then, our first task should be to work on your husband. We must find a means of *cooling* his ardour. Then if he is less anxious for your company, your lover will be less afraid. That will make it easier for us to work on *his* feelings.'

Frances clasped her hands. 'Oh, I am sure you are right.'

'Then we will first work on the husband. Can you arrange that a powder be slipped into his food without his knowing?'

Frances hesitated. 'He is surrounded by his servants. But I might manage it.'

Simon nodded. 'H'm. We will brood on this matter. It may be that we can use some influence to make your life less difficult. But our first step is to give you the powders. These are costly to prepare.'

'I know . . . I know. I am ready to pay.'

'Mrs Turner has explained?'

'Yes.'

'And she is no longer a rich woman. She has given up much time and thought . . .'

'I am ready to pay you both whatever you ask.'

'You must forgive my insistence, Daughter. We must live while we retain our earthly guise. You know Mrs Turner, my dear daughter; she will be your confidante. And when necessary she will bring you to me. It would not be wise for you to pay too many visits to me; but why should you not enjoy a friendship with Mrs Turner? She is a lady, like yourself, although not of such high rank. You will have much in common.'

'Thank you,' said Frances gratefully.

Two little phials were given to her. 'Put the contents of these into his food, and we will see what is the result. I would have you remember that we are dealing with a difficult problem. There may be no results at first; particularly as you may have some difficulty in administering the powders. But we will not despair. I promise you, my daughter, that in time you will have your desire. I repeat . . . in time.'

Frances went away satisfied. She had been greatly impressed by both Mrs Turner and Dr Forman.

When she had left, Simon wrote in his diary: 'The Countess of Essex came today. She is desirous of ridding herself of her husband that she may marry a certain gentleman in a very high place at Court.'

Robert Devereux faced his father and mother-in-law. He was pale and there was a determined line about his jaw.

'I believe I have been patient,' he said, 'but I cannot remain so. Your daughter simply refuses to live with me as my wife. I must ask you to speak to her and to tell her that, although I have waited so long, I am not prepared to wait any longer.'

The Earl and the Countess exchanged glances.

This, implied the Earl, is what comes of allowing the girl to live at Court. She should have remained in the country until her husband came to claim her. Then she would have been willing enough to go away with him. Court life has turned her head.

The Countess shrugged her shoulders. She understood her daughter well, because they were so much alike. Frances was not born to live a quiet life in the country any more than she herself was; and she would have rebelled sooner or later. The pity was that it was sooner.

She herself was far too interested in her own exciting life to worry much about her daughter. Frances must, of course, live with the man she had married — until she could make some other arrangement. It was the duty of her parents to make her understand this.

The Earl said: 'I will speak to Frances. She is young and, I am afraid, wayward.'

'Tell her,' said Devereux, 'that I intend to leave for Chartley within the next few weeks and to take her with me.'

'I shall insist that she accompanies you,' answered his father-in-law. 'Leave this to me.'

As soon as Devereux had left, the Earl sent for his daughter.

Frances stood before him, sullen and defiant.

'You must be mad,' burst out her mother, 'to behave thus.'

'I know you are thinking of my tragic marriage . . .'

'Tragic marriage! With Essex! My dear child, he is an easy young man. If you liked you could have what you wanted from him.'

'There is only one thing I want from him . . . my freedom.'

The Earl spoke gently: 'Look here, my child, you have not given your marriage a chance. You have been spoiled at Court. I would to God we had never allowed you to come.'

'I will not leave the Court with Essex.'

The Earl was aware of his wife's eye on him, a little scornful; he then went to Frances and gripped her firmly by the arm.

'We have been over-gentle with you,' he said. 'That was a mistake. There shall be no more mistakes. You are going to behave like a good wife to your husband. Make no mistake about it.'

'No one can make me,' cried Frances wildly.

'You are mistaken. I am your father and I can make you. I shall have you whipped if need be. I shall have you kept a prisoner in your apartment. I shall have you trussed, if necessary, and delivered to your husband.'

His mouth was grim. Frances knew that like most easygoing men he could be goaded into action; and on those rare occasions he could be stubbornly determined.

She was in despair.

When he left the Earl and Countess of Suffolk, Robert Dev-ereux, feeling sick at heart and deeply depressed, wanted to escape from the restrictions of the Palace. He came out into the fresh air and walked aimlessly, not seeing the river and the crowds, but Frances, the expression of loathing on her face; he contrasted the reality of his homecoming with what he had hoped for, and his melancholy increased.

He had made up his mind. He was not a man to act impul-sively, but once he had decided on a course of action he was determined to take it.

When he had said that he intended to leave Court within a few weeks, he meant it; and when he said that Frances was coming with him, he meant that too.

He found himself close to St Paul's and, still not caring which way he went, he wandered into the main walk where all kinds of business was in progress. The noise was deafening but he did not heed it; several sharp eyes were on him, for he was obviously a gentleman of the Court; his clothes betrayed him. Two pickpockets had their eyes on him and they were closely observed by a third.

A marriage broker called to him as he passed: 'Are you seeking me, sir?'

A pandar with two brazen girls, one on each arm, shouted: 'Would you like a pretty wench to take home with you?'

At one pillar of the aisle a letterwriter was working for a client; a horse dealer was at another; everywhere the prosti-tutes lurked.

Foolish of him to have come to Paul's Walk at such a time. He realized it suddenly. He might as well have gone to the Royal Exchange gallery to be pestered by the stall holders and of course the prostitutes.

He was aware of the crowds pressing about him; the smell of their clothes and bodies was distasteful. A beggar came

near to him and laid a hand on his; the beggar's hand was
hot and there were patches of scarlet colour in his face.

'Pity the blind beggar, fine gentleman.'

He felt in his pocket for a coin and gave it to the man, and
immediately he was besieged on all sides.

He despised himself. He could not manage to take a walk in
the streets without trouble, so how could he hope to tame a
wayward wife?

He gave more alms and crying, 'Enough! Enough!'
struggled out of the crowd. It was not until he was some
distance from Paul's Walk that he realized he had been robbed
of his purse and the gold ornaments on his doublet.

The walk had done him little good. It had brought home to
him his inadequacy. Moreover, there was a stiff feeling in his
throat; his skin was prickling and his hands were as hot as
those of the blind beggar.

Frances and Jennet were alone. Frances' eyes were brilliant.

'It has happened, Jennet. This is Dr Forman's doing.'

'What, my lady?'

'The Earl of Essex is grievously sick of a fever.'

'Is that so?'

Frances clasped her hands together and raised her eyes to
the ceiling ecstatically.

'He is dangerously ill. He has a raging fever. It came upon
him suddenly. Oh, don't you see, Jennet? This is the result of
Dr Forman's work. I was not able to give Essex the powder,
and Dr Forman knew it. So he has been working his spells to
help me.'

'I knew he would help you, my lady.'

'I don't know how to thank him and dear Turner, and you,
Jennet. Because soon I shall be free, and when I am, my Robert
will not hesitate. He loves me but he could not risk a scandal.
That is understandable. The King would be furious; and we
dare not offend the King. Oh, Jennet, this is what I wanted.
You see, until now I had thought that if only Essex would go
away, cease to pester me, leave me at Court with my beloved,
I should be happy.'

'And now my lady wants more.'

'Yes, Jennet, I want more. I no longer want to be married to Essex. And if he were dead, I shouldn't be. And he is dying, Jennet. Soon I shall be free.'

Frances curtsied before the King.

James smiled at her kindly, though vaguely. That was as well for she could not keep her attention on him because beside him stood his favourite, the Viscount Rochester.

'Well, my dear,' James was saying, 'we rejoice with you. A terrible tragedy has been averted. I am told that the worst of the fever is past. You must be a very happy woman.'

'Yes, Your Majesty,' murmured Frances, and she thought: Happy! I must be the most unhappy woman at your Court.

Robert Carr's benign smile, a replica of the King's, only added to her unhappiness. It seemed as though he too were pleased because Essex was recovering from his fever, and that the good which could come to them through the death of Essex had not occurred to him.

She was in despair.

It would have been better if Essex had never caught the fever. Then she would not have glimpsed that glorious possibility; but that it should have come so near only to be snatched away was intolerable.

'And now we are going to lose you, Lady Essex,' went on the King. 'I have talked with your husband and he tells me that as soon as he is quite recovered he is going to take you away from us.'

Speak, Robert! she wanted to cry. Tell him that I must not go.

'We shall miss Lady Essex, eh, Robbie?'

'We *shall* miss her, Your Majesty.'

'Well, my dear, your bonny smile will cheer old Chartley instead of Whitehall. Chartley needs your cheerful presence. It was one of the prisons in which they kept my mother. I think she did not hate it as much as some. You will come to Court again, I doubt not.'

Frances must pass on. She knew what was behind James'

words. This was a command to stop being a recalcitrant wife and obey her husband. She supposed that her father had told the King that she was refusing to leave Court with her husband.

James had spoken and there could be no disobeying the wish of the King.

Never would she forget that dreary journey to Chartley. They rode side by side, not speaking, two young people, their faces set into lines of determination – his to subdue her, hers never to be subdued.

She had ridden to Lambeth before she started on this journey north. It was her only comfort to remember what had taken place there.

'The spirits were not strong enough,' Dr Forman had told her. 'There were other little forces at work against us. It takes time to bring about such a conclusion as we wish for. A little more time and the fever would have proved fatal.'

She had changed in the last weeks. Previously she had been a spoilt girl, anxious to have everything that she desired; she had not thought of death when she planned to rid herself of Essex. She only wanted him to go away and leave her in peace.

But he was so stubborn; and she had changed. She was now a woman who might not hesitate to kill if she had the opportunity.

Secreted about her person were certain powders which had been given her by Dr Forman. Some were to be put in her husband's food; others to be sprinkled on his clothing.

If she obeyed his instructions it should not be long before she achieved her heart's desire.

She believed in Dr Forman, but as she rode farther north her spirits quailed.

Every mile lengthened the distance between her and the Court, between her and Robert Carr. And was he thinking of her while she was absent? He had never loved her with the violence with which she had loved him. And now that she was away from him, suppose others sought to lure him from her with potions and philtres? They might easily do it while she was not there to fight them.

So she was melancholy and would have been even more so but for the thought of Dr Forman and Mrs Turner in London who would, they had assured her, continue to work for her, even though she was far away.

She saw her new home – a castle on an eminence in a fertile plain. She looked with distaste at the circular keep, at the round towers.

Chartley Castle – her prison.

Death of a Prince

ROBERT CARR was relieved to see Frances leave the Court. He was more attracted by her than he had ever been by a woman before, and when he had said that, were there no impediments, he would have willingly married her, he was speaking the truth.

He would have liked to have a son to whom he could leave his fortune and give his name; and Frances had everything that he could look for in a wife – rank, wealth, an influential family, and greater physical attraction than any other woman he knew.

But because she was so vehement in character, because she was already married to a very noble gentleman, he preferred to forget about her.

He was becoming more and more involved in the King's affairs. It was amazing what a difference Thomas Overbury had made to his life. Not only did Tom deal with his correspondence, but he had a way of explaining difficult matters so that they were clear to Robert; he could also advise and make suggestions which Robert passed on to the King, to James' delight.

There was no doubt that Tom was a brilliant man, and he

was in his element, working in the background, knowing that he was having an influence on the affairs of the country. Whenever Robert was in any difficulty he went to Tom and explained it, and there was a firm bond of friendship between the two men.

Robert showered gifts on his friend. At first Tom protested. 'What I do for you, Robert, I do out of friendship.' 'What I give you, Tom, I give out of friendship,' replied Robert.

But when Tom began to see how his suggestions were accepted and Robert received the credit for them, he asked himself why he shouldn't be rewarded. After all he earned everything he received. It was Robert who took the honours, and the King's gifts, so why should Tom hesitate to pick up the crumbs which fell from the rich man's table? He earned them.

His attitude changed slightly. He was as devoted to Robert as ever; but he was beginning to look on him as his creature, a puppet, who danced to his tune.

It was an intoxicating thought that he, Tom Overbury, son of an obscure knight of Bourton-on-the-Hill in Gloucestershire, who had come to Court without any relations to help him along to fame and fortune, should now be an adviser to the King – for that was what he was, even though the King and others did not know it.

Well, he was happy to help a good friend; and his pleasure was to see Robert rise higher and higher in the King's favour, for the higher Robert soared, the higher went Tom Overbury.

It was Tom who understood that the man who was deliberately trying to impede Robert's rise was the Earl of Salisbury.

Robert Cecil, first Earl of Salisbury, was the greatest politician of his day. James had inherited him from Elizabeth, and shrewdly understood that this was a man who would work readily for the good of the country, thrusting aside all thought of self-aggrandizement.

Salisbury disliked the influence the King's favourites held over him; he would have liked to sweep the Court free of them all, and there might have been a personal feeling in this, for the favourites were noted for that personal charm which Salisbury sadly lacked. He was very small, being only a little over five feet in height; he suffered from curvature of the spine which had affected the set of his neck, and earned for him the epithet, Dwarf. Both Elizabeth and James had found nicknames for those about them, and Elizabeth had affectionately called him her Little Elf. James' name for him was less charming. He was Pygmy to him; and he often called him his Little Beagle to his face.

Again and again when James had sought to bestow some post on Robert Carr, Salisbury had pointed out the inadvisability of the action and James had to concede that he was right. The Little Beagle was too clever to be ignored; therefore although Robert Carr had become more firmly established in the King's affection than ever, he still had not attained the posts and honours which could have been his.

Overbury was too clever to believe that at this time he and his friend could set themselves against the Little Beagle; but he did not see why Carr should not in time, when he, Overbury, had a greater grip of affairs, oust this rival from his place; and Overbury believed that eventually the leading statesman of Britain would not be Robert Cecil, Earl of Salisbury, but Robert Carr, Viscount Rochester.

The battle between Salisbury and Carr must at some time come to a head, and this seemed about to happen when the King needed money and asked the Parliament for it. When Parliament refused this, and hinted that if the King was in financial difficulties the first step towards easing the position might be to dismiss his Scottish favourites on whom he lavished a great deal, Robert was alarmed, because he knew that as the leading favourite, this suggestion was aimed primarily at him.

He went into conference at once with Overbury who shared his alarm, and reminded him that, as the King's favourite, he had too many enemies in high places; and he would do well to remember that the King's old Secretary of State, Lord Salisbury, was the first of these.

'You will have to tread cautiously, Robert,' said Tom.

'Otherwise Salisbury will get his way. It would be the end of everything if you were sent back across the Border.'

'I'm afraid of Salisbury.'

'Who would not be? He's a brilliant statesman and James knows that. Oh, how I wish I were there when you talk to the King. You must make him understand that he should not give way to the Parliament. Otherwise they'll have the upper hand and they'll strike against you.'

'But even if the King dissolves Parliament that won't get him the money he wants.'

Overbury was silent for a moment; then he said: 'There could be ways of raising money without the help of Parliament. James believes in the Divine Right of Kings so he would not be averse to trying them out.'

'What ways are these?'

Overbury pondered for a moment or so and then said: 'Well, for one thing, there are many rich men about the Court who lack a good family background. They would give a great deal to possess titles. Why shouldn't the King sell titles? I should imagine that would bring him quite a pleasant sum.'

'Why, that's a brilliant idea,' cried Robert. 'I'll tell James at once.'

'Don't rush in with it. Let it come out casually, as though you've thought of it on the spur of the moment.'

'I will, Tom. My dear, clever fellow. What should I do without you?'

The King's ministers were beginning to think that Carr was a good deal more shrewd than they had suspected. The King had dissolved Parliament when it was rumoured that that body was about to demand the return of certain Scotsmen to their own country. The position would have been extremely awkward for Robert Carr and James if Parliament had ordered the favourite's eviction.

It was a shock to the King's ministers because they had believed that, owing to his dire need of funds, he would not be able to do without their help. Moreover, only the judicious Salisbury prevailed on the King not to send the more troublesome of the ministers to the Tower.

Then it was understood why James could afford to do without his Parliament. He had a new idea which, it was said, had been put forward by Carr.

Any man of means who would like to become a baronet might do so if he would present a little over a thousand pounds to the Royal Exchequer.

From all over the country this offer was taken up. In rolled the money; and if there were a large number of baronets, what did the King care.

He was delighted with his clever Robbie who could concoct such plans to bring his Old Dad and Gossip what he needed.

James was terrified.

He summoned Robert to him, and when he came bade him lock the doors of the apartment.

'I smell treason in this,' he declared.

'My dear Majesty, I pray you calm yourself,' begged Robert.

'I canna help feeling that this is another of their dastardly plots, boy. Have ye heard what has happened?'

'The Lady Arabella has escaped from Barnet.'

'Aye, lad. Escaped and on the high seas. I've ordered that a boat be sent after her from Dover. But if she reaches France and hides there, how can we guess what black mischief she'll be at . . . she and that traitor of hers, Will Seymour?'

'Your Majesty, I feel sure that she will not be allowed to reach France. We shall capture her and bring her back.'

'Ye're a great comforter, boy. But this is how the plots begin. I dream about them, Robbie. I dream they're stacking gunpowder in the cellars again; and that those who wish me out of the way, as the Ruthvens once did, will be putting their heads together. I've had luck so far, Rob. It wouldn't be logical to expect it to go on.'

James was thinking of the ministers of his own Parliament who had recently spoken against him. What were they planning? Wouldn't they seize an opportunity to rally to Arabella; even if the girl did not wish to start a war, they'd make her; she would be a good figurehead. And who could say how ambitious Will Seymour was?

It was a mistake perhaps to have taken her from Sir Thomas Parry with whom he had lodged her when she had disobeyed him by her marriage. She must have been desperate when she heard that she was to go to Durham to be in the care of the Bishop there. She had fretted and her health had suffered so that on the way north she had seemed to become seriously ill and had had to rest at Barnet. Now James saw that that was very likely a trick.

She must have had friends who helped her; she could never have escaped if she had not. Where would she have found French-fashioned hose, and a man's doublet? They must have been found for her; and she, while he believed her to be sick, had dressed herself in these, added a man's peruke, a black hat and cloak – not forgetting a sword – and had, in the company of some of her friends, slipped away. She had reached the Thames where she boarded a waiting vessel and was taken to a French ship which was lying in readiness for her.

This was not all. At the same time William Seymour, also wearing a peruke and a false beard, had walked out of his prison in the Tower down to the river where a boat was waiting for him.

How could this have been done, demanded James, if the pair of them had not possessed friends to help them?

'But mark ye this,' added the King. 'Luck has not gone with them all the way, for I am informed that by the time Will Seymour made his escape, the French ship had already left with the Lady Arabella, fearing to wait longer. Where Seymour is we do not know, but we'll find him. And when these birds are once more my captives, there shall be such a cage made for them that they will never fly away again.'

James' fears were soon diminished. Before her ship touched the shores of France it was overtaken by its swift pursuer, and Lady Arabella was brought back to England.

'Take the lady to the Tower,' said James. 'And this time make sure that she is well guarded. And what of Will Seymour?'

There was no news of Will Seymour for some weeks; and then the rumour came to the Court that he had safely reached France and was sheltering there.

James was uneasy. He would have many a nightmare about that young man. It was good that Arabella was in safe custody, but plots would go on doubtless while Seymour was free.

In her cell Lady Arabella wept bitterly for the ill fortune which was hers. She did not wish to wear the crown of England; she only wanted to live in peace with her husband.

She prayed that he might stay safe in France and that at some time she would be able to join him.

Ready to catch at every hope, she thought of Robert Carr who had seemed to her a kindly man, and had so great an influence with the King.

She took up her pen and wrote to him, imploring him to plead her cause with the King; she begged him to consider her sorry plight, and signed herself the most sorrowful creature living.

Robert was distressed when he read the letter. He had only a casual acquaintance with the Lady Arabella but he had always believed her to be a gentle, harmless lady.

He wanted to plead for her with the King, but first he discussed the matter with Tom Overbury.

'There is nothing you can do,' his friend told him. 'Why even I, to whom the King has scarcely spoken, know how he fears plots. He is in terror of the assassin's knife or the hidden gunpowder. No, Robert, don't be a fool. Your strength lies in your ability to make the King feel comfortable. He wouldn't if you pleaded for Arabella. You may think you can risk offending James. Don't be too sure of that, Robert. Always remember that there are other handsome men waiting to spring into your place. Say nothing of this.'

As usual Robert took his friend's advice. So Lady Arabella continued to languish in the Tower – a melancholy prisoner who had committed no crime – except of course that of belonging to a branch of the royal family. All she asked was to be able to live quietly with her husband, somewhere in the country if need be, well away from Court intrigue.

Alas, for Arabella.

In the upper chamber of the Bloody Tower, Sir Walter was showing Prince Henry plans for a journey he was hoping to make.

Rarely had Henry seen Raleigh looking so well; and he
thought: If he could only regain his freedom he would be as
full of vigour as he ever was.

'Do you know,' he was saying, 'I really believe this time I
shall not be disappointed. I said: Let me serve as a guide in
this expedition and if I do not lead the way to a mountain of
gold and silver, let the commander have commission to cut
off my head there and then.'

'You seem very sure of finding treasure, Walter.'

Raleigh laughed. 'Ah, my Prince. It will be a gamble.'

'You'd gamble your head!'

'Any day, for my freedom.'

'I shall pray for your success.' Henry's eyes lit up. 'Do you
think I might come with you?'

'Not for a moment, my dear friend. The heir to the throne
would never be allowed to risk his life.'

'If I could make my own decisions I should come.'

'When the times comes for you to make your own decisions, your duty will lie here, and not in Orinoco.'

'None will rejoice more than I on the day you return in
triumph; and Walter, when I am King everything that you have
suffered shall be made up for . . . a hundredfold.'

Raleigh patted the young man's hand.

'I shall serve you with my life, my King.'

Henry, feeling too emotional for comfort, hastily changed
the subject. 'You have heard of course that there is a move to
marry Elizabeth to the Prince of Piedmont.'

'I have heard.' Raleigh shook his head. 'I should not care to
see our Princess married to the son of the Duke of Savoy; and
I hear there is another project.'

'That I should marry his daughter. What think you of this
match?'

'It does not please me.'

'Then do not hesitate to speak of your objections.'

'I shall not.'

'There has been a suggestion that Elizabeth should marry the King of Spain. As you know there are many secret Catholics at Court, in spite of the moves my father has made against them; and I believe that some of his ministers are in the pay of Spain. I should protest strongly against a Catholic marriage for my sister, and so would she.'

'A great deal depends on Salisbury's attitude.'

'His desire is for closer alliance with the Princess of the German Protestant union, and the young Elector Palatine is looking for a bride.'

'And Elizabeth, what does she feel?'

'Poor Elizabeth. She is not very old, you know. It is a sad fate which befalls our Princesses. They must marry and go into a strange land. At least that is a fate which we avoid.'

'You are very fond of your sister, and you will suffer from the parting.'

'I shall come to you more often and expect you to comfort me. But perhaps by then you will be on the way to Orinoco. Who can tell?'

Henry saw the far-away look in his friend's eyes, and knew that he was already picturing himself on the high seas.

He is longing to set sail, thought Henry. And when he goes I shall have lost him for a while; and if ill should befall him, perhaps for ever. And if Elizabeth marries and goes away, I shall have lost her too.

There was one other he had lost.

He thought of her occasionally and then he was aware of a nostalgia for the days of his innocence. He had never replaced Frances, having no further wish for a mistress. She could still make him sad. He had believed her to be perfect and his ideal had been shattered on the day when he had learned that Carr was also her lover.

There in the upper chamber of the Bloody Tower he felt a desire never to grow up, if doing so meant that he must lose that which, in innocence, he had cherished.

*   *   *

With the coming of the summer there was much activity at Court on account of the Princess Elizabeth, while one faction worked for a Catholic marriage and another was in favour of the German match.

Northampton, secretly in the pay of Spain, having made a friend of Robert Carr, sought to carry him along with him. On the other hand Prince Henry and his sister were fiercely against a Catholic marriage.

Henry, who loved his sister more devotedly than he loved anyone else, was convinced that she could be happier with a man of her own faith; she too shared his opinion.

The antagonism between Robert Carr and the Prince of Wales intensified, although Robert's pleasant easy-going nature made an open breach difficult. He rarely took offence and was always deferential in his manner to the Prince, but Henry hated the man; whenever he saw him, he pictured him making love to Frances, who, now chafing against life at Chartley, would have felt some comfort to know that she was not forgotten at Court.

Tom Overbury was constantly watching his friend's enemies; and there were two who gave him great cause for alarm. One was the Prince of Wales; the other, Lord Salisbury. But Lord Salisbury was an old man and of late had shown signs of failing health; and Overbury had secret ambitions which he hoped to see fulfilled when the old man died. To whom would fall the Secretaryship and the Treasury? Why not to Robert Carr?

Perhaps this was hoping for too much? But Robert – with Overbury working in the background – would be capable of holding these offices.

Overbury was growing more and more excited during these months.

Salisbury eventually succeeded in making the King see the advantages of the German marriage, and the Princess Elizabeth was formally plighted to the Elector Palatine, Frederick V.

This was in a way a defeat for Northampton of whom Robert Carr had made a friend, and Overbury was dismayed because such a matter was enough to set courtiers asking: 'Is the favourite losing his influence with the King?'

Robert himself maintained his serene attitude and never betrayed by a look or word that he was disconcerted. This was the quality which so endeared him to the King. He always gave the impression that he was at the King's side to carry out his wishes, not to intrude with his own.

Then Salisbury went off to Bath so see if the waters could relieve him, and the Prince of Wales gave himself up to the pleasure of planning the coming visit to England of his sister's suitor.

Robert sought out Overbury, and it was clear that he was excited.

'News, Tom, which will be on everyone's lips ere long. Salisbury is dead.'

Overbury was open-mouthed with astonishment, while slowly a look of delight spread across his face.

'Is it indeed true?'

'I have just had it from the King himself. Salisbury left Bath feeling that no good could come of his stay there. The journey home was too exhausting for him. He reached Marlborough, and there died. The King is mourning his Little Beagle. He says it will be long before we see a statesman of his brilliance.'

'We shall not share in the King's mourning.'

'I had an admiration for the little fellow.'

'He was too clever for us. That's why I am rejoicing that he is no longer here. Do you know that your Little Beagle put more obstacles in your way than the Prince of Wales ever did.'

'He didn't think me worthy of the great posts and he was right.'

Overbury's lips tightened. 'I tell you this, Robert: with me behind you, you are worthy of any post the King could give you. Now we must be careful. We must tread cautiously. They'll all be clamouring round now the Beagle's gone. If you're ever going to be number one in this kingdom, now is your chance.'

'Listen, Tom—'

'No, you listen to me. You're going to have the offices Salisbury has vacated. You have to, Robert. There's no standing still for you. It's go on or fall out. I know and I'm telling you.'

Robert knew his friend was right, because he always had been. Therefore he must accept his guidance.

James looked on with cynical eyes while those about him jostled each other for the dead man's shoes. There was not one of them who would match up to Little Beagle; James would miss Pygmy, but at the same time he was determined not to set up another in his place.

He had made up his mind what he was going to do. Robert Carr was the one who should benefit by the death of Salisbury; Beagle had been unfair to Robbie. Small wonder. The poor ill-favoured creature must have been jealous of one who was singularly blessed with good looks.

Robert would be the ideal Secretary because he would always do what his master wanted. He would not have the title; that would cause too much of an outcry. He, James, would have a chance to put in action that policy which he had always favoured: the Divine Right of Kings to act as they thought best.

Robbie should be the Secretary; he had become a genius with the pen and could always be relied upon to work along the lines his royal master suggested.

As the weeks passed it became apparent that Robert Carr was the most powerful man in the country under the King.

It was what many had suspected would happen, and some had feared.

But there were others who looked on jubilantly.

Among these was Thomas Overbury who saw himself as the secret ruler of Britain; another was the Earl of Northampton, Lord Privy Seal, who had decided to court Robert Carr that they might work together to further Northampton's ends.

The Prince of Wales threw himself wholeheartedly into the

preparations for his sister's marriage. He had convinced her that she was fortunate to have escaped a Catholic match; and because she had always followed him in everything she did, she believed him.

As the summer months were passing the excitement grew. Elizabeth was busy being fitted for new gowns, examining jewels which would be hers. She had received a picture of the Elector Palatine; his looks enchanted her, and she kept this near her bed, each day declaring that she was a little more in love with him.

One day Henry said to her: 'I think I shall come to Germany with you when you leave with your husband. Perhaps I shall find a bride there.'

'Then I should be completely happy, for Henry, there is one thing about my marriage that alarms me: leaving my family. I shall sadly miss our parents and Charles; but you and I have always been closer than the others. I never had a friend like you, Henry. Sometimes I wish that I were not going to be married, for I do not see how I can ever be really happy if I am parted from you.'

'Then that settles it,' said Henry with a smile. 'I must accompany you.'

'In that case I can scarcely wait for the arrival of my bridegroom.'

Henry smiled at her fondly. 'I shall not be sorry to take a little trip abroad. There are times when I feel it will be pleasant to get away from Rochester.'

'He has become more important since the death of my lord Salisbury, I fear.'

'If our father becomes much more besotted he will be giving him his crown. There is little else left to give him. He is at the head of all the functions now. Did you know that he is in charge of bringing our grandmother's remains to Westminster?'

'You mean they are going to disturb the grave of Mary Queen of Scots?'

'That is what our father proposes. He does not care that his mother's remains should be left in Peterborough. He wants to give them an honourable burial in Westminister.'

Elizabeth was silent; her expression had grown melancholy.

'What ails you?' asked Henry, coming over to her and putting his arm about her.

Looking up at him she thought he looked tired and strained.

'Henry,' she said, 'you have been practising too much in the tiltyard. You are tired.'

'It is good to feel tired.'

'I noticed that you have not looked well for some weeks.'

'It has been very hot. Why, what has come over you? Why are you suddenly sad?'

'I suppose it is the thought of what happened to our grandmother. In prison all those years and then taken into that hall at Fotheringay. How dared they, Henry? How dared they!'

'If Queen Elizabeth were alive you might ask her that.'

'I think our grandmother should be left in peace now.'

'Doubtless she would be pleased that our father wished to honour her.'

'But don't you see, Henry, it's unlucky to disturb the dead.'

'Nay, her spirit will rest in peace now that she knows her son mourns her truly.'

'It is all so long ago. Why disturb her now?'

Henry touched his sister's cheek lightly. 'I know what you're thinking of – that old superstition.'

Elizabeth nodded. 'A member of the dead person's family must pay for disturbing a grave . . . pay with a life.'

Henry laughed. 'My dear sister, what has come over you? It is a wedding we're going to have in our family. Not a funeral.'

It was easy to make her laugh. She was about to become a bride; she believed that she was going to fall in love with her bridegroom and that she would not after all have to say an immediate farewell to her beloved brother.

*   *   *

Others were noticing a change in the Prince of Wales. He looked more ethereal than ever, and his face had lost a certain amount of flesh so that his Grecian profile looked more clearly defined. But there was a fresh colour in his cheeks which gave an impression of health although he was beginning to cough so frequently that it was difficult to disguise this. He tried, it was true; and it was some time before anyone discovered that his kerchiefs were flecked with blood.

He did wonder why he could not shake off his cough. He tried to harden himself; he played tennis regularly and swam in the Thames after supper, which seemed invigorating; but at night he would sweat a great deal – and the cough persisted.

He was anxious that his sister Elizabeth and his mother should not know of this change in his condition, and he was particularly bright in their company; but often there would come into his mind Elizabeth's fear when they had talked of the removal of Mary Queen of Scots from Peterborough to Westminster.

A life of a member of the family was the price that must be paid for tampering with the dead. It was quite ridiculous.

Everything seemed more colourful to Henry that summer. The sun seemed to shine more brightly; the flowers in the gardens were more brilliant; he often thought of Frances Howard whom he had loved and who had deceived him; and their relationship now seemed a wonderful experience. He wished that Frances would come back to Court. He was sorry for her, a prisoner in Chartley, for he knew that she had deeply resented being carried there by her husband. But perhaps she was in love with him by now. She was a fickle creature. It was well that she was in the country. If she were back he might be tempted to sin once more. He did not want that. He wanted to live these days with a zest and verve that was new to him. He wanted to enjoy each minute; not one of them should be wasted. He had that feeling.

He did not visit Sir Walter as often as he used to. Sometimes he would sail down the river and look towards the Bloody Tower. He did not want those keen sailor's eyes to discover something which he would rather keep secret.

He did not wish to cast a backward look at what was rapidly overtaking him. He knew that one day it would be level with him; it would stretch out its cold arms and embrace him. There was no eluding that embrace. When it came he would be ready.

The Queen was unaware of her son's condition because he made such an effort to conceal it that he had succeeded.

When she said, 'And how is my beloved son this day?' he always answered: 'In excellent health, as I trust to find my dear mother.'

She saw him flushed from riding and mistook the flush for health. He was a little thin, and she scolded him for this. He must eat more. It was a command from his mother.

He would sit and talk to her, tell her how he had scored in the tiltyard; and she would listen delightedly. He made a great effort to restrain his cough in her presence and often succeeded.

When he could not she would say: 'I should have thought that friend of yours, Walter Raleigh, would have given you some draught to cure that cough. He is supposed to be so clever.'

'I must ask him when I see him next.'

'Do so. I like not to hear it.'

If Anne had not been so concerned with the coming wedding she might have been more aware of Henry's state. The match with the Elector Palatine, who was known as the Palsgrave in England, did not please her, for she thought the man not good enough for her daughter.

'I'd set my heart on her being Queen of Spain,' she grumbled. 'Who is this Palsgrave?'

'I think it is an excellent match, dear Mother,' Henry told her. 'It delights me.'

She smiled at him indulgently, and for his sake tried to hide her disappointment; but she could not manage this completely. When Elizabeth came to them she said: 'So Goody

Palsgrave comes calling on a Prince and Queen.'

'She looks very happy,' commented the Prince.

'Mayhap she has forgotten she was once a Princess. Come along, Goody; you must make a deeper curtsy now.'

But Elizabeth threw her arms about her mother and said: 'Forgive me, dearest Mother, but I think that good wife Mistress Palsgrave is going to be very happy.'

Queen Anne snorted; but Henry was laughing. And it made her very happy to have these beloved children with her.

It was October when Frederick V, the Elector Palatine, arrived in England. The streets of the capital were decorated to welcome him, and the people turned out in their hundreds to greet him.

He was immediately popular, being good-looking and eager to please; and Protestants throughout the country welcomed the union.

When Elizabeth met him she found him all that she had hoped he would be; and there was no doubt that he was as enchanted with her.

For once two people who had been elected to marry for political reasons had fallen in love on sight. It was a very happy state of affairs.

Even the Queen could not help being pleased, although she continued to mourn the loss of the Spanish crown.

Henry had been feeling steadily more ill, and was finding it increasingly difficult to hide this. But during the celebrations he determined to conceal his condition and he plunged into the celebrations with great zeal.

Elizabeth was in love and happy. He wanted her wedding to be something she would remember with pleasure for as long as she lived.

At the tennis tournament he was one of the champions, and everyone marvelled at his skill. Being October the weather was cold, but he played in a silk shirt so as not to be hampered by too many clothes.

When the game was over he was very hot, but almost immediately began to shiver.

The next morning a fever had overtaken him and he was unable to rise from his bed.

The Prince was ill; the news spread through the City. His illness had culminated in a virulent fever which, his doctors were sure, was highly infectious.

The Prince being aware of this implored his doctors not to let his mother, father, his sister Elizabeth or his brother Charles come near him.

He lay on his bed, not being quite sure where he was.

There were times when he believed he was dancing with Frances Howard, and others when he was sailing the high seas with Sir Walter.

The Queen walked up and down her apartment clasping and unclasping her hands while the tears streamed down her cheeks.

'This is not possible,' she cried. 'My Henry! He was always such a bonny boy. This cannot be true. He will recover.'

Nobody answered her. No one believed the Prince could recover, but no one dared tell her this.

'When he was a baby,' she said, 'he was taken away from me. I, his mother, was not allowed to nurse my own son. It was the same with them all. And now . . . this!'

But for all her grief she made no attempt to go to him. It would upset him, she assured herself; and she was terrified of contagion. Yet within her a battle was raging. She wanted so much to go to him; it was meet and fitting that his mother should be at his bedside. But if she should catch this fever . . . if it should run through the Palace . . . She must not be foolish; she must stay away from her beloved son. This was yet another sorrow to be borne.

She called one of her women to her.

'Send to Sir Walter Raleigh in the Bloody Tower. Tell him of the Prince's need. He is a clever man. Let him give him some of his elixir of life. That will save him.'

Then she threw herself on to her bed and wept.

But she felt better. He was wise, her Henry, and he had

always declared that Sir Walter Raleigh was the greatest Eng-
lishman alive – not only a fine sailor, but a scientist of im-
mense power.

Sir Walter loved the Prince. He would not fail now.

When Sir Walter heard the news he was horrified. He had
feared for some time that the Prince was ailing; but it was a
great shock to learn that this well set-up young man was now
close to death, the victim not only of a wasting disease but a
virulent fever.

But Sir Walter was a man of vision. He had always believed
that whatever he undertook would be successful. In the past
he had seemed to be right and it was only when his great
misfortune overtook him, and he lost his freedom, that he
had doubted the truth of his doctrine.

Even so, optimism had prevailed and sometimes he wondered whether he had been made a prisoner that he might
write history instead of making it, that he might preserve life
with his scientific discoveries rather than take it in rash adventures.

He therefore believed that he had the nostrum which would
cure the Prince; and in all confidence he went at once to the
hut at the end of the Walk and brought it back.

Before he dispatched the messenger he wrote a hasty note.
'This will cure all mortal malady, except poison.'

The good news spread through the Palace and City. The
Prince had regained sufficient consciousness to know that the
draught he was given came from his good friend, Sir Walter
Raleigh, and so confident of his friend's powers was he that he
seemed to recover.

Crowds gathered outside St James's Palace; they filled the
streets from the Palace to Somerset House, and some knelt
to pray for the life of the young man whom they all admired,
respected and loved.

There were other cases of fever in the City; people were
stricken, became delirious and in a few days died.

The Queen had left for Somerset House to be away from

contagion; she was inconsolable; longing to be at her son's bedside, yet fearing to be.

When the news came that Henry had recovered a little after taking the nostrum she fell on her knees and thanked God.

The King came to her with Elizabeth and Charles. They were all weeping bitterly and to Elizabeth it seemed unbelievable that, now she was to have a husband whom she could love, she was in danger of losing the brother who had until now held first place in her affections.

'Raleigh's nostrum is working the miracle,' cried Anne. 'Our son will live and we have that man to thank for it. You must reward him with his freedom. I shall never be able to thank him enough.'

James was silent. He was not so optimistic as the Queen; he knew that Henry had revived temporarily, but he believed they should wait awhile before allowing themselves to hope.

'Why do you not speak?' demanded Anne. 'Raleigh says that the mixture will cure everything except poison. Why do you cease to rejoice? Do you believe that our son has been poisoned?'

'Dinna excite yourself so, my dear,' begged James. 'This is a sad time for us. Let us meet it with calmness.'

But how could Anne be calm? If her son recovered she would be mad with joy; if he died she would be demented.

There were loud lamentations in the streets.

The news was out. About twelve o'clock on the night of November 5th, Prince Henry died.

The 5th of November! A significant date in the history of the life of the royal family. A few years earlier, on this very day, the plot to blow up the King and Parliament had been discovered.

In the streets the Catholics were declaring that this was a judgement on the persecutions which had followed the revelation of the Gunpowder Plot. There were riots and fighting in the streets, because there was always the mob which was ready for trouble at any opportunity. But the chief sound that filled the streets that night was that of weeping for the death of the most popular Prince of his House, the young man who had seemed so full of promise and who one day, the people had hoped, would be their King.

When the news was brought to the Queen she could not take it in for some time. She refused to believe it.

But at last she was forced to accept it, and the only way she could curb her great grief was in rage and recriminations.

'Raleigh said it would cure all but poison. Poison! Someone has poisoned my son. Who could have done such a foul thing to one who was beloved by all? What enemies had he among righteous men? None. But he had his enemies. What about Robert Carr whom he always hated? What of that sly shadow of his, Overbury? I always hated Overbury. I do not trust Overbury. He has poisoned my son at the request of Carr. I will prove it. There shall be an autopsy. And if poison is found I shall not rest until I have brought those men to justice.'

Those who heard of the ravings of the Queen did not hesitate to speak of her suspicions. Soon they were being whispered, not only in the Palace but throughout the City.

Even when the autopsy revealed that Prince Henry had died from natural causes, the rumour still persisted that he had been poisoned; and the names of Robert Carr and Overbury were mentioned in this connexion. It was said that the Prince had hated his father's favourite and had stood in the way of his promotion to even greater honours. Carr had a reason for wishing him out of the way; and it was known that Overbury was Carr's creature.

James, who had shown greater courage than the Queen during the Prince's illness and had been at his bedside even though warned of the contagious nature of his illness, scorned these suggestions; and bade Robert put them from his mind.

'Why, lad,' he said, ' 'twas ever the same. A prominent person dies and the word Poison is bandied from mouth to mouth. The autopsy shows the cause of death and in time all will come to accept it.'

Robert was grateful for the King's sympathy but he was uneasy. It was unpleasant to be suspected of murder.

One evening the guards at St James's were disturbed by the figure of a naked man; he was tall and fair, and in the dim light had a look of the Prince.

'I am the ghost of the Prince of Wales,' cried the naked one. 'I have come from the grave to ask for justice. Bring my murderers to the scaffold. It is where they belong.'

Some of the guards fled in terror, but two, bolder than the rest, approached the man and saw that he was not the Prince of Wales.

They hustled him into the porter's lodge and there demanded to know who he was.

'The Prince of Wales,' he answered. 'Come from the grave for justice.'

'This is a trick,' said one of the guards. 'Someone has sent him to do this. We'll find out who.'

They then took a whip and proceeded to lash the fellow until he screamed in agony. But he persisted that he was the ghost of the Prince of Wales.

Ghosts did not allow themselves to be beaten, the guards were sure. They tried to force him to confess he was a human being trying to trick them; but he persisted in his story, and they kept him there through the night, every now and then trying, as they said, to make him see reason and confess the truth.

In the morning news of what had happened was carried to the Palace and brought to the ears of the King, and James himself went to the porter's lodge to see the 'ghost' of Prince Henry.

He frowned when he saw the marks of lashes on the naked body.

'Why,' he said, 'did ye no understand that the man is sick? He's suffering from the same fever that carried off the Prince. He's in need of doctors, not lashes.' He tried to soothe the man whose mind was clearly wandering. 'Don't ye fret, laddie. You'll be taken care of.'

He gave orders that the man should be cared for and inquiries made as to who he was.

It was soon discovered that he was a student of Lincoln's Inn who had left his bed, deposited his clothes in an open grave and wandered on to the Palace.

On the King's orders he was looked after in the porter's lodge; and one evening when his nurses went to his bed, they found he had disappeared.

It was presumed that he had wandered out of the lodge, perhaps in an effort to find his way back to the grave which he believed he had left.

Some boatmen thought they saw him at the river's edge and, as he was never seen again, it was believed that he had drowned himself in the Thames.

The rumour of poison died down; but it was not entirely forgotten. Rather was it laid away to be brought out in the future when people were reminded of it.

Intrigue at Chartley Castle

WHEN ROBERT DEVEREUX, Earl of Essex, travelling from Court with his reluctant bride, was within two or three miles of Chartley Castle he found that the people of the neighbourhood had come out to welcome him. He acknowledged their greeting with bows and smiles and felt wretchedly uncomfortable when he saw their astonished looks directed towards the beautiful but sullen girl riding beside him.

Frances stared straight ahead of her as though she did not see these people. She was not going to pretend that she was a happy bride.

Her beauty must attract attention, for although it was a little marred by the thunderous looks it was no less remarkable.

When they entered the old castle and found the servants lined up, waiting to pay homage, she walked past them and did not glance at one of them, so that it was clear to all that there was something very unusual about their master's marriage.

'The Countess is weary with the long journey,' said Essex. 'Let her be shown her apartments without delay so that she may rest.'

'I am not in the least weary,' retorted Frances. 'While at Court I have been in the saddle for hours without feeling the slightest exhaustion. But let them show me my apartments.'

A dignified manservant signed to two young women, both of whom hurried forward, curtsied afresh to the Countess and turning, made their way up the wide staircase.

'Come, Jennet,' said Frances; and without another glance at her husband, followed the two serving girls.

'What a draughty place this is,' complained Frances. 'One might as well have lodgings in the Tower. They could not be more uncomfortable. Where are you taking me? Is it to the apartments occupied by the Queen of Scots, when she too was a prisoner here?'

'I am not sure, my lady, where the Queen of Scots had her apartments,' said the elder of the servants.

Frances shuddered. 'Poor lady. How she must have suffered!'

They had reached a corridor and were confronted by a spiral staircase. When they had mounted this they came to the apartments which had been prepared for the Earl and his Countess.

The rooms were luxuriously furnished, and from the windows was a view of the lovely Staffordshire countryside.

Frances looked at the big bed and her eyes narrowed.

She turned to the serving girls.

'You had better tell me your names.'

The elder, a girl of about twenty, said: 'I am Elizabeth Raye, my lady.' She turned to her companion who appeared to be about sixteen. 'And this is Catharine Dardenell. We have been selected to wait on you.'

Frances surveyed them intently, trying to assess how loyal they would be to the Earl. It might well be that she would need them to perform special services for her. She decided to try to win their confidence.

'I am sure you will do all you can to help me,' she said; and her face was transformed by the smile she gave them.

They curtsied in a rather embarrassed fashion.

'We shall do our best, my lady,' murmured Elizabeth Raye.

'Go now and bring me food. I am hungry. Bring enough for my maid here, too.'

'Yes, my lady. But a supper is being served in the great hall and the cooks have been planning for days what they would give my lord and lady on this day.'

'I shall not eat in the great hall. Do you understand?'

'Yes, my lady.'

'When you bring the food, knock on the door. It will be opened to you, if the two of you come alone.'

'Yes, my lady.'

'Go now, because I am hungry.'

When they had gone, Frances turned to Jennet.

'Take the key from the outside and lock the door from the inside.'

'My lady . . .'

'Do as I say.'

Jennet obeyed.

'Of one thing I am certain. He shall not come into this room.'

'Do you think that you can hold out against him, here in his own castle?'

'I must hold out against him.'

Jennet shook her head.

'You think he will force me? I have a dagger in this sheath. See, I wear it about my waist as some wear a pomander. I will kill him if there is any attempt at force.'

'Have a care, my lady.'

'Jennet, I am going to be very careful indeed.'

The Earl rapped on the door.

Frances went to it and called: 'Who is there?'

'It is I, your husband.'

'What do you want?'

'To see you. To ask if you are pleased with the apartment.'

'I am as pleased as a prisoner can be with a prison as long as you do not share it with me.'

'Do you understand, Frances, that there will be a great deal of scandal if you behave like this?'

'Do you think I care for scandal?'

'I care.'

'Care all you wish.'

'Frances, be reasonable. My father lived here before me. It is my family home.'

'What of it?'

'I am asking you not to cause a scandal.'

'I'd be hard put to it to provide a greater scandal than your father did.'

'Frances, let me come in, only to talk to you.'

'I have nothing to say to you.'

'You are my wife.'

'Alas!'

'What have you against me?'

'Everything.'

'What have I done to deserve your contempt?'

'Married me.'

'Frances, be reasonable.'

'I am ready to be. It is you who will not be. Leave me alone. Let me go back to Court. If you are so fond of your draughty castle stay and enjoy it. I would not attempt to tell *you* where you should be – as long as it is not with me.'

'I shall not endure this state of affairs. You are my wife and my wife you shall be ... in every way. Do you understand me?'

'You make yourself coarsely clear.'

'Let me come in and talk.'

'I repeat, there is nothing to be said.'

He was silent. He sighed deeply and then said in a sad voice: 'Perhaps by tomorrow you will have come to your senses.'

She did not answer, but leaned against the door listening to his retreating footsteps.

She went back to Jennet. 'You talk of his forcing me. He never would. He has no spirit, that man. He's as mild as milk. Oh, why did they marry me to such a one, when, if I were free . . .'

Jennet shook her head and turned away.

Frances caught her arm and gripped it so tightly that Jennet cried out.

'What are you thinking, eh? Answer me at once.'

'My lady, you're hurting my arm.'

'Speak then.'

'I was thinking that you are not free, and my lord Rochester did not seem to be as desolate as you were when you left London.'

Frances lifted her hand to strike the woman, but thought better of it. Her face crumpled suddenly and she said: 'Jennet, I'm afraid that if I stay here too long, I shall lose him.'

Jennet nodded.

'You think so, do you?' burst out Frances. 'What right have you to think? What do you know about it?'

'I have seen, have I not, my lady? But why do you despair? You saw Dr Forman and Mrs Turner before you left Court.'

A worried frown appeared on Frances' brow. 'I wish they were nearer, Jennet. I wish I could talk to them.'

'You have the powders with you?'

'Yes, but how administer them?'

'It would have been easier if you had allowed him to live with you.'

Frances shivered. 'Never. If I did I believe that would be the end. My lord Rochester would have finished with me then.'

'Did he say so?'

'He hinted it. Jennet, we've got to find a way. We've got to get out of here. I feel shut in . . . a prisoner. I was meant to be free. I can't breathe here.'

'We'll have to see,' said Jennet.

*　　　*　　　*

Essex almost wished that he had not returned to Chartley. Here it was much more difficult to keep secret the extraordinary state of his marital affairs. It was embarrassing for all his retainers to know that he was so distasteful to his wife that she refused to live with him as his wife. He was very young, being not much over twenty, and had had very little experience of women. Frances, two years his junior, was knowledgeable in comparison; she understood him while she bewildered him.

Had he been a stronger-willed man he might have forced his way into her apartments, in order to assure her that he was the master, but his nature was too gentle for him to adopt this method and he hoped he could persuade her to act reasonably.

He even made excuses for her; she was innocent; she was unprepared for marriage and viewed it with distaste. She was after all very young; she would grow up in time; then she would be sorry for all the trouble she had caused him.

The entire neighbourhood was aware of the strange happenings inside the castle. The Countess was never seen out of doors. She refused to leave her apartments; her doors were always locked; though he believed that in the night, accompanied by Jennet, she walked about the castle and in the grounds.

Jennet was always with her; and the two Chartley maids, Elizabeth Raye and Catharine Dardenell, waited on her. They were regarded with great respect by the rest of the servants whom they told that the Countess was in truth a sweet lady, and so lovely to look at that she must be good. She had shown kindness to both Elizabeth and Catharine; and her own maid, Jennet, whom she had brought with her, was devoted to her. Catharine and Elizabeth were beginning to believe that the fault might lie with the Earl.

Essex spent a great deal of time brooding over the situation; and he liked to escape from the castle and often walked for miles trying to think of some solution.

He could, of course, allow her to return to Court and leave her alone; that was what she wanted; and she was ready to be his good friend if he would agree to it. But he was stubborn on one point; she was his wife. Ever since their marriage he had dreamed of coming home to her, because he had carried with him, all the time he had been abroad, a memory of that lovely young girl to whom he had been married. Having built up an ideal of what their life together would be, he could not accept this situation. He would not give up his dream so easily.

As he walked alone, deep in thought, he heard a cry for help which came from the direction of a swiftly running river. He was sharply brought out of melancholy reverie and, turning towards the direction from which the cry had come, he recognized his steward, Wingfield.

'Wingfield,' he called. 'What's wrong?'

Before Wingfield could answer he saw for himself; a man was wading out of the river supporting a young woman whom he had clearly rescued.

The Earl ran to the scene and helped the two men take the woman – who was one of the servants – back to the castle.

It was an hour or so later when Essex summoned Wingfield, with the man who had rescued the girl, to his apartments.

Wingfield introduced this man as Arthur Wilson whom he had invited to the castle for a short stay. Arthur Wilson immediately spoke up for himself.

'Having fallen on hard times, my lord, I seized this opportunity to enjoy the hospitality of Mr Wingfield in exchange for certain services.'

'It is fortunate for that poor girl that you were here,' said the Earl; and noticing that Wilson was a man of education he invited him to drink a glass of wine with him.

When the wine had been brought and they were alone together, Wilson told the Earl something of his history.

'Ever since I was taught to read and write, my lord,' said Wilson, 'I have never stopped doing either. I was at one time clerk to Sir Henry Spiller in the Exchequer office, but I was dismissed.'

'For some offence?'

'The inability to remain on friendly terms with people in a superior position to my own, my lord.'

Essex laughed. He had taken a great liking to this man and he was particularly pleased to have been diverted from his own unpleasant thoughts.

'I thought,' went on Wilson, 'that I could live by writing poetry. That was a fallacy.'

'You must show me some of your work.'

'If your lordship would be interested.'

'Tell me what happened when you left the Exchequer office.'

'I lived in London writing poetry until my money was almost at an end. Then fortunately Wingfield appeared and suggested a short respite here at Chartley.'

'I might offer you a permanent post here. If I did so, would you accept it?'

A faint colour came into Wilson's face. 'My lord,' he murmured, 'you are generous beyond my hopes.'

Friendship had been born in that moment.

Arthur Wilson quickly slipped into his place at Chartley. He was the Earl's gentleman-in-waiting, which meant that he accompanied him on his rides round the estate, hunting or any other such expedition; thus he was constantly in the Earl's company. In a very short time he had become his most confidential servant, and because it so concerned his master, Wilson took a great interest in his relationship with the Countess.

Being such a partisan of the Earl, he was highly critical of Frances. He did not share his master's view of her innocence, and he determined to watch the situation very carefully, without letting anyone know he did so.

Every night when he retired to his apartment he wrote in his diary an account of the day's happenings and the affairs of the Earl and his wife inevitably figured largely in this. He found himself writing glowing descriptions of the Earl's extraordinary patience and goodness to this woman who was behaving so badly towards him. 'The mild and courteous Earl is being tried too sorely,' he wrote.

He began to wonder what dark schemes that woman concocted in the apartment from which she rarely stirred. It was unnatural, unhealthy. There she lived with that woman she had brought with her – allowing only Elizabeth Raye and Catharine Dardenell into the apartment. What were they plotting? If it were harm to the Earl, Wilson was going to be there to prevent it.

He was watching.

'Catharine, my child,' said Frances, 'what pretty hair you have.'

'You'll make the creature vain, my lady,' said Elizabeth Raye. 'She's conceited enough since Will Carrick has had his eye on her.'

'So Will Carrick admires you, Catharine. I can understand that well.'

Catharine simpered. She could not understand why some of the servants were so suspicious of the Countess, when she had always been so gracious to her and Elizabeth. She was so interested in them; and she had more or less promised that when Elizabeth's young man was ready to marry her, she, the Countess, would see that she had a good wedding. A generous lady, a good mistress; and if there was anything wrong between the Earl and Countess, she for one – and she knew Elizabeth felt the same – was ready to put the blame on the Earl.

'I have a blue ribbon which will become you well,' said Frances. 'Jennet, bring it and show Catharine how to tie it in her hair.'

Jennet obeyed.

'It's lovely, my lady,' cried Elizabeth, and Catharine was pink with pleasure.

Frances put her head on one side. 'Elizabeth should have one too. What colour do you think for Elizabeth, Jennet?'

'Pink, I think, my lady.'

'Then get it.'

The girl stood awkwardly while the ribbon was tied.

'How pretty they look!' Frances sighed, and looked sad.

Elizabeth stammered: 'Oh, my lady, we are lucky to serve you.'

Many little gifts passed between Frances and her maids. Any little service she asked of them was performed with delight, and they could not do enough for her comfort. Then came the day when Frances considered that the time was ripe.

'And how is Carrick?' she asked Catharine one day when she was alone with the girl.

Catharine flushed and mumbled that he was as he always was.

'And ready to do anything to please you, I'll warrant.'

Catharine did not answer.

'As page to the Earl it is his duty to attend to his clothes, is it not?'

'Yes, my lady, that is one of his duties.'

'It is a good post to hold and it cannot be long before he asks permission to marry.'

'I know not, my lady.'

Frances patted the girl's cheek. 'You are fortunate. Do you know there are times when I envy you.'

'Oh *no*, my lady!'

'To have someone to love you, of whom you can be sure.'

'But, my lady—'

'I know that my affairs are talked of in the castle. But there are matters which are only known to me ... and the Earl; things are not always what they seem, my child. I am an unhappy woman. Catharine, would you help me?'

'With all my heart, my lady.'

'I can trust you, Catharine, as I can few others. Would you swear to tell no one of what you do for me?'

'But of course, my lady.'

'I am anxious to change the Earl's feelings towards me.'

'But, my lady, it is said that the Earl wants nothing so much as to be a good husband to you.'

Frances frowned. 'It is said! It is said!' she cried sharply. Then her voice softened. 'Catharine, there are things people cannot understand. They cannot look deeply into these matters.'

'No, my lady.'

'When you see Carrick, do you go into the Earl's apartments?'

Catherine blushed. 'Well, my lady, it is only when—'

'Have no fear, my dear. I would always be sympathetic to lovers.'

'Yes, my lady.'

'And Carrick meets you there ... say, when the Earl has gone hunting?'

'Yes, my lady.'

'There is nothing to be ashamed of. No harm has been done. The other servants know you go there and are not surprised when you creep in ... eh?'

Catharine nodded.

'Listen to me. I have a powder here. It is a magic powder. I want you to go ten minutes earlier to the apartment ... before Carrick is due to meet you there. Do you understand? And I want you to sprinkle a powder inside the Earl's garments. His hose ... his shirt ... those which he will wear next his skin. Fold them carefully when you have done, so that none will know that they have been tampered with.'

'A powder, my lady?'

'I said a powder. 'Tis for his good. I have the Earl's welfare deeply at heart. Can I trust you, Catharine, to tell this to no one?'

'Why, yes, my lady.'

'You will have to be quick and careful. If you should be there and find others at hand, you must not do this. It is essential that it should be a secret. You must seize your opportunity, Catharine. I know you are a clever girl and that I can trust you. That is why, when I go to Court, I plan to take you with me.'

'Oh, my lady ...'

'I reward those who serve me well.'

'I will do everything you say, my lady.'

'That is good. Wait here a moment.'

Catharine waited, her hands clasped together; she saw herself riding to London with her generous mistress; perhaps she would be given one of the mistress' cast-off gowns. Who knew? With such a mistress anything might happen.

Frances came back and thrust a packet into her hands.

'Guard it well. You remember what you have to do?'

'Yes, my lady.'

'And you will remember that it is a secret; and that you must await the opportunity.'

Catharine assured her mistress that she would do so.

As gentleman-in-waiting to the Earl, Arthur Wilson took his duties seriously. Essex even confided in him to a certain extent, so that a man of Wilson's perceptions quickly summed up the true state of affairs.

In spite of the cruel conduct of the woman, the Earl was still enamoured of her, and had become obsessed by the need to make her into a loving wife. The woman was possessed of unnatural beauty and Wilson realized that her husband would hear nothing against her, because he wanted to keep his image intact. To the Earl the Countess was a young, innocent girl who had had marriage thrust upon her before she was ready for it. In her extreme purity she could not face the consequences. But that, of course, would pass with maturity.

Well, one must not attempt to enlighten the Earl. Gradually, Wilson believed, he would see the truth.

Meanwhile, Wilson became aware of sinister undercurrents in the situation. That almost besotted devotion of the serving girls? Was it possible that a proud and haughty woman, as the Countess obviously was, would take so much care to ingratiate herself with serving wenches?

Not unless she had some plan to use them.

As gentleman-in-waiting he had access to the Earl's wardrobe, and one day when he was arranging some garments in a drawer he found his fingers beginning to tingle and itch in an extraordinary manner. Looking at them closely he detected some grains of fine powder on them; and it immediately oc-curred to him that this had come from the Earl's clothes.

He took out the neatly folded undergarments and, as he shook them, began to sneeze and cough and there was a burn-ing sensation in his throat.

Studying the garments carefully he saw that grains of powder clung to them. He then examined all the Earl's under-garments and it became clear to him that it was these which had been treated in a certain way.

Alarm seized him. Could it be that this was a poison planned to find its way through the pores of the skin into the blood? He had heard of such things.

His first impulse was to go to the Earl and tell him what he had discovered, but he quickly realized that his master would refuse to suspect the real culprit. Wilson himself had no doubt who that was. This was part of a plot hatched by those diabolical women.

He took the clothes away and washed them himself. He determined that he was going to watch over the Earl's clothes; he would keep an eye on what he ate also, because it seemed to him certain that an attempt would be made to poison his friend and master in a more usual manner.

Frances was in despair. The situation had not changed since she came to Chartley, and she was still waiting for Essex to decide he was weary of her and let her go.

The powder which had been sprinkled on his garments had had no effect. One or two attempts to put other powders into his food had also failed. That man Wilson had taken upon himself to supervise everything the Earl ate; and he was now in charge of his wardrobe. Reports came to her that he was always sniffing here and there and had his nose into every-thing; that he would appear suddenly when any of the ser-vants approached their master.

Frances believed that Wilson suspected something of the truth.

Jennet was right when she had said that if Frances had lived with her husband it would have been a comparatively easy matter to administer the powders; as it was it seemed an impossibility. But not even for that reason would she live with him.

Essex had written to her parents complaining of her conduct, and she had received admonishing letters from them. Essex was her husband and she must recognize this fact. They had sent one of her brothers down to reason with her. This had resulted in long arguments which Frances declared would drive her mad.

'My own family are against me,' she cried.

There was no news of Robert Carr. She might have ceased to exist for all he seemed to care.

In desperation she wrote to Mrs Turner.

'Sweet Turner,

'I am out of hope of any good in this world. My brother Howard has been here and there is no comfort left. My husband is as well as he ever was, so you see in what miserable case I am. Please send the doctor news of this; he told me that all would be well and that the lord I love would love me. As you have taken pains to help me, please do all you can, for I was never so unhappy in my life as I am now. I am not able to endure my misery, for I cannot be happy as long as this man liveth. Therefore pray for me. I have need of your prayers. I should be better if I had your company to ease my mind. Let the doctor know this ill news. If I can get this thing done you shall have as much money as you can demand, for I consider this to be fair play.

Your sister,
Frances Essex'

Wilson was really alarmed. He was certain that the Countess was planning to poison her husband; he knew that she was sending messages to London and he believed that she was either writing to her lover there or to those who were sending her the powders. He, who had lived in London, knew that many professional poisoners existed as well as dabblers in witchcraft; and he was certain that Frances Essex was in the hands of some of these people.

If it were so, the Earl's life was in danger, for he, Wilson, could not hope always to be lucky enough to save him.

As a man of the world he believed there was one way of saving the Earl's life and that was to let the Countess enjoy her lover.

To some extent the Earl confided in Wilson who had become a close friend as well as a servant, and although Wilson was always careful to show no animosity towards the Countess, at length he persuaded the Earl that Lady Frances might be more amiable if they left Chartley, a place which she declared she hated and regarded as a prison.

The Earl saw the wisdom of this and when he proposed a visit to Frances' parents' country house at Awdley-end in Essex, Frances agreed with alacrity.

She was certainly more amiable when they journeyed southwards and once or twice deigned to speak to her husband without first being addressed.

The Earl's spirits rose; but Wilson was as watchful as ever. He did not trust the Countess.

When, at Awdley-end, the members of Frances' family reproached her for her attitude, she listened meekly and then asked for news of the Court.

She pretended to be upset by the death of the Prince of Wales, but she cared nothing for that. She listened avidly for every bit of information about Robert Carr, and she yearned to go to Court. In London she would be able to visit Dr Forman and Mrs Turner, and she believed her salvation lay with them. She would see her beloved Robert again and if he had ceased to think of her during her absence, she was certain that with the aid of the clever doctor and her sweet Turner she could soon win him back again.

She was restless and unhappy but less so than she had been at Chartley.

And at last Essex agreed that they should return to Court.

The Enemies

THE MARRIAGE of the Princess Elizabeth to the Elector Palatine had been delayed on account of the mourning for the Prince of Wales. Henry had died in November and the wedding did not take place until February, which meant that the Elector and his retinue had to be housed and entertained during that period at a great cost to the Royal Exchequer. James reckoned that his daughter's marriage had cost him almost a hundred thousand pounds.

His courtiers had vied with each other to be the most splendidly attired at Court, and James had insisted that his dear Robbie should shine more brightly than any because that was only due to his beauty. Therefore he lavished costly jewels on his favourite; and while his affection was strongest for Robert Carr, he did not forget his other lads, who were handsome enough to show off his fine clothes and jewels.

There was the Queen who, although she was prostrate with grief and in any case was not pleased with the marriage of her daughter, still must be expensively clad; and the cost of her wardrobe was only a little less than the six thousand pounds which had been spent on Elizabeth's wedding clothes and trousseau.

As for James himself, he must remember that he was the King and in the presence of foreigners should make a good show; he was ready to do this as long as his garments were as well padded as they were bejewelled and he was not expected to wash.

So Elizabeth was married in Whitehall Chapel and looked beautiful in her white dress, her golden hair falling about her shoulders, with a crown of pearls and diamonds set on her head. She was led to the chapel by Charles – now growing handsome and with the new dignity upon him of being heir to the throne – and Henry Howard, Earl of Northampton. The Queen had wept quietly while the Archbishop of Canterbury performed the ceremony; and James knew that she was thinking of losing her daughter to a foreigner as she had lost her son to death.

The celebrations which followed the wedding must necessarily be somewhat subdued because although it was three months since Henry's death he could not be easily forgotten.

It was Robert Carr who suggested that the farewell banquet should be held at his own castle at Rochester; and the King, delighted to see his dear Robbie host to the Court, gladly agreed.

The last farewells had been said and Elizabeth had sailed away from England to her new home, while the Court returned to Rochester Castle to be entertained a few days longer by Viscount Rochester before returning to Whitehall.

The castle which stood on the banks of the Medway was a splendid example of Norman architecture; it had clearly been built as a fortress, situated as it was on a hill with its principal tower offering views of the country and river. Robert Carr was proud to possess it, for it had been the scene of many a historic occasion since it had been built in the year 1088 by the Norman monk Gundulph who had been Bishop of Rochester and a celebrated architect. It was an ideal place in which to house the Court and that he could do so was an indication of how quickly he had risen since the death of Salisbury.

Robert was being dressed by his servants in his own apartments when the man whom he had come to regard as one of his greatest friends and supporters asked to be admitted.

This was Henry Howard, Earl of Northampton, who had assiduously courted the favourite since he had realized the firmness of his hold on the King's affections.

'Ah,' cried the wily old statesman, 'I disturb you.'

'Nay,' cried Robert. 'I am all but ready.'

By God, thought Northampton, he is a handsome fellow; and he looks as fresh and young as he did the day he rode into the tiltyard and so cleverly fell from his horse.

'Pray be seated,' said Robert. 'I shall be ready to go to the banqueting hall in five minutes or so.'

'Then we will go together,' said Northampton.

It was well to be seen with the favourite; it reminded his enemies that he had friends in the right quarter. Robert, good-natured and easygoing, never bothered to ask himself why a haughty Howard should be so anxious for his friendship and when Overbury said: 'Why, Henry Howard would not speak to you tomorrow if you lost the King's favour!' Robert replied: 'Why should he?' and left it at that, which meant that while Northampton offered his friendship, Robert Carr was ready to accept it.

Robert dismissed his servants, which was only courteous because he guessed that Northampton did not wish them to overhear their conversation, and since they were both ministers of eminence it was certain that some State matter would be discussed between them sooner or later. Since he had become a Privy Councillor Robert had been aware of the need to watch his tongue before servants.

When they were alone Northampton asked Robert if he knew whether a certain gentleman had been called upon to sign the Oath of Supremacy.

As Robert was able to assure him that this man had not been asked to do so, Northampton was relieved. It was pleasant to be able to ask such a question privately. Northampton was a little worried because he, being a secret Catholic, had no wish to be asked to sign the Oath; and he feared that if the man in question had had such a demand made to him, the invitation to sign might well be extended to himself, Northampton.

The signing of this Oath was a scheme which James had thought up when he was so short of money. It was his plan to force Catholics to sign it and if they refused to subject them to heavy fines or imprisonment. As the Pope had ordered Catholics not to sign the Oath because it contained sentences which were derogatory to the Catholic Faith, to have signed it would have been a denial of faith. Many Catholics had refused and consequently lost their possessions, which was exactly what James had hoped, since it was to raise money that he had thought of the plan.

Robert had not cared for this scheme because he thought it was wrong to penalize people on account of their religion, and would have preferred to see Catholics living in peace beside Protestants.

It was sometimes, however, his duty to write to Catholics ordering them to take the Oath, and this he did because he always obeyed the King; but he never brought a Catholic to the King's notice, and did nothing, except when expressly ordered to do so by James, to enforce this unpleasant law.

At the same time he never implied to James that he disapproved of it. It was alien to his nature to offer criticism; he was well aware that if he did so James would demolish this in a moment with some tricky argument; and he knew that James continued to love his Robbie because he was never what the King called a cantankerous body.

Northampton was aware of this quality in Carr and he knew that he could safely ask for information about the penalizing of recusants. If he, Northampton, had been asked to sign the Oath, he supposed he would have signed it; his political career would always mean more to him than any religious faith; but he preferred not to have to make the decision; and thus it was very comforting to have a friend in Robert Carr.

Northampton decided that he was in no danger and went on: 'I have taken a liberty with your hospitality, and I trust you will not think I have presumed on your friendship.'

Robert smiled his charming smile and said: 'My dear Northampton, it gives me pleasure that you should presume on my friendship. It shows that you are sure of it.'

'Thank you, my dear fellow. The fact is that some of my family have returned to Court unexpectedly. I said they might come to the castle; they will have arrived by now.'

'Any member of your family is welcome.'

'Thank you, Robert. I guessed you would say that.'

'Who are these relatives? Do I know them?'

'I think you know my great-niece. She has been in the country with her husband for some time. Ha, I did not believe the country would suit Madam Frances for long.'

'I perceive,' said Robert, 'that you are speaking of the Countess of Essex.'

'You are right. She is a young woman who likes to have her own way. She implored me to allow her to come here. She could not wait until the Court reached Whitehall. She pleaded that she had been away too long.'

'Why, yes,' replied Robert mildly, 'it must be some time since she was at Court.'

In the great hall she came near to him in the dance.

He had forgotten how beautiful she was. It was true that there was no other woman at Court to compare with her, and Robert felt excited merely to look at her. Their hands touched momentarily in the dance, and for a second she let her fingers curl about his.

'Welcome back to Court, Lady Essex.'

'It does me good to see you, Viscount Rochester.'

'Is the Earl of Essex at Court?'

'Alas, yes.'

Robert turned away to face another partner as the dance demanded. She was still as disturbing as ever.

She was ready for him when he faced her again.

'I must see you . . . alone.'

'When?'

'This night.'

'And the Earl?'

'I know not. I care not. He is no husband to me and never has been.'

'How was this?'

'Because I loved one other.'

'And this other?'

'He will tell me tonight whether he loves me.'

'Where?'

'In the lower apartments of Gundulph's Tower. Those dark

and gloomy storerooms where few people go.'

He was silent while she looked at him beseechingly.

He had missed her; he wanted to reopen their relationship. He had found during the period when she had been away that he could never forget her. There was a vitality about her which was irresistible. If she and the Earl led separate lives by mutual consent what harm was there?

That night when the castle was quiet they met in those lower apartments of Gundulph's Tower! and there they were lovers again.

In the house at Hammersmith Frances sat opposite Anne Turner and told of her anxieties.

'And you are still unsure of him?' asked Mrs Turner.

Frances nodded. 'Yet I believe he needs me more than he did. There is a change.'

'The good doctor has been working for that.'

'I know. But the lord is always aware of that other.' Her face darkened. 'And he is never far away, always threatening. I would die rather than be carried back to the country.'

'My sweet lady, *you* must not talk of dying. Was it so difficult to do with the powders what the doctor suggested?'

'Quite impossible. I kept to my apartments because I could not bear him near me. There were two servants who were ready to do my bidding. I bribed them and they did their best. But he was surrounded by his servants; and there was a man, Wilson, who was too clever for us.'

Mrs Turner nodded. 'It is a sorry business with so many working against us!'

'What I fear is that if there are too many difficulties the lord will be ready to forgo our love.'

'We must bind him so strongly that he cannot escape.'

'Is it possible to do that?'

'With the doctor everything is possible. I think that you should see him again . . . soon.'

'Then I will do so.'

'Let me tell him of your visit and he will name a day when

he will see you. I will manage to get a message conveyed to you.'

'Dear Turner, what should I do without you!'

'Sweet friend, it is my pleasure to help you. I have learned a little from the doctor and I see that the one who is hovering between you and the lovely lord must be removed, because until he is, our efforts will be, to a great extent, frustrated.'

Frances clenched her hands together.

'Would to God I need never see his face again.'

'The doctor will help you.' Anne Turner leaned forward and touched Frances' hand. 'Never forget,' she repeated softly, 'with the doctor all things are possible.'

At a table in the private apartments of my lord Rochester, Thomas Overbury was sitting writing; there was a satisfied smile on his face, and no sound in the room but the scratch of his pen. Thomas read through what he had written and his smile grew smug. He was always delighted with his work.

Seated in a window seat, staring out on the Palace grounds, was Robert, his handsome face set in thoughtful lines.

'Listen to this, Robert,' cried Thomas, and read out what he had written.

'Excellent ... as always,' said Robert, when he had finished.

'Ah, my dear fellow, what would you do without me?'

'Bless you, Tom, where would either of us be without the other?'

Thomas was thoughtful for a second or so. 'That's true enough,' he said at length. But a doubt had entered his mind. In the Mermaid Club he dined with writers, among them Ben Jonson, and they treated him as one of them; there he could hold his own as a literary man; he was someone in his own right, not merely a ghost, a shadow of someone else. He imagined Robert Carr in such company. He would not know what they were talking about. Yet, without Robert, where would he be? What would his writing bring him in? Enough to starve in a garret?

He sighed and repeated: 'It's true enough.'

Robert did not notice the slight discontentment in his friend's expression because he was occupied with a problem of his own.

'Tom,' he said, 'here's something else for you to do.'

Thomas waited expectantly, but Robert hesitated.

'I want you to write to a lady for me. Tell her I shall not be able to see her as I arranged. The King has commanded me to wait on him.'

Thomas took up his pen again.

'Shall I be very regretful? Is the lady becoming an encumbrance?'

'Oh no, no! Be most regretful. I would I could be with her. Say I am sorry.'

Overbury nodded. 'Tell me what she looks like and I will write an ode to her beauty.'

Robert described her so accurately that Thomas said, 'Could this paragon of beauty be the Countess of Essex?'

'Why, Tom, how did you guess?'

'You have made it clear to me. That is well. Now I know to whom I am writing I shall produce a finer specimen of my talents.'

'Fairest of the fair,' he wrote, 'I am overcome by desolation . . .'

Robert watched him while his pen ran on without faltering. How clever to have such a gift of words! If he were only as clever as Overbury, he would be able to write his own letters, work out his own ideas, in fact he would be as clever as the late Salisbury. With *brains* and beauty he could have stood completely alone, sufficient unto himself.

He wondered why the thought had come to him at that moment as he watched his clever friend smiling over his work.

The notion disappeared as quickly as it had come; Robert had never been one to analyse his feelings.

Tom laid down his pen and began to read.

In the letter were the longings of a lover, delicately yet fervently expressed. The poetic strain was there.

Frances would be astonished; yet she would be pleased.

Dr Forman sat at one side of the table, Frances at the other. He leaned forward on his elbows and moved his expressive hands as he talked; and his eyes, bright with lecherous speculation, never left the beautiful eager face opposite him.

In the darkened room the candles flickered.

He was a witch, of course. Frances had guessed this. She believed that he had made his pact with the devil, and should the witch finders suddenly break into the room and examine him they would doubtless find the devil's marks on his body.

She did not care. She knew only an unswerving desire.

She wanted Robert Carr to remain her faithful lover; she wanted to inspire in him a fanatic passion to match her own; and she wanted Essex out of the way.

It was for that reason that she made these dangerous journeys to Lambeth. For the sake of what she so urgently needed she was ready to dabble in witchcraft, although she knew that the cult of witchcraft was a crime; the King believed in the power of witches to do evil and he was anxious to drive them out of his kingdom. Death by strangulation or burning was the penalty. Never mind, Frances told herself; she was ready to run any risk for the sake of binding Carr to her irrevocably and ridding herself of her husband.

Forman's voice was silky with insinuation.

'Dear lady, you must tell me all that happened . . . spare no detail. Tell me how fervent the lord is in his lovemaking.'

Frances hesitated; but she knew that she must obey this man, for it was only if she told him everything that he could help her.

So she talked and answered the questions which were thrust at her; she saw her interrogator lick his lips with pleasure as though he were partaking in the exercise himself. At first she was embarrassed; then she ceased to be so; she talked with eagerness, and it seemed to her that the special powers of this man enabled her to live again the ecstasy she had enjoyed.

When it was over, the doctor bade her rise; he placed his hands on her shoulders and she imagined some of his strength flowed into her. He waved his hands before her eyes and she dreamed once more that she was with Robert in some dark chamber.

Dr Forman drew back curtains in one dark corner of the room to disclose among the shadows what appeared to be the head of a horned goat; he repeated incantations and although Frances could not understand the words he used she believed in their powers.

At length the doctor turned to her. 'What you ask shall be yours . . . in time,' he promised her.

She must visit him more frequently and in secrecy, he went on to explain. He wished to make images of the three characters in the drama. 'The one of whom we wish to be rid; the one whose affections must increase; and the woman. This will be a costly matter.'

'All that you ask shall be given if you do this for me.'

The doctor bowed his head.

'I will set some of my servants to procure what you will need. They too must be paid for their services.'

'I understand.'

'Call me Father — your sweet father, because that is what I am to you, dear daughter.'

'Yes, sweet Father,' answered Frances dutifully.

She was now receiving frequent letters from Robert. Their passion astonished her, and it was so poetically expressed that she read them until she knew them by heart.

'Only a lover could write thus,' she assured Jennet. 'Do you know, he is changing. He is beginning to feel as deeply as I do. Oh yes, he has changed of late.'

'Does he seem more urgent in his passion?' asked Jennet.

'When we are together he is no more loving than he used to be, but it is his letters in which he betrays his true feelings. How beautiful they are! It is due to the doctor and dear Turner. They are making him dream of me, and my image is for ever in his thoughts.'

She thought of the wax images the doctor had made of the three of them. The figure of Essex had been pierced with pins that had been made hot in the flame of candles; and while this operation was in progress, the doctor in his black robe decorated by the cabalistic signs had muttered weird incantations. The figure of Robert had been dressed elaborately in satin and brocade, and that of Frances was naked. The doctor had asked that she serve as a model for it because it was essential that it should be perfect in every detail. She trusted him completely now; she looked upon him as her dear father so that after the first embarrassment she had posed while the image was made.

She remembered the ritual; the burning of incense which filled the room with aromatic odours and vapours. She remembered how the wax male figure had been undressed until it was as naked as that of the woman. The two figures were then put together on a minute couch and made to go through the motions of making love while fresh heated pins were thrust into the wax figure of Essex.

At first Frances had been repelled but gradually she had become elated by these spectacles she was forced to witness.

She believed in the black magic, for had she not noticed a change in her lover since she had begun to partake in it? There was fresh power in his pen, for only a lover could write the letters he was now writing to her; nor did he wait until there was need to write; the letters came frequently, accompanied by poems in praise of her beauty and the joy their lovemaking brought to him.

From an upper window of the house at Lambeth a woman watched Lady Essex ride away accompanied by her maid.

'Quality this time,' said the woman to herself with a smirk. 'I will say this for Simon, he knows how to get hold of the right people.'

She left the window and going to the head of the stairs peered down. All was silence. Where was he now? In that room where he received his clients? Handling the lewd images. Trust him.

What a man!

Jane Forman laughed and wondered how she herself had come to marry him. She had been glad to; there was something about Simon which made him different from every other man she had known. He was a witch.

Once she said to him: 'What if I were to betray you to the finders, Simon?'

And he had looked at her in a way which had made her blood run cold. She knew that if she were foolish enough to do that he would make sure she suffered for it. As if she would! What? When he could make such a comfortable living for them!

She reckoned she had been a good wife to him; she had never grumbled when he had seduced the maids. He had told her he needed a variety of women; it was the command of his master that he should have no virgins under his roof because they would have come between him and his work, bringing a purity into the house, and that was not good when one worked with the devil.

She might have argued that Simon had soon sent virginity flying from his house, so that he need not have worked so hard in his master's cause. But one did not argue with Simon. One was thankful for the good living he made and accepted him, his mistresses and his illegitimate children, of whom that haughty Anne Turner was doubtless one.

The two of them were closeted together for hours at a time. Making plans, he told her, for the treatment of this new client who was the richest that had ever fallen into their hands.

She slowly descended the stairs and made her way to the door of the receiving chamber.

'Simon,' she said, 'did you call?'

There was no answer, so cautiously she opened the door and looked in. The smell of incense lingered, but the curtains had been drawn back now to let in a little daylight and the candles were out.

She shut the door quietly behind her and went to the table. There she stood looking round the room. She saw the large box on the bench and opening it, disclosed the wax figures.

She sniggered.

'What a fine gentleman!' she whispered. And there was the lady, with what looked like real hair. And what a figure!

She could imagine the tricks he got up to with them.

Still there was money in it – and they lived by it.

'Mustn't be caught in here,' she whispered; then she opened the door, looked out, made sure she was unobserved and went quickly and quietly back upstairs.

Robert hurried into the apartment where Overbury sat at work.

'Tom,' he cried, 'write me a letter quickly . . . a letter of regret.'

'To the lovely Countess?' said Overbury with a smile.

'Yes. I had promised to be with her this evening and the King has commanded me to attend him.'

'How inconvenient it sometimes is to be so popular!' murmured Overbury.

'And when it is finished will you take it to Hammersmith for me.'

'To Hammersmith?'

'Yes, I was to meet her there . . . at the house of a Mistress Turner. I cannot stay now, but you know the kind of things. Your letters delight her. Tell her that I am desolate . . . you know so well how to put it.'

Robert went off and Overbury returned to his table a little disgruntled. It was one thing to write the flowery epistles, but to be asked to deliver them like some page boy, was a little humiliating. And Hammersmith! Mistress Anne Turner! He had heard of the name. He believed she was a connexion of Dr Forman the notorious swindler, who might even be a witch. The man had been in trouble once or twice and called upon to answer for his misdeeds. Surely the Countess of Essex was not involved with people like this!

However, there was nothing to do but write the letter and take it to the woman.

An hour later he was riding out to Hammersmith, but his mood had not improved as he journeyed there. Was it absurd for a man of his talents to be employed thus? It was said in some quarters that Rochester ruled the King and Overbury ruled Rochester; and in that case did not Overbury rule England?

He liked to hear such talk. But at the same time it made it doubly uncomfortable to be riding out as a messenger for illicit lovers.

A maid let him into the house and when he asked to see the Countess of Essex without delay, he was shown into a handsome room. He had not been there many seconds before the door was flung open and a voice cried: 'Robert, my dearest . . .' and then stopped.

The Countess was wearing a low-cut gown which after the new fashion exposed her breasts; her long hair was loose; and there was a silver ruff about her neck.

Her expression grew cold as she looked at him.

'My lady, I bring you a letter from Viscount Rochester.'

She snatched it ungraciously.

'So he is not coming,' she said.

'The King commanded his presence.'

Her mouth was sullen and she looked like a child who, disappointed of a longed-for treat, turns her anger on the one who tells her she cannot have it for a while.

'Return to my lord,' she said, 'and thank him for sending you. But you will be in need of refreshment. It shall be given to you in the kitchens.'

'I am in no need of refreshment, my lady, and I do not eat in kitchens. Perhaps I should have introduced myself. Sir Thomas Overbury at your service.'

'Yes, I know you to be a servant of my lord Rochester.'

She turned away, her manner insolent.

Hatred surged up in Overbury. The wanton slut! How dared she. So she had heard of him! Had she heard that he was the man who worked behind the scenes and that it was due to his services that Robert Carr had been able to hold his place with the King's ministers? How dared she offer him such insolence!

She had gone and he was left standing there.

He did not remain; he went out to his horse and rode hard back to Court.

I shall not forget your insults to me, Lady Essex, he thought.

The September day had been warm, and the windows were open to the garden as Jane Forman and her husband sat together while the maids served them with supper.

The doctor was in a mellow mood. The Countess had called that day and that event always pleased him.

Jane wondered how much money he was making from that deal and how long he would be able to keep it going. By surreptitious visits to his receiving room and peeps into the diary he kept – for she could read a little – she knew that the Countess was in love with Viscount Rochester whom all knew was one of the most famous men at Court, and that she wanted to be rid of her husband, the Earl of Essex. Jane knew only one way of getting rid of husbands; also that Simon did not care to sell poisons. He had been in trouble too many times to want more; and supplying poisons could bring him real trouble.

Ah, she thought, one of these days he'll land up on a gibbet.

And that would not be so good for her, for life here in Lambeth was comfortable, even luxurious, and Jane liked her comforts.

She looked at him steadily, and as the light fell on his face she thought he had aged lately; that his pallor was more pronounced and he looked tired.

He had eaten well and was half dozing at the table; she had no idea therefore that he was aware of her scrutiny.

'Well, wife,' he said suddenly, 'what are you thinking of?'

She sometimes believed that he could read her thoughts so she did not lie to him.

'Death,' she said simply.

'What of death?' he asked.

'I was wondering whether you or I would die first. Do you know? But of course you do. You have pre-knowledge of these things.'

'I shall die first,' he said quietly.

She leaned towards him and said quickly: 'When?'

'Next Thursday,' he answered.

Jane leaped to her feet. 'Thursday!' she cried. 'The Thursday that is coming!'

He looked as startled as she did. 'Eh?' he cried. 'What did I say?'

'You said you would die on Thursday.'

He looked aghast, for he was shaken. He had spoken thoughtlessly, and the words had slipped out almost involuntarily. He was alarmed because on the rare occasions when he had forseen the future it had happened in this way.

'Forget it,' he said.

But neither of them could.

He already looks older, thought Jane. A little more tired. A little closer to death. A little closer to Thursday.

On Wednesday Jane said jokingly: 'Well, you only have one more day to live, Simon. I trust your affairs are in order.'

He laughed with her and she was relieved. He had been joking of course.

On Thursday he said he had business to do at Puddle Dock and took boat there. He was rowing steadily when the oars slipped from his hands and he fell forward.

When they brought his body home Jane could not believe it; although she had on occasions known him to prophesy events which had come true, other prophecies he had made had not, so she could never be sure; this she had not believed, so she was stunned and bewildered.

But when she had recovered a little from the shock she went into that room where he had received his clients. Evidently he himself had not believed the prophecy for he had made no effort to put his affairs in order.

I must destroy these things, said Jane as she took out the wax images, the powders and phials of liquid.

She set them out on the bench and went through the drawers of his private cabinet. There she found his diary and turning the pages read here and there.

It was fascinating, for there was an account of many an intrigue and love affair, and Simon had not hesitated to mention the names of the ladies and gentlemen concerned.

What a story this book could tell!

Jane looked at the more recent entries and read an account of the love affair between Lady Essex and the Earl of Rochester with quotations of what Lady Essex had said and done in this room.

She shut the book and then discovered the letters. He had kept every one.

'Sweet Father,' she called him, and signed herself his loving daughter.

Jane made a big fire in the room and sorted out the letters and papers. Among them were spells, incantations and recipes for making certain potions.

Perhaps it was wrong to destroy these things; they might be useful.

So she turned her back on the fire and found a large box in which she placed the images, the recipes, the letters and the diary which gave such lurid accounts of Court intrigues and especially of the most recent involving Lady Essex and the King's favourite.

'Such sad news!' wrote Mrs Turner. 'I beg of my good sweet lady to come to me without delay. We will console each other.'

At the earliest opportunity Frances went to Hammersmith and the two wept together.

'Everything was beginning to work well,' mourned Frances. 'My lord was becoming more in love with me; his letters were wonderful; and I learned that he finds it easier to express himself with the pen than in his actions. I know it is all due to my dear father. What shall we do without him?'

'Do not despair, my dear friend. There are others – though perhaps lacking our father's great skill. But they exist, and I shall find them.'

'Dearest Anne, what should I do without you?'

'There is no need to do without me. Knowing your need I have already been turning this matter over in my mind. My husband was a doctor, remember. That put me into touch with people who handle and understand drugs.'

Frances was thoughtful. Then she said slowly: 'Although the lord has become more loving, that other is a source of great trouble to me. I would I were rid of him. I believe that if I were, the lord would love me even more, for I am aware that the other is never far from his mind. In the course of his State business he often has to write or converse with that other and he does so with the utmost courteousness. The lord is such that he feels uncomfortable at these times and is often a little cooler towards me afterwards.'

'It is one point on which I was not always in tune with our sweet departed father. He wished to work on the lovely lord; and he did so with success. But I always felt that we should rid ourselves of the other before we came to complete success.'

'Oh, to be rid of him!' sighed Frances.

'I have many friends in the City,' went on Mrs Turner. 'There is a Dr Savories whom I believed to be as clever as our dear father. I could consult him. He is expensive . . . even more so than our father; but we cannot hope to go on in quite the same way.'

'You must see this Dr Savories.'

'I will. And there is a man named Gresham, who foretold the Gunpowder Plot in his almanack, and poor man, he suffered for it, because many accused him of being one of the conspirators. But this was not proved against him and was in fact true prophecy.'

'I know that you will do all in your power to help me, Anne.'

'You may trust me,' answered Mrs Turner, 'and together we

will achieve what we set out to – even without our dear
father's help.'

Robert noticed the change in Overbury's manner which had
become cool and withdrawn. He asked what was wrong.

'Wrong?' cried Overbury. 'What should be wrong? All goes
well, does it not? The King is delighted with my work.'

'It seems to me, Tom, that *you* are not delighted.'

'Oh, I have grown accustomed to doing the work and
seeing you get the praise.'

'If there is anything you wish for . . .'

'You are generous,' admitted Overbury. 'You have never
stinted me.'

'And should consider myself despicable if I did. I do not
forget, Tom, all you have done for me.'

Overbury was mollified. He was a little under the spell of
Robert's charm. The handsome looks and the good-natured
serenity were appealing. It was not Robert who had irritated
him, Overbury reminded himself. It was that woman of his.

'I know. I know,' he said. Then: 'Robert, can I speak frankly
to you?'

'You know I always expect frankness from you.'

'I think you are making a great mistake in seeing so much
of that woman.' Robert looked startled and a flush appeared
in his cheeks, but Overbury hurried on: 'There is something
about her which is . . . evil. Be warned, Robert. What of
Essex? You have made a cuckold of him. That would be most
unpleasant if it were bruited about the Court.'

For the first time during their friendship Overbury saw
Robert angry.

He said shortly: 'You have helped me considerably in many
ways, but I must ask you not to meddle in my private
affairs.'

The two men faced each other; both were unusually pale
now for the colour had faded from Robert's face as quickly as
it had come. Then without another word Robert turned away
and briskly left the apartment.

Fool! thought Overbury when the door had shut. Does he

not see where this is leading him? That woman will be the destruction of him.

Another and more unpleasant thought quickly followed: And of me. For never was one man's fortune so bound up in another's as was Tom Overbury's with Robert Carr's.

He paced up and down the apartment. Yet was it so? Many people guessed that the favourite's sudden abilities could only mean that he possessed a ghost who worked in the shadows. Some knew that Overbury's was the hand that wrote the letters, the brain which produced the brilliant suggestions. And if Robert Carr should fall from favour, having involved himself in a disgraceful scandal with the wife of Essex, none could blame Thomas Overbury. People might remember that he had been the brains behind the pretty fellow. That was a comforting thought.

Do I need Robert Carr as much as he needs me?

An exciting idea that, which went whirling round and round in his head.

He went to the Mermaid Club where he was always welcomed as the poet who was also the close friend of the most influential man at Court. It was natural that he should be flattered there for he was richer than most of the Club's patrons and could entertain them with his wit and lively talk of the Court. He had always been cautious, though, never betraying how much he influenced Robert Carr.

But he was reckless that day, and having drunk freely, talked more loosely. With Frances' insults rankling in his mind, with the curt words of his friend mingling with them, he asked himself who had the more to lose, himself or Robert?

And there in the Mermaid Club he talked freely of his association with Robert Carr; and when it was said, 'So the real ruler is Overbury!' he did not deny it.

But the next morning he considered the state of affairs more soberly and he was uneasy.

Is the Earl Impotent?

THE WEEKS which followed were some of the happiest Frances had known. Robert, stung out of his mildness by Overbury's interference, was more loving than he had ever been before. The meetings were more frequent; and Frances was sure that this was due to the spells and enchantments.

She had met Dr Savories and Dr Gresham who had expressed their keen desire to work for her; they were more reckless than Dr Forman had been and agreed with Mrs Turner that it was imperative to work on the Earl of Essex. Frances saw several women, all of whom could procure some ingredients which the doctors had decided were necessary, or had some special powers to work their spells; all had to be paid and they were often pleased to accept a piece of jewellery.

Robert was always loath to make love at Court where the Earl of Essex could not be far away, so Frances arranged that they should meet at Hammersmith; but when she sensed that Robert was not even completely at ease there, because it was the house of Mrs Anne Turner, she decided to buy a country house of her own — a small place which she could look upon as a retreat.

Impulsive as ever she soon acquired a house at Hounslow which had been the property of Sir Roger Aston, and here Robert came frequently as the house was within easy riding distance of Whitehall.

It was here that Robert expressed his dissatisfaction with the state of affairs and explained his uneasiness every time he was in the presence of her husband.

'You need not concern yourself with him,' Frances replied.

'But I cannot help it. He is, after all, your husband; and

when I think of how we are deceiving him—'

'My dearest, you are doing him no harm.'

'But how can that be . . . when you and I are as we are?'

'He could never take your place with me. I have told you that he has never been a husband to me in anything but name.'

'But that seems incredible.'

'Why should it?' Frances remembered those days at Chartley and the lie came to her lips. It was necessary, she told herself, to placate Robert. And what were a few lies compared with all she had done? She repeated: 'Why should it . . . when he himself is impotent.'

She was unprepared for the effect these words had on Robert.

'Is that so then? He is impotent? But don't you see how important that is? Since that is the case I do not see why you should find much difficulty in divorcing him.'

'Divorcing Essex . . .' she repeated.

'Then we could be married. It would be an end of all this distasteful subterfuge.'

An end of scheming! she thought. An end of those journeys to Hammersmith. No longer need she conspire with Savories and Gresham, no longer show her gratitude to women whom she suspected of practising witchcraft.

Escape from Essex! Marriage with Robert, who himself had suggested it!

She was certain that Robert had become spellbound as a result of all the work that had been done. Success was in sight.

Robert himself spoke to Northampton.

'I have often thought that it is time I married.'

Northampton smiled; he was always ingratiating to the favourite. 'I am surprised that James has not found you a worthy bride long ere this.'

'I had no fancy for one . . . until now.'

'And who is the fortunate lady?'

'Your own great-niece. Oh, I know at the moment she has a

husband, but since he is impotent I do not think we shall have any great difficulty in obtaining a divorce. I was wondering whether, as the head of Frances' family, you would have any objection.'

'Frances, eh!' mused Northampton. He thought: Essex impotent! It's the first time I've heard that. He considered his great-niece's marriage. The family had been delighted with it when it had been made, for Essex had rank and riches to offer. But, of course, the man who could offer a woman more than any other was certainly Robert Carr who retained such a firm hold on the King's affections.

'Well?' persisted Robert. 'How do you view this?'

'My dear Robert, there is no one I would rather welcome into the family.'

'Then will you speak to the Earl and Countess of Suffolk?'

'I will with pleasure and tell them my feelings.'

'And I will broach the matter to the King.'

Northampton was elated. He knew that there would be no difficulty with Frances' parents once he made them see what a glorious future awaited her – and the Howard family – when she was married to Robert Carr.

James smiled benignly at his favourite.

'So you have a fancy to be a husband, eh, Robbie?'

'I think it is time I settled down.'

'Well, well, and I never thought ye had much of an eye for women.'

'I have for this one, Your Majesty.'

James patted Robert's arm. 'And she's married. It would have been easier, laddie, if your choice had fallen on someone who was free.'

'Your Majesty, the Countess of Essex should be free. She is bound to an impotent husband and has never lived a true married life with him.'

'Is that so? Essex impotent! 'Tis the first I've heard of that. Never did much care for Robert Devereux. Too serious without the intellect. He always looks as though he's in a sulk.'

'Your Majesty will see that the Countess should be freed from such a man.'

'And given to you, Robbie. I see your point. I see her point. What are Northampton and the Suffolks going to say of this?'

'I have already discussed the matter with Northampton.'

'And he is willing?'

'Very willing, Your Majesty.'

'This is going to be an unusual case, lad. I know not whether it is legal for a wife to sue her husband for a divorce. I am not sure whether his impotence will be counted a reason for granting it. It's an interesting point. I'll look into it myself.' James laughed. 'I'll enjoy having a talk with the lawyers. Dinna fret, boy, I'll swear your Old Dad will find a way out of the tangle. I'll swear he'll give you the girl as he has everything else you have asked him for.'

Robert kissed the dirty hand.

'Your Majesty, as always, is gracious to me.'

'The King is agreeable.' Northampton was walking up and down the apartment while the Earl and Countess of Suffolk watched him. 'Good Heavens, don't you see what great good can come to the family through this?'

'Yes, yes,' put in Suffolk, 'providing they'll grant the divorce. You know how the lawyers like to peck and sniff.'

'Nonsense, man. They'll do what the King expects them to. Robert assures me that James is taking the matter up himself.'

'What bothers me,' said Lady Suffolk, 'is this accusation of impotence. Why Essex was demanding that she live with him when they were at Chartley, and she was locking her door against him. He has pleaded with us ever since to exercise our parental rights to make her share his bed. And you call this impotence!'

'Frances does, it seems,' said Northampton with a sly chuckle. 'Essex might have difficulty in proving otherwise when a girl like Frances is ready to swear to it!'

Lady Suffolk burst into coarse laughter. 'Surely it wouldn't be an impossibility for Essex to prove his potency.'

'You fret over details. Let the King show his eagerness for the divorce and if Essex is a wise man he'll not interfere. After all, his great desire is to get back to the country. Give him a divorce and a new wife who is ready to live the life he wants her to, and he'll be amenable.'

'I'm not so sure,' said Suffolk.

'Come, come,' interrupted Northampton. 'You meet troubles halfway. Carr is the most influential man in this country. James scarcely ever makes an appointment without consulting him. Think what this marriage is going to mean to the Howards. All the important posts in the country can fall into our hands. You have reason to rejoice that you produced your daughter Frances.'

'I am thirsty,' said the Countess. 'Let us drink to the marriage of Robert Carr and Frances Howard.'

A messenger from Hammersmith arrived at the Court; he asked to see the Countess of Essex without delay.

Frances, in a state of bemused joy since Carr had suggested the divorce, and her family had taken up the idea with such enthusiasm, took the note to her apartment and read it twice before she realized the urgency behind the words.

It was from Mrs Turner who asked that she come to Hammersmith without delay. It was imperative that they meet for Mrs Turner had discovered something too secret to put to paper.

At the first opportunity Frances, accompanied by Jennet, rode over to Hammersmith.

Anne Turner was waiting for her, and Frances saw at once that she was distraught.

'I had to see you,' said Anne, and her hands trembled as she embraced Frances. 'A terrible thing has happened.'

'Pray tell me quickly.'

'Do you remember Mary Woods ... but of course you don't. She was one of several. You gave her a ring set with diamonds and she promised in return to give you certain powders.'

'I do not need the powders now that I am to divorce Essex. I no longer care what happens to him.'

'But listen, my sweet friend. Mary Woods has been arrested and a diamond ring found on her person. When she was questioned she said it was given her by a great lady in an effort to persuade her to supply poison, that the lady might rid herself of her husband.'

'She mentioned names?'

Anne nodded anxiously.

'But this is terrible. She said that I—'

'She said the ring had been given her by the Countess of Essex.'

'Where did she say this?'

'In a court in the county of Suffolk where she was brought before the justices.'

Frances covered her face with her hands. It could not be — not now that she was going to be divorced from Essex, not now that Robert was eager to marry her and they would settle down together and live happily and openly for the rest of their lives.

'Oh, Anne,' she moaned, 'what shall I do? There will be such a scandal.'

Anne took her hands and held them firmly.

'There must not be a scandal,' she said.

'How prevent it?'

'You have influential friends.'

'Robert! Tell Robert that I have met such people! He would be horrified. He wouldn't love me any more. There would be no need for a divorce for he would not want to marry me.'

'I was thinking of your great-uncle. He wants the marriage. He is the Lord Privy Seal. I'll swear that he could put an end to proceedings in a small Suffolk court if he wished.'

Frances looked at her friend with wide, frightened eyes.

'You should lose no time,' advised Anne. 'For if this case went too far, even the Lord Privy Seal might not be able to stop its becoming known throughout the country.'

Northampton looked sternly at his frantic great-niece.

'So you gave the woman the ring?'

'Yes, I gave it to her.'

'In exchange for a powder?'

'No, that she should procure the powder.'

'Did you know the woman was a witch?'

'I know nothing of her except that I was told she could find me this powder.'

Northampton was seeing his kinswoman afresh. Good God, he thought, there is nothing she would stop at. She has been trying to poison Essex!

Well, he knew what it meant to have an ambition and see others in the way of it. It was because she was young, so beautiful a woman that he was shocked.

She would never forget that she was a Howard; she would work for the family when she was married to Carr. And marry Carr she must; for now the project was as important to him as it was delightful to her.

'Leave this to me,' he said. 'The case must go no further. Let us hope it has not gone too far.'

He did not wait to say more; he must send orders at once to Suffolk. It was only a matter of time. If the message reached the court before sentence was pronounced he could rely on everyone concerned carrying out his wishes.

The woman must be freed and sent away. An eye could be kept on her and a witch-finder sent to incriminate her later, for she was undoubtedly a witch. But this ring which she had said was a gift from the Countess of Essex must be forgotten.

That was an anxious time, but eventually Northampton was able to send for his niece and tell her that the affair had been hushed up. The woman's case had been dismissed and she had gone off with the ring.

'Let us hope, niece,' he said grimly, 'that you have not committed more acts of folly which will come home to roost.'

Frances was uneasy for a few days; but she could not persist in that state.

She was too happy; all impatience to finish with Essex, all eager desire for marriage with Robert Carr.

Overbury could not believe it. When he had been told the news he had laughed at it.

'Nonsense,' he had said, 'Court gossip, nothing more. Essex impotent! Look at him! That young man is as normal as any wife could wish.'

'Not as normal as the Countess of Essex wished, evidently,' was the rejoinder.

Overbury went to his apartment which adjoined that of Robert Carr.

If it were indeed true, and he feared it was, there could be one reason for it. The Countess of Essex hoped to marry Robert Carr.

If that should ever come about it would be the end of the friendship between Robert Carr and Tom Overbury, for he, Overbury, would never endure her insolence. He thought of all those occasions when he had criticized her to Robert and how his friend had shrugged aside his insinuations.

Robert was so guileless: he did not see behind that mask of beauty. Overbury was ready to grant the lady her attractions; he was ready to admit that she might well be reckoned the most beautiful woman at Court. But he saw beyond the beauty. He saw wantonness, lust, ambition, selfishness and cruelty.

Robert must be made to understand what sort of woman this was and that if he wished to retain his high position he must not marry her.

In the heat of rage against the Countess and anger at the folly of his friend he waylaid the latter on his way from the King's apartments and said he must speak to him without delay.

'What has happened to you, Tom?' asked Robert. 'You look distraught.'

'I have just heard some disquieting news which I want you to tell me is false.'

'Oh? What is that?'

'That the Countess of Essex is planning to divorce her husband on the grounds of impotence.'

A cautious look had come over Robert's face. 'I believe that to be true.'

'The Countess' motives are clear.'

'To you?'

'Yes, and to anyone else who knows what has been going on during the last months.'

'You are over-excited, Tom.'

'Of course I'm over-excited. I see you on the brink of ruin. Isn't that enough to excite me?'

'You've been drinking too much.'

'I am quite sober, Robert. Do you realize that that woman is dangerous?'

Robert shrugged his shoulders. 'I don't want to discuss her with you, Tom. I have told you that before.'

'You're going to discuss her with me, Robert.'

'You forget your position.'

'Nay, I forget nothing. I am the one who wrote the letters, do you remember? I am the one who wrote the poems. I know what has been taking place between you two all the time you have been professing friendship with Essex.'

Robert flushed angrily; it was a point on which he was very vulnerable. He had never been able to dismiss the thought of Essex from his mind even at the peak of satisfaction; and he was so happy now that Frances had explained about the fellow's impotence because that changed everything. He could not feel the same shame at making love to a man's wife when that man was incapable of doing so. And when the divorce had gone through and they were married, they would be quite respectable. That was what he was looking forward to and Tom was spoiling it. He wished he had never allowed Tom to write those letters. Tom knew too much.

'Essex is impotent,' began Robert.

'That's the tale she tells. Why, at Chartley she had to lock her door to keep him out. Ask Wilson.'

'Who is Wilson?'

'Not high and mighty enough for the noble lord's acquaintance, of course. Wilson is a scholar and a gentleman who serves Essex and is his friend.'

'I am glad he has such a friend.'

'Having robbed him of his wife you wish him to have some small comfort I see. Generous of you, Robert.'

'Don't let us quarrel about this, Tom.'

'Quarrel. Robert, you are bemused by that woman. You cannot see clearly. You cannot think. I tell you this: if you marry her she will be your ruin. I am as certain of it as I ever was of anything in my life.'

'You have taken a dislike to her. It is not the first time you have sought to turn me against her.'

'It's not the last time either. Robert, I shall not rest until I have made you see what a noose you are putting your head in. There is something evil about that woman. I do not know what, but it is there. I swear on my solemn oath that I shall work with all my might to stop this marriage. I hope to God the divorce is never granted.'

Robert's habitual calm broke and he showed his anger.

'You presume too much, Overbury,' he said. 'You forget that you would not be in the position you are today, did you not enjoy my favour. You have told me much. Now let me tell you something: If you continue in this way you will no longer enjoy that favour.'

'What? Would you write your own letters? I do not think they would be much admired. And forget not this: you have helped me, but consider how I have helped you. Consider too what I know about you and the lady. I wonder what the King will say when all the Court is laughing at the manner in which Robert Carr, Viscount Rochester, has stolen away from His Majesty's side whenever possible to satisfy his lust with that wanton who now asks us to believe that the husband, who had been clamouring to live a normal life with her, was impotent all the time. I know too much, Robert Carr. Go and tell the lady that. She'll understand, perhaps more than you do.'

Robert strode from the room.

He went straight to Frances and told her all that Overbury had said.

She listened, her eyes narrowed, her mind busy. There was

so much truth in what the odious creature had said; Robert might not realize it, but there was much he could do to harm them. What if he began to pry into her activities. That affair of Mary Woods had been a great shock to her.

She realized that she would never feel really safe while Thomas Overbury was free to ferret into her past, while he seemed to delight in defaming her character.

There was one weapon which Overbury had used with success all his life: his pen. He now decided to use it. He was certain that it would be the end of the career he had planned for himself if Carr should marry the Countess of Essex. The woman hated him and would seek to destroy him. Moreover, he believed that, since she was an associate of Anne Turner, she was in touch with men such as the late Dr Forman. He had heard from Wilson, whose acquaintance he had cultivated, of mysterious powders discovered among the clothes of the Countess' husband. It was possible that the Countess in her ruthless way had made other enemies besides Overbury. There had been a strange allegation from a woman in a Suffolk court. Overbury could see that marriage to the Countess might easily ruin Robert Carr. Perhaps the young simpleton did not realize how easy it was for those who had been at the very peak of success to fall into obscurity – or even worse. In the case of Carr his triumphs did not even rest on his own mental ability. A handsome face, a charming manner and an easy-going nature were the assets which had carried him where he was – with Overbury's help.

No, thought Overbury, I am not to be thrust aside by Madam Countess. I am far more important in this affair than they seem to realize.

Since he had whispered the secret of his relationship with Robert Carr to his friends at the Mermaid Club, they had treated him with even greater respect than they had given him for his writing talent. He had heard it said again and again in his hearing that he was the real ruler of England.

Was he going to stand aside, therefore, and watch this disaster take place?

gone, I have fallen on evil times and I thought that as such a
good friend of the doctor—'

The woman must not know that she was afraid. She smiled
and said: 'Why, if times are hard with you, you must allow me
to help you.'

Give them money. It was easy. There was so much money.

'My lady,' said Dr Franklin, 'the potions I procured for you
were very costly. My experiments demanded a lavish use of
these. I neglected other clients to serve you and, my lady, I
find I have lost two hundred pounds this year because of
this.'

'Two hundred pounds this year?'

'Two hundred pounds a year, my lady, would satisfy me
well, with a little extra for food and my boat hire.'

Franklin smiled at her, the lazy smile of power. These
people were no longer humble as they had been. They had
worked for her and as a result a man had died. That was
something they could not forget.

How many more of them? she wondered. There was Mrs
Turner's maid Margaret, who had run many errands to find
what the lady had needed; there was Mrs Turner's manservant,
Stephen. They all wanted their little rewards – their silence
money.

There was Mrs Turner herself – not that she would do anything so vulgar as to ask for money. But they had been dear
friends, had they not? That friendship must not cease because
they had achieved success together.

'Sweetest lady,' said Anne Turner, 'I'll confess I am never
happy away from your side. We worked well together did we
not? It is foolish of me but I am almost sorry that we have
successfully completed our task and I can no longer be of
service to you.'

Mrs Turner was therefore often a guest at the house of the
Earl and Countess of Somerset and it was a great pleasure to
her to be at Court again.

So, much as Frances tried to forget Sir Thomas Overbury,

these people would not allow her to. It seemed that every day there was someone or some thing to remind her.

She became ill and Robert was anxious.

'What ails you, my love?' he asked her. 'You seem nervous. Are you worried?'

'Nay, Robert,' she said. 'I am well.'

'But you are not,' he told her tenderly. 'You have changed. Others have noticed.'

'I think the long delay over the divorce was more upsetting than I realized. I so longed for it to be over.'

'Well now it is, and we can forget it.'

You may, she thought. But how can I?

She had thought it so simple to murder a man who stood in the way. But it seemed it was not.

Overbury haunted her. He would not let her forget. It was true she saw no ghost; but ghosts took many forms; they did not always have to materialize in order to make themselves felt.

Robert, alarmed for her health, took a house in Kensington for her, but as it did not improve there they went to Chesterfield Park; then Robert decided that she must see the King's physician, and James himself insisted on this. He could not have his Robbie worried after all the trouble they had had to get him married.

So Robert bought a house in Isleworth, and the King's doctor, Burgess, attended the Countess.

He could not understand what was undermining the Countess's health, but he believed she would be well when the spring came.

That was a cold winter; the Thames itself was frozen and there was no escaping the bleak cold winds.

Enter George Villiers

JAMES WAS brooding uneasily when the arrival of Sir John Digby at the Palace was announced.

Money! He could never find enough. It was not that he spent a great deal upon himself. If he asked his Parliament for it they would begin to snarl about his favourites, declaring that they were the ones whose greedy hands depleted the Exchequer.

One of the ministers had said that those handsome young men who were spaniels to the King were wolves to the people. They were eager to drag Robert down; he knew it. They were jealous of Robert on whom he was coming more and more to rely. Robert was the perfect companion, the perfect minister; he never criticized; he never attempted to impose his will. He worked for his master wholeheartedly and through love.

But it was a pretty pass when the brewers were at the door of the Palace declaring they would supply no more goods until their bills were paid. Sixteen thousand pounds they said the Palace owed them and on account of this they were all but ruined; they must have payment. They had even dared to go to law. Such a state of affairs could not be allowed. No tradesman could summons the King. There was only one way of dealing with such a situation if the dignity of royalty was to be maintained. The brewers who had dared act so were sent to the Marshalsea Prison for *lèse majesté*.

But James was a man who must consider a matter from all angles. He saw the brewers' point of view, and recognized that it was unjust that a merchant should supply goods, receive no payment and when he asked for it be thrown into prison. Only James' fervent belief in the Divine Right of Kings would have allowed him to act as he did; and even so his conduct depressed him.

Such were his thoughts when Sir John Digby entered and asked to speak privately to him.

James willingly gave the permission. He was fond of Digby, a personable man in his mid-thirties who had come to Court from his native Warwickshire in the hope of following a career in diplomacy. He had come to James' notice at the time of the Gunpowder Plot when he had been sent to convey a message to the King; James had been impressed immediately by his good looks and intelligence, and Digby had become a gentleman of the Privy Chamber and one of the King's Carvers.

James had recognized the man's integrity – a quality found all too rarely at Court – and had decided on his advancement. Opportunity had come to Digby a few years previously when James had sent him to Madrid as his ambassador to arrange a marriage between the Infanta Anne and Prince Henry. Digby had quickly discovered that the Infanta was already betrothed to Louis XIII of France; and when Philip III had suggested a match between the Prince and his younger daughter Maria, Digby had sensed a lack of seriousness on the part of the Spanish monarch and advised against the marriage. But although that matter had come to nothing Digby had proved himself a worthy ambassador in other ways.

Now his manner was very grave as he bowed before the King.

'Well, Johnnie,' said James, 'I can see ye've brought me news which you're hesitating to deliver. Is it so bad then?'

'I fear, Your Majesty, that this is going to be a shock to you.'

'Well, lad, I've suffered many a shock in my life and mayhap I'll see a few more before I die. So let me hear this one.'

Digby took a scroll from his pocket and said slowly: 'I have prepared this and think it my duty to lay it before Your Majesty. It is to give this to you – and to do it with my own hands – that I am here in London.'

James took the scroll, unrolled it and frowned at it. It was a list of names – all well-known people of his Court.

'I believed, Your Majesty, that certain information was leaking to Spain and I set my spies to watch how this could be. I have now completed my investigation. That list, Your Majesty, contains the names of your ministers and courtiers who are accepting pensions from the King of Spain for the service they do him.'

'Traitors?' murmured James.

'That is so, Your Majesty. I fear that when you read those names you will be deeply shocked.'

James was hastily scanning the list. He knew he could trust Digby, but he could scarcely believe what he read. Yet there it was in detail. The names and the amounts of the pensions.

He would not bear to study the list too closely because he was afraid of finding one name there and if he found it he knew he would never trust any man again.

'Thank you, Johnnie,' he said. 'You're a good servant. Leave the list with me. I wish to examine it closely. You will be hearing more of this, but leave me now, and tell my servants that I wish to be alone.'

When Digby retired James returned to the scroll.

Northampton! The rogue! And Northampton had been a close friend of Robbie's . . . and was now related to him!

The Countess of Suffolk – his mother-in-law! He had never trusted her, knowing her for a rapacious woman.

Thank God! His name was not there.

Of what had he been thinking? Robbie, a traitor! Never. Thank God he could rely on Robbie.

The scroll had ceased to be so very important. After all, was he surprised that he was surrounded by rogues?

But he was glad to have seen the scroll because it had proved to him that he had not been mistaken in Robbie.

James decided to say nothing of the discovery. He had been warned that he was surrounded by men who took bribes from Spain, but he could see no good in making the matter public. He would be cautious in dealing with those people concerned, but it would be very unsettling to have a scandal now. The Essex divorce was still talked about. It was known that recently he had suggested offering baronetcies to any who

could pay six thousand pounds for them; the matter had
come to nothing, largely because there were so few who
would have been ready to pay the price for the title. But some-
how these matters leaked out and were talked of.

No, he wanted no more scandal.

So James gave no sign to those who were in the pay of
Spain that he was aware of this, but he watched them very
closely.

Northampton, meanwhile, was having many a secret meeting with the Spanish ambassador.

Count Gondomar had quickly realized the importance of
this wily statesman, who was now related by marriage to the
King's favourite young man; and as that young man was the
sort to be easily led, Count Gondomar was very hopeful for
the future.

'It would be an excellent thing,' he told Northampton, 'if a
marriage could be arranged between the Prince of Wales and
the Infanta Maria. I believe that if this marriage could take
place, in a few years we should see the Catholic Faith back in
England.'

Northampton agreed with this; he was ready to earn the
pension he drew from Spain and he was against that French
marriage for the Prince of Wales which was now being suggested.

'How does the Earl of Somerset feel about the Spanish
match?'

Northampton smiled. 'I doubt not,' he said, 'that when I
have had a word with him he will feel it to be an excellent
proposition.'

'Then, my good friend, we shall have the King on our side.
For I have heard it said that what Somerset desires today, His
Majesty desires tomorrow.'

'Your Majesty is in urgent need of money,' said Robert. 'Why
should you not fill your coffers with Spanish gold?'

'By agreeing to the Spanish match for Charles, Robbie?'

'Yes, Sire. Philip would give the Infanta a magnificent
dowry.'

'The people are against a Spanish marriage, lad.'

'Because they fear the Catholic religion would be brought back to England.'

'Which it never will be. I know this of the people of England. They remember Bloody Mary and the threat of the Armada. This country made itself the natural enemy of Spain in the days of Drake and Elizabeth. Legends die hard. The English would never have the Inquisition on these shores; and that means they are suspicious of Catholics, and particularly Spaniards.'

'Then Your Majesty does not wish to benefit from the Spanish gold?'

'I wouldna say that, Robbie. There's no harm in your doing a little negotiation with Gondomar. Sound the man. See what they'll offer. Whether we decide there should be a French or Spanish marriage 'tis as well to know all that's entailed. And Robbie, we've been long enough without a Secretary of State. I've decided on Winwood.'

Robert was astonished. Winwood was not the man Northampton had chosen, and therefore Robert had supported. Northampton had thought Sir Thomas Lake would be the man for the job because he was what the old Earl called a Howard man. Robert wondered what Northampton would say when he heard that the King's choice had fallen on Winwood.

Had he chosen Winwood because, as a staunch Protestant and Puritan, he was fiercely against the Spanish marriage?

James waited for Robert to express his disappointment at the choice; but Robert did no such thing. Winwood was the King's choice and although the man would not have been his, as soon as James mentioned it, it became acceptable to him.

How I love this man! thought James. Never shall any other come between our friendship; always the first place in my heart will be for Robert Carr.

Sir Ralph Winwood was overjoyed when he heard of his appointment. It was what he had wanted for a long time. Now he would be in a position to use his voice against all idolaters; and this was particularly important because he knew Northampton was working for the Spanish marriage and had persuaded Somerset to do the same.

In Sir Ralph Winwood's opinion it was his duty therefore to work against the favourite.

He knew that the Queen was a secret Catholic, and this shocked him deeply. It was time a good Protestant had some control of affairs.

He deplored the King's preoccupation with handsome young men. How much better a ruler he would be if he surrounded himself with serious men – men of experience rather than beauty.

Still, it might be that Somerset would not always hold his present position; and the fact that Sir Ralph Winwood had become Secretary of State was a step in the right direction.

Within the Court there was growing friction. The proposed Spanish marriage of the heir to the throne must necessarily be a cause of contention; and now that Somerset was joined by marriage to the Howards, theirs was by far the most powerful party in the country. Northampton, at its head, was a secret Catholic; as for the King, he had known that Northampton took bribes from Spain and yet had done nothing to deprive him of his power. The rulers of England seemed to be Somerset, Northampton and Somerset's father-in-law, the Earl of Suffolk.

The fact that the Queen had become a Catholic made further confusion, for she had always felt a deep resentment towards Somerset and often referred to the death of her son Henry and the suspicions which had been rife at the time concerning Somerset and Overbury.

Somerset's and Howard's party; the Queen's party; the Protestants such as Sir Ralph Winwood; those in favour of a Spanish match for Prince Charles; those in favour of a French one; they were all warring together; and this dissension resulted in insults which led to duels.

James was distracted and turned more and more to Robert

for solace; never had Robert been so powerful and never had so many longed to see him fall.

It was at this time that the King and certain members of the Court made a journey to Cambridge; and because the Earl of Suffolk was the Chancellor of the university there, the arrangements for the entertainment of the royal party were left in his hands. It was an indication of how bold the Howards had become that Suffolk declined to invite the Queen.

Anne was angry, apart from the fact that she loved pageantry of any kind, for she saw in this an insult; and as usual she blamed Robert Carr, although he had had no hand in it.

'Let him wait,' she said. 'I will have my revenge for this.'

There were, in fact, very few ladies present in Cambridge during the King's stay there, apart from those belonging to the Howard family.

Frances was a member of the party, and as she rode out from London her spirits were lifted; she was putting a distance between herself and such places as Lambeth and Hammersmith; Robert was beside her, the devoted husband, who was always solicitous for her health and comfort; she was determined to be gay and enjoy that position for which she had so long fought.

Her father, Suffolk, being the host, was lodged in St John's College, but Lady Suffolk, with Frances and other female members of the family, were to stay at Magdalen, while James and Charles – with Robert – were at Trinity.

The men of the university were determined to provide entertainments for the royal party; the whole town was *en fête*, eager to do homage to the visitors, and banquets were given in St John's College and Trinity; but because this was a university town, there was an endeavour to keep the entertainment on an intellectual level.

One day the company assembled to see a play called *Ignoramus* which was being presented for the pleasure of the King and his friends.

In the play was a youth so handsome, so full of vitality that whenever he was present he attracted the attention of everyone. It was rare that anyone possessed such good looks; there was only one other man at the Court who was so outstandingly handsome; and that was Robert Carr.

The King leaned forward in his chair and watched the play with more interest than it deserved. Or was it the play he watched?

He turned to one of his gentlemen and said: 'Tell me, what is the name of yon lad?'

It was impossible to answer the question for the youth was so obscure that his name was not widely known.

'Find out and tell me,' commanded James.

The gentleman of whom he had asked the question hurried off and a few minutes later returned.

'His name is George Villiers, Your Majesty.'

'George Villiers,' repeated James, slowly as though he wished to memorize it.

Many people noted the incident, some with apprehension, others with glee.

Could it mean anything? Could it be *made* to mean anything?

Perhaps not, for the King did not ask that George Villiers be brought to him; and when he left the Clare Hall, where the piece had been played, he leaned very affectionately on the arm of Robert Carr.

On returning from Cambridge, Lord Pembroke, who had noticed the King's passing interest in young George Villiers, went to see the Queen.

Anne had always been friendly with Pembroke and when he asked for an audience, it was readily granted.

Pembroke found her playing with her frisky miniature greyhounds, which she held by a crimson cord; the ornamental collars about their necks, embossed in gold with the letters A.R., branded them as royal dogs.

'Ah, my lord,' she said. 'I trust I see you well. You are recently come from the Cambridge revels, I believe.'

She pouted with annoyance; *she* had not been invited to the revels. Rarely had a Queen of the realm been so insulted.

But what could one expect when the King gave his attention to handsome young men; and the worst of them all was Robert Carr, who she would always believe had had a hand in the death of her darling son.

She was ready to weep at the thought, and anger shone from her usually mild eyes.

'I came at once to Your Majesty, because I knew you would wish to hear of the revels.'

'I'll swear you were surrounded by Howards.'

'Your Majesty is right. There were scarcely any women present but Howard women.'

'And Lady Somerset?'

'Flaunting her beauty as usual.'

'I never liked her. They make a good pair.'

'Your Majesty, there was a play.'

'A play. Was it good? They know how I love plays and pageants. Do you not think, my lord, that Suffolk should be reprimanded for so insulting me? Not to ask the Queen! Has any Queen ever been treated thus before, think you?'

'Your Majesty's good friends were alert in her interests.'

'And what saw they? What heard they?'

'In the play, Your Majesty, there was a very handsome young man.'

'Another?'

'This one was every bit as handsome as Somerset, I swear it.'

'And the pretty's nose was out of joint?'

'I do not think he noticed, Your Majesty. He has become so sure of himself.'

'He is too sure, my lord. He will discover that one day.'

'Perhaps sooner than he believes possible, Your Majesty?'

'What did you discover, my lord?'

'The King asked his name.'

Anne nodded.

'Moreover,' went on Pembroke, 'he insisted on its being supplied to him.'

'And the name?'

'George Villiers.'

'I've never heard of it.'

'Your Majesty, it occurred to me as I watched the play that you might conceivably hear a great deal of that name.'

'What plans are you hatching, Pembroke?'

'If we could replace Somerset with our man . . .'

Anne's eyes were gleaming. What a glorious revenge that would be on Somerset!

'And you think it possible?' she asked quickly. 'You know how he dotes on that man.'

'I think that with grooming we might do something. This boy Villiers struck me as being one of the few who might in time oust Somerset from his place.'

'Is he so handsome?'

'He reminds me of that head of St Stephen – the Italian model, Your Majesty will remember.'

'Here in Whitehall – I know it well. Is he as beautiful as that?'

'I think Your Majesty will agree with me that he is when you see him.'

'What do you propose to do?'

'Bring him to Court, train him in the way he should go and, when the time is ripe, persuade Your Majesty to present him to the King.'

Anne started to laugh. She picked up one of the dogs and held it against her neck.

'Replace one pretty by another!' she said. 'Well, providing my lord Somerset loses his arrogance, that will please me. Keep an eye on this Villiers, my lord; and bring him to me. I should like to see him for myself.'

After the visit to Cambridge, Frances felt a little better; it always did her good to get away from London, for in London there was too much to remind her. It was hardly likely that she would be followed to Cambridge by some impecunious person who would assure her of all he or she had done to help the Countess to her present state. So at Cambridge she had tried to forget her fears and had joined with her mother and sisters in the gaiety of the occasion; and feeling so much better she began to review her situation with less nervousness. Why should she be afraid of these people who were after all so humble! If she could tell Robert, their importunings could be stopped tomorrow; but of course she could not tell Robert.

But there was one whom she could tell; her great-uncle, Northampton. He would understand, old rogue that he was; and he would tell her what to do.

Having returned to London she decided to visit her great-uncle in his house at Charing Cross.

When she arrived she was told that the Earl was in the Houses of Parliament where she knew stormy debates were taking place at this time, for many of the ministers still clung to their determination to drive the Scottish favourites back beyond the Border. Northampton was putting up a great fight against them. He had no intention of allowing Robert to be sent out of London, since his fortune and that of the Howards was bound up in Robert Carr. Frances felt calm only to think of that. There was a power about her great-uncle which was invincible.

'He will be coming by barge, my lady,' one of the servants told her. 'You will see him arrive ere long.'

Frances said she would go into the garden and watch for his arrival.

The hot June sun shone on the flowery pyramids of loose strife on the river bank and it was pleasant to listen to the lap of oars in the water as the boats passed along. Frances felt more at peace than she had for a long time. How foolish she had been to worry; how stupid to give way to these people who made so many demands! Why had she not thought of asking for her great-uncle's help before this? He would know what to do.

She had strolled down to the river's edge and seeing his barge, hurried to the privy stairs to greet him.

But what had happened? They were carrying him; his face was so white that he did not look like himself at all.

'What happened?' she cried. 'Is my lord ill?'

They did not answer her; they were intent on carrying Northampton ashore.

They said he was dying, but Frances did not believe it; she dared not believe it. She was becoming hysterical at the thought because she had made up her mind that he alone could help her.

She knew that he had a wennish tumour in his thigh; but so many elderly people suffered from such things. Now it seemed it had grown so large and was giving such pain that when he had collapsed in the House he had decided to have an operation. Felton, his surgeon, was coming to Charing Cross at once to perform it, because it was feared that if it were not done it would cost the Earl his life.

He will soon be well, Frances soothed herself. Then he will tell me what I must do.

It was said that when Felton cut open the wen in the Earl's thigh such poison burst forth that Felton himself was likely to die from the very contamination.

As for the Earl he lay on his bed and knew that the end had come.

'There is now no need,' he said, 'for me to keep my religion a secret. Send for a priest that I may have Extreme Unction.'

When the priest had gone Frances went to his bedside and knelt there. But the eyes which looked at her were glazed and almost unrecognizing.

She wanted to say: 'You cannot go like this. You are involved even as I am. You must stay and help me.'

But there were others about the bed and how could she talk of such secrets in front of them?

'This is the end,' said Northampton. 'Who would have thought I should die of a poisonous wen? Bury me in the Castle Chapel at Dover forgetting not that I died Warden of the Cinque Ports. A long procession will leave London and make its way across Kent to the coast, and that will be the last journey of Northampton.'

'Great-uncle,' whispered Frances, 'do not say that. You will recover. You must.'

He peered at her. 'Who is that then? Frances ... ah, the wayward one! But Robert will care for her. Care for each other, Frances.'

'You must not die ... yet,' she cried.

But his breathing was becoming rapid and his eyes were glazed.

Now he did not see her at all. He was preparing to make his last journey to Dover.

They had covered his body with a pall of velvet on which lay a white cross and by the light of candles, his gentlemen took turns to watch over him through the night.

They talked of him in whispers while they watched. It was awe inspiring that one who such a short time ago had been a power in the land was now no more.

In her apartments Frances wept and Robert tried to comfort her.

'You must not weep so, my love,' he said. 'He was a great man, but old; and death is something we must all come to.'

But what could Robert know? He believed she wept for love of the old man; he could not guess that fear of facing the future without his help terrified her.

Frances was angry with herself. What had happened to her? She had always been bold, going after what she wanted and caring nothing for the consequences. Why should she be so afraid because a man had died in the Tower?

She was feeling stronger and her old vitality was returning to her. She would continue to pay these people but she would let them know that if they attempted to get more than what she considered their dues she would find some means of making them sorry.

Robert was too meek. He did not seize his opportunities. James was so devoted to him that he could have anything he wanted; he was foolish not to take advantage of that. The Queen was insolent to him and to her. There was no reason

why they should submit to that. Robert really had no notion
of his power. It was up to her to guide him.

At night when they lay together after lovemaking she
would talk to him of all he might do, all she expected him to do.

'James may be the King but you could command him,
Robert. You are the uncrowned King of England and I am
the uncrowned Queen.'

Robert was so delighted to see her coming out of her
depression that he was ready to agree. She was continually
urging him to act this way and that. Sometimes she would
insist that he did not keep an appointment with the King.
What did it matter? she asked. James would forgive him.

James always did – although he was a little reproachful.

'It's not like ye, Robbie,' was all he said sadly.

And Robert began to realize that Frances was right. He *was*
the real ruler of England because James would always do what
he wanted.

'Now that my uncle is dead,' said Frances, 'you should be
the Warden of the Cinque Ports.'

'The Wardenship has not been offered to me.'

'Then ask for it.'

He did and it was his.

'What of the Privy Seal?'

'I already hold high posts.'

'The Seal should be yours. Ask for it.'

So he asked and it was his.

James was bewildered. What was happening to his sweet
Robbie. His manner was changing; he was a little truculent;
and he had never been so before. He asked that he should be
Chamberlain, and his father-in-law, Suffolk, Treasurer.

James complied with these requests but he was growing
more and more uneasy. For the first time he doubted Robert's
unselfish devotion.

In his residence of Baynard's Castle on the north bank of the
Thames below St Paul's, the Earl of Pembroke called a meeting of his friends.

Pembroke had selected these men carefully and they had

one emotion in common: they all felt they owed a special grudge to Somerset and there was not one of them who would not have been delighted to see him fall.

'Since the death of Northampton,' said Pembroke when they were all assembled, 'Somerset has become more power-ful than ever.'

'Warden of the Cinque Ports,' agreed Sir Thomas Lake, 'and now the Privy Seal and the Chamberlainship. What next, I wonder.'

'The crown,' joked several of the others simultaneously.

'Why should he want that?' asked Lake bitterly. 'It is all but his already; the only drawback is that he cannot wear it.'

'It is no use grumbling together,' insisted Pembroke. 'We should act. And it is for this reason that I have asked you to come here this day.'

'Pray tell us what you have in mind,' begged Lake.

'George Villiers,' answered Pembroke. 'I have seen the King watching him and I think the moment has come for us to do something about it.'

'Your plan is to substitute this Villiers for Somerset?'

'Exactly. We would coach him; he would be our man. He would work for us in the way Somerset has worked for the Howards.'

'These favourites are apt to become overbearing once they are secure in the King's favour.'

'Somerset worked well for the Howards.'

'But he has changed lately; have you noticed?'

'I have,' agreed Pembroke. 'And that is in our favour. He is becoming arrogant. On one or two occasions I have seen a distinct lack of respect in his manner to the King. This gives me hope.'

'Somerset's a fool. One would have thought he would have realized that he kept his place through his gentle good nature. If Northampton were alive he would warn him.'

'Or Overbury.'

'Ah, Overbury. That fellow did all his work for him, if you ask me. Advised him too. Somerset without Northampton and Overbury . . . could be vulnerable.'

'And that,' said Pembroke, 'is why we must act quickly. I have presented Mr George Villiers with clothes in which he will not be ashamed to appear at Court. He was somewhat shabby and although he had good looks enough to make him outstanding in any company, in fine clothes he has the appearance of a young Greek god. The King is aware of him, but hesitates to show him favour because, although I am sure he is turning from Somerset, he turns slowly; and as you know he remains friendly towards those who have once been his favourites, even though others do supplant them.'

'He should be brought more to the King's notice, this Villiers,' said Lake. 'I will buy him a place as cupbearer to the King. What think you of that?'

'Excellent!' cried Pembroke. 'That shall be the next step. And very soon I shall approach Her Majesty – who knows of our plan – and ask her to beg the King to give young Villiers a place as one of his Gentlemen of the Bedchamber.'

The conspirators were now certain that the heyday of the reigning favourite was coming to an end; and they were very gay when they took their leave of Pembroke and rode back to Whitehall.

As they came through Fleet Street, they passed several stalls on which traders had set up their merchandise. On one of these a painter had displayed his work and prominent among it was a picture of Robert Carr.

The party paused to look at it. It was a good likeness.

One of them turned to his groom.

'Take up a handful of mud,' he said, 'and throw it at that picture.'

The groom looked amazed. 'Did you mean that, sir?'

'I meant it. Do it, man.'

With a grin, the groom obeyed.

The painter who had been hovering close by, watching the party of Court gentlemen and hoping for a sale, stared in astonishment when he saw his best picture ruined.

He dashed out and cried: 'Gentlemen, this is a poor joke.'

'We like not your subject,' said the man who had ordered the groom to throw the mud.

'It is my lord Somerset!' protested the painter. 'What better subject in the kingdom?'

'You paint too well, my friend,' was the answer. 'We recognized the fellow at first glance. 'Tis the first of much mud which will be thrown at that man.'

'Having spoilt the picture you must pay for it.'

But the men were already spurring their horses and galloping on.

The artist shouted after them. 'Think not you will escape with this. I know who you are. I shall complain to my lord Somerset. You'll be sorry.'

Robert listened to the artist and as he did so anger flamed within him. He was becoming angry quite frequently now; he was nervous; his relationship with James had changed, and he was surprised at how readily his temper flared up.

He had noticed George Villiers about the Court and it seemed to him that many were trying to bring that young man to the King's notice. He guessed why. He had studied Villiers closely and noticed the fine clear skin, the handsome features, the flush of youth; and that sent him to his own mirror. He had aged since the divorce; perhaps he had begun to age since he had first known Frances and the fact that he and she were deceiving her husband had given him so many misgivings; but he saw now that as far as looks were concerned he could not compare with this fresh young man.

It was too humiliating, because his spies brought him reports that Pembroke and Lake were at the head of this youth's supporters, and he well knew how Pembroke and Lake felt about himself. So it was clear what they were trying to do.

This knowledge was perhaps at the very root of his touchiness. He wanted to prove that his power over James had not changed; that was why he allowed himself to lose his temper so often.

He found himself wishing that Overbury was alive and they were good friends again so that he could talk this matter over with someone of discernment and sympathy.

'Mud!' he exclaimed. 'They threw mud at my picture.'

'Yes, my lord. And 'twas not boys' play either. They were gentlemen of the Court and one of them commanded his groom to do this. The others were all with him though. I shouted after them that it was the best of my pictures, which was so, my lord, being copied from one I have seen of your lordship.'

'They knew it was of myself?'

'They said so, my lord. They said they did not like the subject, and this would be the first of much mud that would be slung at your lordship.'

Robert controlled his rage, rewarded the artist and tried to shrug the matter aside. It was natural that he should have enemies.

When Frances heard what had happened she was furious. She too was aware of George Villiers. She was determined that her husband was going to remain in his present position; he was to be the first gentleman of the Court and she the first lady. It would be ironical if after all she had gone through to achieve her present position, she should lose it to that nobody, George Villiers.

Frances had discovered who the insulting men were. They were of the Pembroke party – those men who were supplying Villiers with new clothes, who had arranged for him to be the King's Cupbearer, who were bringing him to the King's notice on every conceivable occasion.

'You cannot allow this insult to pass,' she stormed at Robert. 'They must be shown that you are all-powerful. It would be the utmost folly to ignore this.'

'It is of no real importance to me, Frances.'

'Then it is to me,' she cried. 'We must revenge ourselves, and in like manner, to let them know that we are aware who did this thing.'

'But how?'

'I have thought of a way. That young upstart will be at the royal table this very day. He will be mincing in the fine clothes which have been bought for him. Just as he is about to rise and serve the King's wine, one of our men shall tip a dish of soup over him. It's a just reward for what they did to your picture.'

'Well, that's harmless enough,' agreed Robert.

Robert was seated on the right hand of the King and James seemed pleased because Robert was in a good humour. Though it was a sad thought that Robert should have become like other lads to whom he had given his affections – subject to tantrums.

The King's eyes strayed to the young Cupbearer who was seated some distance from him. A winsome lad, who might have been a model for the head of St Stephen. His was a rare beauty, and it was difficult to keep one's eyes from that face. But he must not anger Robert. Robert had become very observant and was apt to sulk if he looked too long at yonder lad.

He wanted to say: 'Look here, Robbie, it's some years since you lay with a broken arm on the grass of the tiltyard and our friendship was born. There'll never be another to take your place with me. But why, lad, cannot you be as you once were. Once there was not a sweeter tempered laddie in my kingdom. I want my lad Robbie back. If he will come I'd never as much as glance at yon boy if I thought it pained him.'

James sensed that Robert too was very much aware of that young man who sat there nonchalantly, as though his beauty made him an equal of all men.

The accident happened suddenly. One of the King's gentlemen, who had risen to serve him with soup, had to pass the spot where young Villiers was sitting. As he did so, he seemed to slip and tilting the dish forward slopped it over young Villiers' coat and fine satin breeches.

Villiers stood up, his handsome face scarlet (none the less beautiful for that, James noticed) and did an alarming thing. He lifted his hand and boxed the ears of the gentleman server.

There were several seconds of silence. Robert was aware of Frances whose eyes had widened with delight. He knew what she was thinking. For any man to strike another in the presence of the King was a crime to be severely punished; and the punishment was that the right hand of the offender should be struck off.

Somerset stood up.

He knew that everyone was watching. The Queen, Pembroke, Lake and all those who supported this man believed that by one rash act he had ruined his chances – and their hopes – of supplanting Somerset.

'You young fool,' he said. 'To behave thus in the presence of His Majesty will bring its own reward.'

Young Villiers had turned pale, now looking more like the statue of St Stephen than ever. He knew what Somerset meant because there was not a man at Court who was unaware of the penalty for striking another in the presence of the King. Those watching saw his left hand close over his right as though he would protect it.

'Come here, young man,' said James.

Villiers stood before the King.

'You're over-rash, lad,' James continued.

The clear young eyes looked straight into his. James could not meet them. They were as beautiful as Robert's had been when he was as young as this one. James' eyes rested on that right hand; it was well shaped and the fingers were long and tapering.

Mutilate that beautiful body, thought James. Never!

'A fine coat spoilt,' went on the King and his mouth turned up at the corner.

'Yes, Your Majesty,' murmured the young man.

'But coats, lad, can be replaced; hands cannot.'

He saw the terror in the boy's face; and he was aware of Robert, smiling almost complacently beside him. In that moment he began to turn away from Robert.

'Well,' he said, 'ye're young and a newcomer to Court. Guard your temper, lad, and dinna let such a thing happen again in my sight.'

When the young man knelt before the King and lifted his beautiful face, James was deeply moved. 'Get back to your place, boy,' he said. 'And remember my words.'

There was a rustle throughout the Court, there were sly glances and whispered comments.

Some fell from their horses; some boldly cuffed a gentleman in the King's presence.

It did not matter. One way was as good as another for a handsome young man to bring himself to the King's notice.

George Villiers had indeed come to Court.

There was great exultation in the Pembroke group, particularly when a few days after the incident of the ruined suit, a post in the King's Bedchamber fell vacant.

'It could not be more opportune,' cried Pembroke. 'The time has come to put Villiers in the King's intimate circle. It is the duty of one of us to suggest to His Majesty that Mr George Villiers would adequately fill the post which has fallen vacant.'

When the matter was suggested to James he was excited. He had not forgotten young Villiers and he would have been delighted to comply with the request; but knowing Robert's feelings he hesitated and said he would think of the matter and give his answer in a few days.

This was a blow because Villiers' supporters had believed that James would agree immediately.

Robert still had his friends who knew that if he were supplanted by Villiers their own careers would automatically suffer. So it was not long before Robert heard that Pembroke and his friends were trying to get the Bedchamber post for Villiers.

He talked to Frances about this and her eyes grew dark with anger. She was throwing herself wholeheartedly into the conflict against Villiers; she found it stimulating to have something to work for; also it took her mind off that little band of blackmailers whom she was paying regularly.

'Villiers must not have the post,' she cried. 'If he does, depend upon it, he will be in your place ere long.'

'He could not be. He is too young and inexperienced.'

'You were once.'

'It has taken me years to get to my present position.'

'Villiers looks a sharp one.'

'I see,' said Robert bitterly, 'that you mean I was a fool.'

'You had friends to help you.'

'And so has he.'

'That's exactly what I mean. He has powerful men behind him. You had my great-uncle, but he is dead now.'

'I would to God Overbury were here.'

Frances clenched her hands and screamed: 'He was no good to you ... no good to us. You were a fool over that man, Robert. For God's sake try to have a little more sense.'

She ran from the room and Robert scowled after her.

What had happened to his life? What had happened to him?

Frances was not the sweet and loving woman he had imagined her to be. She was continually goading him. A fool! Was he? He thought of other men who had taken bribes — something he had disdained to do. Had he been a simpleton? He had always agreed with the King ... until now. He had never tried to force his opinions on James.

Did James think him a fool too? Did James think that he could introduce that sly boy into the Bedchamber because he, Robert, was too soft to protest?

He went off to James who had retired for the night and arrogantly entered the private apartments.

'Why, Robbie,' said James, starting up. 'What brings you here at this time?'

'I see, Your Majesty, that you are no longer my good friend.'

'Now, Robbie, what has come to ye, lad. Where's the gentle boy I used to know?'

'Perhaps Mr George Villiers has taken his place.'

'Ah — so it's that, lad, is it. Nay, Robbie, there's none who could take your place with me. Did you know?'

'It does not seem that is so.'

James patted the bed. 'Sit ye down, Robbie, and listen to your Old Dad. You're not the boy you used to be. What's happened to change you?'

'I change?' cried Robert. 'It is you who have changed ...
towards me ... ever since they brought that pretty boy to
your notice.'

James shook his head. 'You grieve me, Robbie. You grieve
me sorely. You come to me in temper at this most unseasonable hour. You bereave me of my rest, it seems on purpose to hurt me. Why have you become sullen of late, Robert?
What has happened to your love for me? I have suffered
through my affection for you. I have prayed for you, because,
my boy, I think that if you go on as you have begun you will
be sorry. I have never prayed for any subject alive but you. I
will speak to you now with great seriousness. You should not
forget that you owe your wealth and your standing here at
Court to me. It is because I have loved you so much that I have
borne patiently with your tempers. Do not try me too much.
Continue to love me, be to me as you once were and hold me
by the heart, Robbie. If you do this you may build upon my
favour as upon a rock. Rest assured that I shall never weary of
showing my affection for you. I have accepted your arrogance
towards me, and I forgive it – although it is something I find
hard to forget. Your fate is in your own hands. Here is the best
and kindest master you could ever have. But if you are un-
grateful, if you forget that although he loves you, he is still
your King, then you will have only yourself to blame for the
consequences.'

Robert listened sullenly to his speech. He longed, even as
James did, to be back on the old footing. He wished that he
were more articulate; he wished that he could explain to this
good friend how everything had changed since he had betrayed Essex through his love for Frances. He believed that
James would have understood more readily than he did himself.

He fell on to his knees then and kissed James' hand and
seeing the sullenness fade from his face, the King was delighted.

'Your Majesty,' said Robert, 'forgive me.'

'We'll say no more of this matter, Robbie. But forget not
what I have said.'

Robert remembered then why he had come here and he said: 'Could I ask one favour of you?'

'What is it, Robbie?'

'A kinsman of mine seeks a place at Court and as there is one at this time in the Bedchamber it would give me the greatest pleasure to offer him that.'

Deeply moved the King answered: 'My dear friend, dispose of the place as you deem fit. And remember this: I shall never suffer any to rise in my favour except that he may thank you for it.'

This was victory. Robert wept with affection and relief; and both he and James were happy because it seemed to them that their love was as firm as it ever had been.

There was disappointment in the Pembroke faction when it was known that the Bedchamber post had gone to Somerset's nephew.

'It seems,' said Sir Thomas Lake, 'that Somerset has not lost a jot of the King's favour.'

'James always clung to his old friends,' agreed Pembroke; 'but he is taken with young Villiers and we must not lose heart. I am going to see the Queen.'

Anne received him, as always, with pleasure and he immediately told her what he wanted of her.

'Somerset is becoming unbearably arrogant, Your Majesty.'

Anne nodded her agreement, being always ready to listen to criticism of Somerset.

'There is only one way of clipping his wings, and that is to turn the King's affection to another.'

'And have another ape Somerset, become as overbearing?'

'Villiers is young as yet.'

'Do not think that youth is less arrogant than middle age. Promote this young man, my lord, and I tell you he will soon be despising us as Somerset does.'

'This young man is of a different nature. He is more ready to learn.'

'He'll not be for long.'

'If he should in time grow like Somerset that time is far distant, Your Majesty. He could not become so powerful for years, and we must bring Somerset down or submit to his rule.'

'You are right in that,' Anne sighed. 'What do you wish me to do?'

'Present him to the King. Tell him that you ask this favour of him, which is a knighthood for George Villiers and a place in the Bedchamber.'

'There was a place in the Bedchamber.'

'Gone to Somerset's nephew, Your Majesty. Soon there will be no post at Court which is not occupied by one of Somerset's men.'

'Well,' said Anne, 'I think you are right in that.' She hesitated. 'I will do as you wish,' she went on, 'and I shall ask Prince Charles to give me his support.'

This was victory. The King was longing to give honours to Villiers; and if the Queen asked a favour how could he refuse her – particularly when it was one which it would please him so much to bestow?

It was St George's Day and outside the King's bedchamber George Villiers waited with his patrons. With James were the Queen and Prince Charles and it was known that the Queen was going to ask a favour of her husband.

At last the summons for Villiers to enter the bedchamber was given and the young man went in.

Robert who had heard a rumour of what was about to happen could not believe it until he came to the door of the King's bedchamber and saw a group of his enemies there – among them the excited young man on whom he knew they had fixed their hopes. He was in time to hear the summons and see the handsome youth walk into the bedchamber, and an impulse came to him to push them aside, to stride into the bedchamber, to upbraid the King before them all; but he remembered James' words when he had not very long ago awakened him at what the King called an unseasonable hour. James had warned him then.

But how could he stand by and see this young man made a Gentleman of the Bedchamber when he had shown the King so clearly that he resented the office being given.

He curbed his anger. Frances would have spurred him on, but she was not with him now; and when he had to make his own decisions he was never as fiery as she would have him be.

He wrote a hasty message to the King, asking James to make Villiers a Groom of the Bedchamber instead of a Gentleman, if he must grant the Queen's favour and give the young man some office.

Haughtily he called a page and bade him take the message to the King.

James received it, read it and thought sadly: Will he never learn his lesson?

He then knighted George Villiers and appointed him one of the Gentlemen of the Bedchamber.

That ambitious man, Sir George Villiers, had no wish to quarrel with the Earl of Somerset who still held the highest offices in the Kingdom. George Villiers knew that he had a long way to go before he was as powerful. If he could make a truce with Somerset, let him know that he had not thought of attempting to step into his place, he was sure he would more quickly climb in the King's favour.

He therefore sought an interview with Somerset. When he heard who was asking to see him Robert was angry, with the most violent of all anger – that born of fear.

The fellow must be sure of himself, since he asked an audience of him. Who did he think he was? Did he imagine that because he was a Gentleman of the Bedchamber he could become on friendly terms with the most important ministers?

Villiers came to him, his handsome face wearing an expression of humility.

'My lord,' he said, 'it is good of you to grant me this interview. I come to ask that I may serve you in whatever way you choose for me so to do. I have always wanted to take my preferment under your favour. I offer myself to you as your most humble servant.'

Robert's anger was suddenly uncontrollable, because he saw himself in this young man, as he had been in those early days when the King had become so enchanted by his grace and beauty. It was a cruel thing to be asked to witness oneself on the decline, the new star about to rise.

'Get you gone from my presence,' he said, his mouth tight, his eyes smouldering. 'You shall enjoy no friendship or favour from me. One thing I will give you – and that is sound advice. Listen, fellow. Attempt to come creeping to me again and I'll break your neck.'

'So this is how you keep your promises to me?' stormed Robert.

'My promises to you?' answered James. 'What mean you? What did I promise and not give you?'

'You have taken that young fool into the Bedchamber.'

'I am the King. I select my own Gentleman, you should know.'

'Gentleman! And who is this gentleman?'

'If you refer to Sir George Villiers, I'd say he was as good a gentleman as Robert Carr was when he first came to Court.'

'I asked you, if you *must* favour him, to make him a Groom.'

James was stern. 'I wished to make him a Gentleman, and must I remind you again that I am the King?'

But Robert could not curb his anger. He was worried about Frances. He was beginning to feel that he was married to a woman whom he did not know. He was losing his hold on the King. His whole world had become insecure; and he was alarmed, though he did not entirely know why. He needed the advice of shrewd men; but those who had advised and befriended him were dead. Northampton! Overbury!

The memory of Overbury depressed him more than ever.

He cried out: 'You are untrue to your promises. You have not dealt fairly with me.'

'Robert,' said James, and there was more sadness than

anger in his voice, 'I dismiss you now. Go to your own apartments, and do not come to me again until you remember that
though I have humbled myself in my regard for you, I am the
King of this realm and as such your master.'

'You have turned against me.'

James laid a hand on Robert's arm.

'Nay. Cast off your sullenness, throw away your tempers.
Only do that and you shall see that my love for you has not
changed. I am a faithful man, Robert; but I cannot say how
long my love for you will last if you goad me so. Go now and
think on what I have said. Reflect well, Robert. Be my good
friend once more and you shall see that my love for you has
not diminished.'

Robert left the King and, pacing up and down his room, he
realized how foolish he had been.

James was his friend and James was a faithful man. He
might in time feel a great affection for Villiers, but that need
not affect his love for Robert Carr. He must be sympathetic,
understanding; he must not give way to these nervous
tempers.

He held the Privy Seal; he was the Lord Chamberlain; he
was still the most powerful man in the Kingdom.

He must regain his old sweet temper; he must explain to
Frances that although the King loved him and had given him
his great possessions, he would be a fool to continue to bully
James who had hinted that he could not endure much more
of it; he must be wise, calm, serene.

And when he endeavoured to be so, James was his
affectionate self once more.

But he was beginning to smile rather fondly on Sir George
Villiers – not, he wanted everyone to know, that this interest
in the young and charming man in any way changed his abid-
ing affection towards my lord Somerset.

James was happier than he had been for some time. He was
delighted with the new young man whom he had nicknamed
Steenie because of his likeness to St Stephen; and Robert was
being his old self, understanding that the friendship between

them was too deep to be disturbed by a new fancy.

James had been on a tour of the South, for it was necessary to show himself to his people from time to time, and was resting at Beaulieu when he heard that Sir Ralph Winwood had ridden from London because he wished to speak to him on an urgent matter.

James had never greatly cared for Winwood but he believed him to be a good minister and he received him at once.

Winwood seemed over-excited and it must, thought James, be news of some importance to have brought him so far to tell it, since James would shortly be returning to London.

'Your Majesty,' began Winwood, 'a strange rumour has come to my ears and it disturbs me so much that I could not rest until I had laid it before you.'

'Let us hear what it is,' said James.

'It comes from Flushing, Your Majesty, where an English boy has recently died in great distress on account of a crime he helped to commit in England.'

'What boy is this?'

'He was an assistant to Dr Paul de Lobel, Your Majesty, and he declares that Sir Thomas Overbury died by foul means in the Tower and that he was bribed to poison the clyster which was administered to him.'

'Ha!' laughed James. 'There are always rumours of this sort.'

'This seemed more than a rumour, Sire. The boy was in great distress and made a full confession on his death bed; he mentions certain people in connexion with the case and I believe there to be such persons living in London as those he named.'

'What persons are these?'

'A jailer of the Tower, and a Dr Franklin . . . a man of shady character, Your Majesty, even perhaps a dabbler in witch-craft.'

At the mention of witchcraft James' face darkened.

'Look into this matter, Winwood,' he said, 'and report to me what you find.'

The Little Fish are Caught

SINCE THE marriage of the Earl and Countess of Somerset, life had been good for Anne Turner. When she awoke in her luxurious bed in some palace or large country house she thanked the day Jennet had brought Lady Essex to her. Anne was a beautiful woman, a fact which had not been so obvious when she was living obscurely in Hammersmith as it was now that she was at Court.

She had even become a leader of fashion and many women had taken up the yellow ruffs which she wore because, as they were so becoming to her, they believed they would be to them.

It was a good life, and all because she had done an inestimable service to a rich and noble lady. Frances would never forget; in fact Anne was determined that she should not, and although she never reminded her that they had committed murder together, she made sure that Frances remembered.

Frances was her friend and patron and she had become one of the many ladies in the retinue of the Somersets. She saw the good life stretching out ahead of her and was determined never to return to Hammersmith.

Her servants came to dress her, and while she sat at her mirror and they arranged her beautiful hair, they chattered to her of Court gossip because she always encouraged them to do this. It was important to carry little scraps of information to the Countess; and now that Sir George Villiers was becoming so prominent, Frances always liked to hear the latest news regarding him.

This day they had another piece of gossip.

One of the maids had a lover who was servant to Sir Ralph Winwood, and Sir Ralph had just returned from a visit to the King. He had left in a great hurry it seemed, and when he had returned had been very busy. He had had long and secret talks with several people – but servants were the great detectives and secrets could not long be kept from them.

'Such a pother, madam,' said the maid, 'and it seems that it concerns a long dead gentleman. He died in the Tower and it was by poison.'

Anne had begun to watch the maid's face in the mirror, but the girl did not notice how fixedly she stared.

'They're going to find out who poisoned him. They're going to follow up the trail because he was once a very important Court gentleman, a friend of my lord Somerset, no less.'

Anne stood up; she was afraid the girl would see that her face had whitened.

'Did you hear this gentleman's name mentioned?' she asked, trying to make her voice sound casual.

'Oh yes, madam. It was Sir Thomas Overbury.'

Since Frances had known that she was pregnant she had felt more at peace. It was true that Sir George Villiers had cast a shadow over her security and would have to be watched; but she felt equal to deal with that young upstart. Each passing week, she reminded herself, took her farther from the divorce and the death of Overbury.

Therefore she was unprepared for the news Anne Turner brought her. As soon as she saw Anne's face she knew that something important was wrong and her heart began to pound with terror.

Anne looked over her shoulder to make sure they were alone.

'No one can overhear,' said Frances.

'A most distressing rumour. Winwood is investigating Overbury's death.'

Frances stared at Anne for the moment, unable to speak, so great was her horror.

'My maid was chattering about it.'

'Maids' gossip.'

'Her lover serves Winwood. I do not think we can afford to ignore this, even if it is only gossip.'

'But why . . . in God's name why . . . *now* . . . after all this time?'

Anne shook her head. 'We must act quickly . . . I think.'

'How?'

'It is certain that Weston will be interrogated. He was his jailer at the time.'

Frances nodded. 'You must see him, Anne. You must make sure that he will know exactly what to say, or I fear he will betray us all.'

'Thank God you have good friends.'

Good friends! – thought Frances. Northampton dead. Robert in ignorance of the plot in which he was involved – and Sir George Villiers standing by, ready to snatch his power.

'Go, Anne,' she said urgently. 'Go at once to see Weston. Warn him. It is always better to be warned.'

In a tavern some miles from London a lady in a cloak, the hood of which partly concealed her face, impatiently waited in the room which the innkeeper had set aside for her to receive her guest.

A Court lady, mused the innkeeper. One could always tell. And this was a secret assignation with a lover. The innkeeper was not displeased. This might be the beginning of a succession of visits from Court ladies and gentlemen; it would be well to let them know that he was an innkeeper who could be discreet.

When the lady's guest arrived he proved to be a disappointment for he was a somewhat shabby fellow. Was the lady having a love affair with her groom? Perhaps this was the reason why they must meet well away from the Court.

Anne's reception of Richard Weston was certainly unlike that of a woman receiving her lover.

'Weston,' she cried, 'so at last you are here! I thought you would never come.'

'You are distressed, madam.'

'So will you be when you hear what I have to tell. We shall all be more than distressed if we do not take the utmost care.'

Certainly he was not. So he took up his pen. He wrote with fire and venom and the verses he produced were called *The Wife*.

These were aimed at the Countess of Essex, and anyone with a slight knowledge of her background and history would know this.

These verses were circulated, not only at the Mermaid Club but throughout the Court.

When Frances read the verses she was furious. Soon he might be openly talking of her. He was a clever man; he had shown that he had already begun to ferret into her past, and there was too much that was unsavoury to be discovered there.

She had little to fear from Essex. While they were at Court he had discovered that his wife was conducting a love affair with Carr, and at last understood that her repulsion to living as his wife had nothing to do with her innocence; it was simply that she wished to be the mistress of another man. He had learned too that the Prince of Wales had been her lover, and it was no innocent virgin whom he had taken to Chartley.

Disillusioned, feeling he had been rather foolish, having listened to vague warnings from Wilson whose judgement he trusted, he had come to believe that he would be well rid of such a woman. He had found comfort in hunting and other outdoor sports with friends of his own sex, and when he heard that Frances was desirous of divorcing him, he shrugged his shoulders and thought that it might be good to be free of her and in time find a wife who was ready to lead a normal life with him.

They had scarcely seen each other for some little time, and now that she believed she would soon be free of him, Frances rarely thought of him.

But another ogre has risen in his place: Sir Thomas Overbury.

She could not tell her lover of her fears because he would laugh at them, not understanding what harm Overbury might do if he discovered too much. Robert would not know how much there was to be discovered. But there was one she knew who would not be shocked by her villainies, providing they could be suppressed and did not cause open scandal; and now that he was working with her, would be ready to use his great power to suppress them. This was her great-uncle, the Earl of Northampton. So to him she went.

He read through *The Wife* and regarded his great-niece severely.

'Yes,' he said, 'this man could make trouble – great trouble.'

'It is for us to see that he does not,' answered Frances.

'You have been very indiscreet.'

'Perhaps. But I am where I am, and it is not for you to reproach me, for you are glad that I am there.'

What a wild creature she was! thought Northampton. Young and inexperienced as she was, and old and experienced as he was, he would not care to have her for an enemy.

'H'm,' he said after a pause. 'We must put an end to this man's activities.'

'I have already tried to do this.'

Northampton's eyebrows shot up. 'What?' he cried.

'I offered a certain man a thousand pounds to engage him in a duel and kill him.'

'My dear niece, you are too impulsive. What man?'

'Sir David Woods, who I knew hated him because he was sure that it was due to Overbury that Robert refused him a post he coveted.'

'And what did he say?'

'He said it was too dangerous, and that only if Robert himself commanded him to do it and would promise him his patronage when it was done, would he undertake it.'

'And Robert?'

Frances laughed. 'It is clear that you do not know Robert. He is so innocent. There is much he does not understand.'

Northampton looked intently into his great-niece's face. 'I believe that,' he said.

She shook herself impatiently. 'Oh, come, it is not for you

to preach to me. Do you think I do not know you take bribes from Spain?'

'Hush, niece, hush.'

'Then do not look as though I am the only sinful member of the family. My mother takes bribes and lovers. And you—'

He held up his hand and looked over his shoulder. 'My dear Frances, be discreet if you can. I am not blaming you for what you have done. I am only asking you to observe the decency to see that you are not found out.'

'That is what I am trying to do. That is why I want an end of Overbury.'

Northampton was thoughtful.

'We must, I think,' he said at length, 'find some means of sending him to the Tower. Safely there he would have little hope of making mischief.'

'Robert would never agree.'

'Robert has quarrelled with him, I believe.'

'Oh, yes, but Robert is still grateful to him. He says he is his friend. The quarrels take place when that snake Overbury reviles *me*. Robert refuses to listen – and for that I must be thankful. Robert thinks Overbury is jealous and you know how indulgent he always is. Please understand this: Robert must be made to see that some action should be taken against Overbury. That is where you come in. If I try to explain he will think I am afraid of the slander Overbury is spreading about *me*. You must make Robert understand.'

'How?'

'That is for you to decide. After all, you stand to gain a great deal from this marriage, do you not?'

Northampton had to admit that that was true.

Northampton made sure that none could overhear their conversation when he opened the subject with Robert in the latter's apartments.

'This man Overbury alarms me,' admitted Northampton.

'Tom? Oh, he has got a little beyond himself, I'll grant you,' said Robert with a laugh. 'He'll calm down.'

'I believe he has uttered insults against my great-niece.'

'For which,' went on Robert, 'I find it hard to forgive him. But he has been a very close friend of mine and I fear he is a little jealous.'

'Robert, you are too good-hearted. You look at evil and see it for good.'

'There is nothing evil in Tom Overbury.'

'It depends on what you call evil. I hear he boasts of his activities and tells his friends that your rise to fame is due to him.'

'We must not take too seriously what he says at this time.'

'But it is serious, Robert. He is against the divorce and your marriage and he has said that he will stop at nothing to prevent it.'

Robert looked shaken. 'Has he said that then?'

'More. He is circulating lies about Frances. That is something I cannot forgive.'

'Nor I,' added Robert quickly.

'In fact, he is dangerous. I know he has been a good servant to you in the past, but he is so no longer. I think we should teach him a lesson. He should have his anger cooled.'

'I will speak to him.'

'You will but fan the flames, Robert. There is one other matter that I have in mind. There were unpleasant rumours at the time the Prince of Wales died; and it was well known that you and he were not fond of each other.'

'He seemed always to seek to bait me.'

'And people whisper that not long before his death he was a strong and healthy man. How was it, they say, that he took sick and died so suddenly?'

'He died of a wasting disease aggravated by a fever.'

'There are some people in London, not far from Whitehall, who know how to make a victim appear to die of a wasting disease.'

'What are you suggesting?'

'I speak of rumours that have come to my ears. If Overbury gave the word, those rumours would carry a great deal of weight.'

'You cannot think that *I* had a hand in the Prince's death?'

'I do not think so. Rumour does not always have to be truth, Robert. At one time the Prince was in love with Frances; the Prince died and she became your mistress. That is not generally known. The King does not know it. He believes that you and Frances have fallen in love because her husband is impotent. He is sorry for you and wants to help you. A little scandal now and who knows what would happen? Who knows who would be accused of what? Overbury is in the mood to make that scandal. He is an arrogant self-opinionated man, Robert. We have to be careful of him. I suggest that if we could put him away . . . oh, only for a week or two . . . just while he cools down . . . well then life would be a great deal happier for all of us.'

Robert was thoughtful. 'If he is going to make mischief—'

'He is making it fast. It should not be difficult to get him a spell in the Tower.'

'But he was my friend . . . still is. I feel I should explain to him.'

'Robert, this is not a matter to be explained. Let us endeavour to get him into the Tower. When he comes to his senses it will be an easy matter to have him released.'

Robert's expression was unhappy. Northampton laid his hand on his arm.

'Think about it,' he said. 'But do not delay too long.'

Robert could not reconcile himself to the plot to get Overbury imprisoned in the Tower. He could not forget their friendship and was certain that Overbury would eventually give up this ridiculous plan to prevent the divorce.

An idea came to him when James was sending new ambassadors to the Low Countries and France. Why not send Tom? It would be good experience for him; he was fully qualified to make a success of the mission; and it would remove him from the scene while the divorce was being arranged.

When Robert suggested this to Northampton he thought it an excellent idea and lost no time in putting it before the King.

James had never greatly liked Overbury. He felt he had too much influence with Robert and was overbearing; Robert had found him a useful secretary, but James had heard how the man boasted of his own importance.

'We shall appoint Sir Thomas Overbury to the Low Countries,' said James. 'Or if he would prefer it, to France. I think he should do well in the post.'

As a result Overbury was summoned by the Lord Chancellor, Lord Ellesmore, and the Earl of Pembroke to come to them to hear the King's wishes.

Overbury, rather startled by the order, was unprepared for the suggestion which was offered.

'Ambassador to the Low Countries or France!' he cried. 'No thank you! I prefer to remain in my own country.'

The eyebrows of the Lord Chancellor were raised in astonishment. 'But it is the King's wish that you should undertake this office.'

'My health is not good enough for me to undertake it.'

'I am surprised,' said the Chancellor, 'for I thought that you were in excellent health.'

'I should not be for long if I went abroad.'

Pembroke said: 'Sir Thomas, you would be ill-advised to refuse this offer. I do believe it to be a prelude to a post in the royal household, perhaps Treasurer. The King wishes to satisfy himself that you would serve him well.'

'The King knows I would serve a master well.'

'Then why do you not give him this further assurance?'

'Because I have no desire to leave England at this time.'

'Is that your final word?'

'You may take it as that.'

When an account of this interview was taken back to the King, he was annoyed.

'I like not the stiff carriage of his fortune,' grumbled James. 'This is an arrogant man. He boasts that he rules the Court and country. He has boasted too often. This is a matter of contempt and punishable by imprisonment. He should not think that I shall allow this to pass.'

Overbury was writing at his table when he heard the tramp of feet outside his door.

He looked up surprised when the door was flung open and he saw the guards there.

'Sir Thomas Overbury,' said the leader. 'I come on the King's command to arrest you.'

Overbury was on his feet spluttering his indignation. 'On what charge?'

'Contempt of the King's royal person,' was the answer.

'I protest. You cannot do this. Call Viscount Rochester.'

The answer was to show the warrant for his arrest.

There was nothing to be done. He could only follow them, out of the Palace, down to the waiting barge.

Along the river they went to the grim grey fortress.

Overbury's heart was heavy with foreboding as he entered the precincts of the Tower of London.

'Overbury is in the Tower!'

The news spread through the Court.

And could not Rochester save him? Did this mean that Rochester was losing his place? Who would step into his shoes?

Robert was dismayed. It had happened so quickly. He wished that he could have saved Overbury from that. It seemed strange because it was exactly what Northampton had wanted to happen. But it was disconcerting to think of poor old Tom in a cell.

He would speak to the King. James had surely acted in a moment of anger, for Tom was too arrogant; he did have too high an opinion of his importance; he really should have taken the post in the Low Countries. He could have come home after a reasonable time.

Robert would have spoken to the King but Northampton, who made a point of seeing him at once, advised him not to.

'Why, Robert,' he said, 'this is the best thing that could have happened. Let him cool his heels against a stout stone wall for a while. It'll do him good. We'll go ahead with the divorce and when that little matter is done with Tom Overbury shall come from prison, a wiser man, I'll promise you.'

Robert could see the reason in that; so he did not speak to the King of Sir Thomas Overbury.

Frances called on Anne Turner at Hammersmith. She looked radiantly beautiful as she embraced her friend.

'Good news, Anne,' she cried. 'Overbury is exactly where we wanted him to be. In the Tower.'

Anne clapped her hands with pleasure. 'That's the best news I've heard for a long time.'

'And not before it was necessary,' went on Frances. 'The man was becoming a menace, I can tell you.'

'That scum of men!'

'Yes, he was determined to make trouble. He had his spies. He was ready to malign me. Anything to turn Robert from me. And that is something I should not endure.'

'I should think not – after all you have done to win his love and keep it!'

Frances sighed. 'I must have more charms, for he is ready to be deterred at the slightest trouble.'

'My poor sweet lady! What trials are yours! Yes, you must continue to hold him.'

'I fear that Robert may visit him there. I fear that he may bring about his release. I also fear what he has discovered. I suspect him of bribing the secrets from people who are willing to sell them. He could stop the divorce. He intends to. Why, if he brought to the King's notice—'

Anne shivered. 'He must be prevented.'

'The King hates and fears witchcraft.'

Anne nodded.

'If he thought that I—'

'My sweet lady, you are over-wrought. He shall never know.'

'How can we be sure?'

'By keeping Overbury in the Tower until he dies.'

'Until he dies,' repeated Frances.

She was staring with wide eyes at her friend. She had made up her mind then. Overbury must not leave the Tower alive.

Murder in the Tower

THE EARL OF ESSEX was astonished – not that his wife desired a divorce, but by the reason she gave for wanting it. She accused him of impotence! He was angry. How dared she make such a statement when she had never given him an opportunity of proving whether he was or not!

If there was any justice in the land she would soon be discovered to be a liar.

Arthur Wilson, who had become his confidant, was not displeased by the news. He believed that he had, by his vigilance, prevented the Earl being poisoned at his wife's order. If Essex was divorced – no matter by what means – he would escape for ever from the evil influence of that woman; he could marry and live a normal life, and that, Wilson believed, would be a very desirable state of affairs.

'My lord,' he said, 'consider this: to be free of the Countess would be the best thing that could happen to you.'

'You are right.'

'Well then, if you stand in the way of this divorce, you will be bound to her for the rest of your life; and while this is so, I am convinced that you are in danger.'

Essex said: 'You have heard the complaint against me?'

Wilson shrugged his shoulders. 'When you are free of her, when you marry again, your children will prove the woman a liar. It will be too late then for them to act upon the discovery. You will be free from her.'

'It would be a great relief to know that I was no longer bound to her.'

'To us both, my lord. I should not have to keep watch for some evil she might do you.'

The Earl laid his hand on Wilson's shoulder. 'I owe you much, my friend,' he said.

'There is no talk of owing, my lord. I give my services for what they are, with all my heart and strength; and in return – but there is no need for returns – I have your friendship. So if there must be talk of payments between friends, we have each given and each taken.'

'God bless you, Wilson.'

'And, my lord, you will not stand in the way of this divorce?'

'I long for my freedom even as you long for me to have it. I shall have to answer questions, doubtless, and must tell the truth; but I shall let all know that I am as eager to sever the bond as she is.'

'Then, my lord, for the first time I shall hope and pray that the Countess succeeds in what she is endeavouring to do.'

The King summoned the Archbishop of Canterbury, a man for whom he had a great admiration.

George Abbot had risen to the highest post in the Church by his great ability, a fact which endeared him to James. He had sprung from humble beginnings, being the son of a cloth worker of Guildford, and had been born in a small cottage. But from the first his brilliance had been apparent although it was commonplace in this family, for George had two brothers, both extremely clever and destined to make their way in the world; but even in such a family George was able to shine.

He had gone to Oxford, taken Holy Orders and very quickly displayed his extraordinary gifts; and, in spite of his lack of family background, over the years he began steadily to rise in his profession until he attained the Bishopric of London.

Brought up in a strictly Puritan manner he had always clung firmly to his principles; James appreciated his integrity and it was his ability to discuss theology which had attracted the King's interest.

When the Archbishopric of Canterbury had fallen vacant. Abbot was more surprised than any that James should have bestowed it on him, although he had supporters in Salisbury, who was then the Lord High Treasurer, and the Lord Chancellor Ellesmore, as well as a rising statesman named Sir Ralph Winwood. It was natural that he should have his enemies also, and these were those who were the secret friends of Spain, led by the Earl of Northampton.

As soon as the Archbishop had arrived at Whitehall James explained to him why he had summoned him.

'My lord Archbishop,' he said, 'the Countess of Essex is seeking to divorce her husband.'

Abbot's mouth tightened; as a Puritan he did not approve of divorce.

'It is a special case,' went on James. 'It seems the Earl is impotent.'

'Your Majesty, I feel bound to express my abhorrence of divorce.'

James waved a hand. 'We all share that abhorrence,' he said quickly. 'But there are times when it is necessary to undertake unpleasant tasks. I wish you to judge the matter and see that the Countess is freed from a union which can find no favour in the eyes of God who commands us to be fruitful and replenish the Earth.'

'Your Majesty . . .'

'I explained that the Earl is impotent and how can the Countess obey that divine command if her husband is incapable of the act?'

'Your Majesty is commanding me—'

'To look into the matter and grant the divorce.'

'Your Majesty, if I am to be judge of such a matter, I beg that other bishops may be summoned to help me.'

James considered this.

It would mean a little delay before Robbie got his wish, but it would be interesting to see the Bishops wrangling together. He would make it understood what their verdict should be, for Robbie must not be disappointed; but it was a fair enough request and one must always be fair.

'Well, whom do you suggest?'

Abbot thought quickly. 'The Bishops of London, Ely and Lichfield I think, and perhaps others.'

James nodded. Yes, it would be amusing to hear them arguing together. Abbot would be a stumbling block, for even though the King made his wishes known he would not go against his beliefs. He was that sort of man. James' ancestor Henry VIII might have had him sent to the Tower, but not James. James had to respect a man's principles – particularly if he had the powers to express them.

He chuckled. He was going to look forward to the arguments; but at the same time he was determined that Robbie was not to be cheated of his wish.

'Go to,' he said. 'Form your Commission. And let there be no delay, for I am eager to see this unsavoury matter settled.'

Frances was disturbed by nightmares; but they were not merely dreams; they had their roots in fact and sometimes she would start out of her sleep remembering some dream, only to realize that the evil of her dream could, by ill-chance, in fact overtake her.

One morning she woke, sweating with fear. Overbury was in the Tower but he was a man who had lived by his pen; he would still be able to use it; and she had dreamed that he had done so against her, with dire results.

Overbury must not be allowed to live; but his death must seem a natural one. He must not suddenly die; his health must be noticed gradually to deteriorate. In the meantime he must be stopped from writing letters to those who could use them against her. She already knew that the Archbishop of Canterbury had been put in charge of the Commission and she was well aware of that old Puritan's views.

They could not afford to take chances.

She went at once to her great-uncle, with whom she was spending more time than she ever had before; over this matter of the divorce they had become fellow conspirators.

'Uncle,' she said, 'we must make sure that any letters Overbury writes shall not reach those for whom they're intended until they have passed through our hands.'

Northampton saw the point of this at once. He did not know how far his great-niece had gone in her attempts to rid herself of Essex; and he did not care to probe because he preferred not to know. At the same time he was as anxious as she was that her past adventures should remain secret.

'How can we make sure the correspondence comes straight to us?' asked Frances.

'Only through the Lieutenant of the Tower.'

'Can you speak to him?'

'I must see what can be done, for we must examine any letters Overbury writes. Leave this to me.'

The Lieutenant of the Tower received the Earl of Northampton in his apartments there.

Sir William Waad, a man of about sixty, who had travelled widely on diplomatic missions and had been Member of Parliament for Thetford, Preston and West Looe was not a man to be intimidated; and he quickly grasped what was behind the Earl of Northampton's request.

'My lord,' he said, with a quiet smile, 'I should be exceeding my duties if I were to pass over to you the correspondence of my prisoners.'

'But this is a special case.'

'Then perhaps the King will give me his orders. I cannot take them from any but His Majesty.'

Northampton was furious. This fool was going to give trouble. How could he go to James and tell him that he wanted to study the letters of Thomas Overbury before they were allowed to reach their destination? Obviously James would want to hear why. Overbury was not in the Tower as a traitor. He had merely shown contempt of the King's orders and was in there to cool his heels for a while. James would be astonished that his correspondence should be so important to his Lord Privy Seal and, being of a curious nature, would want to know why.

'I must see the King on this matter then?' asked Northampton, and his smile was steely.

'That is so, my lord.'

Very well, you old fool, thought Northampton. This shall
be the end of you.

James could always be moved into action by his fear of plots,
and Northampton decided to exploit this in order to secure
Overbury's correspondence.

He sought a private audience of the King and when they
were alone said: 'I paid a visit to the Tower this day, Your
Majesty, and discovered something which greatly disconcerted me!'

'What's this?' asked James.

'The Lady Arabella has been given a key so that she can
leave her apartments there at will. I have to tell your Majesty
that I consider this highly dangerous.'

'Has there been an attempt to rescue her?'

'Not so far, Your Majesty, but I shall have to be very watchful. I have not yet uncovered anything, but I am very suspicious of a Lieutenant who gives such a lady a key.
Particularly when I remember that he was the man who allowed Lady Arabella's husband to escape.'

'I like that not,' murmured James.

'Nay, Your Majesty, and so much am I in agreement with
you that I have been asking myself, since I discovered this
alarming fact, whether it is wise to allow a man, who has
given the lady the key, to continue to be her jailor.'

'You suspect Waad of treachery?'

'I would not go so far as that, Your Majesty. But since she
has beguiled him into giving her a key, I do not feel very much
at peace while that man is in charge of the Tower.'

'Nay, nor I.'

'Would Your Majesty consider it wise to relieve Waad of
his post? If so, I know the man who would fill his place
admirably.'

'Who is this?'

'Sir Gervase Helwys. Your Majesty may remember knighting

him some time in 1603, I believe. A lawyer and a good fellow. Some years younger than that old fool Waad, but still of sober years. Would Your Majesty care for me to summon him that you might judge for yourself?'

James hesitated and Northampton went on: 'He is a man of some means and ready to pay fourteen hundred pounds for the office.'

'Is that so?' said James. 'We could do with the money.'

'I will send Sir Gervase to Your Majesty and when you have given the word I shall have great pleasure in sending that dotard Waad about his business. I shall sleep the happier in my bed of nights to know that he can no longer plot with Lady Arabella.'

It was thus that Sir William Waad was dismissed from the Tower and his place taken by Sir Gervase Helwys, a man determined to serve his patrons, the Howards, who had helped to advance his fortunes.

The Archbishop of Canterbury met the Earl of Northampton in one of the ante-rooms of Whitehall Palace.

'I like not this matter,' the Archbishop said.

'This matter of the divorce?' replied Northampton. 'Why not? It would appear to be a straightforward matter.'

'The severing of a bond between those whom God hath joined together is never a straightforward matter.'

'Come, come, the King has expressed a wish that this matter should be speedily dealt with.'

'I cannot advise my bishops that this should be so. There is a great deal to consider. I have had an opportunity of speaking to my Lord Essex.'

'And he has denied the charge of impotency? Oh, come, my lord Archbishop, what worldly young man would willingly admit such a handicap?'

'He has said that although he has no desire to be a husband to Lady Essex, he would make a good husband for some other lady.'

'What is he implying? That some bewitchment makes him impotent with his wife?'

'I know not, my lord Earl. But I tell you this: I like not this case. Nor do I think it is one which can be settled in a hurry.'

Northampton stamped off in a rage. When he saw his niece he told her that the old Archbishop was against the divorce and they could be sure that he would do everything in his power to delay matters.

Frances was growing anxious. She was terrified of the power of Overbury so she went to see Anne Turner to tell her that something must be done quickly or she would be out of her mind.

'Who knows,' she cried, 'what stories he will tell about me? He came to this house. He will have made inquiries about our friends. How much does that man know about us?'

'We must get to work on him at once.'

'Most speedily. What has Gresham been doing?'

'Alas, my lady, he is very sick. I visited his house in Thames Street but the other day to find him on his death bed. He is certain it is the end and he knows these things.'

'But what can we do now?'

'Do not imagine that, discovering this, I did not get to work immediately. Dr Forman and Dr Gresham are not the only wise men in London. I summoned Richard Weston who was an assistant to my late husband and something of an apothecary himself. He mentioned Dr Franklin to me, and I remembered hearing my husband and Dr Forman talk of him. He is a clever man, and shall I say more inclined to take a little risk than Dr Forman was.'

'Then that is good. We have come to that stage when to take a risk is a necessity. I shall not sleep peacefully until Overbury is dead.'

Anne Turner lowered her eyes. Although murder was in their thoughts, they did not often mention it; and it was an indication of the Countess' state of mind that she did so now.

'My dear friend,' said Anne Turner, 'I know your feelings and I am with you in everything you do. Already I have spoken to Dr Franklin and he understands exactly. He will supply us with what we need, but he says it is necessary that his medicine be administered regularly and over a certain period.'

'That's true,' agreed Frances. 'If Overbury were to die suddenly there would be an outcry and heaven knows where that would lead.'

'Dr Franklin suggests that it be arranged for one of our servants to be introduced into the Tower to wait on the creature and so make sure that what is sent in is given to him and none other.'

'It's an excellent idea. Who? . . .'

'Who but Richard Weston. He is willing, provided you are prepared to pay him well.'

Frances said quickly: 'You know I am. I will pay handsomely for what I want.'

'Then, my dear friend, we have nothing to fear. The way is clear before us. From the moment Richard Weston is in the Tower, we shall begin the work.'

Frances left Hammersmith slightly appeased; she always felt better when she was able to take action.

The next day Frances called on Sir Thomas Monson in the Tower of London. Sir Thomas was the Master of the Armoury and since he had come to Court had been a minor favourite of the King. This had meant promotion which had culminated in the recent bestowal of a baronetcy and the post he now held at the Tower.

He was delighted to see the Countess of Essex because he knew that she was trying to obtain a divorce from her husband and that when she did so would marry Viscount Rochester.

There was one person at Court with whom a man must be on good terms if he hoped for promotion, and that was Viscount Rochester, who was now constantly at the King's side, and it seemed that any applications for any Court post must have his approbation. Naturally if one would please Rochester, one must please the Countess; and Monson could not help being pleasantly excited by a visit from this beautiful young woman who smiled at him so affably.

'I am greatly honoured to receive a visit from my lady,' he murmured, kissing her hand.

'Well, Sir Thomas, I have heard so much of you from my uncle Northampton and my lord Rochester that I wished to speak with you.'

Monson's delight was increased.

'I hear that you perform your duties with great skill and that Sir Gervase Helwys is delighted with his Master of Armoury.'

'Is that so, Lady Essex? I am delighted.'

'And so you should be. I often think of the poor prisoners shut up in this place and shiver for them.'

'You should not distress yourself. Most of them deserve their punishment.'

'I know. But it must be hard to be a prisoner. You have a man here who once served my lord Rochester. How different life must be for him now!'

'You refer to Sir Thomas Overbury?'

'That is the man. My lord Rochester is working for his release.'

'Then I am sure he will soon be free.'

She laughed. 'Oh, not too soon.' The man must not think that Robert could not bring about Overbury's release tomorrow if he wished it. It must not even be presumed for a moment that he was losing his influence with the King. 'I can see you are a perceptive man, Sir Thomas, and that is why I have come to you. I feel – and my lord Rochester feels – that you will readily understand.'

The man looked so gratified that Frances almost laughed aloud.

'You must realize, Sir Thomas,' she went on, 'that Overbury became a little overbearing. I fear he was inclined to think himself more important than he was.'

Monson nodded.

'And my lord Rochester feared for him, because he was making enemies.'

Monson again nodded.

'Therefore, for his own good, this seemed a painful necessity. But I do assure you that it is one which troubles my lord
Rochester as much as it does his one-time servant.'

'My lord Rochester is known to be of a kind and generous
nature.'

'It is true that he has the kindest and most generous nature
in the world. That is why he is so concerned for his friend. He
wants to assure himself that he is well cared for, and to send
him a servant who, we can assure ourselves, will look after his
comforts while he is in the doleful prison.'

'An excellent thought.'

'A man of your sensibilities will grasp the fact that my lord
Rochester does not wish Overbury to know that it is he who
is sending the servant. If he did he would understand that this
imprisonment is . . . not to be taken seriously. You understand
me?'

'Yes, Lady Essex.'

'We should be grateful to you if you would write to Sir
Gervase Helwys and tell him a man named Richard Weston
will come and wait personally on Sir Thomas Overbury. You
might mention . . . not in your letter . . . but perhaps hint it . . .
that it is the wish of my lord Rochester that this Richard
Weston should be allowed to wait on Sir Thomas Overbury.
Would you do that . . . for us?'

Would he? He would do everything in his power for the
sake of pleasing the most important man at Court.

He said: 'Lady Essex, you may rely on me to serve you with
all my heart.'

'I knew it,' she replied, smiling sweetly. 'I told my lord
Rochester that this matter could safely be left in your
hands.'

Now that Richard Weston was established in the Tower as
servant to Sir Thomas Overbury, Frances was eager to get to
work, and Anne Turner arranged a meeting with Dr Franklin.

There was no longer any subterfuge, and Frances clearly
stated her desires.

'What we need,' she said, 'is a poison which will not instantly kill. It must be a slow process so that it seems that the man is dying of some wasting disease. Then no one will be surprised when in a month or so – I think it should be as long as that – he dies.'

'I believe *aquafortis* to be effective,' said Anne Turner.

Franklin shook his head. 'It would work quickly,' he explained, 'and since the plan is that he should appear to be suffering from a wasting sickness, it would be useless.'

'I have heard of white arsenic—' began Frances.

But again Franklin shook his head. 'That would have a similar effect to *aquafortis*. It might be apparent that his sickness was the result of something he had eaten. We must avoid that at all costs. There is powder of diamonds ... which is most costly.'

Frances shook herself impatiently. Why would they keep talking of the cost! Had she not told them that money was of little account, as long as they gave her what she wanted.

'Then get some.'

'My lady. I am not exactly a poor man for my practice is a good one, but I have not the capital to make experiments with such materials.'

Frances immediately took out a purse which she had brought with her and gave to him. 'Buy the powder of diamonds and see if it can be of use, and above all do it quickly.'

'I am at your ladyship's service,' Franklin declared.

And Frances left Hammersmith in better spirits.

When Franklin had his concoction ready the problem was how to get it into the Tower to Weston without arousing suspicion. It was Anne Turner who remembered that Weston had a son, Willie, who might be useful to them. Willie was an apprentice to a haberdasher who was patronized by Court ladies and Frances herself bought fans and feathers from him. Willie could pass information to the Countess when she called at the haberdashers; he could also visit his father in the Tower without attracting a great deal of attention, for what was more natural than that a son should visit his father?

So to the haberdashers went Anne Turner, taking with her a small bottle, the contents of which were to be put into Overbury's food in order to start him on that mysterious illness which in a month or so would prove fatal.

Willie performed his duty with efficiency and reported to Anne that the bottle had been given to his father when they were alone and that his father knew what was expected of him.

Richard Weston felt very honoured to have been selected for this post. He was a humble man but good fortune had come his way at last. Since he had been in the Tower he had begun to dream of power and riches. He did not see why, when he had finished this task, he should not have his own establishment. Why should he not be another Dr Franklin or Forman? To think of the money they had made filled him with a tingling excitement. There was power too in guarding the secrets of the great. And here was he, being of use to the Countess of Essex, a very grand lady, and a member of the Howard family. He had never seen anyone pay so handsomely for a man's services.

Certainly he was coming on in the world, since he was now involved in a plot which concerned people in high places, people who were ready to pay for what was done for them. What would be riches to him, was nothing to them. His fortune was made because when this man Overbury was out of the way some very influential people were going to be grateful to Richard Weston.

He took the little bottle and looked at it. It seemed harmless enough, and all he had to do was to slip it into the broth when he took in the supper.

He had heard a rumour that the Countess was going to divorce her husband and marry Viscount Rochester. Rochester! There was no end to the good that would come to Richard Weston. What if he were offered a post at Court. Why not? Rochester would be grateful to him.

It was quite dazzling when one considered the important people who were in this plot with him – Rochester, the Countess, and the Lieutenant of the Tower Sir Gervase Helwys.

He went to the kitchens for Overbury's supper and when he emerged set down the bowl and took the bottle from his pocket.

He was studying it, wondering whether to put it in at once, when he heard a step behind him and saw that Sir Gervase Helwys was coming towards him. For a moment he had been startled but was immediately reassured because it was Sir Gervase who had allowed him to come here and he himself had been given his post by the wish of the Countess and her great-uncle; therefore they were fellow conspirators.

Weston said: 'Sir, I was wondering whether to put it straight into the broth now, or to wait until the last minute.'

'What is this?' asked Sir Gervase and took the bottle from Weston.

'Well, sir, it's the mixture that has to be put into the broth.'

Sir Gervase turned pale. He was horrified at what he had discovered. He had been given the post to intercept Overbury's letters, not to allow him to be poisoned.

He said: 'I will take this bottle. Give Sir Thomas Overbury his supper and then come to my apartments immediately.'

Weston was trembling so violently that the broth was slopping over the sides of the basin. Sir Gervase had turned and walked away, while Weston, in a growing panic, took the prisoner his supper, cursing himself for throwing away the greatest opportunity of his life.

Sir Gervase looked at the wretched man and said: 'You had better tell me who gave you this bottle.'

Weston's shifty eyes were panic-stricken. He was not going to incriminate his son.

'It was sent in to me . . . with instructions to put it into the broth, sir.'

Sir Gervase looked at the cringing man, but he was not thinking of him. He was remembering his interview with the Earl of Northampton when he had been told what was expected of him.

'This man Overbury,' Northampton had said, 'because of his position with my lord Rochester, will be aware of certain State secrets which, should they fall into the hands of our enemies, could harm our country. It is for this reason that I wish you to pass on all his correspondence to me.'

Sir Gervase had agreed to do this; he was grateful to his benefactor; it was not every man who was selected by the important Howards to work for them. He knew that it was because of this particular prisoner in the Tower that Waad had been dismissed and he been given the post. He had congratulated himself that he had been chosen because of the delicate nature of the task. He was there to prevent the leakage of state secrets, but murder was another matter.

It was a terrible realization for an ambitious man to make. Waad had been dismissed through the influence of the Howards; what would their reactions be if they knew that he was refusing to work for them?

They wanted to be rid of Overbury. They wanted him to be murdered in the Tower. Sir Gervase was a man who was ready to do a great deal to rise in the world — but murder was something he had never considered.

And here was this man Weston, the tool of the great, standing shivering before him, caught in the act. Monson had recommended him and had hinted that it was the wish of Rochester that the fellow should become Overbury's jailer. Rochester wanted to assure himself that his one time friend was comfortable. Comfortable seemed a sinister word.

And here was Sir Gervase — that ambitious man — who saw the road to glory lying straight ahead of him confronted by a gate on which was written Murder.

He must have time to consider. But there was no time. What he did in the next few minutes could be of the utmost importance to his career.

He heard himself saying: 'You know there was poison in that bottle?'

'Why yes, sir,' stammered Weston.

'And you were prepared to administer it!'

'Well, sir, 'twas orders like . . .'

Orders! The question came to the Lieutenant's lips: whose orders? He stopped himself asking it in time. If the man answered that one, what could Sir Gervase do about it?

He must be subtle; he must act with the utmost caution.

'You were about to commit a great sin.' That was it. Words flowed from him. It was not for ordinary men to take life at a whim. What Weston had contemplated doing was an evil thing ... And so on. For five minutes he talked while Weston threw himself on his knees, scarcely listening, seeing himself carried away to a dungeon – one of the noisome underground dungeons where persons of no consequence were sent. This was the end of the good life he had planned for himself – and all because of one stupid mistake.

But to imprison Weston was something Sir Gervase could not do. Had he not been put in his place by Monson at the request of my lord Rochester? Now, there was only one thing a wise man could do in these circumstances, and that was to turn a blind eye on what was going on in the cell of Sir Thomas Overbury.

He would have no part in the murder; neither to assist it nor to prevent it.

He took the bottle of poison and opening his window threw out the contents.

He turned to Weston. 'I see that you are a simple man,' he said, 'and I trust my words have had some effect on you. Have I brought you some understanding of the evil nature of your conduct?'

'Oh, sir,' cried Weston, 'I wish I had died before I had touched the bottle.'

'You have repented. That is good. Go back to your work and we will say nothing of this matter. But I beg you watch your actions in future.'

Watch them in future! So that I do not see what is going on?

Weston's face was illuminated by his relief. 'Oh sir, you are good to me, sir. I swear—'

'It is enough. Remember what I have said.'

'Oh I will, I will, sir.'

Sir Gervase dismissed him and Weston blundered away, bewildered.

After the man had left him, Sir Gervase was thoughtful and very uneasy; it was alarming for an ambitious man to find himself caught up in a plot of murder.

The Commission which had been set up to arrange the divorce were not in agreement.

That eloquent man, George Abbot, Archbishop of Canterbury, was the main stumbling block. He had interviewed the Earl of Essex who was reserved yet determined not to accept the stigma of impotence, although he did agree that as far as his wife was concerned he had no desire. The Archbishop had come to the conclusion that the Earl was by no means impotent but as eager as his wife to have the marriage ended.

He put his view before the Commission explaining that this was a serious matter and they must not allow themselves to be guided by the fact that noble people beloved of the King were eager to see a certain solution. They had to give the right judgement, no matter whom they offended.

Weston was not such a simple man as Sir Gervase had believed him to be; when he had escaped from the Lieutenant and had had a little time to ponder on what had happened, it occurred to him that he had escaped very lightly for a man who had been caught in an attempt to poison a prisoner.

There could be one solution to this: Sir Gervase was either concerned in a plot against Sir Thomas Overbury or he was anxious not to offend those who were. Therefore there would be no real interference from him.

The more he considered the matter, the less fearful he became, and when a few days later he decided to present himself at Mrs Anne Turner's house in Hammersmith, he had made up his mind that Sir Gervase would never dare refer to what had happened, so he told Mrs Turner that he had administered the contents of the bottle.

'And now,' he finished, 'I have earned my reward.'

'Nonsense,' said Mrs Anne Turner, 'there will be no reward

until Overbury is dead. You have merely performed one of your duties. There are others to follow.'

'I do not greatly like this task.'

'Of course you do not. Do you think you would be paid so handsomely for doing what you enjoy? You had better let us hear no more complaints from you. Go back to your duties. You will soon be given further tasks, and if you perform them with zeal, it will not be long before the matter is completed and you may claim your reward.'

So Weston returned to the Tower and waited for further instructions.

Frances was strained and nervous. Every day that Overbury lived she was in danger. That old fool Abbot was delaying the divorce, and seeking reasons for not granting it. If Overbury should get a letter through to him, if it were discovered that she had procured powders from people of ill repute, that would give the Archbishop what he was looking for. It must not be.

She must stir up Franklin. He was planning a lingering death. That would not do. It must be expedited.

She ordered Franklin to appear at Mrs Turner's house and went there to meet him. Anne Turner joined them and the Countess spoke vehemently of the delay which was causing her so much anxiety.

'That which Weston put into the broth produced no result,' she complained. 'He is as well as he was when he was taken to the Tower. I have no intention of paying you if you are not going to do the job.'

'I told my lady that it would be necessary to make certain experiments.'

'Then speed them up, speed them up. I hear the prisoner spends much time writing. What if one of the letters he writes should manage to get through. Then all our work could be in vain. We must make him too ill to be able to use his pen.'

'I think, my lady, we should try white arsenic.'

'It could be put into his salt,' suggested Anne Turner.

'I heard from Weston that he took no salt.'

'Then sprinkled on his food, my lady. It could be used in some way.'

'That should be done. What other poisons could you employ.'

'*Aquafortis*, my lady; and mercury. I have experimented with powder of diamonds and we should use that too. Also lapis costitus and cantharides.'

'Use the lot,' cried Frances; 'but let me hear soon that Overbury's health is declining rapidly. And follow that up with his death.'

If you wished for something you must try to achieve it yourself, thought Frances. It was no use trusting to others.

She called on Sir Gervase Helwys at his apartments in the Tower of London where she was received with great courtesy. As a woman of a noble house, and an extremely beautiful one. she had grown to accept such homage as her right; but lately she had been even more courteously received than before; and she was exultant because she knew this additional respect was due to the fact that she was soon to marry Robert Carr.

'I have come to see you because of my lord Rochester's anxiety on account of one who used to be his friend,' she explained.

Sir Gervase turned a little pale, but Frances did not notice this.

'My lord Rochester has a kind heart I well know,' he murmured.

'So kind that, although this servant has behaved ill, he would not have him suffer. My lord Rochester has asked me to bring him little treats while he is in prison. He knows the poor man to have a sweet tooth and for that reason I want to bring him some of the tarts which he especially likes.'

Sir Gervase shivered imperceptibly. 'You must do as you wish, Lady Essex,' he managed to say.

'Thank you.' Her smile was so bewitching that he could only believe her innocent of any design on the prisoner's life. Rochester and Northampton, the two most important men in the country, were planning the disposal of Overbury, and it was easy to guess that he held some secret, important to them both. And they had decided to use this lovely creature as their unconscious agent!

But what could a man do who was hoping to rise at Court. Only one thing: refuse to think what this could mean.

'Sir Gervase,' went on Lady Essex, 'the tarts I shall bring are for Sir Thomas Overbury alone. I shall send them to you so that you may see they are given to him and no other. It would be a pity to deprive him of that which will do so much to comfort him.'

'No one else shall touch them,' he assured her. 'I myself will see to that.'

That satisfied her and she went away.

The next day the tarts arrived for Sir Gervase Helwys and because he was not there to receive them, his servant took them in. Thus they remained for several hours in his apartment before he found them. By that time they were already turning black and were touched with a strange phosphorescence.

No one would eat such tarts. Sir Gervase would not only be doing Overbury a good turn by throwing them away but those who had sent them, for had any but himself looked at the things that person would have suspected at a glance that some very foul substance had been used in preparing them.

The Archbishop of Canterbury was in despair. When he had put his case before the Commission he had a big following. He was certain then that right would prevail and that there should be no concessions because of the nobility and position at Court of the people concerned.

The King was impatient with the Archbishop. James did not like the case; he wished that Robert had chosen an unmarried girl for his wife; however, since Robert wanted this woman, he must have her. But in spite of James' having made it clear to his Archbishop that he wanted the divorce, still Abbot was arguing against it – and carrying the majority of the Commission with him.

But James had taken one or two of the Commissioners aside and made known his wishes to them; and at the next meeting they no longer supported the Archbishop.

Frances was called before seven chosen ladies who had been instructed to consult her on the intimate details of her married life. Her mother was among them, and being a very forceful woman, and having decided how she intended the inquiry must go, she soon made herself leader of the group. Frances was grateful to her mother and herself gave a touching performance as she explained how her husband had been unable to consummate the marriage.

Essex, questioned by the Commission, was becoming eager to see an end to the proceedings and freedom from a marriage which was growing more and more distasteful as the case progressed; he now seemed ready to accept the slur of impotence for the sake of that freedom.

He was not in truth impotent, he told them, but he had no desire for his wife. He had loved her when he left France and came to England, but he no longer did so, and never could again.

It was suggested that a certain bewitchment might have been put upon him, which would explain why he was able to be a good husband to some woman but not to his wife.

Still the case was not settled and James was annoyed, for now it was being talked of in the streets and it was said that if a woman wanted to rid herself of a husband all she had to do was declare him impotent.

He summoned the Commissioners to Windsor where he was at that time and with them came Frances' father, the Earl of Suffolk, who during the journey had talked with several of the members of the Commission and told them that he and lords Northampton and Rochester were growing impatient. They asked for a simple matter to be settled and these lords deliberately thwarted them. He hinted at rewards which would be given to the acquiescent; punishments which would befall the dissenters.

By the time the Commission appeared before James, several of its members had changed their minds and were opposing

the Archbishop of Canterbury. But old George Abbot was not
going against his principles whatever the advantages ... or
disadvantages.

James was not displeased that there should be this
difference of opinion, because it gave him an opportunity of
debating, an occupation from which he derived much
pleasure, particularly if the subject was a theological one. He
prided himself on being more learned in the scriptures than
any priest and he could always back up his arguments with
quotations.

He summoned George Abbot and engaged him in discussion. The Archbishop was tired and James was alert. Every
point which the priest brought forward James quashed with a
quotation from the Bible and his own subtle argument. He
would have found arguments and quotations to oppose himself had it been necessary; but that was one of the joys of
debate. James could have made a brilliant case for either side.
He was not called the British Solomon for nothing.

It was said in the Bible that a man should take one wife and
cleave to her until death parted them. Ah, but it may well have
been that when that had been written the hideous cult of
witchcraft had not appeared to sully the Earth. What had
happened was that Essex had been bewitched. He was made
impotent as far as his own wife was concerned. When they
had wiped out witchcraft, cases such as this would never
arise.

James was off on his favourite hobby horse. Ever since he
believed he had proved that witches had tried to drown the
Queen and prevent her reaching Scotland, he had become incensed by the very word witchcraft. On account of his hatred
of this, witch-finders were flourishing throughout the kingdom and every day some old woman would be dragged before
the judges and put to the tests.

It seemed to James that witchcraft was behind every evil
scheme that was ever brought to light; and he believed it
possible that witchcraft had made a normal married life impossible now and for ever between the Earl and Countess of
Essex, and therefore the best thing that could happen would

be to dissolve their marriage and let them both find partners elsewhere.

He reminded the Archbishop of events which had taken place when he was but a lad in Scotland. One concerned a woman who had been forced into marriage and ran away from her husband to whom her father insisted that she return.

'And the result, man. She poisoned him and was burnt for it. Ye canna jerk a woman back to a husband and he to her when evil witches have juggled with them. Remember this, and disband the Commission. It shall meet again when you have had time to brood on it. It may be necessary to have a bigger Commission. The more heads to ponder on this the better.'

So there was to be a pause before the new Commission sat; and it gradually became known that the King was ready to reward those who gave the verdict he wished. Honours were given to some who pledged their support; Court wits referred to blessings bestowed as Nullity Honours; and when the Bishop of Winchester – who had shown himself zealous in the cause of Rochester and the Countess of Essex – brought his son to Court to receive an accolade, the young man was jokingly called: 'Sir Nullity'.

It was comforting for Frances and Rochester to know that the King was so fervently on their side.

But they were still waiting for the divorce.

In his prison Sir Thomas Overbury was aware of changes. A lassitude had overtaken him; he suffered from sickness and griping pains.

'I shall die of melancholy,' he said, 'if I remain here much longer. Prison sickness is already beginning to overtake me.'

His weight had rapidly decreased and his face had lost its once healthy glow; his skin was pallid and damp and there were days when he was too ill to rise from his bed.

He wrote to his parents and told them that his health had deteriorated in the last weeks and that if something was not done to bring him out of his prison he feared he would die.

* * *

Sir Nicholas Overbury and his wife were alarmed when they read this letter.

'I cannot understand it,' said Lady Overbury. 'Why have they sent him to the Tower? He appears to have done nothing but refuse an appointment. Is this justice?'

Sir Nicholas shook his head and said that they could only guess at the strange behaviour of people in high places.

'But Viscount Rochester was so fond of him. Our Thomas was one of the most important men at Court.'

'It is the important men at Court who are the most vulnerable.'

'I don't intend to let matters rest as they are. We must go to London and see what can be done.'

Sir Nicholas could see that his wife was determined and as he too was growing anxious on his son's account he agreed that to London they must go.

'I should like to see the King and ask his help,' said Lady Overbury.

That was an absurd suggestion, her husband knew, for humble people such as they were could not call on the King.

'We might send a petition,' he suggested.

'Explaining,' added his wife, 'how anxious we are.'

They did so, begging the King to allow some physician to attend their son.

James read the petition and understood the parental concern behind it. He wrote kindly to the Overburys personally, telling them that he was sending one of his own physicians to see their son.

Sir Nicholas felt that he and his wife had already done some good, and when he heard that his son was suffering from some unspecified disease natural in the circumstances, he was very anxious to see him; he wrote to Viscount Rochester begging him to seek the necessary permission for the parents to visit their son.

Rochester, moved by the letter, was about to say he would arrange at once for the parents to see Sir Thomas, but before making a decision he consulted with Northampton.

Northampton knew far more than Rochester; and he was very suspicious of the prisoner's illness. It could not be long before Overbury began to suspect that the sudden sickness which had overtaken him was not due to natural causes; and then there might be serious trouble. What, wondered Northampton, was Frances up to now? He was certain that she would never let matters take a natural course and she had far more reason to fear Overbury than she had allowed even him to understand.

On no account must Overbury's parents be allowed to see him.

'My sweet lord,' he said, 'Overbury is sick; he has been a prisoner for some weeks; you can be assured that he is angry with you. How can we know what lies he will tell against you? I have heard it whispered that he is in the Tower because he is in possession of a dark secret which involves you, and that it concerns the death of the Prince of Wales. By God and all his angels, Robert, if such a tale were bruited abroad – false as you and I know it to be – it could be the ruin of you. Even James would not be able to save you.'

'I cannot believe that Overbury would so lie about me.'

'Nor would he, when he was your friend. Now he is your enemy and never was an enemy so bitter who was one time a close and loving friend. Overbury is a dangerous man. Nay, Robert, let us get the divorce done with and then we will come to terms with him. We will give him his freedom in exchange for his promise never to utter a word against you.'

'But what of his parents? What can I tell them?'

Northampton considered. 'That very shortly he is to be released, and that if you are to bring this about it is better for him to be quiet and say nothing that might jeopardize your plan. At the moment he is in prison and resentful. You do not wish to tell him how near his release is, just in case it should take a little longer than you hope to bring it about. Therefore, let matters rest as they are.'

'Very well, if you think it is necessary.'

'Necessary, my dear fellow. It is essential to your future –

yours and Frances'. Believe me, my greatest desire is to see you two happy together.'

'Then I will write to Sir Nicholas and Lady Overbury.'

'Do so. They will be delighted.'

'Others have asked permission to see him. Some of his kinsmen.'

'Tell them the same. It is the best way. And it is true. For as soon as the divorce has been granted, Overbury shall have his freedom.'

So Robert wrote as directed; and that was all the satisfaction the Overburys and their anxious relations received.

A terrible realization had come to Thomas Overbury.

He would never escape from the Tower.

There were days when he was too ill to think clearly; but these were sometimes followed by periods when, although his body was weak, his mind was active.

Why should he have been imprisoned merely because he refused to take an appointment overseas? It was unreasonable – and it had happened just at that time when he had quarrelled with Robert about that evil woman of his.

What was the real truth behind his imprisonment?

His pen had always been a comfort to him and he used it now. He was going to write down everything that had happened since the day he met Robert Carr in Edinburgh; and he was going to send copies of this to his friends and ask them to read it and see if they could discover what had led to his imprisonment in the Tower.

The idea made him feel alive again, and he felt his strength coming back.

He wrote a letter to Robert – a long bitter letter of reproach and recrimination in which he accused him of throwing away their friendship for the sake of an evil woman. He told him that he had written an account of their relationship, his fears and suspicions, and was making eight copies of this which would be sent to eight of his friends. He did not believe Rochester could deny one word of what he had written; and he wanted people to know that he suspected he had been put into the Tower because of what he knew concerning Rochester and that evil woman who had been his mistress, and whom he now desired to make his wife.

When Northampton saw the letter which Robert showed him, he ordered Helwys to be more vigilant than ever. Eight letters which Overbury was writing must be brought to him and by no means allowed to reach the people to whom they were addressed.

Northampton was very uneasy. The divorce, thanks to the Archbishop of Canterbury, was being delayed. Overbury was becoming suspicious and truculent, although Helwys reported that he was growing more feeble every day.

There was a time of great anxiety when two physicians recommended by the King examined Overbury, and great relief when they reported that the prisoner was suffering from consumption aggravated by melancholy.

James' sense of justice was disturbed when he received this report. Overbury had been put into the Tower for a flimsy reason. He had angered the King by a curt refusal to take a post abroad and James knew that if he had been another man his anger would have been shortlived. He had seen something of the friendship between Robert and Overbury and he knew Overbury to be a clever man; the truth was he was a little jealous of Robert's affection for the man; and that was why he had, at Northampton's instigation, treated him more harshly than the offence warranted.

He sent for the eminent physician Dr Mayerne and asked him to do what he could for Overbury.

Dr Mayerne attended Overbury once, saw no reason to doubt that he was suffering from consumption intensified by melancholy, and since he did not intend to spend much time on a patient who was after all in disgrace, appointed his apothecary Paul de Lobel to attend Overbury.

Each morning Frances would wake from disturbing dreams. She was so near achieving her heart's desire, yet it could so easily be snatched from her.

She could not endure the waiting; it was unnerving her.

There was a meeting in the house at Hammersmith when she opened her heart to Mrs Turner.

'I begin to wonder whether Dr Franklin is as skilful as we thought,' complained Frances. 'All this time and the man still lives!'

'He is loath to administer stronger doses for fear of discovery.'

'Afraid! These men are always afraid. My dear Turner, if they cannot give us what we want we must do without them.'

Anne Turner was thoughtful; then she said: 'I heard that Paul de Lobel is attending him.'

'Well?'

'I sometimes visit his establishment in Lime Street and I have noticed a boy there who is very willing to do little services for me . . . for a consideration.'

Frances was alert.

'Yes, dear Turner?'

'Overbury has had several clysters since he has been in prison and de Lobel administers these. They would be prepared in Lime Street before taken to the Tower. If I could speak to this boy . . . offer him a large enough sum . . .'

'Offer him twenty pounds. He would surely not refuse that.'

'It would be a fortune to him.'

'Then tell him that he will receive the money when Sir Thomas Overbury is dead.'

'Three months and seventeen days I have been in this cell,' said Overbury. 'How much longer shall I remain?'

Dr de Lobel looked at his patient and thought: Not much longer, by the look of you. For if the King does not release you, death will.

He said: 'Any day, sir, you will get your release. That's how it is with prisoners. I come some days to a prisoner to find that he is no longer here. "Oh," they tell me, "he was released last week." '

One day you will come here, Doctor, and find that I am gone.'

'I hope so, sir, I hope so.'

'Oh, God, let it be soon,' said Overbury fervently.

'And how are you feeling today?'

'Sick unto death. Such pains I have endured! But let me be free of this place and I'll recover.'

'You have been writing too many letters. You have tired yourself.'

'In a good cause.' Overbury smiled. They would be reading his letters now. They would learn the nature of the man for whom he had done so much and who now left him miserable in his prison. They would know something about the evil woman who had changed one of the best of men into a fiend.

'This clyster should do you much good.'

'Another clyster?'

'Sir, it is my pleasure and duty to make you well again. Come, prepare yourself.'

It was shortly after the clyster was administered that Sir Thomas Overbury was overtaken by such sickness as he had never known before.

He no longer wished for liberty and revenge; he only wished for death.

The next day the sickness continued and he lay panting for his breath.

What has come over me? he asked in his lucid moments. What has happened to make me thus?

No one could answer him. They could only shake their heads and tell each other that the wasting sickness of Sir Thomas Overbury had taken a more virulent turn.

For seven days he lay groaning in his cell; and on the eighth day when his jailers came to him, he did not answer them when they spoke to him.

They looked closer and saw that he was dead.

The Wedding

OVERBURY DEAD!

Frances was dizzy with glee. But what of the divorce? Oh, if it were only possible to give the old Archbishop a clyster.

She heard from Robert and her great-uncle that but for the Archbishop of Canterbury they would have the divorce by now. It seemed the old fool had a conscience and even the fear of the King's displeasure could not make him offend that.

Why, in God's name, if two people wanted to divorce each other, couldn't they? demanded Frances. What had it to do with old men who had finished with life and could not understand the passions of the young?

The King, eager to have the matter done with, because it was causing too much talk throughout and beyond the Court, sent for his Archbishop and asked how the cause was going?

George Abbot looked grave.

'It is a cause for which I have little liking, Your Majesty,' he said.

James looked impatient. 'Why, man, we all find ourselves facing distasteful problems at times. Then the best advice is to do the work with all speed and have the matter done with.'

'Your Majesty this is not a matter which can be settled with a yea or a nay, and it grieves me that you should reproach me for listening to my conscience.'

'What grief can there be to your conscience if the Lady Frances is no longer the wife of the Earl of Essex?'

'It is no concern of mine, Your Majesty, whether the Lady Frances be the wife of the Earl of Essex or another. But I cannot give a verdict which I do not believe to be just. That is my problem, Sire. I am fifty-one and have never yet muffled my

conscience when called upon to do my duty. It grieves me that
I must displease Your Majesty and it is a matter of desolation
that this verdict should be of importance to you. But if I said
yea when I meant nay, then you might say that a man who did
not serve his conscience could not be trusted to serve his
King.'

James saw that the Archbishop was deeply moved and his
sense of justice forced him to admit that the priest was right.

But what a pother to make about the matter! And Robert
would not be happy until he had his bride; the Howards were
also eager for the match.

Nevertheless he laid a gentle hand on the Archbishop's
arm.

'You're an honest man, I know well. But it is my wish that
the Lady Frances should be divorced from the Earl of Essex.'

The Archbishop was on his knees. This was indeed a trial of
strength. If he fell from royal favour through this matter, then
fall he must. A man of God must obey his conscience.

He felt strengthened when he rose; he knew exactly what he
would say to the Commission when it assembled. He was
going to show those men that there was no true reason why
this marriage should be severed except that two people – one
a woman belonging to a family of influence, the other a
favourite of the King – desired to marry. If this divorce were
granted it would be a blow to marriage throughout the
country. It would never be forgotten; women would be accusing their husbands of impotency when they sought to
marry someone else. Everything that he, as a man of the
Church, had ever believed in, cried out against it.

He could feel the power of his eloquence. He was certain
that he could sway those men the way in which they must go;
even those who had received favours from the King, and
those who were promised more, must surely reject them for
the sake of their immortal souls.

He knew he could count on five honest men, and these were
led by the Bishop of London. No matter what the consequences to themselves they would vote as they thought right.

But the remaining seven? He was not sure of them – though he knew that some of them had already taken their bribes.

With great confidence he awaited the arrival of the Commissioners at Lambeth. He was well prepared for he was certain he had been inspired. He would work on them with the zest and fire of truth; he would make them see the sin they were committing by selling for wealth and honours their right to decide.

When they were all assembled he rose to speak, but before he could do so a messenger from the King arrived and said he had a command from His Majesty.

'Pray tell us this,' said the Archbishop.

'That, my lord, you spend no further time in talking one with another. It is His Majesty's command that you give the verdict and that alone.'

The Archbishop felt deflated. The brilliant speech he had prepared would never be uttered. He saw that the men who he suspected were going to vote in favour of the divorce were delighted; they were eager to have done with the business and retire, their favour earned.

One could not disobey the command of the King. The vote was taken.

Five against the divorce; seven in favour of it.

'A majority!' cried Northampton when he heard the news. 'At last we are triumphant!'

Frances received the news with rapture.

Overbury dead! Herself no longer the wife of Essex and free to marry the man she loved!

Everything that she had longed for, schemed for, was hers.

'I am the happiest woman in the world,' she told Jennet.

James was thankful that that unsavoury matter was at an end. Now let it be forgotten. Let Robert marry as soon as he liked; and let everyone forget that Frances Howard had ever been Frances Essex.

There were other troubles. It was a sorry thing to see tradesmen calling at the Palace and threatening the servants that they would deliver nothing more until their bills were paid. Small wonder that people compared this Stuart with the Tudors. Imagine anyone asking Henry VIII or Elizabeth to settle a bill!

James had little royal dignity; he was too ready to laugh at himself and see the other person's point of view. All the same, having tradesmen demanding payment of bills was something he could not tolerate.

He told Robert about it. 'A sorry state of affairs, Robbie. And here am I wanting to give ye the grandest wedding the Court has ever seen!'

'Your Majesty must not think of me. You have already been over generous.'

'You've had nothing more than you deserve, lad. You look sad. And you about to be a bridegroom!'

'I am sad because of Your Majesty's plight.'

'Why, bless you, boy, Old Dad has been in difficulties before. We'll think of a way.'

Robert did think of a way. He gave twenty-five thousand pounds to the Treasury.

When James heard of this he wept with emotion.

'The dear lovely laddie,' he kept saying. 'God bless his bonny face.'

He knew of a way to reward his lad.

'Robbie,' he said one day, 'it seems Viscount Rochester is a title hardly worthy of you.'

'I am grateful for receiving it at Your Majesty's hands.'

'I know that, lad. But I'd like to see you on a level with the best. You are, of course; but I want them to have to recognize it too. Ye're going to be an Earl.'

'Your Majesty!'

'My wedding present to you and the lady.'

'Your Majesty, how can I? . . . What can I? . . .'

'Ye deserve it, boy.'

Robert's eyes were bright with excitement. How pleased Frances would be!

A few days later James created him Earl of Somerset.

*   *   *

Frances was being dressed by her women. She had chosen white for her wedding gown and she wore diamonds; with her golden hair about her shoulders, she had never looked as beautiful as she did on that day.

She refused to think of the dead body of Sir Thomas Over-bury, but it was significant that she had to admonish herself on this point. Why should she think of a man who was dead? What was he to her now?

'Oh, my lady,' cried one of the maids, 'there could never have been such a beautiful bride.'

Jennet was settling the white ruff about her neck, her eyes downcast.

'Just as a bride should be,' went on the garrulous maid. 'White for innocence, they say.'

Frances turned sharply to look at the maid; had she caught a glance passing between her and one of the others? Were they whispering about her in corners?

She had to suppress an impulse to slap the girl's face.

She must be watchful.

She turned to Jennet; Jennet's eyes were still lowered. Was that a smile she saw curving her lips?

They wouldn't dare, she assured herself. She was over-wrought. But was this how it was going to be in future? Must she be watchful, furtive; must she always be asking: How much do they know?

Frances was led into the chapel at Whitehall by her great-uncle Northampton and the Duke of Saxony, who was visiting England.

This wedding was attracting as much attention and almost as much pageantry as that of the Princess Elizabeth. The King had expressed his desire that no expense should be spared; Whitehall was to be the setting; and the Banqueting Hall was festooned and decorated with a brilliance rivalling that dis-played for the wedding of the King's daughter.

Robert Carr's desire for a wife had in no way diminished the King's affection; and now that the favourite had his earl-dom it seemed that he could climb no further. His task in future would be to hold his place at the very heights of power.

Chief advisor and favourite of the King, joined through marriage to the most powerful family in the land – it seemed that at last he was secure.

Frances could not help thinking when the Bishop of Bath and Wells married her to Robert, of that occasion when the same man had married her, in the same place, to another Robert. She dismissed the memory as hastily as she could; she need never again think of Robert Devereux. It must be as though they had never met. He could now go his way and she hers.

She *must* be happy. Here was Robert smiling beside her; and there was no doubt of his satisfaction. He was respectably married; no more secret meetings, no more furtive messages.

No more fear – only ecstasy.

In the Banqueting Hall was a scene of great magnificence. The King, Queen and Prince of Wales had taken their seats, and beside the King sat the bridegroom and beside the bridegroom his wife.

A curtain was drawn back to display a scene of such fantasy that all those watching gasped with astonishment. Above was an impression of cleverly painted clouds, and below this, a sea on which boats appeared to move as though with the wind. On either side of the seascape were promontories, rocks and woods. Now the dancers came forward, each significantly garbed to indicate a certain quality. First came the villains: Error, Rumour, Curiosity; these were followed by Harmony and Destiny, the latter represented by three beautiful girls. Then there were Water and Fire, the Earth and Eternity, followed by the continents – Africa, Asia and America. The costumes were brilliant in colour and planned to give a clue to the watchers as to what their wearers represented before they sang their songs of explanation.

Queen Anne, who enjoyed such pageantry more than any other member of the royal family, watched intently, waiting for the moment when she would be called upon to play her little part, for she could never bear to be left out of these occasions; and when the three Destinies brought towards her a golden tree, she plucked a branch from it and presented it to one of the knights who came forward to kneel and receive it. This was the moment for a chorus to appear and break into song, extolling the virtues of the newly married pair.

Then from pillars of gold which had stood on each side of the big stage, maskers appeared; there were six of them and their garments glittered as they came before the royal party and the bride and bridegroom.

They began to dance, twisting, turning and leaping; and as they danced they sang:

> 'Let us now sing of Love's Delight,
> For he alone is Lord tonight.
> Some friendship between man and man prefer,
> But I the affection between man and wife.

> 'What good can be in life
> Whereof no fruits appear?
> Set is that tree in ill hour
> That yields neither fruit nor flower.

> 'How can man perpetual be
> But in his own posterity.'

Everyone applauded this, even the King, who might have thought it a slur on his own nature but for the fact that his own son, tall, handsome, becoming as charming a prince as the brother who had died, was sitting there with himself and the Queen.

The curtain fell and when it rose again a scene of London and the Thames was displayed, with barges from which merry sailors alighted to perform their dances and sing their songs

Frances watching all the pageantry which had been arranged for her delight, determined to thrust aside those niggling little

worries which beset her. The future was going to be glorious.
There would be no question of her living in the country with
her new husband. It would be the gaiety of the Court all the
time; and there would not be a woman more respected than
the Countess of Somerset, for her husband was, in all but
name, the ruler of England.

How happy I am! she thought; but it was necessary to keep
reminding herself that she was.

Robert had no such qualms; he was in truth happy. The
wretched divorce was over; he was truly married to the
woman he loved, and James was behaving like a benign father
who could not honour a beloved son enough.

It was true he had enemies, but that was inevitable. Many of
these people gathered here tonight who had brought costly
wedding presents would be ready and eager to turn against
him tomorrow if he were to lose the King's favour. That was
human nature and something every man must be prepared for.

Northampton was his friend. He was sure of that. There
was a family bond between them now, and it was good to
have such a strong man for a friend. The presents he had given
showed the world how much he approved of the wedding.
The gold plate alone must have cost some fifteen hundred
pounds; and the sword he had presented to Robert had a hilt
and scabbard of pure gold. James' gifts of course had excelled all others; the earldom was not universally recognized
as a wedding present, so there had been ten thousand pounds
worth of jewels from the King.

They were rich; they were powerful; they were in love.
What could they lack?

There were some men though who made Robert uneasy.
One of these was Sir Thomas Lake, an ambitious man who
had been at Court in the time of Queen Elizabeth and had
acted as secretary to Sir Francis Walsingham. Lake had assiduously courted the new Earl of Somerset, and had given six
beautiful candle sticks as a wedding present; but he was
eagerly watching for advancement and Robert did not entirely
trust his friendship.

There was Sir Ralph Winwood who had shown great

deference but there he was in his plain garments, refusing to put on silks and brocades or fine jewels. He was a stern Puritan and wished all to know it; and his speech was as plain as his garments. For all that, he was an ambitious man; and on returning to England from service abroad had quickly seen that if a man would advance in England he must be a friend of the King's favourite.

There was another who caused Robert to feel uneasy. This was Count Gondomar, the new Spanish ambassador, a very handsome gentleman, with attractive manners, always fastidiously attired, gallant in the extreme, but with a pair of alert black eyes which missed little.

Robert suspected that Gondomar had those eyes trained on him; and among the presents which arrived was a casket of jewels which he suspected to be worth at least three hundred pounds. The Count of Gondomar dearly wished, said the accompanying note, that his little gift would give pleasure to the bridegroom.

The sight of those jewels had startled Robert because he had heard it whispered that some ministers actually received bribes from Spain. That was something he would never do; and the more he looked at those jewels, the more uneasy he became, for it seemed to him that there might be more in the little casket than a wedding gift.

He had written at once to the Count to tell him that it was good of him to send such a handsome gift, but that he never accepted anything without first having obtained the King's permission to do so.

Such a comment must have been very unusual to the Spanish ambassador who had so many good friends at the English Court. It meant that this Earl of Somerset was a most extraordinary man because he was not to be won by bribes.

When Robert told James of the incident the King had smiled tenderly.

'Take the jewels, Robbie,' he said. 'I know you to be beyond bribing. So you wrote to the Spaniard, eh? Well, well, it'll be good for him to know there's one honest man at Whitehall.'

So Robert accepted the jewels, but seeing the Count at the wedding festivities he remembered the incident.

He would have to go very carefully now that he no longer had Overbury to help him.

Frances was watching his perplexed looks and she whispered: 'Does aught ail you, sweetheart?'

He smiled quickly. 'Nay, I was thinking of poor Tom Overbury and it made me sad to remember how we parted and that I shall never see him again.'

A shiver ran through her.

This is our wedding day, she wanted to cry. We have won. We are together. Are we never to forget?

So they were together at last. Robert was happy.

'No longer now,' he said, 'need we fear that we are being spied upon. We are legally married. This is how I always longed for it to be.'

'And I, my love,' she told him.

If he but knew how she had worked for this; how she had schemed and planned, first against Essex, then against Overbury!

She longed to tell him that he might understand something of the measure of her love for him. She wanted to cry: 'This I have done for you.'

But she dared not tell him. He would be shocked beyond expression. Perhaps his feelings would change towards her if he knew.

No, she must enjoy this perfect night – for perfect it must be.

Yet when he made love to her she could not shut out of her mind those waxen figures – the naked woman with the hair that looked like real hair, lying on the minute couch with the naked model. She could almost smell the overpowering incense which had burned in Dr Forman's room.

And it was as though a mocking ghost was in that room. The ghost of Sir Thomas Overbury who, not so long before, had been murdered in the Tower of London.

*   *   *

But the next day she was the gay young bride. The Christmas festivities and those of the wedding took place at the same time, for the couple had been married on December 26th. There followed a week of merrymaking for the New Year was at hand and James would have the New Year celebrated with as great a show of masking and feasting as Christmas.

Frances was so proud sitting in the tiltyard on New Year's Day – a member of the King's party, which she would be now, for Robert was always near the King and in future she would always be near Robert.

'Never, never to part,' as she had told him.

All the noblest of the lords were tilting on that day; and they thought it an honour to wear the yellow and green colours of the Earl of Somerset or the white and mulberry of the House of Howard.

This is how it will be in future, thought Frances. Everywhere we go we shall be honoured.

The Lord Mayor of London, at the King's command, entertained the royal couple, and the people watched the processions as they rode through the street.

There was some murmuring in the crowds, and men and women joked together: 'If you're tired of your husband, ladies, just complain that he's impotent. You'll be in noble company.'

'Who is this Scotsman?' asked others. 'Why should we be taxed to buy his jewels? It's time the King grew out of lapdogs.'

But they enjoyed processions, and the young Countess of Somerset was a beautiful bride; she smiled and waved to the people in a friendly fashion and they forgot to be angry when they looked at her.

One of Frances' presents was a handsome coach but neither she nor Robert had horses fine enough to draw it and could not procure them in time for the procession. As Sir Ralph Winwood was a connoisseur of horses and had some of the best in England in his stables, Robert asked him if he would lend them two pairs for this occasion.

Sir Ralph's reply was to send the horses without delay. 'So great a lady as the Countess of Somerset should not use borrowed horses,' he wrote, and he begged her to accept them as a gift.

Frances, delighted, showed the note to Robert, but he frowned.

'My love,' he said, 'we must be careful from whom we accept gifts.'

'But he has so many horses and he wants to give them.'

'He wants a post at Court. The Secretaryship, I believe. I cannot have him think that by giving you four fine horses he can buy my support.'

He immediately wrote a note of thanks to Winwood telling him that his wife could not accept such a costly gift; but Frances was so disappointed and Winwood so eager to make the present, that at last Robert relented; and Frances rode through the city in her fine coach drawn by four of the most magnificent horses ever seen.

And Sir Ralph Winwood, watching her, congratulated himself that he had done a very wise thing.

She should have been happy, for Robert was a tender husband; she loved his simplicity; and it seemed a marvellous thing to her that one who had been so long at Court should have retained an innocence.

He was so different from her. Was that why she loved him so passionately? Perhaps. For her love did not diminish with marriage; rather did it grow.

Yet she would sometimes wake at night, sweating with terror. How strange this was, when before she had not had a qualm of conscience! When she had been working towards her goal she had thought of one thing only — success. And now she had achieved it she was unable to forget the road she had come to reach it.

What had started this? Was it a look in the eyes of Jennet when she had spoken sharply to her? Was Jennet reminding her that she knew too much?

Jennet had always been a saucy girl; she had shown respect

it was true, but there had often been a suggestion of mockery beneath it.

'Jennet,' she had said, 'would you like this gown? I have scarce worn it and I think it would become you.'

Jennet had taken it with less gratitude than a maid should show to her mistress.

'I'll swear you've never had such a gown,' said Frances.

'No, my lady.'

'Yet you do not seem surprised to possess it.'

'I know my lady is grateful to me. We have been through so much together . . . to reach this . . . happiness.'

Then Frances remembered the darkened room, the incense, the low almost caressing voice of Dr Forman; and Jennet watching in the shadows.

She would like to rid herself of Jennet; but Jennet knew too much. She dared not.

She, Frances Howard, dared not rid herself of a servant!

It was small wonder that she sometimes awoke in fright.

'My lady, there is a female to see you.'

'A female? Ask what she wants. No . . . no . . . One moment. What sort of a female?'

The fear had touched her again. She must go carefully. There was so much to hide.

'A respectable-looking female, my lady.'

'I will see her. Bring her to me.'

They brought her; and the door was shut on them leaving them alone together.

'My name is Mrs Forman, my lady. You were a friend of my husband's, the late Dr Forman.'

'I think you are mistaken.'

'Oh no, my lady. You wrote to him often you remember. He called you his daughter and to you he was "Sweet Father".'

'Who told you this?'

'He used to show me his letters. I have them still. You see I was his wife and I worked with him. That is why, now he is

She then told him of the rumour.

Weston turned pale and began to tremble. 'I only acted in this under orders,' he burst out. 'It was nothing to me whether Sir Thomas Overbury lived or died.'

'You were eager enough to help when you knew how well paid you would be.'

'I was acting as a paid servant, remember.'

'This is no time for such talk. We have to decide what we shall say if we are questioned, for it is imperative that we all tell the same tale. If anyone asks how you acquired your post in the Tower, you must tell them that Sir Thomas Monson recommended you for it.'

Weston nodded.

'And you must find out how much Sir Gervase Helwys knows of that matter, and when you have done this, send a message to me by way of your son. I will go to order some feathers and he must tell me then. We must be very careful. This may be an idle rumour but should it be more than that we must be prepared. You should in no way mention my name or that of the Countess. Do you understand?'

Weston said he did. He was perplexed. How was he to sound Sir Gervase who, he was certain, knew that there had been an attempt to poison Sir Thomas Overbury? Had he not intercepted Weston when he was actually carrying poison? Had he not taken it from him?

But of course Weston had never told Anne Turner this.

It was all very unsettling.

Sir Ralph Winwood was pondering on the Overbury matter. It was true, of course, that there were always rumours of poison to accompany any death, and Overbury would be no exception – particularly as he had been a man of some standing in Court, had been sent to the Tower on the smallest of accusations and had died there.

He could question Weston, who had undoubtedly been Overbury's jailer; and if Overbury had been poisoned, could this have happened without the knowledge of Sir Gervase Helwys who, after all, as Lieutenant of the Tower, should know what was happening to his prisoners.

If he were going to look for reasons for Overbury's death he would more likely find them among the people of some position rather than the underlings.

Sir Gervase had become chief suspect in the mind of Sir Ralph Winwood; and while he was pondering this the Earl of Shrewsbury invited him to his house at Whitehall.

By a strange coincidence. Shrewsbury told him that he wanted him to meet, among others, Sir Gervase Helwys, the Lieutenant of the Tower, a man of many qualities, added Shrewsbury, but stopped short seeing the expression which crossed Winwood's face.

'You do not agree?' asked Shrewsbury.

'I am in no hurry to meet that man . . . at a friend's table.'

'But what is this? I do not understand?'

'First,' said Winwood, 'I would like to know that he is not involved in an unpleasant scandal.'

'What scandal?'

'I am thinking of the death of Sir Thomas Overbury. There is a rumour that he died by foul means and as Helwys was Lieutenant of the Tower at that time it seems likely that he was involved.'

'But this is shocking,' cried Shrewsbury.

And when Winwood left him he called at once on Helwys and told him of his conversation with Winwood.

Helwys was horrified. His one idea was to absolve himself from blame. He knew that there had been something very suspicious about Overbury's death and had been prepared to keep silent in order to please important people. Now he felt the need to break that silence to please Sir Ralph Winwood.

He went to him and asked to speak to him alone.

Winwood regarded him coldly and Helwys burst out: 'Sir Ralph, my lord Shrewsbury has talked to me of your suspicions. This is a terrible thing and I hasten to tell you that I am in no way to blame for the murder of Overbury.'

Ah! thought Winwood. He admits it is murder.

'I think,' said Winwood, 'that you could best help me and yourself by telling all you know.'

'Weston is the man who can help you,' cried Helwys. 'He was sent to work at the Tower for the purpose.'

'It was you who engaged him?'

'Yes, because I was asked to do so by some important people.'

'What people?'

'Sir Thomas Monson, Master of the Armoury, asked me to allow the man to wait on Overbury.'

'So the important person was Sir Thomas Monson, you believe?'

'No, no. I meant someone of great importance. It was the Countess of Somerset — then the Countess of Essex — who asked Monson to arrange this. I believe that while this request came through her it was in truth made by the Earl of Northampton and my lord Somerset.'

Winwood was astounded. He had not expected to hear such names mentioned at this stage.

He was delighted with this revelation and his pleasure showed itself. Misconstruing this, Helwys was relieved. All would be well. The matter would pass over him. After all he had only obeyed the orders of those greater than himself. What more could a man do?

'Thank you,' said Winwood. 'You have been of great help to me.'

'If there is anything else I can do . . .'

'There will be, I have no doubt. I am very grateful.'

Helwys watched his visitor depart, assured that what he had feared would be a dangerous interview had turned out very well for him.

Winwood took barge from the Tower to Whitehall. He felt exultant. Somerset and his Countess! And it fitted so well. Overbury and Somerset had worked closely together. Overbury would be in possession of secrets which Somerset would not want betrayed. They had fallen out. Oh, there was no absence of motive.

What could this mean? The end of Somerset? The end of the Spanish policy? No Spanish Infanta for the Prince of Wales? In his hands he held the key to the future.

He would go straight to the King.

But he must be careful. James was enamoured of young Villiers, but he was a faithful man and Somerset was still his beloved friend, for James did not cast off old friends when new ones appeared.

The King must not yet know how far this had gone; he must not know yet that the name of Somerset had been mentioned. That must not come out until it was too late to withdraw.

James received him at once and he told the King that he was greatly disturbed by the confession of Sir Gervase Helwys.

'I think, Your Majesty, that there can be no doubt that Sir Thomas Overbury was murdered.'

James was grave. He felt a twinge of conscience because he had sent Overbury to the Tower for such a small offence. The least he could do now was to avenge his death.

'Let Helwys write down all he knows of this matter,' he said, 'and when he has done so bring what he has written to me. We shall then see how to act.'

Sir Gervase, eager now to work in the cause of justice and at the same time save himself, wrote an account of what he remembered; he told of the occasion when he had intercepted Weston with the poison; he told that Weston had admitted to him how Overbury's death had been brought about by the clyster and that the boy who had poisoned the clyster had been paid twenty pounds. He mentioned that a few weeks ago Mrs Anne Turner had asked Weston to meet her in an inn and there warned him that investigations were about to begin.

When James read this he was very perplexed. He knew that Mrs Turner was in the service of the Countess of Somerset. But he did not for one moment believe that Robert could be involved in murder; and he saw no reason why his Countess should be.

Winwood was watching him intently.

There must be justice in the realm, thought James. We

cannot afford such a scandal at this time – and scandal there would be if it were believed Overbury were murdered and nothing done in the matter.

'We must unravel this mystery,' said James. 'I will summon the Lord Chief Justice without delay and will put the matter into his hands.'

It could not be better! thought Winwood. Stern old Sir Edward Coke would never allow any consideration to stand in the way of justice.

The end of Somerset! prophesied Winwood secretly. The end of the Spanish menace!

Sir Edward Coke went to work with enthusiasm. His first act was to arrest Weston and put him through an intensive cross-examination. Unaware of all that had been discovered Weston at first attempted to lie, but he was soon trapped, and seeing himself caught, betrayed everyone.

The names came tumbling out: Dr Forman, Franklin, Gresham; Mrs Anne Turner, Sir Gervase Helwys, and behind it all the late Earl of Northampton and the Countess of Somerset.

Frances, aware that terrible revelation was at hand, did not stir from her apartments. She made the excuse that her pregnancy was responsible for her state of health; but when the news was brought to her that Mrs Anne Turner had been arrested she broke down, and Robert found her lying on her bed so unnerved that he realized she had some fearful secret on her mind.

She knew that she could no longer hope to keep the whole story from him. Sir Gervase Helwys was now being questioned; Franklin had been taken up; soon she knew, the Lord Chief Justice would be pointing to her.

'Robert,' she said, 'I am terribly afraid.'

He looked at her steadily. 'Is it anything to do with Overbury?'

She nodded.

'They are saying he was poisoned,' went on Robert.

'I know.'

'You mean you know that he was poisoned?'

'I know that too,' she answered.

Horrible understanding was coming to Robert. He whispered: '*You?*'

She only looked at him, but he knew the answer.

'Mrs Turner . . . Weston . . . Monson . . . Helwys. . . .' Robert enumerated them.

'I used them all.'

'And the boy who confessed to poisoning the clyster?'

'I paid him twenty pounds to do it,' said Frances wearily.

'Oh, my God,' cried Robert.

'You may well call on God to help us. No one else will.'

'So you are . . . a murderess!'

'Don't look at me like that, Robert. I did it for you.'

'Frances! . . .'

'Yes,' she cried passionately, 'for you! For this life of ours . . .' She beat on her body with frantic hands. 'That I might bear you children. That we might grow in power. That we might be together for the rest of our lives.'

'And Overbury?'

'He was in the way. He was trying to stop us. He knew that I had obtained spells from Dr Forman.'

'Spells?'

'To rid myself of Essex.'

Robert covered his face with his hands. What a fool he had been not to see. Fools paid for their folly. And then he began to think of those months when Overbury was in the Tower. He himself had sent in tarts and delicacies to him. Had those tarts been poisoned? Had he not arranged that Overbury should be sent to the Tower? Had he not wanted it because he was angry with him on account of his attitude to Frances? Frances! It all came back to Frances. But how deeply was *he* involved?

He was trying to look back to those months of the imprisonment. Had the knowledge been with him that all was not as it seemed? Did he not prevent Overbury's family from seeing him? Was he too ready to listen to Northampton's advice?

He would never have condemned to horrible death a man

who had once been a friend. But had he thrust the thought of murder from his mind because it was convenient to do so?

How much was he to blame?

He looked at Frances — her eyes enormous in her pale face. She was talking wildly, missing no detail. The letters she had written to Forman, the images he made — the lewd obscene images — the efforts to bewitch Essex; all those horrid practices which had culminated in the murder of Overbury.

And now the story was out, and the Lord Chief Justice would be taking his findings to the King.

The King! thought Robert, with whom his relationship this last year had become strained, the King whose eyes dwelt too fondly on the handsome features of Sir George Villiers.

But James was a loyal friend. He must see James; he must protest his innocence in the matter.

Frances was clutching at his coat with shaking fingers; he wanted to throw her off. He could not bear to look into her face.

Murderess! he thought. She murdered poor Tom Overbury. And she is my wife.

'Robert,' cried Frances, 'remember this always: I did it for you.'

He turned away. 'I would to God,' he said bitterly, 'that I had never set eyes on you.'

James looked sorrowfully into the face of his old friend.

'Your Majesty believes me?' said Robert, his face contorted with emotion.

'My dear Robbie, how could I ever believe that you would take part in such a dastardly plot!'

'Thank you. With Your Majesty's confidence in me I can face all my accusers.'

'Are they accusing you, Robbie?'

'There is talk of nothing else in the Court but this hideous affair.'

James laid his hand on Robert's arm. 'Don't grieve, lad,' he said. 'Innocence has nothing to fear.'

*   *   *

Sir Edward had had many people brought in for questioning. Weston, Franklin, Helwys and Anne Turner would be obliged to prove their innocence, although Sir Edward did not believe they would be able to do this. The servants of these people had been questioned so thoroughly that they had betrayed what he wanted to know.

Northampton was dead and could not be brought to justice, although Coke believed he had had a hand in the murder. But there were two who were living and whom he believed to be at the very centre of the plot: the Earl and Countess of Somerset.

Coke, bowing to none in his determination to lay the guilt where it belonged, summoned Robert Carr, Earl of Somerset, to appear for examination in connexion with the poisoning of Sir Thomas Overbury.

When Robert received the summons he was horrified. For so long he had been treated as the most important man in the country. Did Coke think that he could summon him as he would an ordinary person?

Robert went to the King and angrily told him what had happened, showing him the summons.

James took it and shook his head sadly.

'Why, Robert,' he said, 'this is an order from the Lord Chief Justice of England and must be obeyed.'

'But surely—'

'Nay, lad. If the Lord Chief Justice summoned *me* I must needs answer it.'

Robert was distressed because he had been counting on James' help to release him from such an unpleasant undertaking, and seeing this a great fear came to James. He could not help wondering why, if Robert were entirely innocent, he should be so distressed.

He took him into his arms and kissed him tenderly.

'Come back soon, Robert,' he said. 'I shall be waiting eagerly to welcome you. Sorely shall I miss you and you know my heart goes with you.'

Robert saw that it would be useless to plead with the King. He was summoned by the Lord Chief Justice and he must go.

James stared after him and there were tears in his eyes.

'Goodbye Robert,' he whispered. 'Goodbye, my dear one. Something tells me I shall never more see your face.'

Frances waited for doom to touch her.

Those whom she had paid to help her were all in the hands of the law, and perhaps even at this moment confessions were being extorted. The story of Sir Thomas Overbury's death would be surely unravelled. The attempt on the life of Essex might also be revealed for this was a prelude to the other.

Who would have thought such ill luck could come after all this time?

She had believed Sir Thomas Overbury long since dead and buried – in all respects. She had assured herself that in time even she would cease to dream of him.

And now everyone was talking of him; and the most insistent question of the day was: How did Thomas Overbury die?

What had happened to the life which was going to be so good? She could feel the child move within her – hers and Robert's, the heir to all their greatness, she had once thought. Would the child be the heir to all their sorrows? Would it go through life with the stigma on it: Your mother was a murderess?

Life was intolerable. Her servants were silent in her presence; how could she tell what they said of her when she was out of hearing? How could she know what was said to them of her?

Robert was no longer with her. He had been summoned to help the Lord Chief Justice in his inquiries.

One of her servants came in to her and told her that a messenger was below asking to deliver something into her hands.

She shivered. Every messenger nowadays filled her with fear.

'Bring him to me without delay,' she commanded.

He came, and after giving her a document, withdrew.

She guessed what it was when she saw the signatures. They

were all members of the Commission set up to inquire into
the death of Sir Thomas Overbury, and among them was the
name of Sir Edward Coke.

She was required to keep to her house at Blackfriars if that
was ready for her, or go to the house of Lord Knollys, near
the tiltyard. She might choose from either residence but
when she had made her choice would be required to keep to
her chamber without suffering the access of any person other
than her necessary servants until she was acquainted with His
Majesty's pleasure.

This was what she had dreaded.

She was a prisoner.

As she paced up and down her chamber Frances could hear the
bells ringing.

She was large with child now being in the seventh month of
her pregnancy; and there were times when she wished she
were dead. She would be allowed some respite until the child
was born; that had been promised her, but when she had
recovered from the birth it would be her turn.

Jennet was with her; sometimes she felt she could not bear
to see the woman's eyes fixed on her. They were no longer
truculent. Jennet was as frightened as she was. It was clear that
Jennet was wishing she had never taken her along to see Anne
Turner.

'I wish those bells would stop,' she said.

'They are for Richard Weston,' answered Jennet.

'They sound joyous.'

'They are meant to be ... because a poisoner has been
discovered and sent to his death.'

'Be silent.'

'Did you expect London to mourn for Weston, my lady?'

Frances did not answer. She sat, her head bent, her fingers
pulling at her gown.

'What did he say, I wonder, when they questioned him.'

'He was ever a coward, my lady.'

Frances was overcome by further shivering and Jennet
brought her a shawl.

'Jennet,' said Frances, 'go out and see his end, and come back and tell me all that happened.'

Jennet rose obediently. As she pushed her way through the crowd to Tyburn, she had convinced herself that she was not to blame. She had done nothing. There was no law against introducing one person to another; and if these people plotted murder together that was no concern of hers.

It was disconcerting to see a man one had known, riding in the cart, and Jennet wished she had not come. The people were all talking about Sir Thomas Overbury.

'I hear he only gave the stuff and was paid well for it.'

'By those that could afford to pay him.'

'Did you hear what he said? It was that he believed the big fish would be allowed to escape from the net while the little ones were brought to justice.'

'Oh, there's more to this than we have heard. My Lord and Lady Somerset . . .'

'Somerset!'

'The King won't have Somerset hurt . . .'

Jennet was almost swept off her feet, so great was the press.

She looked at the scaffold with the dangling rope. Weston was talking to the priest who rode with him in the cart; the moment had almost come, and the noose was about to be placed round his neck, when a group of galloping horsemen arrived on the scene.

There was a gasp of surprise among the watchers when it was seen that these were led by Sir John Lidcott, who was Sir Thomas Overbury's brother-in-law.

The hangman paused and Sir John was heard to say: 'Did you poison Sir Thomas Overbury?'

'You misjudge me,' answered Weston.

Sir John addressed the crowd. 'This man is sheltering some great personages.'

But the hangman continued with his task, saying that he had his orders and Weston had received his sentence.

'The matter shall not rest here,' shouted Sir John. 'This is but a beginning.'

The crowd was silent while Richard Weston was hanged.

Jennet made her way back to her mistress. She had little comfort to offer her.

It was indeed a beginning.

A month later Anne Turner was brought out from her prison, after having been found guilty, and condemned to be hanged. She looked so very beautiful in her yellow starched ruff, the fashion and colour she had always favoured and which many had copied, that it was a silent crowd who watched her go to her death and scarcely one voice was raised to revile her.

But every woman who possessed a yellow ruff made up her mind that she would never wear it again; and the fashion Anne Turner had made died with her.

In the early stages of her cross examination she had done her best to shield Frances, but when she realized that the truth was known, when the letters which Frances had written to Forman were produced, when the waxen images were shown to her, she understood that there was no point in attempting to conceal that which had already been discovered.

Then she had cried bitterly: 'Woe to the day I met my lady Somerset. My love for her and my respect for her greatness has brought me to this dog's death.'

She died bravely, making a further confession on the scaffold; and her brother, who held a good post in the service of the Prince of Wales, waited in his coach and then took her body to St Martins in the Field that he might decently bury it.

The next to die was Sir Gervase Helwys. His crime was that he had known efforts were being made to poison Sir Thomas Overbury but had done nothing to stop the crime; in fact he had made of himself an accessory by allowing the murder to take place under his eyes.

He was followed by Franklin.

There was a little time left to her, Frances knew, because of the child she carried.

They would not bring a pregnant woman into the Court.

'There is only one thing I can do,' she told Jennet; 'and that to die. I shall never survive the birth of my child.'

Jennet could not comfort her, she was too fearful for her own safety. Weston had been right when he had said that small mercy was shown to the little fish.

But everyone was waiting for the big fish to be caught in the net; and there was growing indignation throughout the country because four people had been hanged already for the murder of Sir Thomas Overbury and the chief murderers had as yet not been brought to trial.

'What shall I do?' moaned Frances. 'What can I do?'

On a dark December day her child was born.

Her women brought the baby to her and laid it in her arms. 'A little girl,' they told her.

She looked at the child and pity for her state was so great that the tears fell on to the child's face.

'The child is born,' she said, 'and I still live. Oh, what will become of me?'

She was in great despair because she knew now that soon she must be brought to justice.

It occurred to her then that if she named her daughter Anne the Queen might be pleased and would surely do something to help her namesake; and how could she best help this child than by showing a little comfort to her mother?

So the Lady Anne Carr was christened; but Queen Anne and all the Court ignored the event.

Frances now understood that there was to be no special treatment. She must face her judges.

The Trial of the Big Fish

WHEN JENNET came to tell her that the guards were below, Frances began to weep quietly.

'They will separate me from my baby,' she said.

'The child will be well looked after,' Jennet assured her.

'They will take me to the Tower, Jennet.'

'My lord Somerset is already there, my lady.'

'What will become of us all?' moaned Frances.

Jennet thought of the dangling bodies of Weston, Anne Turner, Sir Gervase Helwys and Franklin, and she was silent.

Along the river from Blackfriars to the grim fortress. Never had it looked more forbidding. Under the portcullis; the impregnable walls closing about her.

Here they had brought Thomas Overbury. How had he felt when they brought him in? It had never occurred to her to wonder until now.

Thomas Overbury, who had been brought here for no crime, who had been sentenced to death not by a court of law but by Frances, Countess of Somerset!

She was overcome by a chill fear.

What if they were to take her to the cell where he had died in agony? What if his ghost remained there to haunt her in the dead of night? He had haunted her since his death in one way; but what if he were to come to her when she was alone in her cold cell?

She began to scream: 'Where are you taking me? You are taking me to Overbury's cell. I won't go there. I won't.'

The guards exchanged glances, believing those to be the protests of a guilty woman; but she was so beautiful even in her grief, that they were sorry for her.

'My lady,' they said, 'we are taking you to the apartments recently vacated by Sir Walter Raleigh.'

'Raleigh,' she repeated; and she thought of Prince Henry who had talked to her of that great adventurer and told her that he had often visited him in prison.

How life had changed for them all! Henry dead; Raleigh preparing to leave for Orinoco; she herself a prisoner about to stand her trial for murder.

She looked about the room over the portcullis; she sat at the table where Raleigh had worked and she buried her face in her hands.

What will become of me? she asked herself.

It was late May when Frances was brought from the Tower to Westminster Hall. Crowds had gathered in the streets because the case had aroused greater interest than any within living memory. The people were angry that the humbler prisoners should have been so promptly brought to justice while the Earl and Countess, who, it appeared, had been the authors of the crime, were allowed so far to go unpunished.

'Justice!' grumbled the mob. 'Let us have justice.'

This was a State trial and all the trappings of ceremony must be observed. Many of the foremost lords led by the Lord Chancellor Ellesmore had been summoned to appear; everyone wanted to be at the trial; and many of the lesser nobility travelled up from the country for the express purpose of seeing the Countess of Somerset brought to justice.

The bells were chiming as the Lord Chancellor followed the six sergeants-at-arms, all carrying maces, into the hall. After him came all the dignitaries of the court. The Lord High Steward and the peers of the realm. There was the Recorder, sombrely clad in black; and Sir George More, the Lieutenant of the Tower, who had taken the place of the executed Helwys, was already at the Bar.

The Sergeant Crier demanded silence while the indictments were read; and when this was done he cried in a voice which could be heard all over the court: 'Bring the prisoner to the Bar.'

The Lieutenant of the Tower disappeared for a few minutes and when he returned he brought Frances with him.

She was very pale and her lovely eyes betrayed her fear. She was dressed in black with a ruff and cuffs of finest lace; and as she stood at the Bar and raised her eyes towards the Lord High Steward she looked so exquisite that she might have stepped, exactly as she was, from a picture frame.

'My lords,' began the Lord High Steward, 'you are called here today to sit as peers of Frances, Countess of Somerset.'

A voice echoed through the court: 'Frances, Countess of Somerset, hold up your hand.'

Frances obeyed.

The accusation of murder was then read to her in detail and when it was finished the Clerk of the Crown cried in a resonant voice: 'Frances, Countess of Somerset, what say you? Are you guilty of this felony and murder, or not guilty?'

Everyone in the hall was strained forward to hear her reply.

She gave it unfalteringly, because, knowing her letters to Forman and Anne Turner were in the hands of her judges, there was only one answer she could give.

'Guilty,' she answered.

The trial was not long. Because she had confessed her guilt, there was no need then to bring out those lewd wax figures, those revealing letters. But it did not matter; many of these people had already seen the images, heard the letters read.

There was nothing she could say in her defence. The whole cruel story was known: the attempt to bewitch Essex, and everyone believed, murder him, which had failed. The attempt to murder Overbury which had succeeded.

The Chancellor delivered the sentence.

'Frances, Countess of Somerset, whereas you have been indicted, arraigned and pleaded Guilty, and have nothing to say for yourself, it is now my part to pronounce judgement ... You shall be carried hence to the Tower of London and from thence to a place of execution where you are to be hanged by the neck till you are dead. The Lord have mercy upon your soul.'

As the Chancellor was speaking Frances saw a pair of brooding eyes fixed upon her from among those assembled to watch her tried.

Robert Devereux, Earl of Essex, could not completely loathe this woman who had tried to make such havoc of his life, and as he looked at the prisoner at the Bar he could not shut out of his mind the memory of a laughing girl who had once danced with him so merrily at their wedding.

Frances turned away. She did not wonder what her first husband was thinking of her now. Her future loomed before her so terribly, so frightening that the past meant little to her.

Out into the fresh air. Once again to enter the gloomy precincts of the Tower.

When next she left it—

But Frances could not bear to contemplate that terror.

She lifted her face to the May sun; never had it seemed so desirable; never had the river danced and sparkled so brightly; never did the world seem so beautiful as it did now when she was condemned to leave it for ever.

The next day the scene at Westminster Hall was similar but this time there was a different prisoner at the Bar.

'Robert, Earl of Somerset, hold up your hand.'

'Robert, Earl of Somerset, what say you? Are you guilty of this felony and murder whereof you stand indicted, or not guilty?'

Robert could give a different answer to this question from that which Frances had been compelled to give.

'Not guilty!' he said firmly.

Robert's trial was longer than his wife's; she had admitted her guilt and condemnation had come swiftly; but Robert was determined to prove his innocence and to fight for his life.

So the days passed while the evidence was brought and considered; and the letters were read once more and the images displayed.

Some of the most sorrowful moments were those when he must listen to the words Frances had written to people such as Forman and Anne Turner; when he must hear an account of the orgies in which she took part.

He realized then that he was only just beginning to know the woman who was the mother of his child; and he felt lost and bewildered.

There was one friend from whom he longed to hear; but James had nothing more to give to a man who could stand accused of such a dreadful crime. And innocent though he might be, he was allied to the woman who had admitted that she was one of the most wicked in England.

The court was against him. Robert sensed it. He knew before they gave their verdict that they would find him guilty; that they would condemn him to the same fate as that which they had decided on for Frances.

He was not surprised when it came, when he was led from the hall out into the sun, to make, as she had made, that journey back to the Tower.

The Retribution

BUT NEITHER the Earl nor the Countess of Somerset were hanged by their necks until they died. That was something which the King could not tolerate.

He had loved that man and he understood that it was ill fortune, circumstances, fate — whatever one cared to call it — which had brought Robert Carr close to the scaffold; it was not Robert's nature. He had been easygoing in those days when his life had been uncomplicated; and that was how it was natural for the lad to be. He had been trapped though, as young men will be, by a scheming woman; and it was she who had brought him low.

'Robbie shall not hang,' said James to himself, 'because he was once my good friend; and as long as my friends seek not to harm me they remain my friends.'

As for Frances – she was a member of the great Howard family who had, at times, served their country well and she had shown herself to be truly penitent.

No, they had sinned and they had suffered; they must be punished but not by death.

In the streets the people murmured.

'It is one thing for the humble to commit murder and quite another for noble lords and ladies.'

'Who were the true murderers? Tell me that! And they are to be pardoned, while lovely Anne Turner hung in her yellow ruff until she died.'

'Weston said the big fish would break out of the net and the little ones be caught. Weston was right.'

It was a sad state of affairs. No public hanging for the Countess and the Earl. What a spectacle that would have been! Mrs Turner in her yellow ruff had not provided half the excitement they would have had at the hanging of the Earl and Countess of Somerset.

Frances was hilariously gay when she heard the news.

She realized now how she had dreaded the thought of death. She was young; she was vital; and passionately she wanted to live.

And now she would live; and in time she and Robert would be back at Court.

The King was enamoured of this boy Villiers – but let him wait.

Would she say in time that all had been worth while? A few weeks ago she would have believed that to be impossible; but now she was going to live again, richly, gloriously.

But when she discovered that, although the death sentence was not to be carried out, they were still prisoners and might not leave the Tower, Frances' joy diminished considerably and she was subject to fits of melancholy. How could she plan for a future which was to be spent within the precincts of the Tower of London? What hope had she of taking up her place at

Court, of regaining her old influence, when she was a prisoner who was expected to be grateful because she was not dead.

Her baby was in the care of Lady Knollys who had been a good friend to her; and often little Anne was brought to the Tower to be with her mother.

Nor was she kept apart from Robert; but gradually she began to understand that she could not resume her old relationship with her husband.

Every time he looked at her he saw the waxen images which had been displayed in court; every time he heard her voice he remembered the words she had written to her 'sweet father', Dr Forman.

In place of the beautiful young girl whom he had loved, he saw an evil woman, whose hands were stained with the blood of a man who had been his closest friend.

She no longer attracted him; he found even her beauty repulsive.

His feelings were obvious to her, and she wept and stormed, threatening to end her life; she was angry with him, and bitterly sorry for herself.

But it was of no use.

Sometimes she would awake at night and fancy she heard the laughter of Sir Thomas Overbury.

Robert spent his time in writing pleading letters to the King.

He asked forgiveness and leniency; he asked that he might be permitted to leave the Tower with his wife and retain his estates.

James was always upset when he received these letters. He longed to forgive Robert although he had no wish to see him again. To have had him at Court would have been too embarrassing; besides young Steenie would not have tolerated it.

Yet James did not forget the old days of friendship; and on occasions — when Steenie was a little overbearing — he thought with longing of the early days of friendship with Robbie, when the lad had been so modest and happy to serve his King.

But he could not bring him back to Court. The people would never hear of it. They had been angry when a pardon had been granted the Earl and his lady. They had said then that there was no justice in England. There had been an occasion when a noble lady in her carriage had been mistaken for the Countess of Somerset and that poor lady had narrowly escaped with her life.

No, Robbie and his wife must remain prisoners, until such time as they could be quietly released; but of one thing James was certain; Robert must never come back to Court while James lived.

It was not until some six years after their pardons that James thought they could safely be released; and in order that they should not come to Court, one of the conditions of their freedom was that they should reside only in places which the King would choose for them. These houses were Grays and Cowsham in Oxfordshire and they must not travel more than three miles' radius of either.

Robert came to Frances' cell to tell her the news.

'We are to leave the Tower. I have the King's letter here.'

'Freedom at last!'

'Nay,' he said coldly, because his voice was always cold when he addressed her, 'this is not freedom. Rather is it a change of prison. It is a concession because in these houses we shall not be treated as prisoners and shall have our own servants.' His face lit up with pleasure as he added: 'We shall have our daughter with us.'

Frances' joy turned to indignation. She had set her heart on returning to Court.

Yet it would be pleasant to leave the Tower and all the evil memories which she longed to thrust behind her.

'I always hated living in the country,' she said.

'Then you must perforce learn to like it,' retorted Robert.

He was less unhappy than she was. He hated his wife but there was someone whom he could love; and during the last years he had become devoted to his little daughter.

One day, thought Frances, was so like another, that she believed she would die of very boredom.

How tired she was of green fields! How she longed for a sight of Whitehall! She would dream that she was seated at the King's table, that the minstrels were playing and the dance about to begin. Everyone was seeking her favours because not only was she the wife of Robert Carr, Earl of Somerset, who held more sway over the King than any ever had, but she was the most beautiful woman at Court.

Then she would wake to the sound of wind sweeping over the meadows, or the song of the birds, and remember with bitterness that Whitehall was far away – and not only in mileage.

I shall die, she would say, if I never see Whitehall again.

Then she would weep into her pillows, or storm at her servants; hoping to find comfort from either action. But there was no comfort; there was only regret.

Each day she must live with a man who could not hide his feeling for her. He could never see her without remembering some evil deed from her past; he could never forget that he owed his downfall to her. His only happiness was to shut her from his thoughts.

For months they lived in wretchedness, dreading to be together, yet unable to avoid it; each day Robert's loathing grew a little stronger; each day her anger against him grew more bitter.

But Robert found a way out of his despondency. Sometimes from her window, Frances would watch two figures in the paddock; a sturdy little girl and a tall, still handsome man. He was teaching her to ride. The child's high laughter would come to her ears and sometimes Robert's would mingle with it.

They were always together, those two.

Frances could find no such joy. She had never wanted children, only power, adulation and what she called love – but that did not include the love of a child.

She continued to fret while Robert learned to live for his daughter.

Occasionally news came from the world beyond them; it was like, thought Frances miserably, looking at a masque through a misty window; a masque in which one was barred from playing a part. This was no life; she was poised between living and dying.

Life was the Court where people jostled for power and wealth; but she was no longer of it; nor could she break through to it; she must live out the dreary years in a limbo, poised between vital life and a living death.

They were still in exile when Raleigh returned from his ill-fated journey and when, soon after, he laid his head on the block in Old Palace Yard. And when Frances heard that her father and mother had been summoned to the Star Chamber and there sentenced to a term in the Tower for embezzlement, she was not deeply moved. That life now seemed so far away.

When Queen Anne died of dropsy, no one was surprised. She was in her forty-sixth year and had been ailing for some time; a certain Dr Harvey discovered the circulation of the blood and confirmed this by his experiments; a comet appeared in the sky to cause great consternation and speculation but even this could not interest Frances.

Sometimes Robert thought wistfully of the old days; he wondered whether there would be a Spanish marriage for Charles after all, or whether that sly Gondomar would have worked in vain. It would have been good to be there in the thick of intrigue.

He pictured himself with the King, proudly bringing forward a girl who was growing to be as beautiful as her mother, yet with a different kind of beauty.

'My daughter, Your Majesty.'

He could almost see James' emotional smile, almost hear his tender voice: 'So ye've a lass now, eh, Robbie. And a bonny one!'

He would have asked for favours for her. He wished he

could have given her great wealth and titles. But what did she want with them? She had her horses to ride – and she was already a good horsewoman; she had her father to be her companion. *She* did not ask for more, so why should he?'

It was not often that they spoke to each other; they avoided each other's eyes. They both wanted to forget and they were a constant reminder to each other.

But one day she could not restrain herself. 'My lord Buckingham I hear is going to Spain with the Prince.'

'Is it so then?'

'My lord Buckingham – that upstart Villiers. A Duke no less!'

Robert shrugged his shoulders. But he pictured the scene at Court so well: James, grown older now, but no less affectionate, he was sure; and at his feet the handsome man, seated on the stool once occupied by himself.

'They say there is no end to the honours that man has taken to himself.'

'It may well be.'

'You do not care?'

'I am past caring.'

'I am not then. And never shall be.'

'That is a tragedy for you.'

She turned on him angrily; his calmness maddened her, the knowledge that he had been able to build a life for himself out of these ruins, while she had failed, was more than she could bear.

'It might never have happened. You could have persuaded James. You should have been more subtle ... a little more like his newest friend, my lord Buckingham.'

'And you, madam,' he retorted, 'should never have stained your hands with the blood of my friend.'

She turned away and ran to her bedchamber where she locked herself in and wept until she believed she had no tears left. Tears of rage and frustration.

'Better would it have been if they had taken me to Tyburn,' she cried. 'Better if they had hanged me by the neck as they did poor Anne Turner. Anything would have been more desirable than this life of mine.'

After that they avoided each other. It was better so.

In one of his favourite palaces – Theobald's in the parish of Cheshunt – the King lay dying.

James had no illusions; he knew this was the end. He was in his fifty-ninth year and had been a king for almost the whole of his life: James VI of Scotland since he was little more than a baby and his mother's enemies had insisted that she abdicate in his favour; James I of England for the last twenty-three years.

'A goodly span,' he murmured, 'and when a man suffers from a tertian ague and gout it is time he said goodbye to earthly pleasures. Perhaps I have been overfond of my wine, but it is no bad thing to be overfond of the things life has to offer.'

It was characteristic of him that he wondered what posterity would think of him. The British Solomon! How much had his wisdom profited his country? Would they remember him as a wise ruler, or the King who had gone in terror of the assassin's knife since the Gowrie and Gunpowder Plots? Would they remember him as the King who was excessively fond of his favourites?

Steenie had not always been a comfort. He had grown arrogant like the rest. Steenie would look after himself. He was already a friend of Charles and they had jaunted to Spain together when Charles went to woo the Infanta. And Charles was affianced now to Henrietta Maria the daughter of Henry IV of France and sister of the reigning King Louis XIII. It would be a Catholic marriage for Charles which might cause trouble; there could clearly be no more persecution of recusants with a Catholic Queen on the throne. But that was Charles' affair – no longer his.

It was strange to think of the end. No more hunting, no more golf, no more laughter at the pranks of Steenie and the rest; no longer would he sign to a handsome young man to give him his arm to lean on.

The old life was passing.

And as he thought back over the years there was one whom he could not forget, and had never forgotten. Often during the years he had longed to recall him. Yet how could he recall a man who had been condemned for murder?

'Robbie was no murderer,' he told himself, as he had often during the hours of the night when he had awakened from some vague dream of the past, haunted by a handsome affectionate young man. 'I'll bring him back. He shall have his estates back.'

But by light of day he would say: 'I canna do it. It would serve no good purpose. How could Robert take up his old place now?'

It was nearly ten years since he had seen Robert, and that was a long time for a King to remember. And for all those years Robert had remained virtually a prisoner.

There was one thing he would do before he died. Robert should have a full pardon. His estates should be returned to him. As for the woman – she must have her freedom. He could not keep one prisoner and not the other.

It must be his first concern to pardon Robert.

The pardon was given; and the documents drawn up which would make Robert a rich man once more.

But James had not known how little time there was left to him, and he died before he could sign those documents.

But for Robert and Frances there was change at last: and that March of the year 1625 when James died in Theobald's Palace, they were at liberty to go where they would. James' last gift to them was freedom from each other.

The Solace

THE EARL OF SOMERSET was no longer a young man; it was nearly thirty years since he had been found guilty of murder by his peers; yet there were times when it seemed even longer. Looking back, it appeared to him that he had been three people: an ambitious young man looking for a place at Court; the most powerful man in England; and a man who had learned to understand himself and life, and had contrived to make something worth while out of disaster.

It astonished him often that the last phase of his life had been the happiest; was that the reward of a successful life? To have learned one's lessons; to have come to an appreciation of the true blessings the world had to offer?

He believed so; and when he was with his daughter – so like her mother and yet how different! – he was content.

Yet even after he had received his full pardon, life had been uneasy.

Frances had gone often to Court, but she had not been happy. She did not enjoy the glory under Charles and Henrietta Maria that she had known when James and Anne were on the throne. Who was this Frances Howard? was a constant question. Wife of the one-time favourite who had fallen from grace; daughter of the Earl of Suffolk and his Countess of whose reputation for fraud all were aware; great-niece of that old rogue Northampton who had died in time to save himself from scandal; and worst of all – a self-confessed murderess.

She was angry; she was frustrated; she was melancholy; but she could not stay away from Whitehall.

Back and forth to Court; growing older, sullen, always seeking what could never be hers; resenting that growing love between her daughter and husband, who had found happiness together.

There was no happiness for Frances. Fears had come with the gnawing pain which at first she ignored; but eventually it would not be ignored. More insistent it grew until it dominated her life.

There were no more visits to Court; there was only pain that grew worse with every day.

Sometimes she lay on her bed and screamed in her agony; sometimes she lost consciousness; at others she would wander in her mind and those who attended her would hear her say: 'So you are there ... mocking me? You are telling me you suffered such pains. Is this your revenge, Tom Overbury?'

It was a relief when at last her pains were no more. She had lived thirty-nine turbulent years; and sixteen had elapsed since she had faced her judges.

But when she was no longer there the memories began to fade. The days were happier; there was the girl nearly seventeen, a lovely blooming creature with a deep affection for the father who, because of their exile, had been closer to her than parents often were.

He was poor by comparison with what he once had been, for his only possessions were now a house at Chiswick and a small income.

'It is enough for our needs,' Anne told him; and he rejoiced in his daughter.

He would have been completely happy if she could have remained in innocence, but there had been documents and books written about the case of Sir Thomas Overbury and it was inevitable that one day something of this nature must fall into Anne's hands.

He found her one day staring before her, the book having slipped to the floor; and, seeing the horror in her face, he knew what she had been reading.

'My darling,' he said, 'you must not let it grieve you.'

'My mother ... did that!'

'She was young; she had been too indulged.'

How explain Frances Howard to her daughter?

He thanked God that Anne was a sensible girl. After the first shock, after they had talked together and he had told her the story as he had known it, she was able to put it out of her mind. He was innocent and her guilty mother was dead. It was because of what had happened that they lived here together away from the Court. It was past; no amount of grieving could change what had happened.

He was glad that she knew because he had lived with the fear that one day she would meet someone who would tell her the story. It was better that she should hear it from him.

She was growing into a very lovely woman, with the features of her mother, made more beautiful by the kindliness of her expression, the modesty of her manners and the virtue which shone from her. He knew that he should not let her remain shut away from the world. It would have been pleasant to keep her to himself for she asked no other life. But he loved her too well.

He had one or two friends who had remained constant throughout his exile, and they helped Anne to see a little of society; but it was with reluctance that she left him to go on an occasional visit and she always returned to him with pleasure. It was during one of these visits that she met Lord William Russell; the attraction was mutual and immediate; and William, eldest son of the Earl of Bedford, was certain that the only wife he would have was Anne, daughter of the disgraced Earl of Somerset and his notorious Countess.

One could not expect life to go on in the same gentle groove for ever. Robert knew now that this was the end of his cherished companionship with his daughter; she would either marry Russell or, if she did not, spend the rest of her life grieving for him. It certainly seemed that she would not have Russell for Bedford had angrily declared that there should be no marriage between his heir and the daughter of such parents.

Bedford stormed about the Court and the old scandal was revived. Anne had lost her gaiety and that was more than Robert could bear; he knew that he would give everything he had to buy her her happiness, and would even be prepared never to see her again if that were necessary.

William Russell was a determined young man who had no intention of giving up the woman he loved, and being a friend of the King soon enlisted his sympathy and that of the young Queen Henrietta Maria. It was difficult for Bedford to refuse a request from the King to be kind to the lovers, and at last he agreed, but on a condition which, knowing Robert's poverty, he did not believe would be complied with.

His son's wife must have a dowry of twelve thousand pounds. That, he declared, was a reasonable suggestion when she was marrying into one of the most important families.

Anne was desolate. 'He knows it is impossible,' she mourned. 'That is why he has set this condition.'

Twelve thousand pounds! mused Robert. By selling everything he had perhaps he could raise that sum. It would mean he would live the rest of his life in poverty; but he was ready to buy Anne's happiness on any terms.

When the money was raised Bedford had no more excuses and so the Lady Anne Carr was married to Lord William Russell and although he knew that their intimate companionship was over, that was one of the happiest days of Robert's life.

He had had little possessions of his own for as long as he lived, which was for eight years after Anne's marriage. They were happy years, for he was often with his daughter and he saw her the mistress of great estates and, what was more important, a happy wife and mother. Often when his grandchildren climbed on to his knee they would make the eternal plea: 'Grandfather, tell me a story.'

And he told them stories of the splendour of Courts and the exploits of knights; but there was one story he never told; and he trusted that by the time they heard it – which in course of time they must – they would see it as a tragedy of figures become shadowy with time, and that they would not judge too harshly the grandfather whom they had known in the days of their childhood.

Other Pan books that may interest you
are listed on the following page

Susan Howatch
Penmarric £1.25

'I was ten years old when I first saw the inheritance and twenty years old when I saw Janna Roslyn, but my reaction to both was identical. I wanted them.'

The inheritance is Penmarric, a huge gaunt house in Cornwall belonging to the tempestuous, hot-blooded Castallacks; Janna Roslyn is a beautiful village girl who becomes mistress of Laurence Castallack, wife to his son . . .

'A fascinating saga . . . has all the right dramatic and romantic ingredients' WOMAN'S JOURNAL

Cashelmara £1.25

A glorious, full-blooded novel, brimming with memorable characters, which centres on Cashelmara, the coldly beautiful Georgian house in Galway, ancestral home of Edward de Salis.

Charged with emotion, the fast-moving plot follows the turbulent fortunes of an aristocratic Victorian family through half a century of furious encounters, ill-advised liaisons and bitter-sweet interludes of love.

'Another blockbuster from Susan Howatch' SUNDAY TIMES

You can buy these and other Pan books from booksellers and newsagents; or direct from the following address:
Pan Books, Cavaye Place, London SW10 9PG
Send purchase price plus 15p for the first book and 5p for each additional book, to allow for postage and packing
Prices quoted are applicable in UK
While every effort is made to keep prices low, it is sometimes necessary to increase prices at short notice. Pan Books reserve the right to show on covers new retail prices which may differ from those advertised in the text or elsewhere